Hazel Osmond has been an advertising copywriter for many years. In 2008, she won the *Woman & Home* short-story competition sponsored by Costa. In 2012, *Who's Afraid of Mr Wolfe?* was shortlisted for the Romantic Novelists' Association's (RNA) Romantic Comedy award. While she is overjoyed to be a writer, a tiny part of her would like to have been an artist in Paris during the nineteenth century. Without the grinding poverty and syphilis, obviously. She is currently writing her fourth novel.

Also by Hazel Osmond

Who's Afraid of Mr Wolfe?
The First Time I Saw Your Face

playing grace

HAZEL OSMOND

Quercus

First published in Great Britain in 2013 by

Quercus
55 Baker Street
7th Floor, South Block
London W1U 8EW

A CIP catalogue record for this book is available
from the British Library

PB ISBN 978 1 78087 373 2
EBOOK ISBN 978 1 78087 374 9

10 9 8 7 6 5 4 3 2

Printed and bound in Great Britain by Clays Ltd, St Ives plc

Typeset by Ellipsis Digital Limited, Glasgow

In memory of my mother, Josie Derrick
(1926–2012)

CHAPTER 1

Right at that moment, Grace could have done with the United Nations dropping in and working their magic. The Americans were getting restless and the smiles of the Japanese were growing more and more mask-like. True, the New Zealand couple looked pretty laid back as they studied the statue of the Greek god who obviously favoured doing his hunting naked, but the way that Monsieur Laurent, the French guy, was gripping the gallery guide suggested he was having a hard time with his *savoir faire*.

At the ticket desk, Lilly gave her an uncharacteristically sympathetic smile, although Grace knew that if her little Tower of Babel continued to clutter up the entrance hall much longer, she'd suggest that Grace take everyone outside to wait.

She glanced at the gallery clock and saw the minute hand jump another segment to the right. It was heading for the powdered wig, now faded and crazed with age, of a young man who had been painted on the clock's face.

He was loitering against a backdrop of straggly trees and Grace had always suspected that he was waiting for some rose-lipped country wench to trip into view for some al fresco seduction. But his intentions today were of minor concern. The more pressing problem was that when the minute hand reached that wig, it would be exactly ten minutes since her tour should have started. By now they ought to be exploring the 'Leading Lights of the Impressionist and Post-Impressionist Movement' in one of the Paddwick Gallery's wood-panelled rooms upstairs.

Grace heard the large double doors open. She had given up all expectation of anyone from the United Nations appearing, but was still hopeful that it would be the tardy Tuscelli family – the reason they were all loitering about on the flagstones. It was an elderly woman walking with the aid of a stick. She made a slow progress towards the ticket desk and then an even slower ascent of the oval stone staircase that spiralled up through the centre of the building, carrying people from the Reformation to the Renaissance to the early twentieth century. The minute hand moved to poke the powdered wig and Grace knew, without having to look, that the Americans, Evangeline and Scott Baldridge, would be on the move too.

Lodged at the 'intensely demanding' end of the client spectrum, the Baldridges treated any glitch or deviation in the advertised sched-uuu-le (said with a deep Texan drawl) in the same manner: Mrs Baldridge would get one side of Grace, Mr Baldridge the other, and in a whinging pincer movement they would complain fulsomely about the tour, the company, the other people in the group and the UK in general. Mrs Baldridge had a voice like a buzz saw in a biscuit tin and Mr Baldridge a tendency to express opinions that other people would not even dare to think, and so it was with much unease that Grace turned to face them.

'Late,' Mr Baldridge pronounced, pointing towards the clock before bringing his hand down to rest on his hip, or where his hip must have been when he was younger and several stone lighter. 'Well, ahh saw it comin', of course. Always the same with them Eye-ties.'

'Yup,' the buzz saw agreed, tilting her head towards her husband.

Racial stereotyping did not sit well with Grace. After nearly four years of gallery tours with Picture London, she had to concede that there *were* certain characteristics you could loosely assign to particular nationalities, but anything more was an insulting straitjacket. In her experience, people were as individual as you allowed them to be and the Tuscellis were unfailingly punctual. She would wait a few more minutes and then try Signor Tuscelli's mobile.

But how to stop the Baldridge duo saying something even more inflammatory in the meantime? Grace sensed tension already building – most of the members of this particular tour had met on a previous trip around the National Portrait Gallery, during which allegiances had been formed and dislikes taken. The Baldridges were definitely not going to be asked to swap addresses with anyone. The moue on Monsieur Laurent's face suggested he was bracing himself to defend his own nation should Mr Baldridge tire of insulting the Italians and move sharply northwest towards France.

Grace saw that Mr Baldridge was now going for the double-hand-on-hip approach. 'Ahh do hope,' he said, 'that if this delay means less of a tour, wheel be gettin' a refund.'

Mrs Baldridge's nod made the creased wattle of her neck wobble.

'Oh, don't worry about that,' Grace said in best head girl mode, 'we'll simply tack the lost time on at the end . . .' As she saw the next objection forming in Mr Baldridge's skull, she added, 'But before we get into that, what about last night, hmm, Mr Baldridge? Magnificent, magnificent performance!'

Mr Baldridge looked as if he had been caught doing something illicit. Over at the ticket desk Lilly tilted her head in an attempt to eavesdrop, making her large earrings wobble.

'Ma'am?' Mr Baldridge's confusion was underlined by his failure to close his mouth once the question had been asked. There was a nervous shift of his eyes towards his wife who, unable to mirror her husband's expression, merely assumed the appearance of somebody who had been slapped in the face with a wet haddock.

'I'm talking about the baseball, Mr Baldridge,' Grace explained. 'The Rangers. Good win over the Rays.'

'Well, yeah . . . yeah, they did good . . . did you . . . do you?' Mr Baldridge was a small truck that had suddenly stalled.

'I take an interest.' Grace gave a self-deprecating laugh and forgave herself for bending the truth – to describe her knowledge of baseball as an 'interest' was like saying Leonardo da Vinci knew how to apply a mean undercoat. She knew a vast amount about the players, the management teams and could reel off a list of reasons why the Rangers were likely to win the World Series that year. She could also have chatted about various American football teams, athletes, TV programmes and films. In fact, with the exception of the no-go areas of politics and religion, there were few aspects of American life that she couldn't have whipped out to plaster over a nasty moment.

As Mr Baldridge opened his mouth again, Grace sensed the need to bring in reinforcements. She smiled over at Mr Hikaranto.

'Baseball,' she said with a brief nod of her head instead of a bow. 'Mr Baldridge supports the Texas Rangers. But I believe your team, the Yomiuri Giants, has also had a good year?'

Mr Hikaranto beamed in a modest way. 'Very good team, Texas Rangers. And yes, so kind, the Giants are playing . . .' He turned to his wife for help.

'Like giants,' she said softly, with a shy glance up at Grace.

Mr Baldridge raised his eyebrows. 'You into baseball?'

'Yes, thank you,' the Japanese couple replied, in unison.

Hoping that the Baldridges might now be fully occupied, Grace turned her attention to the next potential flashpoint – Monsieur Laurent's grip on his gallery guide was leaving indentations.

'We don't really play baseball in Britain,' she said, before feeding him a line she knew would be snapped at: 'Although perhaps we should. Might be better at that than—'

'Football,' he said and accompanied it with a Gallic smirk, thereby proving one of Grace's rules governing the discussion of sport with foreign clients: you could yabber away forever about their local teams but the only national team you should ever discuss was your own. This facilitated a psychological exchange known as 'assuming the position of underdog in order to make visitors feel superior'.

She rewarded Monsieur Laurent with her 'What-can-you-do-about-our-overpaid-footballers?' expression.

'Don't s'pose you'll wanna talk about rugby either?' Mrs Macintosh, the New Zealander, said, breaking off from her close examination of the nude hunter's buttocks.

Her husband laughed. 'Now, love, don't rub it in. Just 'cos they're going through a rough patch.' As Grace found Mr Macintosh attractive in a big, outdoorsy kind of way, she decided to forgive him and his wife with a gracious smile.

With the march of time apparently forgotten, this would have been Grace's opportunity to slip outside and ring Signor Tuscelli's mobile, but she was saved the effort by the arrival of the latecomers themselves, who appeared in a flurry of padded coats, spiky boots and sunglasses, the double doors slamming shut behind them. They rushed across the flagstones towards Grace, both adults talking so fast and so much over each other that it took Grace a few seconds to understand why they were late.

'I said Temple, to get off,' Signor Tuscelli was assuring Grace, his hands chopping out the words, 'but Gisella,' he indicated his daughter, 'she said it was Charing Cross. And so we have had to run, run up the . . .'

'The Strand,' his wife supplied.

'Yes, the Strand. So fast.' Signor Tuscelli blew out his cheeks.

'So hot.' Signora Tuscelli was shrugging off her coat.

A heady perfume reached Grace as Gisella of the large, dark eyes and very tight jeans said, to the group in general, '*Scusi*. It was all my fault.'

Everyone muttered that it was OK, although Monsieur Laurent in particular looked as if he'd like to hear more of Gisella's pouty apology.

Mr Baldridge, as usual, spoilt the party. 'The name of the toob station was clearly written on our itin-er-rary.'

'Ah, but these things are so much harder when your first language is not English,' Grace said quickly.

Mr Baldridge jerked his thumb at Mr and Mrs Hikaranto. 'Well, our friends here managed.' Only the way Mrs Hikaranto gripped the handle of her Prada bag suggested the Japanese couple were not keen on that 'friends' label.

Signora Tuscelli was beginning to look affronted, so Grace suddenly threw her arms wide – a gesture that always distracted people long enough for her to change the subject.

'The London Underground is a confusing place,' she said so brightly and so loudly that she got an admonishing frown from Lilly at the desk. 'Yet for all its confusion, it's an adventure too. An experience. And talking of experiences, there is another wonderful one waiting for us now. This building was largely completed in the eighteenth century and stands on the site of what used to be a Tudor Palace. Constructed on neoclassical lines around a central courtyard it housed a variety of government departments before it became an art gallery. I think you'll agree it is both elegant and stately, dominating the Strand on one side and a large stretch of the Thames on the other. Quite simply it is a masterpiece in Portland Stone.' She laid her hand on a portion of the wall to make her meaning clearer to the Hikarantos. 'A masterpiece housing other masterpieces, because here are names that are famous the world over. Monet, Renoir, Cézanne. The paintings of Van Gogh and Manet. We have so much to see, so let's not waste a moment. Mr Baldridge, if I could ask you to lead the way, please? Up the stairs and then sharp left into the first room . . .'

Sometimes Grace felt like a games mistress who had inhaled too much muscle rub, but faced with all her eagerness and confidence, even the most recalcitrant complainer usually rolled over and gave in. She watched as Mr and Mrs Baldridge vied momentarily on the bottom step to be the first up the stairs and then it was Mr Baldridge who, having gallantly elbowed his wife aside, led the group on the climb upwards.

Grace watched and thought of all the people whose feet had worn down those stone steps. The earls and lords on the way up to adventure and down to the scaffold; the ladies, their skirts lifted just high enough or way too high; the government spies, the civil servants and now the art lovers, tourists and students.

As she moved to follow them, she mouthed a quick 'thank you' to Lilly who replied by jerking her head in the direction of Mr Baldridge, who had now reached the first-floor landing.

'You be able to get all the way round without World War Three breaking out?' she asked with a chuckle making her earrings do some more wobbling.

'Of course. Some people just need careful handling and a lot of distraction. It's all under control now.' Grace had reached the bottom of the staircase. 'Besides, they're about to see some of the most beautiful art in the world – that's bound to make them happy. It's not like we're going to come face to face with anything that stirs everyone up or provokes them, is it?'

Perhaps if she'd had any inkling that she was one hundred per cent wrong about that, Grace would not have run lightly up the steps to join her group with a confident smile on her lips. She would have turned around and headed back out of the double doors as fast as she possibly could.

CHAPTER 2

It was after Monet and just before Manet that she noticed him. He was what her boss, Alistair, called a 'floater'. Grace felt that description carried far too many toilet overtones and preferred the more poetic name of 'shadower'.

You got them on almost every tour: the member of the public who would loiter near the group to listen to what the guide was saying while trying to appear as if they weren't. Sometimes they would pretend they were studying a different picture, or station themselves on a nearby bench and shut their eyes as if gallery fatigue had overtaken them.

A woman Grace had attracted last week had developed some problem with her shoe which necessitated taking it off and peering at the heel as Grace explained why Gauguin had felt compelled to leave France and paint in Tahiti. The moment Grace stopped talking, on went the shoe and off went the woman.

Alistair got very shirty about the whole thing, reasoning that if someone wanted to listen to a tour they should damn well put their hands in their pocket and pay for one, but Grace took a more relaxed approach. None of the shadowers stayed long and barely any followed from one room to the next. If they did, Grace stared at them and asked, with a concerned expression, whether they were lost. That invariably sent them slinking away.

This particular example of the species was different. Positioned just behind the Tuscelli family, he was making no effort to hide the fact that he was following them. He moved on exactly when the group moved, stopped when it stopped.

Grace guessed that he wouldn't have had much success trying to be inconspicuous anyway. He was more of a show-off than a shadower. His shaggy blond hair, finger-combed she suspected, made her wonder if he was Scandinavian or perhaps spent a lot of time outside in the sun. He might even be a surfer, but his clothes had definitely never been anywhere near the sea. He seemed to be wearing a formal evening dress jacket with tails, its sleeves pushed up to reveal a jumble of brightly coloured wristbands from music festivals. Under it was a purple T-shirt and on his bottom half were, well, Grace was not sure what. She would have said pinstripe trousers but, if they were, they were incredibly old-fashioned, the kind that you'd expect to see topping spats in a black-and-white film. His were teamed with black biker boots, chunky and looking as though they'd been scraped along the road, possibly where he'd fallen off a bike.

There was something deeply familiar about that kind of appearance – the off-the-wall rather than off-the-peg clothes and the way they had been put together – and Grace didn't like it at all. Not one bit. It made her feel that everything she had worked to dampen down in herself over the last nine years might be in danger of taking light again, and while her mouth continued to explain about brush-strokes and artistic influences, in her chest there was a sense of unease that felt as solid as if she had swallowed something down without chewing it properly. She continued to talk, the group continued to listen, but there was mad Fred Astaire at the back, his blond hair blaring out at her every time she let her eyes stray that way.

Her sense of unease intensified as she got beyond his hair and clothes to his face. It wasn't a disturbing face in itself – strong nose, green eyes, usual number of lips – but as she talked it was obvious from the range of expressions animating it that he was intensely, mind-numbingly bored. His body language was shouting that too – now he was crossing his arms, now uncrossing them. He examined the palm of his hand, turned it over and seemed to find fault with one nail. If he did look at the painting they were gathered around, it was with an expression that suggested not only boredom but also irritation. It was followed by more fidgeting.

All that energy. All that restlessness. Hard to contain.

Once or twice she caught him watching her and then his expression became even more morose, a frown making him suddenly look more Viking than beach boy.

Not knowing the Swedish or Norwegian for 'Are you lost?' and hoping that he would simply drift away, she shifted position so that he was not in her sight line. A quick check on the group confirmed that nobody else was really concerned about his presence yet. Except for Gisella Tuscelli: she was running through what Grace supposed was her flirting repertoire, alternating hot glances with shy dips of her chin, her body being subtly displayed in the blond guy's direction. He gave her a half-hearted once-over and returned to examining his fingernail.

'So,' Grace said briskly, 'that's the first of Manet's paintings we'll be looking at this afternoon, and now, for the second.' She gestured along the wall. 'It's perhaps one of the best known in the world.'

Everyone turned to look.

'A Bar at the Folies Bergère,' Mrs Macintosh said, as if she couldn't believe it was here, just a few feet away. Grace saw that a few others had the same star-struck expression on their faces and waited for the customary scramble to get the best position. She beat them to it and asked them to move back a few steps, mindful of a previous client who had been so caught up in the moment, he'd reached forward and would have touched the painting if Grace had not stopped him.

The blond guy had followed them and the unchewed thing in her chest got bigger.

'So strange to see this in front of me,' Mrs Macintosh said, the sense of wonder still in her voice, 'I had a poster of it on my bedroom wall when I was a student.'

'I also.' Monsieur Laurent nodded at the woman in a black-and-white dress standing at the centre of the picture. 'She is beautiful.'

Beautiful she might be, but Grace had always felt the woman seemed distant, as if she were protecting herself from all the frenetic activity around her in the painting. Perhaps that was why she loved it so.

'This is a painting that is very much rooted in a particular time and place,' Grace said, her enthusiasm genuine. 'It's full of details that make the famous Parisian nightclub come alive.'

She heard a sigh from the blond guy and turned to see him wander over to a window and stare out through the glass. He was putting his hands in the pockets of his trousers, a flash of a silver ring on one thumb. Everything about him said bored, bored, bored. He remained there, chin down, looking glumly out at the courtyard.

That was the point when, if Grace had been one to indulge strong emotions any more, she would have lost her patience. As it was, she contented herself with hoping he might force the window open and jump out, and returned her attention to Manet.

'Painted in 1882, this was Manet's last major work, and although he's not strictly classed as an Impressionist, this painting conveys beautifully the new trends in painting at the time. Most importantly, Manet has done some intriguing things with perspective and reflection.' Gisella was again turning and flirting, occasionally glancing slyly back at her parents to make sure they hadn't noticed. Well, Gisella's parents had paid for her to learn about the paintings in this gallery and as far as Grace was concerned that was a binding contract.

'Now,' she said, raising her voice, 'I mentioned the many wonderful details in this painting so perhaps I could ask Gisella . . .' She was amused to see the girl's head turn sharply to face front as if she were a schoolgirl caught dreaming in class. 'Gisella, would you like to come here and look in the top left-hand corner of the painting? Tell us what you see.'

Gisella's parents helped propel her forward, and she hesitantly approached the painting, leaned in closer and peered into the corner. There was a sharp exclamation.

'Feet,' she said, looking round at the group, the astonishment evident. 'Green feet on a . . . a . . .' She deferred to Grace.

'A trapeze,' Grace said, '*trapezio*. It's one of the entertainments in the nightclub: an acrobat. I love the way he, or she, is just tucked away up there. I've seen some posters of this cropped so badly that the acrobat isn't even on there.'

'That'll be the one I bought,' Mrs Macintosh said with a wry shake of her head.

Gisella went back to her parents and after one or two others had come up to peer at the feet, Grace began to talk through other details about the painting: a way of leading everyone gently towards the bigger things Manet had been trying to convey. She pointed out that there was champagne and beer at the bar and that the beer was Bass Pale Ale, so the tastes of British tourists were obviously being catered for. She showed them where the painter had signed his name on one of the bottle labels.

'Damn clever,' Mr Baldridge said.

'Indeed. So, remember I was saying about perspective and the use of reflection? Well, if you look behind the barmaid and off to the right, do you see the back view of a woman and a man in evening dress?' Grace could not stop herself from glancing towards the blond guy and his take on evening dress, and was pleased to see he had not moved from his contemplation of death by jumping. 'Now, if this is meant to be a reflection of the barmaid here, talking to a customer who would be standing where we are now, it's in the wrong place. It should be right behind her – that's how reflections work. Does that mean Manet wasn't that good a painter? Or has he deliberately played with perspective to create a kind of before-and-after situation – two realities? Look closely at those figures off to the right. The man is bending in to ask the barmaid something and even from the back she looks engaged, animated; but here at the centre of the painting, the barmaid we see staring out at us appears distant. Are we seeing her reaction to what the man in the reflection has asked her for?' She paused. 'It's only one reading of the painting, but it makes us question her status and her relationship with the man.'

Grace usually left it there and let the grown-ups draw their own conclusions, but she had barely got the word 'man' out when a bored American voice said, 'Oh come on, cut to the chase. What you mean is, has he just asked her for sex because she might be the kind of barmaid who's also a prostitute?'

The voice came from behind the Macintoshes this time and was accompanied by a hike of eyebrows and a grin suggesting that the blond-haired guy had started to enjoy himself and was fully aware of the effect his words would have. Nearly all of the group were now staring at him rather than at the painting, except the Hikarantos, who had their phrase book out and were no doubt searching for the word 'prostitute'.

Grace knew that at least one of Mr Baldridge's hands would be on a hip. His wife's mouth looked as if she'd drunk hot varnish.

If Grace weren't careful, this was going to descend into something unpleasant. But would trying to get rid of the blond guy be even more disruptive? She checked along the gallery to the seat usually occupied by Norman, a large, amiable attendant, but it was empty.

'Thank you so much for that interesting comment,' Grace said, hoping that beneath her sweet delivery the blond guy would hear the sarcasm. She followed up with her iciest stare, the one which unfailingly told anyone getting too close to retreat. The guy just stared right back and, if anything, seemed even more amused, but whether it was by Grace or the reaction his speech had just provoked, she could not tell. For the first time in a long, long while, she was tempted to stop being well behaved and say exactly what she thought, something along the lines of 'Bog off, you smug freeloader.'

She quashed that idea and said politely, 'I'm sorry, I think you might have mistaken us for your group. I did notice another one in the "Italian Masters" section. If you go through that door—'

'Nice try,' the blond guy said, 'but I'm right where I'm meant to be.'

'You think?' Mr Baldridge cut in. 'You paid to be part of this group, son?'

'Nope.' The tone was laconic.

'Well, we have.' Mr Baldridge raised his chin. 'Paid in full, up front.' Others in the group nodded.

Mr Baldridge upped the ante with a double-hand, double-hip stance and the blond guy responded by pointedly folding his arms and lowering his chin. Monsieur Laurent was strangling his leaflet again off on the sidelines.

'I think,' Grace said slowly, calmly, 'it would save time if we left chatting about payment until after we've viewed the paintings.' The blond guy opened his mouth, no doubt to say he wasn't paying for anything, but she had regained the group's attention and she wasn't giving it back. She was already moving. 'Come along then. It's Van Gogh next. No time to waste; remember there's so much more to see.'

Like a fussy mother goose with her brood, she got them out of the room and on to the next one. She talked brightly to cover up any lingering embarrassment and spotted where Norman the attendant was roosting today. Slumped on a seat next to the wall, he had his eyes closed, but at the sound of their feet on the wooden floor, he opened them and mouthed, 'All right, Grace?'

She was going to mouth back, 'Not really,' when she saw that the blond guy had not followed them.

The unchewed thing in her chest dissolved slightly, but even while she was talking them through the self-portrait of Van Gogh, she kept an eye out for that blond hair. She explained about the painter's extraordinary use of colour and the huge influence he had on artists who had come after him. She waited. No interruption; still no sign of him. Gradually she felt her muscles stop clenching and, as she relaxed, she could see the group was doing the same. If one of them felt at ease enough to ask a question, she knew all was well again.

'I hear,' Signor Tuscelli said, 'Van Gogh did not sell any paintings when he was alive.'

She flashed him a grateful smile. 'That's very nearly true, Signor Tuscelli. He sold just one – *Red Vineyard at*

Arles. Tragically, much of the time he *was* struggling against poverty. And now . . . well, the highest price ever paid for a Van Gogh was $82.5 million back in the 1980s.'

'So sad,' someone said. 'Such a pity.'

There was an exasperated, 'Only if you think an artist's worth is measured in money.'

'You back?' Mr Baldridge snapped and the blond man, now towering over the Hikarantos, said, 'No fooling you, is there?' did a pirouette and wandered over to a bench and sat on it. He made a big show of turning in the opposite direction, but when Grace started talking again it was obvious he was listening. At one point he sighed loud enough for everyone to hear, before stretching out his legs and wiping something off his boot. Grace could see he was unsettling people once more – every now and again someone would turn to check what he was doing.

She carried on, refusing to lose what felt like a battle of wills. When they moved from Van Gogh to Cézanne, she saw Blondie lie down on the bench and cross his hands over his chest as if he were dead. She increased her volume and animation and when she looked again she was pleased to see that Norman had hauled himself off his chair and was standing near the bench, presumably asking the blond man to sit up. He did so like a lamb, but as he turned his head to look at Grace, she heard him say, 'Hey, she's the one who put me to sleep. Tell her off.'

Grace fought the temptation to walk over and ping all the wristbands on his arm to wipe that lazy grin off his face. She could feel her muscles, particularly those in her jaw, start to tighten up again. She would ignore him, talk louder.

The next time she checked, the source of her irritation was leaving the room, methodically folding and unfolding his gallery ticket as if that was the only thing that would prevent him from falling into a coma.

'I think we're safe now,' Grace chanced saying in a con-spiratorial whisper to the group, as the noise of his heavy boots receded, and was pleased to get back laughter and smiles and a comment from Mrs Macintosh that she didn't know how Grace had stopped herself from 'slugging the guy'. Gisella gave Mrs Macintosh a look that suggested she'd like to strangle her, ditch her parents and follow the sound of those boots.

For a while, there were no further incidents, and Grace should have headed straight upstairs to 'Impressionist Landscapes', but she wanted to introduce the group to a painting hanging on the wall in a darkened side room. Although, if she was truthful, her detour had more to do with her need than the group's: she could no more have walked past the room than a mother could have ignored a child pulling at her skirt.

'If you'll forgive me,' she said, as she led them into the room, 'I'd like to show you this recent acquisition. It's a fifteenth-century icon from what is now Macedonia. I think if the people at the front move along a bit, we can all fit in. That's it . . . Mrs Macintosh, you here, and you, Monsieur Laurent. Please mind your footing; it's a little darker in here to protect the colours.'

Even in the low light the vibrant blues, golds and purples sang out and Grace gave the group a few seconds to take in what they were seeing.

'The Madonna with child is a common, much loved subject of religious art,' she said when she gauged the time was right, 'but this painting, with its quite tender and animated pose, is more unusual. The child hugging his mother with his back to the viewer looks natural, but the mother's response does not. She's looking straight at us, not at him, and we see how worried she is – you get a real sense of what's to come.' Grace fought to keep her voice steady and carried on. 'The intimacy of the relationship between the Virgin Mary and—'

'Jesus!' It was the blond guy, leaning against the door frame. He prised himself away from it and there was a shake of his head suggesting he thought that she was crazed. 'What, you're going backwards now – you plannin' to do cave paintings next?'

As he came further into the room he caused a general shuffling to make room for him.

Grace closed her eyes, hoping that when she opened them not only would he somehow be gone but that this dizzy feeling slowly spiralling up from her feet would have disappeared too. She opened her eyes to find him still there, and everyone was looking from her to him and back again.

She should concentrate on the colours, finish what she was going to say.

'Do you have a problem?' she heard herself ask sharply.

All heads swiftly turned to him.

'Well,' he said, squinting at the icon, 'as you ask, and apologies if you're religious, but an icon? Really? You've got everyone all cosied up in here for this?' Now he was really screwing up his eyes as if assessing the painting. When he opened them again it was obvious what the assessment had been.

'This icon,' Grace said, aware of the heads snapping around to look at her as if they were watching some kind of point-scoring, art-based tennis match, 'this icon is interesting and relevant in so many ways. Its survival, for a start, is miraculous in the face of all kinds of historical upheavals – war, communism, the black market. Icons like these used to be slashed with knives, dumped in rivers, sold abroad only to disappear into private collections. Even . . .' she was going to say *loaded on to bonfires* but couldn't get the words out. She took a deep breath and set off again before he could butt in. 'And, yes, they are an aid to prayer, but icons have also had a huge influence on all kinds of painters. Matisse, to name but one, loved their colour and spontaneity and they influenced his own work.'

She came to a halt to see the blond guy was smiling at her and his expression had a warmth to it which made her feel more uneasy than everything else about him.

'OK, OK,' he said, 'I get it, you like the icon. Boy, you've got some real passion going on there. Makes a nice change from all that painting-by-numbers spiel earlier.'

Grace did not hear that last bit, because at the word 'passion' she suddenly had such a strong vision of a beach that she had to put her hands behind her and press on the wall. There were waves too, baby ones, running up and back. She could feel the sand under her bare feet, even though when she peered down she was wearing the shoes she had put on that morning . . . blue shoes to match her blue suit. She lifted one hand from the wall and placed it on her jacket to check it was still there and had not been replaced by something made of cheesecloth.

She knew that she had to do something, but she was running into the sea, Bill behind her. She was splashing him before he caught her in his arms. 'You're pretty quick for an old guy,' she whispered into his neck and he laughed and let her go. 'I'll show you who's an old guy,' he said, turning and sprinting out of the water and back up the beach, and she knew there was only one way to stop him – she was reaching for the hem of her dress and peeling it up and off, chucking it back over her head into the waves. Tips of her thumb and third finger in her mouth, she whistled sharply and saw Bill turn; her heart gave a jolt at the way he veered to a halt, seemed unsteady. 'My God, you can't do that here, there are people,' he shouted, but he was coming back to her. 'Look at you, look at you, Venus out of the waves,' and she stood there feeling the sun all over her, his gaze all over her, beautiful, adored, free. Sublimely, crazily happy.

'Are you OK?' she heard an American voice say and she looked at the man in front of her and wondered how it was possible that Bill had grown younger. And then she was pushing herself away from the wall, leaving the beach behind, shaking the sand from between her toes.

'Yes, I'm absolutely fine,' she said, staring into green eyes and ignoring the puzzlement in them. 'And it's been incredibly nice having you along, but I'm sorry, we have to say goodbye now.'

He was looking like a Viking again. 'You doin' that "we" thing when you're really talking about yourself.'

'I'm also sorry I've been unable to show you anything that interested you.'

'Oh, I wouldn't say that,' he shot back, doing a flicky movement with his eyes up and down her and then giving her such a direct stare she was forced to look away and busy herself with apologising to the Hikarantos for talking so fast.

She heard him move, saw him stretch. 'Anyway,' he said, 'don't sweat it . . . it's just my taste in art isn't so—'

'Sophisticated?'

A flash of green eyes. 'I was gonna say conventional. I like something more modern. Challenging.'

Grace should probably have let him go then – she sensed the majority of the group were growing restless – but that arrogant assumption that his taste was better than hers was crying out to be deflated. She reached into her bag and extracted a Picture London leaflet and held it towards him. 'We do other tours,' she said, 'Hepworth to Hockney, Bacon—'

'I was thinking of something a bit edgier. Installations, happenings. What's on the streets right now.'

'Ah.' She put the leaflet back in her bag.

'Ah?' he echoed with a short laugh. '"Ah" as in "how great" or "Ah" as in "I don't like it"?'

'I saw a Gilbert and George exhibition once,' Monsieur Laurent announced. 'And Damien Hirst and a man called Angsty.'

'Banksy,' the blond guy corrected him, looking delighted that someone else was on his wavelength.

'I did not like them,' Monsieur Laurent went on, shaking his head sadly. 'They did not speak to me. Inside.' He placed his hand over his heart as if to make absolutely clear that he did not mean any other part of his anatomy.

'They don't damn well speak to me either,' Mr Baldridge blustered, pushing people aside to get to the blond guy. 'And even if they did, I couldn't hear them with your voice yapping on, son. How about you shut the hell up and let us get on with this tour? We've got time to make up, you know.'

'It's all right, Mr Baldridge,' Grace said softly, 'this man is just leaving.' She turned back to the shadower, who was looking at Mr Baldridge as if he wanted to tell him to have a go if he thought he was hard enough, or whatever the equivalent American expression was.

'I suggest you try the White Cube gallery,' she said. 'Or the Serpentine Gallery, the Institute of Contemporary Arts, or any number of artist spaces in Hackney, Tottenham, Hoxton . . .'

Suddenly Gisella was standing next to Grace. 'Hackney, Tottenham, Hoxton, are they far?' she said, the place names sounding both exotic and erotic in her mouth. Grace tried to think what the Italian was for 'on heat'.

'Not far,' the blond guy told Gisella, but the look of triumph in his smile seemed only for Grace.

'The gentleman is right,' Grace said, feeling a part of her old self scrabble up and out. 'These places are not far and, of course, your parents will probably have heard about them on the news – they became quite famous after the riots there.'

Gisella was soon standing back between her fussing parents and Grace dropped an 'ooh, sorry, look what I did' smile on the blond guy. 'Nice move,' he said, after which he just kept staring at her in a way that made her wonder if somebody had turned up the heating in the little room.

'Goodbye,' she tried, in absolutely her firmest voice.

There was a bit of a stand-off before his face relaxed. 'OK, I'm taking the hint. I'm goin'. But hey,' he gave her a megawatt smile that she hadn't expected, 'it might not be goodbye. We might bump into each other again.'

'I very much doubt it.'

'Small world out there.' He moved towards the doorway. 'Never say never.'

As soon as he'd gone, Mr Baldridge said loudly, 'Damn kook from New York.'

There was a beat before that blond head appeared back round the door frame. 'Nope, Rhode Island,' the head said with a grin and disappeared again.

'Rhode Island? That's even worse,' Mr Baldridge shouted after him. 'Bunch of pot-smoking Democrats.'

A laugh drifted back, along with the sound of heavy biker boots on a wooden floor, before gradually fading away.

After that there were no more sightings of him and Grace got the tour safely upstairs and focused on the art, as she always did, until the blocked feeling in her chest was gone. By the end of the day the irritating American would be no more than a memory, filed away by force of will on her part, the emotions he had stirred up pushed back down again.

When it was time for the tour to end, Grace took her group slowly back down to the gallery entrance. Some of them had further questions, either about the art they'd seen or other tours her company offered. There were questions about London too: how to get to a particular theatre; requests for recommendations about authentic pubs. Mr Macintosh needed some advice about an emergency dentist. Grace was not one of those guides who got sniffy about being asked to supply this kind of information – she saw it as an opportunity to build up some brownie points for

London and Londoners; small kindnesses that might be remembered in the face of whatever truculent waiter or gobby taxi-driver was encountered later.

After that it was time for goodbyes. The Baldridges were, unfortunately, already booked on her 'The Nation's Best-Loved Paintings' tour at the National Gallery next week. Other people she was unlikely to see again. She had a feeling she'd always remember the Tuscellis, though, especially Gisella, who even now was acting as if Grace had personally ruined any chance of her future happiness.

Hands were shaken, tips were handed over, and Mrs Hikaranto also gave Grace a paper wallet and an origami crane.

'How was Norman?' Lilly asked when Grace had seen the last member of the tour out of the double doors. The question was accompanied by a customary jerk of the head towards the upstairs rooms that always made Lilly look as if she were trying to dislodge something stuck in her ear.

'He—'

'Sitting down with his eyes closed?'

'Well . . .'

'Worn out. Caught him asleep yesterday. That new wife, Lavinka, Ludmilla, whatever she calls herself, she's always wanting this new and that new. Running him ragged.' The energy Lilly had brought to that speech caused a piece of hair to work itself free from the artful arrangement on her head and she poked it back into place with a finger before smoothing first one and then the other eyebrow. After that, the finger did a quick check along her bottom lip and Grace knew that if she were not standing there, Lilly would be getting out the hand mirror she kept under the desk and reapplying her lipstick. Lilly frequently refreshed her make-up, swivelling to face away from the gallery door to do it, which did not make it any less noticeable. Whereas in the morning she simply looked like a woman of a certain age putting on a good show, as the day wore on it began to seem as though the make-up was wearing her.

Grace had overheard guides with other companies referring to Lilly as 'The Painted Lady' and once, a guide who had suffered under the sharpness of her tongue, had called her the 'The Daubed Drab'.

Grace refused to laugh or smile at the nicknames, feeling that women who worked in a largely male world had to stick together. Unfortunately Lilly herself did not always buy into that view.

'It's all right with *your* hair,' she said, poking at her own again. 'Your hair's so neat it stays exactly where you put it. But mine's full of life, see.' Lilly was smoothing down her jacket, giving the cuffs of her blouse a tug to get them to peek out from under the sleeves of her jacket. 'And this uniform, well, it's not cut right for a figure like mine.' She looked over at Grace. 'Designed more for a boyish figure really. You'd have no trouble with it.'

'Thanks,' Grace said as pleasantly as she could, but her face must have showed some kind of negative response to those backhanded compliments because Lilly added, 'Nice get-up though that, Grace.' She waved a manicured hand at Grace's suit. 'And how do you get your hair so glossy?'

'White vinegar in the final rinse.'

Lilly nodded. 'Suppose you need that shine on it or a cut like that could look a bit severe. My hair wouldn't hold a bob, see.' Lilly was jerking her head towards the stairs again. 'Norman's wife, she's got a bob, evidently and she definitely wouldn't fit in this jacket.' She lowered her voice. 'Silicone job.'

Grace replied with a non-committal, 'Oh,' and before Lilly could add anything else felt the need to retrace her steps past the desk and up the stairs, heading for that small, dimly lit room again. It was empty of other visitors and she stood looking at the tenderness with which the baby was holding on to his mother, one foot twisted in his blanket.

She checked again that she was alone and then bent forward.

'Sorry about the American,' she said very quietly, 'not the Texan – the one from Rhode Island.' She leaned in further until her nose was almost touching the paint. 'And while I'm here, I'd like to say again how sorry I am about everything else too.' She hesitated. 'Desperately, desperately sorry.'

CHAPTER 3

Grace came out of the gallery, turned left and headed off down the Strand, retracing the route the Tuscellis had puffed along a few hours earlier. Deftly she negotiated her way around the bus queues and the groups of strolling tourists, dropping some money in the cup of the woman in the striped knitted tea-cosy hat and matching blanket who, as usual, was hunkered down in the doorway of the long-gone photo-processing shop. A few yards further on, she spotted the young guy with the cans of Special Brew arranged in a rough pyramid next to his feet. By this time in the afternoon he would invariably ask her to get her breasts out, although he used a more earthy expression. It was absolutely no consolation that he did the same to any woman who passed by, even the tea-cosy lady. Grace brought her perfected avoidance technique into play: quick look over right shoulder to ensure no traffic, skip into the gutter checking nothing nasty lurking there, walk rapidly while looking into bag as if hunting for something and then, when out of sight and earshot, a hop quickly back on to pavement.

Once breast man had been circumnavigated, Grace was again moving rapidly. Being able to walk fast after the ambling gait necessary in the gallery felt like a kind of freedom and she breathed in deeply. Autumn was mild this year; there was, as yet, no coldness to the air and there was a brightness to the light that Grace loved even more because once October was properly underway it would be replaced by a washed-out dreariness and then early dusk. The street today had the look of a film set – buses, people, taxis – the energy of it all making a canyon of busyness rolling down to Trafalgar Square, side routes splitting off to head down to the river or up to Covent Garden.

She inhaled deeply again. Was she the only person in London who found the smell of the traffic, the dirt, the din and the jostling of the people comfortingly mind-numbing?

She passed Charing Cross on the left and saw the tops of the cranes stretching above the buildings opposite, signs of a new development way off to her right. Just down the road she knew there was a statue of Charles I. That was the thing about London: history was forever shifting around you. In one stretch of pavement you could be in the present, then given a glimpse of the future before being yanked right back to the past.

The threat of being yanked back to the past spurred Grace on until she was at the heaving, noisy scrum of people and traffic and pedestrian crossings that was the junction of Northumberland Avenue and the Strand. Among those waiting for the lights to change were some Spanish college students, each wearing identical hoodies bearing the name of their college. Hanging from most of their hands were also identical carrier bags from one of the gift shops that lay in wait along this particular stretch of road. Grace guessed that within those bags lay various combinations of beefeaters, black taxis, red buses and perhaps postcards of Will and Kate. As the traffic stopped she saw the boy nearest her extract a mask of the prime minister from his bag. He seemed highly delighted with his purchase and she wondered why until she heard him shout 'Simon Cowell' and hold it over his face. There was no time to laugh at that because now it was a half-run, half-walk to get to the safety of the next traffic island before the impatient drivers, revving their engines, surged forward as the lights changed again and mowed you down.

Cutting across Trafalgar Square and squinting to see what was on the fourth plinth, she scattered pigeons and headed for the domed and columned mass of the

National Gallery. A quick check of her watch – no, Gilbert's tour would not have finished. If she was quick, she could catch him in action. Making slow progress against the flow of visitors already exiting, she reached the stairs and climbed them to arrive in the run of rooms dedicated to sixteenth-century European paintings. The atmosphere was hushed, reverential almost, as she approached a gallery in which, at the far end, she could see Gilbert and his tour of four people. They were gathered around a picture of a portly woman whose hand was resting on a stone balustrade.

In his pink shirt and pale linen trousers, his jacket slung over one arm, Gilbert could have been any urbane man in his sixties who, judging by his slight paunch, was too fond of a good meal and a good drink. Yet close up, the half-moon glasses, the intensity of his tone and the way he was talking as much with his hands as with his mouth hinted at a more cultured, perhaps studious, person. Grace watched him illustrating Titian's vigorous brush-strokes.

Heads moved in closer to the picture. There were nods, noises of consideration.

'And here,' Gilbert said, moving along to the next painting, the blue of his eyes still vivid behind his glasses, 'one of the most influential paintings of the Renaissance: *Bacchus and Ariadne*.' He surveyed the group and left a pause of a few seconds before confiding, 'Of course, Titian's religious paintings of the period exhibit this same vibrancy.'

There was more nodding as if those listening had known this all along and were happy that Gilbert had been able to confirm it for them.

Grace was going to move closer when she saw one of the gallery attendants walk slowly towards her, raising a hand in greeting – Samuel, his curly dark hair grey in places, but his friendly, open demeanour still managing to make him look much younger than she guessed he was.

'Puttin' them all in a trance,' he said in a soft aside, his accent lilting and tripping and somehow at odds with his sombre gallery uniform.

Grace nodded. 'Kind of mesmerises you, doesn't he?'

They continued to stand, side by side, as Gilbert moved his group along to the next painting. As he did so, he caught sight of them and lowered his head and peered over the top of his glasses, but did not smile. Gilbert liked to maintain a serious persona with his tours, but when he had all of his group firmly established in front of the next painting, she saw him lift his hand and place it on the back of his head as if smoothing down his hair, before splaying his fingers wide and then wiggling them.

'He's telling me he's got another five minutes to go,' Grace said in response to Samuel's quizzical look.

There was a low-throated laugh. 'He's a clever one, that Gilbert. Yeah. Really clever.'

A suggestion of something in Samuel's voice made Grace turn to look at him. That 'something' was in his eyes too, soft and watchful.

'I'll wait for Gilbert outside,' she said and walked away as quietly as she could, thinking about Samuel and what that soft look meant and whether Gilbert had any inkling at all.

Out on the steps, she watched the people in Trafalgar Square before tipping her head back to peer up at Nelson. Did he dream of Lady Hamilton up there, a soft gleam in his eye like the one in Samuel's? Or did he look down at all these nationalities and now and again spit on the heads of French visitors? She should warn Monsieur Laurent.

She was still thinking of that when Gilbert appeared at the top of the steps with his tour group. He was putting on his jacket, chatting with one of the women, and there was a handshake during which a tip was obviously being handed over. Gilbert was charming in the way he accepted it, but still managed to convey the impression that he was doing the giver a huge favour by taking the money. Slowly the group descended the steps with him and there was a gradual parting.

'Art group from Whitstable,' Gilbert said, coming to join her. 'Phil, Philly, Philippa and Phyllis.'

'Oh, come on, Gilbert, they can't all be Philistines. They were really paying attention, enjoying it.'

Gilbert sighed. 'You're right. They weren't a bad bunch. And no one did that bloody awful "Bless you" when I first said Titian.' He reached in the pocket of his jacket and pulled out his watch. Its strap was broken – had been broken for months – and Gilbert was in the process of getting it mended. Gilbert's processes for anything took time and involved more thinking than doing.

'Look,' he said, returning the watch to his pocket, 'I've got to come back to the office with you. Alistair's cocked up my payment again. Moved a decimal point . . . and not in a good way. Don't suppose I could tempt you to a coffee? I feel the need.'

Gilbert hadn't had to tell her that, she could hear it in his voice, and she suspected that his weariness was not actually due to the people from Whitstable or the wandering decimal point.

'Violet?' she asked, and when he closed his eyes as if pained, she transferred her handbag to her other shoulder and linked her arm lightly through his. Gilbert was not at ease being hugged or patted on the back, but he would take this level of intimacy from her. They set off, Grace saying nothing and knowing that Gilbert needed time to unburden himself, just as he needed time to get his watch mended. They walked in step, having to slalom to avoid those coming towards them and Grace wondered if they looked like father and daughter to the passers-by. Gilbert was as neat as she was; his white hair, still clinging on for dear life, was cut well, his shoes gleaming as normal. Gilbert had a vague, slightly bored air about him, though, which bore no resemblance to her approach to life, and whereas his blue eyes lent an air of bright intelligence to his face, her dark brown ones hinted at a more contemplative nature.

'Turkish or Italian?' she asked when they reached a gap between a ballet shop and an antiquarian bookseller's.

'Turkish, definitely.' They turned into the gap and down a paved alley that became broader the further along they went. Here there were a couple of shops selling coins and stamps, but they appeared dusty and lifeless. Acar's further on was a different matter – under a green awning was a collection of tables occupied by men smoking and drinking coffee and, although Grace could not understand more than a few words of Turkish, it was obvious that life was being chewed over, sometimes vehemently.

'Would you mind?' Gilbert gestured towards an empty table and patted his other jacket pocket. It was a pat that meant he wanted to smoke. 'Of course not,' she said, and before she had even got her bottom into contact with the seat, a young waiter appeared. He was carrying a tray on which were two china cups, a conical copper jug with a narrow saucepan-like handle, and a small glass plate holding baklava and revani.

The waiter put the tray down on the table. 'All right there, Gilbert?'

'Not really, Hakan.'

There was a sympathetic laugh. 'Like that, is it? Never mind, this'll bring you back to life.' Hakan spooned out the dense foam from the top of the jug into each cup and then delicately poured a stream of thick, rich coffee on top of it. He placed one cup in front of Gilbert and handed the other to Grace, asking her, as he did so, how she was doing.

'Oh, I'm fine . . . are those for us?' She nodded at the glass plate still on the tray.

Hakan darted a look at a large guy in a striped shirt that was straining at its buttons. He was, for the moment, engrossed in his game of backgammon.

'They're meant for him, but you can have them. Reckon he can live off his blubber a bit longer.' That seemed to amuse Hakan greatly and he put the plate down with a great show of rebellion before gathering up the tray, holding it in front of him like a steering wheel and driving himself back inside the restaurant.

'Bottoms up,' Gilbert said without much emotion, and, raising the cup to his mouth, sipped rapidly. Grace let her coffee sit a while before sipping at the cardamom-infused sweetness. For a time there was only the sound of the others talking and the clunk of backgammon pieces on board, but she could tell the coffee was refuelling Gilbert and that soon he would speak.

When he did, he said, 'Had all the kitchen cupboards out yesterday,' and Grace did not need to ask who had. 'Scrubbed them clean, washed all the jars and tins and packets. Convinced there are mice in the house. I have instructions to return home bearing traps and poison.'

Grace knew better than to start any question about Violet with the word 'why' as it suggested there might be a logical explanation for her actions. 'She's seen droppings then? Caught sight of something furry?' she tried.

Gilbert gave her a look that suggested even her careful choice of question was way off the mark.

'My sister, as you know, has highly sensitive hearing. She has heard them talking – not scrabbling and squeaking, mind you, but actually discussing our food supplies.' He picked up his coffee cup again and made to lift it to his lips, but paused. 'If they start bloody dancing, I shall ring Hollywood.'

She allowed herself to laugh at that, knowing Gilbert would not find it insensitive – she was one of the few people to whom he confided about Violet and her ever-shifting patterns of phobias and neuroses. Grace suspected that this was because she did not offer him platitudes or possible solutions. Also, when he told her about some particularly bizarre behaviour – only eating food that started with 'f' being one of the most extreme ones – Grace did not try to smooth out his worries and pretend it was 'nothing'. Having seen other people do this, she knew it simply made him angry and once or twice had caused him to doubt whether it wasn't he who had the problem, not Violet.

One other thing she had learned never to do was use the word 'issues' – it transformed Gilbert from cultured gentleman to carpet-chewing maniac. Once Grace had been present in the house during a visit from a well-meaning soul from the borough's social services department. They had not only uttered the dreaded phrase 'Violet's issues' but used their fingers to make inverted comma shapes in the air around it. Grace had taken herself upstairs to the bathroom, but had still been able to hear Gilbert hectoring the offending person and telling them to 'stop soft-soaping everything with that namby-pamby baby talk.'

Gilbert was perhaps the only man in London who could

use the expression 'namby-pamby' and make it sound like hideous swearing.

Grace picked up a revani, and while endeavouring to get it to her mouth without the syrup dribbling down her hand, also tried to navigate a route through Gilbert's black mood. 'So, the clearing out of cupboards? Discover anything?'

'No. Except . . . except . . . that's not strictly true. I found the rail ticket to Cambridge I bought for that weekend away that Violet did not want me to go on, some empty bottles of sherry that she's embarrassed about me taking for recycling, and, oh yes, I discovered that if you wash packets vigorously enough, they disintegrate, and labels on tins start to come off, which means that no doubt I will find myself eating rice pudding on toast one of these days.' Gilbert picked up a piece of baklava and broke it apart. 'I also discovered that if you stay up till 2 a.m. poking the sofa with a knitting needle just in case mice are nesting in there, the next day you can feel more than a little churlish about life.' Both parts of the broken baklava were put in his mouth and chewed and Grace hoped that the honey would sweeten his mood. When he spoke again, he said, 'Sorry, I'm being a pain and I'm being disloyal to Violet. I shouldn't make fun of her.'

'You're not. You're poking fun at the situation, aren't you?'

'Dear girl.' Gilbert gave her a brave smile and then rooted about in his jacket pocket and brought out a pack of thin cigars. He put one to his lips and, scanning the men at the tables either side of them, stood up and went and asked for a light.

'Not getting too cold are you?' he asked, sitting back down.

'No, I'm fine . . . and Gilbert, if you fancy a bit of a break this weekend, I could possibly pop round. If she'd let me.'

Gilbert smoked without speaking and Grace knew he would be weighing up how likely it was that Violet would contemplate a change to her routine. She had not been out of the house she and Gilbert shared for many years and would allow few visitors because visitors brought in dirt, a constant source of vexation. Grace had, however, been summoned there for the first time, quite out of the blue, not long after she joined Picture London. During that initial visit it had been obvious that Violet had wanted to ascertain if Grace had romantic designs on Gilbert. That his own sister did not understand Grace was completely the wrong sex for Gilbert had made Grace feel even sorrier for him than she already did.

'It's a very kind offer,' Gilbert said, as he stubbed out his cigar. 'But there may be a tiny light at the end of the tunnel this weekend. Vi is, when not worrying about mice, back on her research project. As well as traps and poison, I will be bearing home some virginal scrapbooks and travel literature from Chinatown's finest bookstores.'

'Ah, so she's finished America.'

'Yes. And now it is China's turn.' Gilbert waved towards the door of the café and did the universal writing-on-hand mime to call for the bill.

Grace suspected that Violet's interest in other countries was a way of compensating for the fact that her own world had shrunk to a three-bedroom semi and a small back garden with pots.

Gilbert reached for his wallet and waved away Grace's suggestion that they should split the bill. 'I am hopeful that if the mouse thing calms down, I could manage a couple of hours out and about on Sunday while she cuts and pastes her way around Beijing. I thought I might go and see a film, have a walk along the South Bank, browse the book market.' He shook his head slowly. 'Stupid place to go really. Too many memories of Tony.'

'Oh, Gilbert,' she started to say, but Hakan appeared with the bill. They did not speak again until they had retraced their route down the alley and back to the street. Gilbert fleetingly touched her arm and said, 'Ignore me, Grace. It's just summer going, autumn, then winter . . . you know.' He was looking around at the darkness coming in and Grace felt that even with the street lamps on and the light from the shop windows blooming across the pavement, Gilbert's mood was darkening again.

'There will be other Tonys,' she said, wanting to mention Samuel and that soft watchful way he had been looking at Gilbert, but knowing she had to pick absolutely the right moment. Besides, Gilbert was talking again.

'I doubt there *will* be other Tonys,' he said. 'I'm not much of a catch these days, and I come with baggage, if you'll forgive me referring to Vi in such terms.' He stopped to button up his jacket and lifted his chin. 'No, I've put all that behind me, if you'll pardon the pun. Anyway, enough of that . . . how's Mark?'

'Fine. Back for a few days end of next week, then off again for a couple of months.'

'Returning to Brazil?'

'No, one of the stans . . . Tajikistan, I think. Or it could be Uzbekistan. Hard to keep track.'

The noise of traffic and the crush of people made it difficult to say any more, but when they finally broke away from the main thoroughfare again, Grace felt that she should try to cheer Gilbert up before they got back to the office.

'I've had a trying time today too – a weird shadower, floater, whatever you want to call them. An obnoxious, opinionated American. Looked like a surfer, dressed like some demented Fred Astaire complete with dinner suit and biker boots. First of all he acted as if I was boring him to death, then he kept butting in. Had to keep him and that couple called the Baldridges apart. And cheek, he also made it clear that he thought I ought to be giving the clients a taste of edgier, more contemporary stuff.'

'God spare us,' Gilbert said in a dowager voice, 'from having to enthuse about bits of burned wood and melted plastic and cool ideas expressed in neon. Or video installations of a woman trying to iron a shoe. While it's still on her foot. People climbing up and down a fire escape with paper bags on their heads.' He was getting into his stride, already sounding more perked up. 'Save me too from things floating in jelly. Things made from poo. Old bits of tyre with diamonds pushed into them. Broken dolls' heads made into coats.'

'Gilbert, you're dreadful. There's more to modern art than that.'

'Wouldn't swap a warehouse full of it for one Titian.' He suddenly had hold of her arm. 'And for pity's sake, don't mention this to Alistair. He'll have us trotting out to Hackney to explore crappy galleries run by dreadful women with asymmetrical fringes.'

'Oh, Gilbert, have I ever mentioned how fond I am of you? You just say exactly what you think.'

'Now, now, don't start on with all that modern huggy-kissy business. I depend on you never to embarrass me with that kind of thing. You're far too sensible and down to earth.' He pulled out his watch. 'Come on, Alistair will be wearing a groove in the floor waiting for you to return. Fancy a wager on what his first words will be when we open the door?'

'No.'

'Spoilsport. I was going to take a hazard on "Grace, you have only twenty-four hours to save my company from a meteor!"'

'Idiot.'

Even as she laughed, Grace knew that Alistair *would* have some problem or another waiting for her. It seemed that these days she spent as much time sorting out his mistakes or, as he referred to them, 'oversights', as she did explaining the major movements in western art.

Picture London occupied the second floor of a three-storey building in a street just far enough away from Covent Garden not to be funky or fashionable or even particularly attractive. Here the buildings were of old London brick and only a measure of squinting was needed to cut out the traffic and imagine yourself back in Dickensian times. On the ground floor was Far & Away, a travel agency, and on the top floor a shop that offered watch and camera repairs. Alistair liked to make a clumsy joke about Time and Travel, into which he then tried to jemmy an art reference. Both Gilbert and Grace had heard this joke repeated so often that the pain was almost wearing off.

How Alistair could afford premises in this part of London had been a mystery to Grace until she had become friendly with Bernice, whose family owned the travel agent's. According to her, the building belonged to the dour Frank, the watch and camera mender on the top floor. His daughter had been Alistair's first wife, a fact that Alistair kept very quiet. Evidently, the lease for the floor occupied by Picture London came to Alistair as part of the divorce settlement, but how long it was his, or on what terms, were still unknowns.

As they approached the large window at the front of the building, Gilbert's progress faltered.

'Remind me what day it is?' he said craning his neck to try to peer into Far & Away's window before his feet reached it.

'You're safe, early closing. No Bernice.'

Gilbert stopped craning his neck and sauntered past the darkened window and the posters advertising individually tailored itineraries.

'Thank God for that,' he said. 'The eighteen-month build-up to the wedding I could just about cope with, but if I have to hear any more about the house restoration, about cornices and picture rails and damp courses I . . . well, I may book myself on one of her holidays and never return.'

He held the door open for Grace.

'Leave Bernice alone.' She walked along the hallway, past the glass-panelled door of the travel agency and then up the stairs. 'She's just enthusiastic about everything to do with her and Sol's life together. I like hearing about it. And, you know, she'd be as enthusiastic about Violet's projects if you only told her about them. She could get you some really good stuff on China – you wouldn't have to buy all those expensive travel guides. Why don't you ask?'

'Not likely.' Gilbert's tone was so sharp that she turned on the stairs to look down at him.

'Really? That's a shame because while you were talking to Bernice about China, you could also apologise for crawling past her door on your stomach earlier in the week so she wouldn't see you.'

'I've never done such a thing.' Gilbert executed an impression of an innocent man before patting his stomach. 'How would that even be possible?'

'How indeed?' She resumed the climb up the stairs until she reached the first turn where there was a window and, more importantly, a wide window sill where Gilbert liked to stop. He said it was to look at the view, but they both knew it was to get his breath back. She waited for him to puff into place and, when he had, he flicked the latch and pushed open the window. The sound of someone warming up their voice, running first up and then down a range of scales, drifted across from the dressing rooms of the nearest theatre.

'Did Bernice really spot me?' Gilbert asked, still looking out of the window. 'Has she said something?'

'No, I saw you; just happened to look down the stairwell. But it could very well have been her.'

'Point taken, Mum.' Gilbert closed the window again, but seemed in no hurry to set off up the remaining flight of twelve stairs that led to Picture London's front door. From here they could see the white lettering on the black paint and the wonky drawing of the London skyline that Alistair swore was 'refreshingly naïve'. Gilbert and Grace felt, with the way Big Ben was afforded such prominence, that it was vaguely rude, as though a gargantuan and very wonky penis were menacing the capital.

'So,' Gilbert gave her a gentle prod, 'last chance to bet on Alistair's current crisis. On what is now unfolding behind that black door.'

'Stop it, Gilbert.'

'Oh, Grace, Grace. Just for once you should let him disappear in his own paper storm; work your contracted hours and see where that leaves him. Or at least point out that making sure his backside engages with his office chair more often might improve things.' Gilbert's expression became more knowing. 'And another thing: where does he keep nipping off to these days? And why has he started locking his office door? Has he got another woman?'

'Hardly. He and Emma seem very happy.'

'Ah, yes, your friend Emma. Gives every appearance of being normal and then goes and does something stupid like marrying Alistair.'

'Ignoring you, Gilbert,' Grace said, going on ahead. She heard him get up and slowly follow her to the door.

'Right, last chance,' he whispered. 'I am going to put my bet on Alistair screeching, "Grace, I appear to have a spare trouser leg and keep toppling over."'

Despite trying to maintain a disapproving expression, she laughed at the picture of Alistair with both feet crammed down one leg of his chinos. Gilbert laughed too before placing one hand flat on the door and one on his forehead, suggesting it enabled him to tune into what was happening inside the office.

'No, no,' he said in a stage whisper, 'I was wrong about the trousers . . . hang on, it's coming through, yes, what he's actually going to say is, "My God, Grace, we haven't paid this bill, the bailiffs could arrive at any minute to strip the place."'

With that, Gilbert put both hands on the door handle, turned it and let the door swing open.

'My God, Grace,' Alistair's voice called out, full of fret and worry, 'we haven't paid this bill. They could cut the electricity off at any minute.'

'Ah, so close,' Gilbert said, and then stepped aside to let Grace enter the office before him.

CHAPTER 4

Grace believed that everyone had a distinguishing charac-
teristic. Whenever she thought of Alistair, she thought of
paper – he was always waving it about, stuffing it in his
pockets or sifting through the drifts of it that accumulated
on his desk. On rare occasions he would even get to grips
with writing on it. Today he was clenching an envelope in
one hand and a couple of sheets of paper in the other and
there was more, in a rough roll, protruding from the pocket
of his chinos. Grace recalled the paper crane Mrs Hikaranto
had given her and smiled. Alistair, her origami boss.

'The brown stuff's really going to hit the fan, Grace,' he
was saying, thrusting the papers towards her. 'Except there
won't be any power for the fan, so it'll just—'

'Slide to the floor,' Gilbert said behind Grace.

Alistair's colouring, already stormy, darkened. 'Yes, thank
you, Gilbert. This is no time for your mordant wit.'

Gilbert came into the reception area and shut the front
door behind him, which meant Grace had to tuck herself

in between the leather sofa and the coffee table. The reception, with its art magazines and designer lamps, was furnished to impress clients, but was not spacious enough to accommodate Alistair and his two staff when Alistair was 'achieving orbit'. This consisted of standing with his feet planted wide apart in the centre of a room while brandishing whatever was offending/upsetting him at the time. As he was fairly bulky to start with, and brandishing was accompanied by finger jabbing, Grace and Gilbert were often corralled into a tiny portion of the space not laid claim to by their boss.

'Perhaps if you just let me see what you've got there,' she said, soothingly, 'I'm sure—'

'It's red, I tell you, Grace. Red.'

It took her a moment to realise that he was talking about the colour of the bill, and not that he'd run his eye over it and she needn't bother.

'How in God's name has it got this far, Grace?' Alistair's voice was getting louder, rising in pitch. 'Why didn't you bring it to my attention earlier?'

There was a sound of barely concealed exasperation from Gilbert at the way nothing was ever Alistair's fault, even though he opened all the post and was meant to pass Grace anything that needed action. It was a system that could have worked smoothly if Alistair didn't have the organisational skills of a drunken gorilla. Sometimes Grace imagined he dealt with the post by standing in a corner of his room with his eyes closed and hurling it in the direction of his desk. While Grace tried to work around this by surreptitiously tidying up when he was out of the office and actioning things she found mouldering in the far reaches of his room, sometimes something important would elude her. This could be due to a mishap, such as Alistair letting post fall down the back of a piece of furniture or taking it home in his pocket and never bringing it back. Other times he was more imaginative in his stupidity. Once he'd even managed to sandwich incoming letters between outgoing ones and lobbed the whole lot into the postbox together.

Luckily for Gilbert, Alistair did not hear that exasperated noise, being deaf now to all but his own hysteria. Judging by the way he had screwed up the envelope and thrown it on the coffee table and was using both hands to shuffle through the offending paperwork, that hysteria was on the rise.

'I'll lose business through this,' he was saying, 'and more money because we'll have to get reconnected.'

'Alistair, I'm sure it's nothing that can't be sorted.' Grace wasn't sure of that at all, but calming him down was her first priority. Getting out of her prison between the sofa and the coffee table was her second.

'How about we go to your office?' she said, indicating one of the two doors in the wall opposite. 'I can't see what you're worrying about while I'm trapped over here by the sofa.'

'No, not my office . . . not just now.' Alistair looked as evasive as it was possible for anyone to look without actually pulling up a trench coat collar and ramming a trilby down over their eyes. He moved towards the other door in the wall. 'We'll go into yours. But it doesn't really matter where we go, Grace. This is beyond sorting.'

He opened the door and stepped into her office.

'Why can't we go to his?' Gilbert said very quietly. 'Do you think he's got a fancy woman in there now? Over the desk?'

Grace didn't reply, but she couldn't help wondering what kind of mess Alistair's office must be in if he didn't want her to see it. God knew, she'd seen it in some terrible states.

Alistair replanted himself, but at least this time there was more space around him. Here too there was room enough for a desk, a couple of filing cabinets, an easy chair in which Gilbert took up residence whenever he was visiting and a wooden table holding everything needed to make tea or coffee, including a battered kettle. There would have been even more room if Alistair had not cut corners, literally, when overseeing plans to have this floor of the building converted. As a result, the place was Partition Heaven, which meant that instead of offering a layout where there was a spacious office leading off the reception area via one door, there were two less spacious rooms leading off the reception area via two doors. Alistair's office was narrow at the front, but widened out near the back, a feat achieved by nicking a big square of space from Grace's. Things were further complicated by the fact that the only way to get from one office to the other was to go back into the reception area and start again. Even more inconveniently, the only way to get to the toilet was through Grace's office, and the only way to get to the kitchen was through Alistair's. Neither of these arrangements was really convenient, particularly when Grace had to put up with clients trooping back from the toilet, sometimes only a few feet ahead of any smell they had created.

Grace took off her coat and hung it from the hook on the back of the door and saw Gilbert lower himself into the easy chair. She wondered if sitting at her own desk would give the impression that she wasn't taking Alistair's problem seriously enough. She remained standing, but reached over and turned on her computer.

'Don't fuss with that,' Alistair snapped, 'we're meant to be getting this sorted.' He waved the papers at her again.

Alistair's mood was now morphing from fretting into tetchiness and it was possible there would be a short detour through snitty later. There had been a time when incidents like this one happened only every couple of months and between them he would simply be disorganised with overtones of bright and breezy. These days he got worked up about the slightest thing.

'If you could just let me have a look.' Grace tried reaching out for the papers, but Alistair did not appear ready to hand them over.

'Perhaps,' Gilbert said from the chair, 'before you get bogged down in that, we could discuss my last payment?' He pulled an envelope from his pocket. 'I've brought in the invoice I submitted and the cheque you sent. Now, if you compare one with the other, you'll see—'

'I will not bloody see anything,' Alistair shouted, his eyes flaring. 'You don't get it do you, Gilbert? This,' the papers were waved again, 'this is serious.'

'So is my payment.' Gilbert's tone was affable, but Grace saw Alistair's colour heighten further and he stopped moving, even stopped waving the papers. It was always a dangerous sign that he was about to take his tirade up another notch. Gilbert obviously thought that too, because he shoved the envelope back in his pocket, got to his feet and said, 'How about I make us all a cup of tea?' He had gathered up the kettle from the small wooden table and was carrying it out of the room before Alistair could wind himself up any more.

Grace took her chance and got hold of a corner of one of the pieces of paper in Alistair's hand, but as she pulled at it, he jerked away. 'You've given me a paper cut,' he said with a yelp and stuck his thumb in his mouth.

'Sorry, Alistair. Really sorry . . . but I'm just trying to help. I can't understand why you've got a bill. You pay by direct debit.'

He took his thumb out of his mouth. Stared blankly. 'Do I? Yes. Or . . . or did I change it?'

Grace wondered how Emma put up with constantly having to iron out problems and sort out hiccups. At least Grace was getting paid for it. Well, some hours of it.

She held out her hand for the papers again. 'Stop worrying, Alistair. I'm sure the electricity company has to leave twenty-eight days between sending a bill and a disconnection notice. Even then there has to be about a week before they actually do anything.'

'Ivecheppedvedake,' Alistair said, around the thumb that was now back in his mouth. Grace interpreted this as 'I've checked the date.'

'And?'

Alistair wiped his thumb on his pullover. 'End of August.

That's six weeks ago, Grace. Which means that they might have sent a disconnection notice already and if I've . . . we've mislaid it, well . . .'

Gilbert came back into the room with the kettle. He glared at Grace in a meaningful way before saying to Alistair, 'Your door is locked.'

'So?'

'So I can't get through to the kitchen to top this up.' Gilbert shook the kettle.

'That bloody kettle shouldn't be in here anyway,' Alistair stormed, 'it should be in the kitchen along with the rest of that junk on the table.'

'But we don't like to disturb you by coming through your room every time we want to make a hot drink,' Grace said, trying to calm him down.

Gilbert stirred him up again. 'Even when your office isn't locked it's a bind.'

'Now, look—'

'Perhaps I could just fill it from the toilet.' Gilbert grinned. 'Not the actual lavatory, of course, but the hand basin. If I tilted it to get it under the taps . . .'

Gilbert was acting out the extreme difficulties this would present when Alistair said very slowly and very softly, 'If you do not put that kettle down, I will take it and shove it right up—'

'I think there's probably enough water in there already for two cups, Gilbert,' Grace said hastily. 'I'm not bothered about having anything.'

Gilbert gave her a little bow as if to underline how accommodating she'd been and what a pain Alistair was.

'So, happy now, Gilbert?' Alistair asked. 'Good. Well, if it's not too much trouble, perhaps you'd keep quiet from here on in, let Grace and me sort out this great big stinking mess?'

Gilbert raised his eyebrows at the tone, but carried the kettle back over to the wooden table.

'I'm sure it's not a mess, Alistair,' Grace soothed. 'I will ring the electricity company. I'm presuming you haven't done that?'

'When have I had the time?'

She did not say, *during the two-hour lunch breaks you seem to be taking these days*, and she ignored the way Gilbert was rolling his eyes, secure in the knowledge that with his back turned to Alistair, he would not be seen.

'If we pay by direct debit,' Grace said reasonably, 'then this bill is obviously a mistake. If we don't, we'll simply send them a cheque, explain the problem. There's no way the electricity is going to go off.'

At that moment there was a clunk and the lights went out.

Alistair bellowed into the darkness, 'I was right, but oh no, you wouldn't have it. And now look.'

'She can't look, it's gone dark,' Gilbert said from somewhere near the wooden table and there was a stumbling noise and then an 'Ow, bugger,' which Grace hoped wasn't Alistair attempting to find Gilbert and grab him by the throat. The sound of china hitting against china suggested Gilbert was trying to move around too.

'Stay still, both of you,' she said, 'you're going to hurt yourselves. Let your eyes get used to the gloom. And Gilbert, did you just switch the kettle on?'

'I did. And then the lights went out . . . Ah.'

'It's tripped the switch on the fuse box, that's all. There's obviously something wrong with it. Nothing to do with the red bill.' She started to feel around her desk until she reached the drawers. Pulling open the middle one, she extracted a torch and, when she had turned it on, shone it first at Alistair to make sure he was still upright, and then at Gilbert. 'Unplug the kettle, will you?' she said, 'I'll just go and turn the electricity on again. I'll only be a couple of seconds. Don't move.'

She picked up her chair and, carrying it and the torch, made her way slowly back out into reception. The electricity box was high up on the wall just outside the front door and soon, by climbing on the chair, she had opened it and found the switch that was in the 'off' instead of the 'on' position. She flicked it back up and there was that clunk again, and then light. She blinked at the brightness and closed the front of the box.

When she got back to her office, Gilbert was sitting on the edge of her desk with his trouser leg rolled up, examining a red mark just below his knee.

'Desk or easy chair?' she asked.

'Both,' he replied.

Alistair appeared to have calmed down. 'Thank you, Grace,' he said and looked shamefaced. This was the nice Alistair, the one who, although frustrating to work for, made up for it by being kind and funny. The other Alistair appeared to have melted away into the dark.

She put the torch carefully back in the drawer exactly where it had been lying before and held her hand out for the papers. This time Alistair gave them to her and she put them on her desk and flattened out the creased evidence of all the waving and fretting to which Alistair had subjected them.

A quick skim over the figures left her none the wiser, and then something caught her attention.

'Alistair, this bill isn't ours. It's not even for anyone in this street. Saracen Place, that's quite a hike away.'

Alistair came and looked over her shoulder.

'But the bill came to me.'

'When? I've never seen it. I'd have noticed if it had been hanging around since the end of August. Where did you find it today?'

'My in tray.'

'This isn't making sense. Your in tray has been cleared out many times since August.' She didn't say by her. 'When I had a quick peek last, you were more or less up to date.'

Alistair picked up the papers again. He was frowning, but as Grace watched she saw a tiny relaxation in the frown as if he'd just had a thought.

'Unless . . .' he said, 'unless it was among those papers I found at the bottom of my briefcase. You know the briefcase I take to the Chamber of Commerce meetings? I haven't used it since the last one and I was clearing it out ready for yesterday's meeting and . . . yes . . . I remember taking some papers out of the bottom of it and placing them on the floor.' He beamed at her. 'Yes, that's probably it.'

Grace knew that was the best explanation she was likely to get. Asking him how he'd managed to open someone else's post, continue to think it was his, file it in his briefcase even though it was a red bill and then wipe its existence completely from his mind was pretty pointless. She just hoped that the people in Saracen Place weren't still groping around in the dark because of him.

'Perhaps I ought to take a look at those other papers that were in your briefcase as well,' she said.

He nodded vigorously. 'Yes, of course, Grace. Good idea. I'll get them now.' Another smile and he trundled from the room.

'That,' Gilbert said, rolling down his trouser leg, 'was a classic, even by Alistair's standards. He's getting worse.'

'Shh.'

When Alistair came back, he was not holding any papers but he had put on his coat. The offending briefcase was clutched to his chest.

'There's not another Chamber of Commerce meeting now, is there?' Grace asked, staring at it.

Alistair appeared to be ignoring her. 'I won't be long,' he said brightly. 'Can you just hang on till I get back?' He called across to Gilbert. 'You too . . . as you're here anyway.' He started to leave the room.

Grace followed him. 'Those papers, Alistair, remember you were going to fetch them?' But the front door was already closing behind him.

Back in Grace's office, Gilbert had taken up residence in the easy chair again. 'Marvellous. Now I'll have to wait for him and I'll end up rushing around to get Vi's supplies. And he's forgotten all about my payment.' He gave her a sly smile. 'I don't suppose, Grace, that you could take a look?'

Over the next twenty minutes, Grace sorted out where Gilbert's payment had been messed up, and when she tried Alistair's office door and now found it open, left him a note on a large piece of paper about the new cheque he needed to write for the outstanding amount. On the floor was what she assumed were the other papers he had found in that briefcase. She sifted through them and the in tray to make sure none of it was toxic. She answered a couple of letters on Alistair's behalf, putting them in envelopes ready to drop in the postbox on her way home. She checked the answer phone and dealt with what she could, leaving Alistair another larger note about a couple of things that only he could sort out.

In the kitchen she emptied the fridge of everything looking past its best, put it all in the bin and then, carrying the full bin-liner through to the reception area, left it near the door to take downstairs when she went out. She walked back through to her office to give Mrs Macintosh, the New Zealander, a quick call to see how her husband had got on at the emergency dentist and, finally, she pulled down the blinds on the two windows overlooking the street and had a bit of a clean around with the duster and polish kept in her drawer next to the torch.

'For goodness' sake, Grace,' Gilbert said, 'just sit down and relax. Have a cold cup of tea. You do not get paid to

do all this extra stuff. Remind me again how many hours
of office admin are in your contract?'

Grace didn't answer.

'All I can say is that Alistair hit pay dirt when he found
a woman as dedicated to order as you are.'

'We've talked about this before, Gilbert,' she said, carrying on with the polishing. 'I'm not necessarily doing it
for Alistair. I like things to run smoothly, be in the right
place. Anything else makes me feel unsettled.'

'Never think of initiating a coup though, Grace? Storming
his desk, taking over the company? You could run it better
than he could with your eyes closed.' Gilbert did a camp
pause. 'Actually, I think that is how Alistair runs it most
of the time – eyes closed, fingers in ears, brain up his—'

'Don't be daft, Gilbert.'

'Or looking for something else, something with a bit
more power? Yes,' he lowered his voice, 'you could set up
a rival company. I'd come and work for you like a shot. Bet
quite a few of the other art guides in London would too.
I can see it now.' Gilbert swept his hand through the air
in an exaggerated arc. 'Guided by Grace. Got a certain ring
to it, don't you think?'

'No, I don't. I'm perfectly happy pootling around here.
Suits me, Gilbert. I like the routine.'

She didn't know if that sounded a bit defensive, but the

soothing strains of Mozart emitting from Gilbert's phone distracted him. His face suggested he was anything but soothed.

'Ah, what fresh hell is this?' he said in a weary tone before answering it. For a long time he said nothing, and when he did it was obvious he was really having to fight to get even one or two words out.

'No . . . I did tell you he would be coming . . . Yes, we discussed it . . . to read the meter. He should have had an identification thing round his neck . . . well, that's all right then . . . no, what? Wait . . . so he hasn't read the meter? Well, yes, it could have been forged . . . but . . . No, I'm not cross . . . just . . . look . . . I'll be back soon. Yes, I'll remember.'

'Another day in Paradise,' he said, coming off the phone, and Grace tried to head off what threatened to be a return visit from the black cloud of Vi by wondering aloud what was so urgent that Alistair had to leave as quickly as he had. It was almost furtive. And why did they have to stay until he got back?

'Perhaps he's gone to see a man about a Doge,' Gilbert said laughing hysterically and then apologised immediately. 'Too long spent in the Venice rooms this afternoon.'

They batted a number of increasingly daft ideas about before deciding that it was probably something mundane

– perhaps he was picking up proofs of the new leaflet from the printers and wanted them to stay back to check them over?

Which was when they heard the door downstairs slam.

'Brace yourself,' Gilbert said, and they sat and waited for Alistair to climb the stairs. They heard the door to the reception area open and Alistair say, 'Just through here.'

'He's got someone with him,' Grace whispered.

Gilbert laughed. 'Bit heavy-footed for a fancy woman.'

The door was flung wide.

'Ah, here you are.' Alistair seemed very jovial. 'I've got someone I'd like to introduce. Someone who's going to bring a bit of new blood to the team. Here he is: Tate Jefferson.'

Before she saw him, Grace knew it was going to be the guy with blond hair. And here he was: striped trousers, evening dress jacket, rubber wristbands, biker boots.

'There you go, Gracie,' he said, giving her a double thumbs-up, 'told you we might bump into each other again.'

CHAPTER 5

'It's Grace, not Gracie,' she said, but Tate Jefferson gave no indication of having heard her. She was going to repeat it, but decided she could not summon up enough politeness to make it sound anything less than aggressive. She smiled serenely instead, as if she were pleased to see him again, but her heart was somewhere at the back of her throat and her mind already laying out the framework for a coping strategy, some way of minimising the presence of this disturbing, memory-stirring, testosterone-exuding man grinning away at her.

She continued to smile serenely as Alistair made a speech about how it was a new era, how he'd had to think hard about ways to widen the company's appeal and how Tate (boyish slap on the blond guy's back) would attract a completely different group of clients.

'Tate,' Alistair said, laying down his briefcase, 'will do more cutting-edge tours, show people the up-and-coming artists – even the ones no one has heard of yet. It'll be contemporary, in your face, challenging.'

He rocked back on his heels and executed a weird kind of swing at an invisible baseball with an invisible bat which Grace assumed was a movement designed to make him seem go-getting and modern. It was as embarrassing as watching your dad grooving his way on to the dance floor at a wedding.

There was the slightest of double-takes from Tate at Alistair's puzzling body language, and then he turned his attention back to Grace. Suddenly his hand was out towards her for shaking. It was the hand with the silver ring.

She took it graciously and refused to listen to any of the nerves in her body and what they were shouting at her. One shake and she would drop this unsettling hand, but its owner seemed quite happy to let it linger round hers.

'What's Tate short for?' she asked, trying to pull her hand free. 'Mutate?'

'Grace!' Alistair said, but her words had the desired effect on Tate: she felt him let go of her hand as he laughed.

'Gracie's pissed with me,' he said, turning to Alistair. 'We had a run-in earlier. You know you suggested I tag along on a tour; see how they're done? Well, I tagged along with Gracie.'

'Grace.'

'And, well, cut to the chase, we didn't see eye to eye.'

'Ah,' Gilbert said getting up. 'So you're the obnoxious, opinionated American Grace was telling me about.'

Tate looked down at his boots and then back up at Gilbert.

'Yeah, guilty of that.' He did not look guilty at all. His hand was out again and Gilbert came over and shook it with every appearance of being amused.

'I suspect Tate is short for Tate Modern, hmm?' Gilbert said. 'Or have you heard that a million times?'

'A million and one times now.'

They both laughed, before Tate added, 'Suppose you get people asking if you're half of Gilbert and George?'

'Only once.'

There was more laughter and Grace wondered what Gilbert was doing. That ready handshake felt like disloyalty towards her somehow, the jokey chat almost as if he were flirting. And Alistair: was he mad? What had possessed him to hire this brash idiot? This was all wrong . . . wrong! Didn't they see how disruptive a guy like this would be? How threatening to the smooth running of . . . everything?

And how was she going to consign 'the blond guy' to the dumping-ground section of her brain if, at this very moment, he had a name and was standing in the office, by her desk, chatting and looking like he felt at home?

She needed some time to get her composure back.

'I'll make us all tea,' she said, and before either Gilbert or Alistair could stop her, she had plugged the kettle in again and switched it on.

There was a 'phutt' noise and everyone disappeared into calm cloaking black.

Grace could hear Alistair huffing away, asking how she could forget so soon that the kettle was faulty? Gilbert joked about Tate needing to get used to being kept in the dark in this company, which Alistair responded to with something blustery before Tate cut in with, 'Hey, Gracie, think you got your night-time routine turned around. You put me to sleep this afternoon, now you're switching the lights off. What next? You gonna do some tucking into bed?'

However soothing the dark was, it couldn't stop Grace feeling aggrieved by that smug familiarity, and she turned in Tate's direction and pulled a face before doing the 'penis on the forehead' mime for a dickhead. It felt pretty good, until there was the sound of a match being struck and Tate's head and shoulders were illuminated in a glow of light. She wasn't sure she'd put her hand down quickly enough to avoid her rude gesture being spotted.

The match burned down and they were back in the dark.

'I'll get the torch,' she said, fumbling for her desk, and

all at once being in the dark didn't seem such a good idea. Someone was moving; she could hear them. She worked her way around her desk, her hands feeling clammy, and Gilbert started to whistle. He sounded as if he were still standing right where he had been when the lights went out. She listened again. Someone was definitely moving around – there was the scuff of a shoe, or a boot, on the carpet not far from her.

'Remind me to take that kettle out with the rubbish when I go tonight, Alistair,' she said, just to gauge from his answer where he was now standing.

Exactly where he'd been before, judging by the uninterested, 'Right,' she got back.

Pulse ricocheting about, she bent down quickly and grabbed the handle on the middle drawer and pulled. She felt for the torch and then squawked.

Someone had just blown in her right ear.

'What's the matter now?' Alistair called.

'Nothing, nothing,' she said, swiping through the dark off to her right with her hand, but only connecting with air. 'I touched something sharp in the drawer. No damage done.'

This time she managed to get the torch and held it in her not very steady hand to turn it on. In the beam she could see that Alistair and Gilbert were indeed where they had been when the lights went off, but Tate was closer to her desk. His face was a lesson in how to look innocent.

She asked Gilbert to unplug the kettle again and repeated the whole process of carrying the chair out through reception before balancing on it to reach the fuse box. As she did, she listened to the flow of conversation between the three men. It stopped and started as if they felt a bit self-conscious talking into the dark.

'So, what's your background?' Gilbert asked Tate, who replied, 'Art Institute of Chicago. Then a gallery in New York for a few months . . .'

Grace flicked the switch back up, the lights came on and she carried the chair back into the room.

'Wanna hand?' Tate said, nodding at it.

'No, thank you. I can manage a chair.'

'But not a kettle?'

Grace was careful not to plonk the chair down and when she opened the drawer to drop in the torch, she did it gently. Years of training herself to keep the lid on her more extreme emotions were paying off.

'Good job you had a flashlight,' Tate went on, raising his eyebrows. 'Can get pretty scary in the dark.'

She ignored the subtext of that, even though all of a sudden she wanted to put her hand to her ear.

'Oh, I'm prepared for most things,' she said brightly and then wished she hadn't as, rather than making her sound like Superwoman, she felt she had come across like a very old, faintly pathetic female Scout. The kind of person who carries a Swiss army knife around just in case anyone needs something gouging out of somewhere.

'We depend on Grace to get us out of any mess,' Gilbert said, making her feel worse. 'So, you have matches. Please say you're a fellow smoker? Normally I'm exiled in the yard alone. Be nice to have some company round the back.' He left a beat. 'If you'll pardon the pun.'

Yes, Gilbert was definitely flirting and Tate seemed to be flirting back in a kind of metrosexual way that was something else Grace knew she was going to grow to hate about him. Empty, easy charm. The worst kind.

'Yup, I'll keep you company,' Tate said, 'but I'm really trying to kick the habit. Cut right back in the summer, but now . . .' He turned to Grace. 'Guess you've never been a smoker?'

'No, afraid not. And now, Alistair, sorry to interrupt, but there are a couple of things on your desk I'd like to talk to you about. Shall we?'

She waved in the direction of Alistair's office, which was always a tricky manoeuvre and meant you had to decide in advance whether to be literal and do a zig-zagging thing with your arm to indicate the route into the reception area and back out again, or go for the simple option and, with a sharp jabbing motion, suggest a theoretical route straight through the office wall.

She had gone for the jabbing, which seemed to rouse Alistair. He picked up his briefcase, but before detaching himself completely from the others announced, 'I used to smoke quite a lot.' A schoolboy snigger. 'Not tobacco.'

Gilbert winced and as Alistair did that weird baseball action again, made even clumsier by the presence of his briefcase, Tate caught Grace's eye just at the moment she was remembering Mr Baldridge's comment about 'a bunch of pot-smoking Democrats.'

She looked away. He could forget about building little connections between the two of them based on in-jokes. She was busy building a high wall to keep him out, with possibly a moat beyond.

In his office, Grace saw Alistair glance at the notes she had left him about Gilbert's payment and the phone messages, and push them to one side.

'Seems . . . interesting, Tate,' she said, knowing an oblique approach to any issue was always best with Alistair.

'Mmm. Challenging, bit brash maybe, but I can see his potential.' Alistair did that face Grace suspected he had read about in management technique books – the one he imagined made him appear inscrutable. In reality, it made it look as if he had a piece of food stuck between his molars and was trying to extract it surreptitiously. 'I can see him really connecting with the funky young clients,' he went on. 'Making us the go-to company for hip tours.'

Grace studied Alistair's V-neck sweater and the striped shirt under it, one side of his collar buttoned down and the other breaking free, and gave thanks he had not used the terms 'wack' or 'well baaad'.

'Have you been thinking of getting someone like this in for a while?'

'Oh, yes. I mean, I know people think I sit in here just faffing around, but I've been thinking strategically. Our competitors aren't standing still, Grace; they're all offering a wider range of tours than us. And no offence, but neither you nor Gilbert is able to fill this gap in our services: Gilbert's at home in the sixteenth century, the seventeenth at a pinch, and you're far too busy keeping me in line.' He leaned back in his chair. 'Don't think I don't appreciate it.'

When he was like this, she could understand what Emma saw in him. He dressed far older than his years and he could do with shifting a bit of weight, but he wasn't bad looking in a scrubbed, pens-in-his-top-pocket way. And he was decent. Not a flake. Not like Tate Jefferson.

'So, he's employed on a freelance basis? Same terms as Gilbert?'

She saw the beginnings of a look that suggested it was none of her business. 'Uh-huh,' Alistair replied with a mistimed wave of his hand, which Grace guessed was meant to suggest nonchalance. 'Kind of a no-risk approach on my part.'

Grace very much doubted that.

'And he has a Blue Badge?'

'No. But what he does have is lots of contacts – artists, gallery owners, curators.'

She would not show how irritated she was that Alistair had put Tate's extensive address book on a par with the tourist qualifications Gilbert and she had sweated and studied for.

'And he has all the right paperwork, you know, for being employed in the UK? I expect you've seen his qualifications? You interviewed him formally somewhere?'

She could tell from Alistair's face that the answer to those questions was 'don't know', 'no' and 'yes, in the pub'.

'Grace, Grace.' He folded his hands in his lap. 'Sometimes you have to take a leap. Push back the boundaries. We all get so bogged down in making sure every "t" is crossed and every "i" dotted. Don't you sometimes feel that you have to shake off the shackles of how things have been and move on to how things will be? A life lived with regret is a life not lived at all.'

She wasn't really sure where Alistair was going with this; certainly not towards any practical considerations. Like whether Tate had the tact and patience needed to deal with tricky people. Tricky people who weren't him. Or if his organisational skills would enable him to make sure he had the right people at the right place at the right time.

'I suppose he understands all the health and safety issues?' she tried.

'He's doing art tours, Grace,' Alistair shot back, 'not potholing.' He got up and put an arm around her shoulder and she realised he was going to usher her out of the room. 'I know what all these worries are about.' His tone was kindly. 'They're just manifestations of a teensy bit of jealousy.' She went to remonstrate, but he held up his finger. 'And I understand, I really do. We've been a settled team for a while and this younger, trendier guy turns up. Charismatic. But really, Grace, you have nothing to fear. He won't be stealing away any of your potential clients – totally different market. He won't even be in the office much. It's not like he's going to share your desk or anything.'

'Right.'

'So, let's welcome him on board. I told him we'd all go out for a quick one after work. Get to know each other.'

'That's a good idea,' she said, despite having absolutely no intention of doing a quick anything with Tate

'And after the weekend, first thing Monday, we'll get to grips with publicising him and his tours, eh? Update the website, do some emailers, amend the leaflets.' He took his arm from round her shoulders. 'Right ho. Out in a minute.'

She found herself back in reception and there was a click behind her as Alistair locked his door.

Locking himself in now, as well as locking them out?

Grace returned to her own office, but hesitated in the open doorway. Tate was sitting at her desk and Gilbert was perched on a corner of it.

'I went to Chicago once,' Gilbert was saying, 'very disappointed.'

'Yeah?'

'Well, it wasn't windy. That's like going to Manchester and finding that it's not raining.'

Tate spotted her. 'Alistair mentioned about going for a drink tonight,' he said, standing up. 'Gilbert's up for it. What about you?'

'Oh, real shame, I'm afraid. I need to see my parents tonight . . . urgently. Bit of a crisis. Sorry.' She avoided looking at Gilbert.

Tate still had one hand on the back of her chair, the one

with the silver ring on the thumb. There was no way she was sitting down, even though he had angled the chair as if inviting her to.

'Sure you're not still sore, you know, about me in the gallery?'

'Absolutely not. I deal with difficult people all the time.'

He gave her a look that suggested he had got the insult. 'Well, as long as you're OK about it. No hard feelings? 'Cos some people might be tempted, you know, to make faces at me when they think I'm not looking? Perhaps even suggest I was a bit of a dickhead?'

She thought back to him blowing on her ear in the dark and stooped down to get her bag before executing a quick turn to unhook her coat from the back of the door. 'I'll give you a ring on Monday, Gilbert,' she said back over her shoulder, 'let you know when Alistair's written that cheque and, Tate, you have a lovely weekend, enjoy your drink and I'll see you soon. Not sure when your first tour will be; expect Alistair has it all under control.'

'Doubt it,' Gilbert said, 'and, Grace, are you sure you can't just come for one drink?'

'Love to, but can't. Sorry. Have fun.'

She didn't wait to hear any replies, just got herself out of the room, into reception, picked up the bag of rubbish and opened the front door. Disposing of the kettle could wait until Monday.

She heard them start talking again and felt forgotten already. Forgotten and miserable about being forgotten.

She went back to the door of her office. 'Sorry to interrupt. I just felt I ought to remind you, Gilbert, about that stuff you had to get.' She let her gaze drift to Tate. He was already back in her chair. So much for not having to share her desk with him. She added, with feeling, 'You know, especially the traps and the poison.'

'Nice try, Gracie,' Tate said, 'but it's gonna' take more than a few traps and some poison to get rid of me.' He swivelled the chair towards her. 'And don't think I'm getting in that trash bag without a fight.'

'Ha, ha.' She failed to make it sound anything other than forced and Tate stopped swivelling his chair and nodded at the bag. He wrinkled his nose.

'That one of your jobs too? Taking out the trash?'

'No . . . I . . .'

'Shouldn't be hauling that stuff about.' He stood up. 'You wanna chuck this kettle?' He grabbed it and in a few strides was standing in front of her – she did not have time to tell him it didn't matter and she could manage. As if to prove she couldn't, the strap of her handbag betrayed her and slid down from her shoulder.

'Here,' Tate said as he slid it back up her arm and repositioned it, giving it a pat into place. He was smiling at her as he did it and she tried to look nonchalantly over his shoulder despite the proximity of his face, his breath. Him.

'Gonna hand it over then?' he asked.

'What?' She looked at her handbag. Did he mean her handbag?

'The trash.' He laughed. 'Unless, you know, you're attached to it?'

'No, no.' She held it out towards him and the strap of her bag came down again and this time she managed to clamp her arm to her side to halt its progress. It was a bad move, because it forced her to cling on to the rubbish bag and took her attention away from trying to avoid any part of his body touching any part of hers.

More amusement from him, more embarrassment from her.

He was tugging at the rubbish bag now and she let it go and saw him transfer both it and the kettle to one hand, and then he was putting her wayward strap back up on her shoulder at exactly the same time as she was trying to do it herself.

'Oh, sorry,' she said, flapping to pull her hand away. He said nothing, but she saw from his eyes he had registered her awkwardness. When she did manage to disengage her hand, it seemed a gauche thing to do, as if she were a nervous virgin, an impression underlined by the way she flinched when he again patted her strap into place on her shoulder.

'Thank you,' she said primly and saw his lips give a definite hitch up.

Gilbert appeared behind Tate's shoulder. 'You two are making this look like some ancient bag-transferring ceremony. Have you quite finished? Because if you have,' he patted the pocket where he kept his cigars, 'I might tag along with you and sneak a crafty one. If you'll pardon the pun. Give me that kettle, Tate; I need an alibi for my trip out if the smoking police should happen to emerge.' He looked towards Alistair's door.

Grace could have kissed Gilbert at that point. 'Excellent,' she said, 'that's really helpful. You can show Tate where the rubbish goes and I can nip off.' She did a quick turn intending to head out before them and get down the stairs as quickly as she could.

'Need something from you before you go,' Tate said, making her turn back.

'Yes?'

He nodded slowly and she couldn't help reading the signs. He was interested in her, perhaps more than interested. There was a light in his eyes that was trying to spark something in her. She dropped her gaze to the cuff of her coat as if whatever was there, invisible to anybody else, had to be examined that minute.

'Sorry?'

She heard the rustle of the bag and worked out that he was about to lift it up and over his shoulder. She imagined he must look like a pinstriped robber when he got it there, but she wasn't going to check.

'Your flashlight, Gracie,' he said. 'Wanna lend it me? Gonna be dark round the back, I guess.'

'No,' she said to her cuff, refusing to rise to his teasing. 'The security light will bounce on when you arrive.'

She was moving as quickly as she could without appearing to run and pulled open the door, jabbing the doorstop under it so she wouldn't have to stand there and hold it open for him.

'See you Monday,' she called back as she traversed the landing and headed down the stairs, noting with satisfaction that Tate had only just ambled to the open door, Gilbert a couple of steps behind him.

'Bye, Grace,' Gilbert called after her.

'Yeah, mind how you go, Gracie,' Tate added. 'And you get plenty of rest over the weekend.'

Grace didn't want to think what Tate meant by that hanging sentence and instead concentrated on heading, like a person seeking sanctuary, out of the building.

CHAPTER 6

Alistair locked the door behind Grace and returned to his desk but made no attempt to sit back down. He only had a few minutes before Gilbert would come looking for him.

He relived the red electricity bill incident. That had been bad, a real cock-up. Not concentrating enough, that was the trouble. All that shouting and prancing about he'd done. He moved around the desk as if the change of position could shift the memory of his earlier histrionics.

Still, not much use dwelling on it; he'd never been particularly good at that aspect of business, even when his mind was focused on what he was doing. Give him the bigger picture to think of and he was fine, but all that checking and attention to detail, all that keeping the plates spinning – not where his strengths lay. Thank God for Grace standing there catching the china. Like Emma.

No, best not to think about Emma at the moment.

He bent down and got hold of his briefcase, remembering how he'd told Grace he'd emptied it out to take to the

Chamber of Commerce meeting. She'd never know he only got there in time for the last two items on the agenda. Other fish to fry.

His heart began to pump harder.

He placed the briefcase carefully on his desk, laying it flat and staring at it, feeling the scurries of excitement in his stomach. Typical Grace just now, asking him all those questions. When she locked those dark eyes of hers on to his, he felt as if he were being interrogated. And he knew what she was getting at: all the things he hadn't done by the book; all the things that could go wrong with Tate. Fear of change, that was her problem.

And that jealousy: who'd have thought it?

Easy for people to feel undervalued, overlooked when someone new comes along. He'd have to watch that. Pay rise? Maybe not. New kettle instead.

He laughed at that. He could still manage a laugh.

He turned the numbered dials next to the left-hand lock on the case and it clicked open. He had started on the other side when the phone rang and he almost took a chunk out of his tongue.

To answer or not to answer? Could be Emma. He saw his hand reach for the phone, his brain pull it back before he could pick up.

Guilt had replaced anticipation. He needed to calm down. Just answer normally. Everything was normal. He needed to tell her he was going for a drink after work, he'd be late. It was only fair or she'd worry.

He picked up the phone.

'Alistair Sawclose.'

'Hello there. It's me. Nothing wrong, just checking what time you're likely to be home. I've made coq au vin. Was going to put it in now . . .'

'Lovely, lovely,' he said, thinking how normal all those plans sounded, how light her tone.

'Are you all right? You sound a bit . . . a bit . . . oh, I don't know.'

'Just rushed into the office to answer the phone. Sorry. I'll take some deep breaths . . .' He hammed it up. 'There. Better?'

'Uh-huh. Oh, how did the Tate thing go? Grace OK with it?'

'Think so, although, Grace being Grace, she wanted to know it was all done by the book . . .' he stopped himself going down that route; if he mentioned Grace's questions about qualifications and paperwork, Emma might want to know about them too.

'She'll keep you right. So . . . home time?'

He glanced at his watch, felt the available free minutes

left to him ticking away. First anticipation, then guilt. Now? Frustration. His constant companion these days.

'I'm going to be a while,' he said. 'We're taking Tate out for a drink, just so everyone can get to know each other a bit better. Try and be home by eight.'

There was a noise that might have been exasperation or disappointment, and then, 'OK, well, I'll put it in anyway, it won't spoil.'

'What won't?'

'The casserole, silly. Are you sure you're OK?'

He wanted to scream, 'No, I'm not, so get off the phone!' and instantly felt remorse. None of this was Emma's fault.

'I'm fine, darling, just a bit tired. Get that bottle of Merlot open, the good one out in the garage . . . we'll sink that when I get in. Have to go . . . Bye.'

'Bye.'

'Putting the phone down now . . . Bye.'

He looked at the briefcase and finished unlocking it, his heart speeding up again. His hand, he saw, was trembling as he reached in and placed it on the carrier bag hidden there. Just doing that made his mouth dry. A quick look towards the door and he'd opened the bag, tipped the green silk blouse out into one hand. The colour would look fantastic on her. Match her eyes. He couldn't wait to see her wear it. He disappeared into the prospect of that for a while.

The sound of people entering reception hauled him back. Tate and Gilbert. Had they left and come back? Why? When? How long had he been standing there?

Reluctantly he put the blouse back in the bag. The bag back in the briefcase. The briefcase back under his desk.

Now the blouse was out of sight, the pull of the woman it was meant for was lessened and for one insane moment he thought of ringing Emma back, confessing everything. Coming clean.

He steadied himself against the desk and imagined her staring at him in disbelief. She'd want to know what she'd done wrong.

No, he couldn't do it. What you didn't know couldn't hurt you.

He moved towards the door. Better unlock it just in case Gilbert tried to open it and made another loaded comment. He knew they'd started talking about it, him and Grace. Wondering why.

Perhaps he should just get a secure cabinet, easier to explain a locked cabinet than a locked door. He'd make up some reason for getting it – something about keeping client details secure at all times, advice from the Chamber of Commerce, data protection . . . blah, blah, blah.

Yes, that might work – after all, they needed to guard against a nosy client who might rifle through a drawer, find someone else's bank details, home address.

Besides, there was only so much you could fit in a briefcase.

The prospect of seeing her in that blouse resurfaced and made him feel lightheaded.

He put on his coat. Yes, a lockable cabinet was a good compromise. The others would get back their access to the kitchen and he'd get a lot more peace of mind. Wouldn't have to lug that briefcase around whenever he nipped out, either.

Right, he said to himself as he opened the door, and then shouted it again as he stepped through into reception. 'Right. First round's on me. Chop-chop, time's wasting.'

CHAPTER 7

Grace nudged the hot tap on with her toe, waited until the bath water returned to optimum temperature and then nudged it off again. Leaning back, she breathed in the perfume of white musk and amber from the candles burning on the windowsill, held it for a few seconds and then exhaled slowly. The process was repeated carefully, rhythmically, as she worked out a way of minimising the risk that Tate Jefferson posed to her well-ordered life. To her hard-won stability.

'He is,' she said to the taps, 'just passing through. He doesn't want to be a tour guide. He's doing it for the money. What he is, plainly, is a flashy, look-how-Bohemian-I-am artist. It's written all over him.' She contemplated the taps as if they'd said something and she was obliged to listen before nodding. 'Yes, we're a staging post before he's off somewhere warmer and cheaper. The question is, how long will he stay?' She gave the taps another knowing look. 'And, more importantly, how much upset will he cause before he goes? His type just loves stirring things up. He won't be able to stop himself from pointing out that we could do with a bit more of his carefree, rule-breaking attitude in our lives – our bourgeois, hidebound lives. Or, as we who have to live in the real world call it, "normality".'

She splashed her feet around in the water and then stopped and laughed – a weird noise in the candlelight. It sounded fake even to her. Tate Jefferson didn't make her feel like laughing. He made her feel like running very fast to a place where he wasn't. He reminded her of Bill and being reminded of Bill would lead her to remembering all kinds of other things.

'Nope, not going there,' she said to the taps. 'Not that person any more. No.'

She closed her eyes and concentrated on letting the white musk and amber soothe her enough so that she could think rationally again.

'What people like him need,' she said, when she opened her eyes again, 'is something or someone to kick against. And it very much looks as if he has you in mind for that person. You've been too starchy, too uptight with him. He caught you on the back foot. So, come Monday, Grace, my girl, you will be polite and helpful. You will show real interest in his tour and smile serenely even when he winds you up. What you will not do is answer back, engage in verbal sparring – in short, you will not rise to the bait.' She paused. 'Particularly when he starts up with all that "do you never feel like kicking off your shoes, Gracie? Cutting free? There's a whole world out there?" crap.'

Well her days of kicking off her shoes were over. She slipped down into the water to mouth level and blew a long breath full of bubbles before gurgling, 'Play it right and he'll be so bored, he'll be gone by Christmas.'

Now she had a strategy, she felt the hard edges of the Tate Jefferson problem start to waver. Besides, this time she was the older one. What was he? Twenty-three at most? So she had at least six more years life experience under her belt than he did.

Only idiots made the same mistake twice and she wasn't an idiot, she had to remember that. As she did, her uneasiness seemed less and less distinct until she imagined it a wispy, insubstantial thing drifting to the ceiling along with the steam.

That just left Alistair to worry about. He'd never been slavishly addicted to the concept of the work ethic, but recently the hours he hadn't been putting in had made her believe he might be losing interest in the business. Yet here he was, talking of fresh challenges and hiring someone to break into a new market. Even if that someone was the wrong kind of someone entirely.

She swished the water around with her hand and didn't let her mind stray to those other tricky questions about Alistair's behaviour. Like why he had taken to locking the office door? Or carrying around an air of furtiveness which seemed clamped to him as tightly as that briefcase had been yesterday? And what about all those trips out and about, unexplained and inexplicable? If he was cheating on Emma, that would make life tricky for someone who was stuck bang in the middle – employee of one, friend of the other.

Grace mulled over Alistair a while longer before deciding that talking to him about these things smacked of interference. And if there was nothing she could do, no strategy she could follow, it wasn't worth her worry.

She glanced across to her watch propped up on the back of the sink and congratulated herself. Two hours ago she had arrived back at the flat with her nerves, courtesy of Tate Jefferson and London Transport, feeling as if they had been stretched, twisted and then sandpapered roughly. Now everything was smoothed out in her mind and her body.

She remained in the bath a while longer before pulling out the plug and looping the chain around the taps. Standing slowly, she stepped out on to the bathmat and let the water drip down her body. A towel was pulled from the heated rail and she dried herself, methodically, slowly, before dropping the damp towel in the dirty-linen hamper. She peered at her toes, making a note to revamp her nail polish before Mark came back and, when the bath had emptied and been rinsed out, she finally undid the clip that held up her hair in a barely-there, neat twist. It was put back in the bathroom cabinet and a fresh towel wrapped around her body, the loose end tucked down between her breasts to keep it in place. She thought of Lilly's comments about her boyish figure and smiled. Slim would have been a nicer way of putting it. Pulling back her shoulder blades, she comforted herself with the knowledge that she still had enough happening up front to keep a towel in place.

She gave the bathroom a last critical look and turned out the light. This was the point at which, if she still drank, she would have walked barefoot to the kitchen and poured herself a large glass of wine. Instead she walked barefoot to the kitchen and felt around in the back of one of the cupboards and pulled out a large biscuit tin. She prised off the lid and examined the contents. Wrapped in a cheesecloth shirt was a packet of cigarettes and half a bottle of whisky. Under that were a couple of CDs of Spanish disco hits. Two joints, stubby and loosely rolled were shedding dried-up strands of tobacco in one corner. She wrinkled her nose at the unmistakable aroma of old dope and lifted the whisky bottle out of its cheesecloth wrapping and tilted it, hearing the liquid glug. She felt the balance of it change in her hand as she tipped it first one way and then the other and then she stopped abruptly. It was making her feel nauseous – the sound, the feel of the glass, everything. She put it back in the shirt and studied the joints as if they were some kind of archaeological find, interesting but not relevant to her life. She forced herself to think of Tate Jefferson – the way he dressed, his smile, that easy charm. Good, she was still feeling sick. She put the lid back on the tin firmly with a sense of victory, as if she were containing him just as successfully. With a hearty push, it was sent to the back of the cupboard again.

Minutes later she was back in the bathroom giving the grouting behind the bath a good going over with a stiff toothbrush she kept just for that purpose. She hummed as she worked.

The phone rang once and Grace let it ring. On checking her messages, she found it was Emma, sounding a tad squiffy and asking if she was all right, only Alistair had thought that Grace was going for a drink after work with everyone, but then found she had left already and Gilbert had said something about having to deal with family stuff that couldn't wait? Was everything OK? Just the normal dramas? And did Grace fancy a pizza and a catch-up later in the week?

Grace felt momentary guilt that she had lied to Gilbert about her reason for not joining everyone for a drink and that this lie had now spread out to Emma. She sent her a text saying she was a bit tied up at the moment, she'd explain everything later, maybe Thursday night, the pizza place by Victoria station? By the time Thursday came she would have come up with a better story to shore up the lie she had told.

Later, as she lay in bed, Grace felt a warm, heavy-limbed tiredness that she knew would soon take her under. She thought of the two free days ahead, with nobody to please but herself, and the prospect of seeing Mark at the end of next week. She turned on to her back. Everything was as it should be – calm, ordered, manageable. She and the world were safely under control.

At precisely 2.23 a.m. Grace sat up abruptly in bed and slammed her hand down on the snooze button of her alarm clock. It took her several seconds to understand that the buzzing was not coming from the alarm clock, but from the intercom next to her front door. Pushing off the duvet, she stumbled out of bed, located her dressing gown and flailed around trying to feed an arm into a sleeve. The deep calm and serenity of those moments before sleep had not survived the shock of being ripped from it. She was loath to move out into the hallway: even though there were two flights of stairs and five doors between her and whoever was ringing her bell down on the street, the age-old anxieties about friend or foe circled. When she did move towards the intercom, she misjudged the top step of the little run of six that led down to her front door and had to steady herself by grasping the banister rail.

The buzzing had settled into some kind of rhythm as if the caller were playing a tune. No, not a tune; three short buzzes, three long, three short again – S.O.S.

She jabbed at the intercom button. 'Dad, are you all right? What are you doing? What's happened? Dad?'

There was only the empty echo of the street and a lone engine, idling, before her father's voice came through, loud and aggrieved. 'She's gone and done it this time. Felicity. Your mother. Crossed the line. We've had a right old set-to . . . things have been said.'

Grace was unable to imagine what kind of lines her mother could possibly have crossed to upset her father. His normal way of operating was to smile benignly as Felicity, his wife, kicked up her heels and sailed over each and every line he'd ever drawn, her hair swaying with the speed of take-off.

'I'm opening the door, Dad. Come on up.'

'Right. And Nadim's here too. In his van.'

Grace heard a faint, 'Hello, Grace.'

'Van?' she said slowly. For a three-letter word it seemed very long and very difficult.

'Yeah. He's giving me a hand with some of me things.'

She moved her finger from the intercom button to the one that released the lock on the main door downstairs.

The buzzer on the intercom went again. It was Nadim's voice, not at all faint this time. 'You couldn't come down, give us a hand? We've got quite a bit of stuff. Don't wanna leave the van. I know this is Putney, but . . .'

Grace was already aware of the muffled sounds of her father's progress past the dental surgery on the ground floor, through the fire door and upwards.

Quite a bit of stuff?

'OK,' she said. 'I'll pop on some clothes and be right down.'

She glanced back over her shoulder at her sitting room and saw her pale sofa and one lovingly chosen statement armchair, the low coffee table with slate top, the rug. She pictured her bedroom with the muted colours and soft textures. Her gaze lingered on the delicate hall table with the polished wooden bowl holding three alabaster eggs. They suddenly looked as if they belonged to a species under imminent threat of extinction.

'Calm, calm, calm, Grace,' she intoned softly and unlocked the door of her flat. She pulled it open and listened. There was a noise as if someone had just snagged stiff cardboard along painted wall. Without pausing, she turned for the bedroom and some clothes, resisting the urge to detour via the bathroom and lock herself in forever.

CHAPTER 8

Grace was sitting at the kitchen table looking at her father, but her attention was on the boxes ranged along the hallway. Boxes that used to contain wine and toilet rolls and now contained books, magazines and rolled-up lengths of paper. There were three more boxes piled one on top of the other in the tiny sliver of a storage room in which Grace kept her ironing board, her shoe collection, a drying rack, a single duvet in a plastic cover and a suitcase. The room's inventory now included the polished wooden bowl from the hall table, with its clutch of three alabaster eggs recently divided into two whole eggs and two halves.

There were also plastic rubbish sacks and Grace could see the bunny ears of the largest one which was balanced at the top of the stairs leading to her front door. It was a friend of the three in the kitchen which, judging by the shapes Grace could make out pressed up against the plastic, contained clothes and shoes. On the table between Grace and her father were two other items: a toilet bag, slightly frayed and with a zip that would not meet over the things inside it, and a West Ham United mug which up until tonight had lived in a house in Newham, and which now lived, for a time unspecified, in a flat in Putney.

Grace wondered what the collective noun was for what she had littering her flat. A mess of boxes? A storm of sacks? A muddle of toiletries? One thing she did know: that mug was singularly horrible.

The expression on her father's face was not easy to read. It could have indicated that the bluster which had sent him storming out of his own house with boxes, sacks, bags and mug had shifted into a sickly realisation of what he'd done. Or perhaps it was simply another strain of the almost deferential nervousness he tended to display around her. She knew she was something of a mystery to him these days: his only conventional, wage-earning, property-owning daughter.

He glanced at her and away. Quick and alert were good descriptions of her father. Compact was another, and sometimes with his small stature and those deft movements he looked like some kind of busy bird. His dark eyes and sharp features only added to that impression, as did his fine plumage because, come marital calm or storm, he was dapper. It was what attracted her mother in the first place. 'Knew how to wear a suit, did your dad.'

Even though he was a bit creased and crushed at the moment, it was one of his good suits that he was wearing, accompanied by a shirt and tie. He had always worn a tie, even when she was a child and he was just taking her to the park or the cinema. His one nod to casual dressing would be letting go of his jacket and putting on a jumper.

He did a jerky movement of his head in the direction of the hallway.

'Let me pay for it, that egg.'

She again assured him that it didn't matter, it wasn't important; what was important was telling her the reason for the major spat with her mother. As opposed to all the previous minor ones.

'Only I know you like the place just so,' he went on, staring doggedly at his toilet bag.

'Dad—'

'I mean, I wouldn't have bothered you, but with your sisters away . . .'

He ground to a halt, no doubt realising that pointing out Grace wasn't top of his list of sanctuary providers could be seen as tactless, especially when she was all that lay between him and sleeping in Nadim's van.

'It's not a problem, Dad, even . . .' she checked the clock, 'at 3.45 in the morning. But come on, what's wrong? What's so bad that can't be solved by the usual shouting from you, flouncing and sulking from Mum and then some kissing and making up?'

Her father was still looking at his toilet bag, but she saw a softening of his mouth at the mention of kissing her mother. Perhaps it was the precursor to confessing all.

'Those dentists downstairs, the married ones,' he said eventually, 'how are they getting along?'

Grace slowly leaned forward, picked up the teapot and gave it a shake, as much in frustration as to see if there was any tea left. The pot was dry and cold.

'They're away at the minute. Holiday to see his mother in Copenhagen.'

'Money in teeth,' he said, as if it were a universal truth, and then he was getting up. 'Tell you what, as they're not here at the minute, the dentists, I could touch up that bit of paint I knocked off just by their door. You got any paint?'

Even for her father this was a major avoidance technique. She formed the words, 'Sit down, Dad,' but he was rushing on as if, like a skater on thin ice, moving forward quickly would prevent everything around him from cracking.

'Have to set it right, love. Couldn't look them in the face if it's not. Don't want to have to skulk about when they get back, trying to avoid them. That's not—'

'When they get back, Dad? They're in Copenhagen for seven days. There's no possibility that you'll still be here then, is there?'

'We-ell . . .' Her father was sliding his West Ham mug towards himself as if he needed a talisman. 'We-ell, I wouldn't bank on it, Grace. I might be here for a while.' He held his hand up. 'And don't ask me again what's going on between your Mum and me. It's her that needs to do the explaining. She's the one at fault.' He lifted his chin. The bluster was back. 'I'm telling you, Grace, things have been done. Terrible things.'

The phone on the worktop suddenly sprang into life and her father sat down again.

'It'll be her,' he whispered, his dark eyes going back and forth from the phone to Grace. 'Heard us talking about her.'

'Dad, if she was that telepathic she wouldn't have to use the phone. She'll be checking to see you're safe.'

'Taken her time about it.' He shut his mouth with the kind of precision that suggested he wasn't going to open it again for a while, so Grace stood and picked up the phone. Telepathy *was* one of the many off-world skills her mother laid claim to, but presumably the connection between north and south of the river was weak tonight.

'He's there, isn't he?' Her mother sounded, this time of

the morning, more like a female member of the Kray family than the boho, vaguely ethereal persona she normally adopted.

'Good morning, Mum. Yes, he is.'

'Knew he would be. What's he told you?'

'Nothing.' She saw that her father was pretending he wasn't straining to hear what was being said at the other end of the line. 'So perhaps you'd like to enlighten me, Felicity? I mean, I know you two like to fall out now and again, your Yin versus his Yang. Something to keep your relationship spiced up.' Grace had to work hard to keep the wince off her face. 'It doesn't normally involve him decanting his possessions into a neighbour's van, though. So come along, someone owes me an explanation. I'm the one with my flat full of half your house.'

'I'm not explaining anything to anyone.' Her mother's voice was wearing its righteous indignation. 'Your father is in the wrong. Sooooo in the wrong. The things he's accused me of; the tone he's used. He should be down on his knees begging me to forgive him. I've barely been able to get up off the sofa to ring you.'

As always, that tone of voice managed to reach down into Grace and pull up handfuls of irritation.

'I'm sorry you've been laid low by this,' she said. 'Perhaps you'd better go and find if there's an all-night shaman who can get your chakras realigned? Or massage your inner being?'

'Don't you take that snitty tone with me, Grace Surtees. And don't you take his side.'

'I'm not taking anyone's side, except my own. Come on, Mum, you normally can't wait to spill every single detail of your life.'

There was a pause and Grace imagined Felicity trying to think of a suitable come-back. On his chair, her father moved uneasily from one buttock to the other.

'I am going to ignore that, Grace,' her mother said finally. 'I am going to ignore it because I know you can't help being jealous of the way I'm in touch with my emotions. The way I feel deeply instead of hiding things away in boxes . . .'

'Talking of boxes . . .'

There was a whump as her mother slammed the phone down.

'What she say?' her dad asked.

'Nothing that made any sense. So no change there.'

Grace returned the phone to its base. She had intended to quiz her father some more, but it seemed as if he had become more round-shouldered since that phone call. She noticed how much his hair was thinning, the flecks of dandruff on his collar.

'Dad, you look really tired. Come on.' She picked up his toilet bag and handed it to him. 'Go and find your pyjamas. Let's get you to bed.'

'I'll just kip on the sofa.'

'No, you won't.'

After a tussle, he agreed that he would use her bed but there was no need to change the sheets. She wouldn't hear of it and he gave in and retreated to the bathroom.

While he was in there, Grace stripped her bed and put on a fresh sheet, duvet cover and pillowcases. She dug out the spare single duvet from its plastic case in her store room and made herself a bed of sorts on the sofa.

From the bathroom came the noises of her father's night-time routine – him flushing the loo, cleaning his teeth; silence while he wetted his comb and shook off the excess water before passing it through his hair; gargling. In a while he would use his inhaler and there would be a bout of coughing followed by nose-blowing.

She looked around her sitting room. Perhaps if she half closed her eyes it wouldn't seem so much like a temporary housing shelter. There was no way she could stand this disruption for longer than one night, two at the most.

Back out in the hallway she waited for her father to finish rubbing his ointment into his heels and idly picked up some books from one of his boxes. *Unsolved Crimes of the*

1960s, In Jack the Ripper's Footsteps, City Fraud: The Big Players. Returning them, she moved to a different box. Magazines this time, a sheaf of ones from the *In, Out and Undetected* series. A shuffle through them before unfurling one of the rolls of paper. It was a graph showing violent crime, borough by borough, from 2009 to 2012. Another roll showed a plan of the streets around a warehouse, bits of coloured paper indicating the position of cars. *The Haringey Heist*, her father's jagged writing read along the top. Down the side there were various notes, including, *Warehouse manager? Address now? Any signs of a sudden rise in living standards/habits?*

Her poor dad. He had wanted to join the police since he was a boy, but the height requirements at the time and his asthma had defeated him. 'Short of height and short of breath' the family mythology had it.

He'd made the best of it, getting into insurance and finally investigating claims, but it hadn't fulfilled his need to be involved with the more hard-core kind of crime. Especially unsolved crime. Grace suspected that in his head he was a streetwise, slightly maverick detective high up in the Met, picking up on the leads that everyone else had missed. She put 'The Haringey Heist' back in its place.

Her family had always treated this hobby-cum-obsession with fond resignation – if the books and magazines, the charts and statistics helped him cope with that lifelong disappointment of not being a policeman, that was OK. Sure, being dragged along to the site of famous robberies had got a bit boring when she was younger, but it didn't compare to being one of those sad Neighbourhood Watch people ringing the police at every noise and pinning up *Do Not Breathe* notices on lampposts. And, as a hobby, it was less embarrassing than morris dancing.

Quite sweet really that he'd wanted to bring it all with him when he'd stormed out. It suggested he couldn't bear to be parted from it. The words *however long he's going to be here* slotted themselves on to the end of that sentence and she quickly called out, 'Goodnight Dad, the bed's made. Just let me know if you need anything else,' before going into the sitting room.

As she got under the duvet, Grace remembered how she had lied about having a family crisis just to get out of going for a drink with Tate. And now here she was with a real family crisis. Her mother would say she'd tempted fate with that lie, and while she wasn't buying into any of her mother's pronouncements on how the universe was ordered, she couldn't shake the idea that somehow the disruptive powers of Tate Jefferson had already begun to get to work.

CHAPTER 9

Alistair got off the train at Waterloo and tried to remember the last time he'd been up this early on a working day. Failing to manage that, he let himself be swept along by the other commuters as they surged up the platform, negotiated the ticket barriers and spewed out on to the concourse.

He imagined Emma still at home, probably only just getting into the shower. It had taken a lot of willpower to detach himself from her warm body in bed, but he needed that hour alone in the office to calm his thoughts before Grace arrived.

Over the weekend he'd decided that this thing with the other woman had to stop. He felt sick even thinking of losing her, but it was madness. A one-way ticket to . . . he stopped suddenly and got an elbow in his back and a snappy, 'For God's sake,' from the guy behind him.

He wasn't going to think about the destination of that one-way ticket. No need now anyway. He started walking again. He had cast-iron willpower and he was going to end it today. Finito. No messing around with locked cabinets, locked anything. He was going to go in now and think it through calmly and then just get on with growing the business. Throw himself into that and into Emma. That was where the future lay. No good would come of going back to the old ways.

He repeated these mantras to himself as he caught the tube to Leicester Square and then made his way to the office. He felt resolute, chirpy even.

And then he realised that he wasn't heading to the office, he was veering away from it. He stopped in front of a jewellery shop. Not yet open, its window had been cleared of the most expensive pieces, but a pair of earrings caught his eye, each a cascade of silver feathers. He imagined them in her ears and his resolve had gone, replaced by a juddering pulse. He put the palm of one hand on the glass as if he could push through and gather up the earrings, and when he moved his hand again, it left a damp mark on the window. He walked to the door of the shop and checked the opening times.

Moving away, he passed a shop selling shoes; the grille was down but he could see the straps and heels, the pointed toes.

He forced himself to start walking again. It was hopeless. He knew he'd be back later. Everything beautiful reminded him of her. Why had he thought he could break away?

He speeded up, desperate to get to the office and lock himself in before Bernice from downstairs arrived and spotted him. Good, she wasn't in yet. He unlocked the main door, disarmed the burglar alarm and sprinted up to the first floor, feeling strung out with anxiety. But there was excitement there too . . . he was going to see her again. And he'd get those earrings for her. For next time.

He was in the wrong; he knew it. And he was only storing up trouble, but everyone had their drug of choice – alcohol, cocaine, premier league football. She was his.

CHAPTER 10

In Far & Away, Grace watched as Bernice laid the chintz material over her arm, between the wrist and the elbow, then the pink elephant cord higher up and the hard-wearing cotton with swirly red pattern over her shoulder.

'For the sofa,' Bernice reminded Grace, screwing up her eyes and giving the fabrics a quick once-over. Her free hand disappeared back into the drawer and a square of shagpile was brought out. Grace sensed Bernice's hesitation about where to place the carpet, short of balancing it on her head, before she trapped it in the crook of her arm, between chintz and elephant cord.

'That help?' she asked.

Bernice's renovation of her and Sol's house in Finchley had progressed as far as the breakfast room, so to make a proper decision regarding the curtains, Grace not only had to factor in the shagpile but also the colour scheme in the kitchen and hallway.

It was the least she could do seeing as Bernice had

happily put up with her appearing just as she was unlocking the door and had listened as Grace explained about her father turning up in the middle of the night and not being able to get any sense out of either parent about what was going on. Bernice's practical outlook on life made her the ideal person in whom to confide. She did not apportion blame; she was not interested in digging up motives or pawing over the possible emotions involved. Bernice simply helped you think of workable ways to deal with your current predicament so that you could return to where you had been. This often involved a level of honesty that wasn't entirely welcome, and an absence of dithering and soul-searching that was.

Sitting here at this time of the morning, Grace was once again hopeful that things would get sorted out quickly. That hope had become tarnished over the weekend by her mother's refusal to answer her phone and her father's insistence that Grace was not to go and broker some kind of truce. Grace had ignored this and taken herself over to see her mother on Saturday, only to find she was not in. Having sat and waited for a couple of hours, she left her a note and came away. Grace had another go at tracking her down on the Sunday, spurred into action by the way her father's possessions were stealthily migrating from the boxes and bags in the hallway and how Jack the Ripper and his mates were now in piles all over her bedroom floor. There was still no Felicity at Newham, but the fact that the note Grace had left now had a *Not talking. Tell him to make his mouth work* scrawled across it showed she'd been there at some point. Grace had waited again but finally had to concede defeat and had returned to her flat to find her father's books on one of the worktops in her kitchen. They had been arranged neatly, and in alphabetical order, but they were there nonetheless. Her father had been apologetic and given Grace an assurance that his charts and plans would not find their way on to her walls, but she knew the longer he stayed, the more the flat would look like a series of police incident rooms.

She glanced out through Far & Away's large plate-glass window, past the sales notices where she could read, in reverse, just how cheap it was to fly to any of the Swiss ski resorts and hire your ski gear. The street was quiet: London, or at least this particular bit of it, was only just shaking itself to life and venturing out, and this morning that felt vaguely uplifting too, as if she had a head start on everyone. When she went upstairs in a minute and unlocked Picture London's door, she knew that there at least it would be calm and ordered until the phones started to ring. If she was lucky, Alistair wouldn't appear until mid-morning.

Or perhaps the resurgence of her optimism was just the result of being faced with racks of brochures showing a permanently sunny world. She studied the notices in the window again and the word 'only' kept catching her eye, reinforcing the sense that the entire world was within quick and easy reach; freedom just a matter of a few pounds.

In fact, the only grey cloud in this bright scene was standing just to the left of Grace's chair: Esther, the other person who worked in the travel agency.

Esther was a bleached-out version of Bernice – light and lank-haired where Bernice was dark and glossy; pallid where Bernice was rosy-cheeked; concave where there were mounds and rolls and dimples. Probably in her mid-forties, Esther very rarely said anything and, as far as Grace could see, didn't seem to do an awful lot either. What role she played in the company, or whether she was from Sol's side of the family or Bernice's, Grace had no idea. She had a languid air about her and leaned a lot – against desks, filing cabinets, anything really that was more stationary than she was. The only explanation Bernice had ever given for Esther's pathological lack of vitality, lack of conversation, lack of anything that approached a personality, had been a mouthed 'tube trouble' and a hurried nod at an area below Esther's waist.

Grace presumed this meant some kind of gynaecological problem and not that something unpleasant had happened to her on the Underground.

For someone who was largely silent, Esther had a way of involving herself in any conversation that bordered on the intrusive. Standing too close to you, she would, by tiny movements of her head and the way she worried at her bottom lip with her teeth or fingers, convey her reactions to what was being discussed. It was impossible to resist the urge to look and see which particular lip–head combo she'd employed as the result of something you'd just said.

It was obvious to Grace that Esther and Bernice did not like each other much, but that they followed the long-established British procedure of never actually bringing that dislike into the open. Only now and then did it seep out in a too icily polite request from Bernice and feigned deafness on Esther's part – deafness to add to her bouts of playing dumb.

Currently a frowning Esther had her bottom lip scrunched up into a cupid's bow between her thumb and middle finger as she examined the various pieces of material and carpet.

'Pink, do you think?' Bernice prompted, giving Esther a hacky look.

'Oh yes, I like the pink. Very much,' Grace said hurriedly and caught Esther give her lip a particularly hard scrunch.

Bernice nodded. 'Good choice, Grace. That's what I told Sol. He liked the chintz, but I said modern's the look we're after here, Sol. Not your auntie in Camberwell's front parlour.' Bernice's voice had got louder as her speech had progressed, leaving Grace to wonder if Sol and his wife had ever had that conversation or whether Bernice had made the whole thing up to put that scrunched mouth in its place.

When the pieces of material and carpet were whisked back into the drawer, Bernice started to rummage around in a plastic bag on the floor while still keeping up her conversation with Grace. This necessitated much swivelling and talking over her shoulder on Bernice's part as her hands continued to search the bag. For anyone else this might have been problematic, but it was a doddle for Bernice, who could carry on two or three conversations and any number of tasks at the same time. As if to prove that, she suddenly said, 'Worse than toddlers, parents. Here we are: paint.' She hauled a litre tin up on to her desk, along with a small buff-coloured cardboard box, before reaching for the phone. 'Hang about, need to make a call.' The computer screen was nudged round to the right angle.

'Shouldn't be on the sofa, Grace,' she said as she tapped in a number. 'If your dad's all cosy in your room, he'll be in no rush to get things sorted with your mum.' A pause. 'Yeah, Mr King, yeah, Bernice here. No, not bad, going to rain later. So, stopover at Dubai, twenty-two hours and a four-star hotel . . .' Bernice held the phone a little away from her mouth and whispered, 'Got an air bed you could borrow.' The phone went back to her mouth. 'No . . . no, five star's going to take you over budget . . . unless you miss out something when you get to Sydney.' Her hand went over the mouthpiece of the phone. 'Sol says it makes him feel queasy when he sleeps on it, but then he gets seasick walking over Blackfriars Bridge . . .' The hand came off the mouthpiece. 'Yeah, what about dropping the sky walk, just doing the champagne sunset harbour tour?' Bernice was reaching for a calculator, tapping in numbers, squinting at the computer screen. 'Enough for one night in a five star. Sending you over some recommendations . . . there they go. So, talk to your wife, get back to me. 'S'a really good price . . . can't guarantee it past eleven.'

The phone was put down. 'Takes no time to pump up,' she said without missing a beat.

It was the kind of performance that drove Gilbert mad. Multi-tasking was a jarring concept to him that smacked too much of the modern world.

Bernice was patting the paint tin. 'Four-leaf clover green, but it's hard to see how deep the colour is just from the label.' For one horrible moment Grace feared that meant Bernice was going to prise off the lid and daub some paint up her arm to display it to best advantage. No, the tin was simply turned so the label was facing Grace. Bernice then made a big flourish of opening the buff-coloured box and when it had been tilted forward, Grace saw two stencils, one of a B and one of an S. 'Sol's idea. Finishing touch,' Bernice explained, her face radiating something that might have been pride.

Grace had never met a straight man so interested in home decorating as Sol.

She sensed she was meant to say something at this point, so she said, 'Wonderful.'

She hoped visitors to the morning room would understand B and S were Bernice and Sol's initials and not abbreviations for something else. A quick check on Esther confirmed she had moved her fingers and brought her top lip way down over her bottom one. It gave her the appearance of a duck and suggested that she too had wondered about the BS motif and might even be finding that funny if laughter were not too physically exhausting for her.

Bernice was watching Esther too and was obviously suspicious of that mouth. She raised her chin before stowing paint and stencils back under the desk.

There was a hiatus where Esther stopped leaning on a filing cabinet and went to lean against her desk, and Grace was so engrossed in wondering how you could move that slowly without actually going backwards that she was not aware until Bernice spoke that she had, in turn, been studying Grace.

'Look tired, Grace. You need to show your dad how selfish he's being, so that's why an air bed's ideal.' Bernice nodded at her own wisdom. 'You can't just dump some pillows and a duvet on it and call it a bed like you can a sofa. You got to find room for it. Pump it up. You got to put a bottom sheet on it. Next day you got to unmake it. Deflate it. Stow it away.' She pointed at Grace. 'It all shows him how he's putting you out. Makes him uncomfortable up here,' she pointed at her forehead, 'without making him uncomfortable here.' Bernice seemed unsure what to tap so just pointed over her shoulder and down her back.

Esther was tapping her lip with a forefinger. Did that mean she agreed with Bernice or thought she was being too tough?

'But he's sixty, Bernice,' Grace said, hesitantly, 'I'm not—'

'If that fails, make up a story about some visitors coming to stay . . . Oi!'

This last word didn't seem to be addressed to either Grace or Esther. Who it was addressed to was clarified when Bernice got to her feet and rapped on the window. A man leaning against it, wearing what looked like an RAF greatcoat, exhaled a big feathering of cigarette smoke and turned round, his blond hair ruffling in the breeze.

He squinted at Bernice, who was now telling him to shove off and stop lowering the tone, and with the cigarette still in his mouth, lifted both hands in a 'don't shoot me' gesture. Then he spotted Grace, took the cigarette out of his mouth and threw both arms wide. 'Gracie, baby,' he shouted, 'no good hiding. I've fought a hangover to get here early, make a good impression on you.'

'You know him?' Bernice looked uncharacteristically confused.

Grace nodded, and just at the edge of her vision she saw Esther tilt her head and bite her bottom lip with her little pointy teeth.

CHAPTER 11

It was a good twenty minutes later that they climbed the stairs to the Picture London office, Grace seething quietly about what Tate had just done in Far & Away.

He'd started by bursting through the door to introduce himself before she'd been able to head him off because, as he said, 'I bet Gracie hasn't told you about me yet. Likes to keep me as her dirty secret, does Gracie.'

Esther had found the energy to shake his hand, limply, before retreating into lip-biting silence. What she was thinking either involved savaging Tate or nibbling him. Grace did not want to picture that second option, but would have quite happily bought tickets to watch the first.

Bernice's opinion of him was easier to read. She had started off as outraged shop owner and stayed in that mode to lecture him about lolling against her window and tut at his smoking habit.

'Gotta die of something,' he had said earnestly and then undercut it with one of his laughs.

Bernice hadn't liked that and she hadn't liked his clothes either. Sol, whenever Grace saw him, was dressed in a manner that placed him neatly among the ranks of the safe and dull, where many thousands of men, even here in London, were happy to loiter. There had been a tie he'd once owned that had caught Grace's eye, but other than that her overall impression was of grey and white; sharp creases at the start of the week and crumpled ones towards the end.

Tate, on the other hand, was today wearing black jeans with a white shirt tucked into them that might previously have been the property of a consumptive poet. It may have even been filched from his lifeless body. It had flounces and when he took off his coat it became obvious that it also had voluminous sleeves, the cuffs of which came down over his knuckles. The neckline, a flapping, deep V, would have shown a distracting amount of chest were it not for the black scarf wound round his neck, with the two ends left dangling.

Bernice couldn't stop staring at the ensemble when she wasn't staring at his eyes because, unmistakably, he was wearing a smudge of kohl on the outer corner of each one.

Bernice was clearly thinking *dissolute* and possibly also *questionable sexual orientation*. God knew what Esther was thinking.

Grace dared her brain to engage with how Tate looked or what he wore, although some part of it registered that despite the billowing and eyeliner and scarf, the reading coming off him was still resolutely, disconcertingly male. Perhaps it was the biker boots.

Grace was pleased at Bernice's negative reaction – it confirmed that the Tate worship which had infected Picture London had not spread downstairs. And it made her feel as if she had an ally; they could talk about it later and reinforce each other's views. If she was really lucky, Tate would call Bernice 'Berni' like he called her Gracie and blood might be spilled.

Tate was walking over to the display of brochures. 'Good range of stuff here,' he said. 'Looks small from the outside but you've packed a lot in.' He reached out and grabbed a brochure and leafed through it. 'Like that tardis thing. You know . . . ?' he turned to them. 'You have that TV programme over here?'

'We invented it,' Bernice said tersely, watching Tate as if she expected him to pocket the brochure.

He grinned. 'Yeah, I know. Just kidding.' He replaced the brochure on a shelf and picked up one about Florida, opened it, closed it again and swapped it for another about California. Grace saw him do a quick check on Esther then a quick check on Bernice as if trying to work them out.

'So, what's the most popular place you send people then, Bernice?' he said, waving the brochure. 'The good old US of A, or more exotic?'

'America is very popular.' Bernice's tone inferred that if more of her clients saw Tate they might not be in a rush to head there. 'But the Far East, that's up and coming. Cambodia, Vietnam . . .'

'Unspoilt until you send the tourists there, eh?'

Grace watched Bernice's spine straighten.

'Not at all,' she said, in what even Grace felt was a prim voice. 'We stress the need for responsible tourism in this office.'

'Good for you.' The California brochure went back on the shelf, there was another check on Esther, and Grace was torn between wanting to see Tate get slapped down and trying to preserve the peace.

'Perhaps we ought to head off upstairs,' she suggested, and Tate did his soft laugh and said, 'Hang on, Gracie. I'm not that kind of guy. You're going too fast for me, honey.'

Grace smiled politely, remembering the promise she had made to herself in the bath, but it took a great deal of willpower, especially when she saw Esther press her lips together as if stifling a smile. Bernice had obviously spotted this bit of mutiny too and glared at Esther. She might even have been about to say something, but she was distracted by Tate coming across and perching himself on her desk.

'So, do you get to go any of these places?' he said, putting down the brochure he'd been holding. 'Don't like to think of you just watching other people having all the fun.' He was looking at her intently, his voice devoid of any of the earlier cheekiness, and Bernice gave him a nervous check, as if there were a trap lying somewhere in his words.

'I . . . get to go to a few places,' she said slowly.

He nodded. 'Where?'

It was the tone of someone taking confession and Bernice's posture, which had been all elbows and defensiveness, seemed to soften, but her voice still sounded guarded. 'Well, I went to Bali – that was for my honeymoon. And we've done a lot of Europe, of course . . .'

'Bali? Awesome. Go on.'

The tone was still gentle and encouraging, and the way Tate was looking at Bernice, as if she was the font of the greatest wisdom, the most spellbinding entertainment, was obviously confusing her. She darted a glance at Grace, as a person would reach for a lifebelt.

'I used to go to Israel a lot, to see family,' she said unsteadily. 'And I've done the Rockies. California. Some other parts of the USA too . . .'

'Not my part I guess? Rhode Island?'

Bernice shook her head and Tate gave her a forgiving smile before slowly leaning towards her.

'But where would you *really* like to go, Bernice?' His tone had a still intensity about it that was more entrancing because of the energy that had gone before. 'If you could choose anywhere in the world, where would it be?'

'New Zealand.' Bernice had the appearance of someone going under anaesthetic and Tate nodded and said, 'Good choice,' patting her hand as if she'd done well.

Grace had no time to wonder if Bernice was climbing over the barricades and into the enemy camp before Tate had turned to Esther.

'And you, Esther, what about you? Ever dream of heading off somewhere?' He dimpled encouragingly, all blond hair and lively green eyes.

Bernice blinked, as if resurfacing. 'Oh, Esther's very shy.' She waved a dismissive hand, but before that hand had finished its return journey to the desk, Grace heard Esther say, 'No, I'm not. I'm just quiet. And it's South America, actually. I would love to go there. Dream of it. Never had the opportunity. Never.'

Bernice did a lot more blinking. 'You've never mentioned you wanted to go to South America.'

Out of a cat's bottom version of her mouth, Esther said, 'You've never asked me.'

'I have, plenty of times . . . well, not asked exactly, but I'm always saying about South America, clients going there, and you've never shown the least interest. Not the least.' Bernice sounded affronted. 'And now you "dream" of going. Why keep that to yourself? You work in a travel agent's, for goodness' sake. Sol and me, we could have worked out a good deal for you.' She looked at Tate as if pleading her case. 'We could have got you the best deal around. Called in favours. You are family, after all. How do you think this makes me feel, saying that? You sitting there, "dreaming" of South America?'

Esther shrugged. 'I have no idea.'

'You have no idea? That's rich. I never know what you're thinking, standing there doing things with your mouth that don't include speaking. Dreaming of South America! Like I've trapped you here. If you weren't so secretive . . .'

Grace tuned out Bernice and watched Tate. Whereas she felt uncomfortable, he didn't appear disconcerted at all by the scene unravelling in front of him; he seemed intrigued, like a child who had wound up a clockwork car as far as it would go and was now studying the way it zoomed around on an unpredictable, unstoppable drive.

Just as she suspected, he liked to stir things up and see what happened.

He caught her eye and the look was mischievous, not

malevolent. 'Guess it's time to go,' he said, jumping to his feet and returning the brochure to the stand. She caught the wry lift of his eyebrows.

'Bye, Bernice,' he said as he headed for the door. 'Bye, Esther. Hope you get to make your dream happen. Don't leave it too long. Been to Peru. Mind-rocking.' As Grace followed Tate, Bernice was still berating Esther and gave a barely-there wave goodbye, but Esther looked almost animated. As Grace passed her, she noticed those little teeth were back on her lip again.

CHAPTER 12

On the door of Picture London, Grace found a note that could not have surprised her more if it had said, *There is a mongoose living in the printer.* It was from Alistair, informing her that she wasn't to worry about the door being open – he was in early.

She must have stared at it a couple of seconds too long because Tate said, 'Something up?'

'No, not at all.'

Tate followed her into reception, shouted, 'Pepperoni pizza for Mr Alistair Sawclose,' and with a neat sidestep and a huge laugh disappeared into Grace's office. She watched him go and wanted to drag him back and shake him. She waited, irritation zinging around in her, for Alistair to emerge and, when he didn't, she tried his door. It was locked. She knocked.

'Yes, yes,' he called, 'be out in a minute. Got some things I need to crack on with. Didn't want to be disturbed. Left you some stuff on your desk.'

Grace stared at the door handle. Did he mean disturbed by her? He must – she was always first into work. She walked back to her own office. What was so secret that she couldn't see it?

Tate was sitting in the easy chair, his coat over his lap, looking as if even ice cream wouldn't melt in his mouth.

'Al safely under lock and key?' His tone told her he knew the answer to that and she was working on ignoring the mangling of another name when she became distracted by the cardboard head and shoulders of a smiling Chinese woman balanced on a broken milk crate between the two front windows. A wrapper stating *Full-fat cheese* had been stapled to her mouth like a speech balloon.

'Like it?' Tate asked. 'Found it round the back when I was putting the trash out. One of Bernice's old displays, I guess.'

Grace knew it was a test, but even so was finding it hard to make her mouth into any other shape but one that said, 'Yeuch.'

'Al said I could stamp my mark on the place if I liked . . . through here. You don't mind, do you?'

How dare Alistair let him junk up her office? 'It's very unusual,' she said, turning her back on it, which unfortunately meant facing Tate.

'Unusual? That's right up there with interesting as a cop-out. You hate it, don't you?'

'Of course not. Oh, what's this?' She fell on the small pile of papers on her desk with relief. There was another of Alistair's notes: *Been busy over the weekend. Suggested copy for the website, for the leaflets and for the emailers. Run it past Tate when he gets in too, will you?*

She skimmed through the copy and saw Emma's hand in it. Much too well written and to the point for Alistair. She handed it to Tate with the note and took her coat off. She saw him look across at her and waited for him to say something, but he just went back to reading the copy.

'May I hang your coat up for you?' she asked.

He shook his head. 'Nope, don't expect you to do that for me, even if you did ask so nicely.' He nodded at the papers. 'Yup, looks fine to me. He's called me challenging. Haven't been called that since seventh grade.'

Grace doubted that were true, but laughed in the appropriate place and, after hanging up her coat, took the papers back from him. She opened the blinds, turned on her computer and got some Sunday supplements out of her bag to swap with the out-of-date ones in reception. Tate took one from her and started to skim through it.

'So,' he said, not taking his eyes from the magazine,

'never got a chance to ask you downstairs where you'd like to head off to, Gracie?'

She was checking her emails, thinking about her father and how much of his hobby he would be strewing around her flat while she was out; she was thinking about Mark and where they might go to eat when he came back. She was not engaging with Tate Jefferson and whatever game he was playing with her now.

'It's Grace,' she replied sweetly. 'No "ee". And I'm a city girl: Milan, Paris, Berlin. Anywhere with a five-star hotel, good restaurants, fantastic galleries. A spot of shopping. That's me.'

He lowered the magazine. 'Really? You live in a city and you want to get away to other cities? That's what gets your pulse racing? All that shallow, big-bucks stuff? Don't want to see more of the world than that? Don't want to kick off your shoes and relax?'

Grace lowered her head to hide her smile. It had taken him less time to arrive at the subject of kicking off shoes than she had thought.

He was shaking his head. 'Never want to lie on a beach, swim in the sea, stand on top of a mountain?'

Memories of doing all three, sometimes naked, sidled into Grace's brain and out again.

'Never want to just cut loose? Don't tell me you didn't

even bum around for a bit before college.' He leaned forward. His green eyes seemed to have a sharper glint to them. 'Gilbert said you were up in Edinburgh.'

'Oh, I'm not into cutting loose . . . I thrive on keeping busy. We're all different, aren't we? But that's enough about me. What about you? Where would you go if you could?' She feared that adding *back to America?* might sound too barbed.

'That's easy.' He threw the magazines on her desk and stretched out in the chair, his hands behind his head, his eyes closed. 'Anywhere the sun shines most of the time and I can jump in some cool water, haul myself out and just dry off in the heat.' He had the air about him of a very contented blond cat.

Grace felt a wobble in the force field she had built around herself as she watched him – a recollection of listening to cicadas in the evening by the pool at the villa and still being able to feel the heat of the day on her skin. Luckily Alistair appeared in the doorway at that point, and the force field stopped wobbling.

'Morning, campers,' he said, appearing almost feverishly bright, and Tate opened his eyes, sat up and looked at Alistair as if he had no idea what the hell he meant.

Alistair was oblivious. 'Didn't expect you so early, Tate. Good weekend?' Not waiting for a reply, he turned to Grace. 'What did you think of the copy?'

She told him it was fine, then turned to Tate and he nodded.

'Great,' Alistair said. 'So, Grace, can you get those amends done . . . set in motion? I have some other things to sort out.' He was going for the door, but stopped and came back to make a big show of checking his watch. 'Oh, and could you give Tate a quick scoot round how we operate? You know, booking people into tours, taking payment, that kind of thing. Just show him the ropes. I would do it myself, but something has cropped up. A meeting. I have to go out now and then I'll be back fleetingly before my Salvador Dali tour at one. OK? As you were.'

He did a weird salute that got another double-take from Tate and was on his way back to his office.

Tate was still looking at where he'd been standing.

'Always as jumpy as that?' he asked.

'Jumpy?'

'Like he's got fifty thousand volts jazzing round his system or a serious coke habit? He's wired.'

'I hadn't noticed.' She pretended she had found something really interesting on her screen so she did not have to see the disbelieving face Tate turned towards her. She felt pretty incredulous about Alistair's behaviour herself. A meeting? This early?

She heard Tate move and then he was hanging up his coat and dragging the easy chair around to her side of the desk and positioning it right next to her. The difference in the height was a good six inches and when he plonked himself down into his chair he had to look up at her.

'So, getting the idea it's you runs this place, Gracie,' he said. 'Am I right?'

'No, no. Alistair's very much a . . . hands-on boss . . . owner . . . person. He . . . he sees the bigger picture. I just deal with the details.'

There was a disbelieving laugh. 'Imagine you're always hauling Alistair's ass out of the crap.'

'That's not how I see it,' she said carefully. 'Now, can we get on?'

'OK, Gracie.' Tate's tone was softer now. 'Ignore me . . . just wanted to make sure you were happy, you know.'

Grace ignored the cold, hard shimmy in her stomach at that. 'Yes, quite happy. So—'

'So, these ropes you're gonna show me.' He clasped his hands together and held them towards her as if he were offering her a gift. He lowered his voice even further. Looked more intense. 'Tight as you like, Gracie. I promise not to cry out. I won't ask you to stop, whatever you want to do to me.'

She stared down at his face and couldn't think of one single bright and breezy thing to say, and what might have started as a joke on his part shifted into something darker and more disturbing.

No. More exciting.

He wasn't speaking either and she knew she needed to do something to sweep away the silence which had a life of its own – like an electrically charged fog. She was no longer aware of anything except his hands held out to her and the look in his eye.

'Stepped over some kind of invisible line there, huh, Gracie?' she heard him say and it roused her enough to answer, 'No, not at all,' before she managed to stop looking at him and concentrate on her computer screen. She tried harder, managed to dredge up, 'I was just a bit confused about what you meant. Hah, very good . . . ropes, tying. Get it now. You'll have to excuse me. Bit slow this time of the morning.'

It was gibberish, but like a godsend, Alistair was back at the door.

'Forgot to say, Grace, I've ordered a secure cabinet for my room. New regulations . . . Chamber of Commerce alerted me to it. Confidentiality of client information, getting much stricter . . .' He waved towards the reception area. 'Especially in premises that are open to the public. It won't come today, of course. Just mentioning it. Off now.'

He was gone. She heard the outer door close.

She waited for Tate to take up where he had finished off with her, but he was frowning. He was still looking at the spot where Alistair had been standing.

'Cat on a hot tin roof, our Al. Seems nervy about something. Gonna have a heart attack if he goes on like that.'

'He's fine, just a bit excitable.'

'I'll say. So, you gonna show me your stuff?' Tate raised his eyebrows and grinned, and Grace silently thanked Alistair for breaking the mood and steering them safely back into harmless innuendo. She slowly began leading Tate through the process of taking bookings and how clients could pay through the website, by phone or by popping into the office. If they did phone or visit, she emphasised how important it was to make sure the details were put on the computer: it had to be kept up to date. And no accepting bookings without payment – Alistair was very definite about that, having been stung a couple of years ago by a group of eight that took the tour and melted away before payment. She could see Tate nodding away as she showed him the website, but she sensed that he was amused by her earnestness. He would have her down as a 'rules first, last, every time' person.

'We limit the tour size to sixteen people, and this programme will tell you if you're trying to go over that,' she explained, pointing at the screen with her pen. 'It's more to do with the galleries than us; most won't countenance really large groups.'

'Yeah, and there's only so many people you can put to sleep at one time, Gracie,' he shot back with his laugh.

She graciously inclined her head, able to deal with wanting to spike him with her pen. 'So, basically, you can't go wrong as long as everything goes on the computer. I tend to print off the names of the people beforehand, just so I have an idea who to expect. Language requirements, that kind of thing. Gilbert usually rings in a couple of hours before his tours and I tell him the names over the phone.'

'Yeah, Gilb. Interesting guy. Said he works for other companies. Does some kind of history tours too.'

She nodded. *Gilb*?

'He does. Now, your tours . . . we'll need to set up a separate page for them and show where you're taking people. Um, you've got the gallery names here: Whitechapel, the Institute of Contemporary Arts, the Saatchi Gallery, White Cube . . . yes, quite a few, but what about the studio visits?'

He went over to his coat and dug around inside it, coming out with a small notebook. When he was sitting back down, he opened it and showed it to her.

'I've drawn up a rolling programme, see, depending on the size and location of the gallery. If it's a big one, I won't

do any studio visits. Where it's a smaller one, I'll fit in a couple
of studios as well, maybe three if they're all close together,
like in Hoxton or Hackney. I wanna make sure all these places
get a bite at the cherry . . . need to mix it up a bit.' She knew
he was studying her. 'Hey, Gracie, you're looking at me like
I'm a dog that's just proved it can dance on its hind legs.'

She realised she had been, amazed that he had obviously
been doing some planning. Good planning.

'I was only thinking how complicated it is for you, that's
all,' she said blandly. She carried on, explaining how important it was to make it clear where he would meet the clients
and what to do if they were late or didn't arrive at all.
What to do about complaints. Some basic health and safety
issues. As she talked, she was aware he was starting to
fidget, and as she finished explaining what the policy was
regarding tips, he stood up.

'Nope, this isn't working for me,' he said, dragging the
chair back to its original home and giving one of the legs
a tap with his foot. 'Too low – feel like I'm getting a lesson
from a teacher. Don't move,' He collected his coat off the
hook and was gone without any further explanation.

Grace didn't know whether to be happy that he'd compared her to a teacher or not, but she was happy to be shot
of him for a while. She started to create a page for him on
the website.

It was barely a quarter of an hour later that she heard him coming back up the stairs. He sounded as if he were making heavy weather of the trip and when he appeared in the doorway of the office she could see why. He was carrying what appeared to be a torn and battered office chair with wheels. He lowered it to the floor and Grace saw the seat was slashed, the foam exposed.

'What are you . . . ?' she started to say and then remembered she was meant to be non-confrontational and deadly dull, so she simply watched as he got a roll of silver tape out of the pocket of his coat and with great gusto pulled a long strip of it free before tearing it with his teeth and starting to patch up the slashes in the seat. He worked quickly: rip, tear, stick, rip, tear, stick, his teeth white against the silver of the tape whenever he tore it. She quashed the thought that he was good with his hands – and mouth.

'Saw it in a dumpster on my way in this morning,' he said, twisting the chair around when he'd finished and proudly surveying his work.

To Grace, it was a battered old wreck made even worse by the fact its seat was now all silver tape, but he seemed pleased enough – the tape was back in his coat pocket, his coat was back on the hook and he was lowering himself on to the seat. He rocked from side to side and back and forth.

'Great,' he said and then he scooted the chair towards her and it came to rest with a bump that made her grab at the edge of her desk. He was laughing and she wanted to get the tape and wind it round his head. How much more of London's rubbish was going to end up in her office?

'That's better, isn't it?' she said as if she really meant it. 'What a good idea.'

'You think?' He cosied the chair up even closer. 'Only I thought you might worry I was lowering the tone.'

'Don't be silly.'

She detected a slight narrowing of his eyes, but he didn't say anything and so she resumed her explanation of how the office worked, ignoring how close his face was to hers now and how she could smell cigarette smoke on him as he'd presumably had a smoke on the way to the Skip of Plenty. She outlined how Gilbert invoiced for his hours, how he liked to be paid by cheque, and Tate said that would be fine for him too. They talked about work permits and tax details and he told her he had 'a handle on all that stuff': he'd been living and working in England for a while already.

Alistair was back. Grace willed him to notice the skanky chair but he was too puffed up with what looked like smugness.

'What do you think of the new addition?' he said, beaming.

Grace looked at Tate, who looked straight back at her.

Alistair had cocked his head as if trying to nudge a response from her. Surely he wasn't expecting her to comment on Tate, give some kind of a verdict on his personality, right there in front of him?

It seemed as if he was. He was still tilting his head encouragingly in her direction.

'I think . . .' she began, casting around for an adjective that wasn't pushy, brash or obnoxious, 'I think he's very enthusiastic.'

Alistair suddenly stopped beaming. 'What on earth are you talking about, Grace? I wasn't asking you about Tate.' He actually tutted. 'The idea! I was hoping you'd noticed that.' He pointed to the tea tray and Grace saw for the first time that the old kettle had been replaced by a new one – same model, slightly shinier.

Tate started to laugh – not his normal laugh but a loud one from his belly – and as his seat was now rammed up against hers, she could feel his laughter vibrating up her body.

Alistair was looking aggrieved.

'Sorry. I hadn't noticed,' she floundered. 'I had a couple of cups of coffee with Bernice earlier, you see, so I didn't even . . .' She knew she was waffling and decided the only safe thing to say was, 'But that's great, you know, that you managed to get a new one so quickly. I'll go and fill it, shall I? Make a cup of tea?'

She escaped to the kitchen, giving Alistair's desk a particularly scouring look as she went through his office. There didn't seem to be anything out of the ordinary on it.

In the kitchen she halted when she saw that the bottom half of the Chinese lady who was in her room was taped to the wall as if she were climbing up it. One of her feet had a dirty old piece of material wound around it. She peered closer. In pencil, Tate had written on the wall, *With one bound, she was free.*

Grace took a long time to fill the kettle and wondered if Alistair and Tate had made some kind of pact to drive her up the wall too?

When she got back, Alistair was saying something about Tate trying to build up to three tours a week.

Grace nodded enthusiastically. That still meant two completely Tate-free days. It was essential to look on the bright side.

Alistair retired to his office again and only reappeared to tell her he would post Gilbert's cheque out to him. He had his briefcase clutched tightly against his body as if he feared being mugged, even in his own office.

'See you around three,' he said and was gone.

Grace was relieved of the burden of having to talk to Tate any further by the phone ringing. He watched her take the booking from a couple interested in Gilbert's next visit to the Renaissance Masters and then another for three people wanting to join her tour of the Wallace Collection (French Art, 1700–1800). When she put the phone down she asked him if he wanted to answer the next call.

'You know what?' he said yawning, 'pretty early start for me this morning. Might just get back to you on that answering the phones thing. Gonna put my head down for a bit.'

She had to clamp her mouth shut not to let *Whaaaaat?* escape.

He ambled through to the reception and she heard him lie down on the sofa. When she leaned forward she could see his feet through the open door, ankles crossed and resting on the arm. WITH THOSE STUPID BIKER BOOTS.

She felt three warring urges: one to point out politely to him that at any minute a client could come in; one to stay calm and say nothing; and yet another to go and give his stupid great feet a hearty shove.

She tried to take her mind off his barefaced cheek by catching up with her emails again. There was a new one from Emma asking her if she was all right, to which, truthfully this time, she replied that she had parent problems and her father was staying with her, so their planned pizza evening was looking even more attractive. There was also an email from her mother headed up '*If you knew how I've suffered*'. She found her finger itching to press the delete button, but opened the email and scrolled through it just in case it might contain any hint about what was happening with her dad. It was the usual "scream" of consciousness, tripping from one point of martyrdom to the next and seeming to take as its theme the way that neither Grace nor her father understood what a sensitive person she was. Grace was not sure how this could be as they'd had to hear her tell them that for years. She noticed as she sent it to the recycling bin that the email had been copied to her sisters. Great. Any time now she could expect three more emails expressing sisterly concern and offering the usual range of bizarre advice.

She immersed herself in creating some emailers to announce Tate's arrival and amending the leaflet copy ready to send out to the printer after Alistair had checked it through one last time. As she worked she was pleased to discover that the second or third time she glanced out at Tate's biker boots, the stab of indignation was cutting nowhere near as deep as it had – after all, Tate asleep was better than Tate awake. She just had to get used to him being around. Him and his dismembered Chinese woman.

The phone rang again.

'Hey, Gracie,' a laconic voice drifted in from reception, 'you wanna start mentioning my tours to whoever calls? I know they might be wantin' you or Gilbert, but you never know, once they hear about mine, they'll probably change their minds.'

'Yes. They might,' she replied.

She took two phone calls in quick succession after that and did manage to interest one person in Tate's tour. Tate's tour! Why couldn't he have a normal name so that you didn't have to make it really clear that it wasn't a tour of the Tate, but by a guy named Tate? Even his name was irritating.

When she put the phone down the second time, she could hear Tate talking to someone. She went out to reception to find two young Austrians eyeing Tate uneasily as he chatted away to them horizontally.

She suggested they come through to her office.

'See ya,' Tate said and closed his eyes again.

Grace managed to sweet-talk the couple into a tour of the Royal Academy, but she would not have been surprised if, as soon as they left the office, they cancelled the credit card payment. The woman had been sitting on Tate's seat and when she stood up to leave, she had to give her skirt a fierce tug to free it from a section of tape that had come unstuck. After they'd left, Grace took a pair of scissors and tidied up the chair as much as it was possible to tidy up something that had known a lot of backsides and been living in a skip until a couple of hours ago.

Tate continued to sleep through more incoming calls and the outgoing ones she made to the various hotel concierges who regularly pointed their guests in the company's direction.

'Oh, yes, he's very challenging and dynamic,' she assured them while looking at his lifeless feet. 'It'll be a fascinating tour.'

Whenever she felt the irritation levels rising and considered how satisfying it would be to push his feet off the arm of the sofa, she reminded herself that he would love that. As a distraction, she went and tried Alistair's door and found it unlocked. She had a quick look in the post tray. Nothing of interest and then, on a whim, she picked up his phone and rang Julie, the woman who acted as secretary at the Chamber of Commerce meetings. When Grace said she was just checking if there was any paperwork on these new client confidentiality rules, it was obvious that Julie didn't know what she was talking about. Grace winged it, not wanting to drop Alistair into anything, but just before she finished the call, Julie said, 'Do you think you could subtly mention to Alistair that he needs to ring us in future if it looks like he's going to be late for a meeting? We hung on and waited a good ten minutes for him before we gave up and got on with it. Just as well really, seeing as he never made it until Any Other Business.'

Grace put the phone down more worried than she had been when she had picked it up. Why had Alistair lied about new regulations that didn't exist? And about going to a meeting of which he'd only caught the tail end?

This time she determined to 'accidentally' nudge Tate's feet as she walked through reception and to hell with the consequences – except his feet weren't there. They were up on her desk and he was lounging back in her seat, on the phone.

'Yup. Just started today, so, as I said, if you like your art edgy, give me a shot. If you like the same old, same old, try one of the others.' He swivelled in the chair and gave her a wave. 'Alrighty then.' He sat up and put his feet to the ground and, with the phone trapped between his ear and his shoulder, placed his hands on the computer keyboard. 'Here we go, firing up the machine. So, what are you called? Real name, mind you, no aliases.' There was more of his laughter and Grace had to walk out of the room again. She sat on the sofa and listened to him being too familiar, too pally, altogether too unprofessional. It became apparent that the person booking the tour was Australian as at one point Tate said, 'Streuth,' in a mock Aussie accent and there was more laughter. She heard him taking the credit card details, telling the person to slow down with the numbers – didn't they know he was American and didn't speak Australian? Grace coaxed the magazines on the table into a neat pile, picked them up and gave them a good hard tap to make sure they were all perfectly in line. There were ways of doing these things, of speaking to the clients. She heard him put the phone down. She slapped down the magazines.

'Another four people for my tour,' he shouted through to her. 'I bet you I can get it up to five days a week.'

'Wouldn't that be great?' she called back.

She braced herself to go back in and face him, but there were more people coming up the stairs. She hurriedly gave the cushions a rough plump up.

'Good morning,' she said as the door opened and immediately knew that these were Tate's friends and not potential clients.

'Hi, we're looking for Tate,' a girl with an addiction to kohl said, and Grace wondered if it was the same stick of kohl that Tate had used on his eyelids. The girl bounced herself down on the sofa, her black coat and black tights merging with it so that all that really stood out about her was her purple Doc Martins.

'Yeah. Tate.' That was from an intense-looking, thin guy with a beanie hat pulled down low over his eyes. He was hugging himself through his black leather bomber jacket and looked as though he had been asleep only minutes before.

The third person who came in through the door simply said, 'Tate, baby,' in a honeyed drawl, and as Tate came into reception she enfolded him in her arms. Grace did a bit of female stocktaking that went: long blonde hair, size 10 body, suede pelmet skirt, legs of an attractive racehorse. There was a fair amount of kissing of both women and some strange, high-fiving, low grappling hand stuff with the guy.

Tate turned to Grace. 'Hey guys, this is Gracie,' before counting off, 'this is Joe, Corinne and Bebbie.' Handshakes did not seem to be in order and so Grace just did a curl of her hand.

'Gracie does tours of the old guys, for the old guys,' Tate said, and his visitors assumed a range of expressions of which pity seemed to be the unifying theme. 'Likes her art in a frame, don't you?' Tate said, addressing her directly.

It made her feel one hundred and seventy-two. One hundred and seventy-two on a bad day.

'Sorry,' she said and did a self-deprecating laugh, which, as she'd calculated, meant they lost interest in her.

The kohl-eyed girl, who Grace now knew was called Corinne, was retrieving some paper bags from her black rucksack and unwrapping croissants and pastries. Grace expected them to be black too. Soon the magazines were being used as plates.

'Cor-i-nne,' Tate said in a tone that suggested she was a genius.

Joe rubbed his hands. 'Coffee would be good.'

'Yeah.'

'Good idea.' Tate turned to Grace. 'You mind making some coffee?' He sat down next to Bebbie and she put her hand on his arm and was whispering things to him before Grace could even work out how she was going to stop herself from screaming, *Yes, I do very much mind making your friends some coffee. And there are grease marks on the magazines and crumbs on the table and soon they will be all over the floor. And stop looking so damn pleased with how avant garde you think you are, as if you'd just bloody invented it.*

'No problem,' she said, siphoning her irritation into a quick walk back to her office. She collected the kettle, and when she passed through reception on her way to the kitchen, nobody looked up. When she returned with a full kettle and some more cups, it was as if she did not exist. She glanced at the floor around the table. She had been right about the crumbs.

She took two more phone calls as the kettle was boiling and wondered if she too had steam escaping from the top of her head. She listened to them discussing the club they'd been in the night before; how Joe had got 'wasted'; whether Tate was going to be a no-show again or actually make it out tonight. She stopped feeling invisible and started to feel threatened, but could not pin down why. Was it because if they came spilling into her office she did not know whether she would be extra starchy or do something unpredictable?

She heard music, and when she carried the cups of coffee through to them, she saw someone had taken out a laptop, which was now churning out a dense beat. Standing there dolling out the coffee, she experienced that feeling of being under threat again, as if she were afraid one of them would start dancing and she might get up on the table and join in, so that when Tate suddenly reached out and got hold of her hand, she could not prevent herself from jumping.

'Hey Gracie, you're as nervy as Al. What's up?'

'Sorry, I was miles away.' That, at least, wasn't a lie. Miles and years away.

He was still holding her hand, still looking up at her, 'Where's your coffee? I thought you'd join us? Come on, take a break.'

All that enthusiasm. She felt the skin of his hand against hers, the beat of the music. She had to get away.

'Sorry,' she said, slipping her hand from his. 'That's really kind, but I've got to nip out . . . and I won't be back before my tour.' Had she pitched it right? Not come across as too stroppy or sulky? 'I'll leave the answerphone on – I can pick up any messages later, so you needn't do anything much . . . unless a client comes in, of course.' She couldn't help her eyes straying to the mess on the table.

'Hey, no problem,' Tate said, standing up. 'I've got it covered.'

There was a lot of disbelieving laughter from the others.

'Ignore them,' he said, 'I'm not going to ruin the business while you're away. What is it this afternoon? Your tour?'

'Rubens,' she said, backing away from him to go and get her coat.

He winked. 'Try not to put anyone in a coma this time.'

Determination and a false smile saw her through the business of getting on her coat, setting the answerphone, going back through reception and giving a cheery, 'See you later, have fun,' and then she was out on the stairs and heading for the windowsill.

She tried to zone out the beat of the music and hoped they were still all sitting round that table when Alistair came back and he could see what a mistake he'd made. Tate had no respect for anything; he was lazy too, by the looks of it. She caught herself and tried to stop seething by looking out at the mass of rooftops and glimpses of street.

She heard the outside door downstairs slam and the slow upward progress of footsteps. Gilbert. Sure enough, his head and shoulders and then the rest of him came into view. She was reminded of the Chinese woman in her office.

'Locked out?' he asked.

'No, just taking a breather – I'm going to have an early lunch. Have you popped by for anything?' As she spoke, a buried 'must do' from her list resurfaced. 'Oh, Gilbert, I'm sorry, I meant to call you, tell you Alistair had posted your cheque out. You've had a wasted journey.'

That was Tate's fault, disordering everything, changing the routines. She had to concentrate harder or everything would fall to pieces again.

'No matter.' Gilbert lowered himself next to her on the windowsill. 'I've just had a quick canter through the Great Plague and the Fire of London so thought I'd look in on the off-chance. How are the parents?'

She made a face, but his attention was on the Picture
London door. 'Can I hear music?'

'Tate's entertaining people.'

'A tête-à-tête?'

'Very good.'

'Thank you. So, what do you make of him?'

'Seems nice enough.'

'Yes. despite an unfathomable enthusiasm for video art.'
He caught her enquiring look. 'He "does" video installations; that's what the gallery in New York specialised in.
Now he wants to see the world, earn some money and
perhaps get some sponsorship for a big video installation
project he's come up with.' Gilbert shrugged. 'I thought
most of those things were shot in someone's front room,
but they're quite costly to make and stage, evidently. Had
a good chat about it Friday evening. I imagined he'd have
told you?'

'We haven't really had time to talk.'

'No? Well, play your cards right and he might give you
a walk-on part. I told him I'd do anything short of appearing
naked or wearing a lobster on my head.' Gilbert's laugh
and the way he was still looking towards the black door
told Grace he wanted to be on the other side of it.

'I'll see you,' she said standing up, 'maybe a coffee later
in the week?'

He nodded but he was still looking at the door. 'Yes, I think Tate's certainly going to liven things up around here.'

Grace said nothing and went swiftly down the stairs and into the street, not even looking towards Bernice in Far & Away.

CHAPTER 13

Violet leaned forward and reached out with the picker-upper. Not its real name, but she couldn't bring that to mind at this precise moment. Gilbert was forever telling her what the device was really called, explaining how it was designed to retrieve small things from hard-to-reach places.

Or things you didn't want to touch. And one had to be so careful with the post – all those hands who had, well, handled it.

It was only good for letters. Padded envelopes were hopeless: the claws on the picker-upper did not open that wide. Padded envelopes meant rubber gloves.

Violet manoeuvred the device so that one claw was underneath and one on top of the first envelope on the mat; she then moved the handles of the device together and watched as the envelope was gripped and held tight.

Carefully, she straightened up and, still holding the picker-upper away from her body, one of her arms braced against the other to keep it steady, she tiptoed to the kitchen. Tip-toeing was so much less wearing on the carpet, and as Gilbert positively refused to do it and went about purposely stamping his feet if she asked him, she had to do it for both of them. He was such a boy sometimes.

In the kitchen she put her foot on the pedal of the bin, waited until the lid was fully up and then stopped holding the handles of the picker-upper together so that the claws opened. She watched the envelope fall. Removing her foot from the pedal, the lid of the bin descended into place with a satisfying clank.

It wasn't the normal rubbish bin, which was out of sight under the sink – this was a special one Gilbert had bought. A special post bin.

She wished it *was* the rubbish bin and she wished she could put it directly under the letterbox because letting anything into the house was always troublesome. Even letters. Letters invariably meant bad news or bills. She'd tried to explain that to Gilbert last year – was it last year? – when she had put all the letters directly into the recycling and he'd found them and been very cross with her. The kind of cross where he went out a lot and stayed out late and didn't bother taking his shoes off when he returned.

So now she had the special bin. It was only when he brought it home that they started speaking again.

She headed back to the porch, but stopped just by the television in the sitting room. There was a crumb of something on the carpet. How had that got there? Had Gilbert been eating in this room? He knew he mustn't eat in this room. Violet sat down on the chair, trying to catch her breath.

'Deep, slow breaths, Vi,' she heard Gilbert say in her head, and so she listened to him until she wasn't breathless any more.

She was in charge, not the dirt. She would simply clear it away.

She went back to the kitchen and detached the sucking-up thing from the wall. The vacuum cleaner – there, she had the words. It was better than the big one, not so heavy, but it just pecked at things – you couldn't do a good clean. She turned it on and thought it looked like a gun.

'Bang, bang, crumb,' she said and advanced on it, placing her feet and her hands like she had seen on the television programme where the policeman was pointing his gun at a suspect on the floor.

She watched with satisfaction as the crumb seemed to cling on to the carpet and then give up the ghost and whoosh up the nozzle. She turned it off and blew across the nozzle, not sure why really. Perhaps there had been another programme, a western, where they had done that.

'We could have had that crumb,' the mice said, and she stuck her nose in the air and ignored them. If she thought about something else, they'd shut up. They'd shut up all together when those traps got them. She wished Gilbert hadn't decided against the poison.

Perhaps he had been worried she'd put it in his tea. She laughed at that and was still giggling as she retrieved the picker-upper and got the second buff-coloured envelope safely from porch mat to post bin. Quite worn out now, she sat down in the sitting room. That was what it was for. Sitting. And watching television. Not eating.

She leaned back in the chair, but not too heavily or it would leave a crinkle in the fabric, a dent in the anti-macassar.

She thought about the letters, bringing things into the house – news and demands. If only she and Gilbert could seal up the house and stay here just the two of them – him looking at his paintings and her with her scrapbooks.

'That's not possible, Vi,' Gilbert's voice said. 'I don't want to lock myself away. Besides, what would we eat?'

'You're very talkative today.'

'Must be a nice change from the mice, Vi . . .'

She had had to agree with that. And she knew Gilbert had to have a life away from her. Sometimes. She'd got used to his work. All the names of all the people he brought back into the house. But every now and again, every once in a while, there was a new name. A name she worried about.

He had come home on Friday smelling of drink and whistling and with no poison – just traps and one or two, frankly, lacklustre guides to China. When she'd asked him why he hadn't been to the travel agent's downstairs, he had become very wayward. When she'd asked him why he smelled of drink, he said he'd only had one Chablis and began to behave even worse. When she'd asked him why he was whistling, he'd said nothing.

Tate. An American. Modern art. Those were the three facts she knew about him. Four really: she knew he was a man.

She picked up the television remote. Things came into your house through the television, but she didn't mind that. They were like ghosts – touched nothing, left nothing. But she didn't know if she was going to mind this Tate. If there would be more whistling from Gilbert. Worrying whistling.

She put down the remote again. She hadn't liked the idea of Grace at the start and then she had turned out to be nice. Very well behaved. Knew about coasters under glasses and shoes at the door. Grace wasn't the kind to take Gilbert away from her. She wouldn't lead him astray by introducing him to other, more dangerous, women either. And that other name, Alistair . . . well, he was an idiot, everyone knew that, so there was no danger of Gilbert being influenced by him.

But this Tate – he might influence Gilbert. Might take him places he liked better than this place. Introduce him to women who weren't as nice as Grace. Women who didn't understand that Gilbert always had to come home to her.

She felt breathless again at that and the only way to stop it was to have a plan. Know your enemy. If Gilbert wouldn't tell her any more about Tate, perhaps Grace would. It was a while since she had visited.

It would mean a lot of work – plates put out, cups and saucers, bread cut. She'd have to charge the vacuum cleaner up as there would be crumbs – Grace was a neat eater, but there were always crumbs.

'More for us,' sang the mice.

'Do be quiet,' Violet said and snapped on the television with the remote, letting herself get used to the picture before she turned up the sound. The mice were still discussing the possibility of crumbs. 'You're wasting your time,' she said to them, 'I cannot be bothered with you today. I have a plan. And there will be no crumbs for you – only for the vacuum cleaner.'

CHAPTER 14

Grace sat in Green Park and watched the first of the leaves spiralling downwards. The temperatures must have been low enough the night before to start the annual ritual of leaf parting with tree. In no time at all there would be rough russet and yellow collars around the base of each trunk, but for now it was just the odd leaf leaping forth into the unknown.

Her tour had finished half an hour ago and had swept away all that pent-up frustration at the way Tate Jefferson, after only one morning, seemed to be taking over the office. It had been a good group – no annoying Baldridges and no blond-haired gatecrasher; just an appreciative couple from Ohio and a family from Brussels. She'd had a pleasant enough conversation with Lilly on the ticket desk and even Norman had seemed animated, chatting on about it being his wife's thirtieth birthday soon and how he had bought her something he knew she would like this time.

He had been smiling like a boy when he spoke. He obviously doted on her.

So all in all a good morning and now there was only a wisp of unease remaining about Tate's colonisation of her office and her starchy reaction to it. If she was going to cope with this, she had to relax into this role of uninteresting Grace. Nothing he had done threatened her – the chair, the sleeping, the friends, treating her as a waitress. She watched another leaf elegantly pirouetting to the grass. Even those jibes of his weren't nasty, more teasing. His behaviour in Far & Away, however, had been pretty calculated. And Gilbert . . . Gilbert who had been eager to go and join in the happy throng upstairs. What was she feeling about that? Jealousy, perhaps, but also a sense of unease that made her wonder again whether she shouldn't, the very next time she saw him, mention Samuel and that soft look. The kind of soft look Norman had on his face when he talked about his wife.

She watched some more leaves, a woman pushing a boy on a tricycle, some foreign students joking and eating sandwiches. She should stop fretting. It was only possible for Tate to make her feel as if she was staring down at a very steep and slippery path, if she let him. The first morning had been a bit of a baptism of fire; things would get easier. Forgetting to phone Gilbert about his cheque didn't mean she was losing it again. Everyone forgot things now and again, even, she laughed to herself, the mighty Grace.

She got out her mobile and did a countdown in her head. As she reached one, it rang.

'Hi there, gorgeous,' Mark said.

'Hello, yourself. Punctual as ever. How are things?'

'Fine, fine . . . Look, can't stop long, lots to do before I pack up and ship out. I'll be on the flight that gets in at 4.30 – Heathrow, not Gatwick this time. So that means I should be at your place about 7, 7.30.'

'Right. Lovely . . . but Mark . . .'

'Something wrong?'

'Probably not . . . just thought I ought to mention that I have my father staying at the minute. He should be gone by Friday, but he's had some kind of falling-out with Mum, major one this time—'

'For God's sake,' he said sharply, 'your Mother! You know, Grace, she really needs to grow up.'

Grace felt the momentary indignation that arises when you hear anyone else voice a criticism of your loved ones, even if you are quite happy to hear it come out of your own mouth.

She heard Mark sigh, imagined the quick flick of his eyes skywards. He was probably regretting having rented out his own flat, a father-free zone in Chiswick.

'So, when you say he should be gone by Friday, you only mean that you hope he will be? It's not definite?' Mark's tone still sounded aggrieved, causing Grace to say, with as much conviction as she could, 'I'm sure he'll be back home by Friday. Really sure. My flat isn't big enough for me, him and his hobby.'

'I don't know, Grace.' There was silence and then, 'Look, let's forget about your flat. Let's book into a hotel. What's the name of that nice one, near the park in Kensington? Let's go there.'

'Are you sure? It's quite pricey.'

'Doesn't matter. I've been working hard, I need a bit of luxury. Besides, it's only a couple of nights. Book us in there, will you?' The sharpness in his tone was now replaced by the one he used to show he was in charge of the situation. Grace very much liked that voice of his, confirming as it did her own view that any obstacle could be overcome if you had the determination to do it. Mark laughed. 'I'll come straight there from the airport. You can get the bed warmed up before I arrive.'

'I'll do my best.'

'And we'll have room service . . . the whole weekend. I want the kind of weekend where we won't even know what the weather's doing outside the window. Sound good?'

'Sounds wonderful.'

Grace heard a phone ring in the background. 'OK, Grace, I better answer that. You get it booked, yeah? I'll sort out the money later. See you Friday. Cheers.'

'Bye, Mark. Safe journey.'

She waited to hear if there were any last endearments brewing, but he had gone. A few minutes later she had booked the hotel and walked back through the park, bending to pick up a leaf on the way and twirl it between her fingers. She hadn't been lying to Tate when she'd said a posh hotel ticked a lot of boxes for her. Mark understood that, understood her to the exact level she wanted to be understood and no further.

The prospect of Friday and Saturday night with Mark and a bit of luxury was still shimmering away when she dropped the leaf back on the grass and went out into Piccadilly, cutting through the backstreets to return to the office. She passed the end of a curved row of buildings and stopped. It would take hardly any time to build in a small detour. She retraced her steps, walked to a mid-point in the curve and smiled at the wooden doors with their brass, art nouveau handles and door plates. A weird hybrid gallery, this one; started by a father who collected everything from Hogarth to Hockney, the Shillingsworth was now run by the son who was only interested in anything produced after the year 2000. She had seen it on Tate's list of the galleries he intended to tour.

Pushing open the doors, she walked into the hushed interior, the girl on the desk with her short blond bob and her take on a salwar kameez barely giving her a glance when she paid her entrance fee. Grace headed for the back of the building where the original wall had been removed and replaced by massive sliding glass doors leading to a cobbled courtyard. A large, hunched-over metal figure, with the head of a unicorn and the body of a man, turned slowly in a pillar of water pouring over it from a gold brain. Grace surveyed it through the glass, noticing how the water ran down the body before splashing into a pond full of metal snakes and finally emptying via a small square drain. The explanatory blurb next to the sliding door assured her the sculpture represented man's higher nature being sublimated by his animal needs and the serpent's call of sin. Grace didn't recall the serpent's call of sin being exactly like that, but the hunched-over nature of the figure was definitely touching a nerve.

She moved away and went to find what she had come here for. And there she was, off the main galleries, almost as if the current owner was building up enough gumption to get rid of her all together but had not quite managed it yet. She wasn't as opulent as the icon in the Paddwick Gallery, and the infant she was holding seemed less life-like, but he still held his cheek against his mother's and she still looked out at the world as if hoping that someone would stop what was about to happen. Grace stayed for a while, not even looking at her watch. Let the world wait.

'I know you're probably not ready to draw a line under it all,' she whispered to the icon before she left, 'but can I just say how much I appreciate you listening.'

Back out in the street she walked more purposefully and had decided, by the time she reached the office, that she would ignore her father and get herself over to Newham once again. Mark was right: her mother needed to grow up, and her father too, come to that. If they were both acting like children, it was up to her to be the parent.

She waved at Bernice as she went past the door. Despite being on the phone, Grace saw her pull a face and mime something at the ceiling. Grace took it as a comment on Tate upstairs and made a similar face back. Esther twitched her lips in what could have been a scowl or smile.

Grace continued upwards, wondering what she might find when she arrived. Perhaps a full-scale party, a trashed office, Alistair tearing bits of paper into snowstorms in anger? No matter, she would sail resolutely through it all. The dangers were too great to tempt her to get emotionally involved in any way.

On reaching the office, she got a pleasant surprise – apart

from the grease stains on the magazines, all was as it should be. She heard Alistair's door open.

'Ah, Grace,' he said, coming towards her at a canter, 'just the person. Checked the copy for the leaflet: fine, fine. And thank you for amending the website, doing the emailers, you've been busy.'

'No problem, Alistair.' She moved to go into her office, but he put his hand up.

'Actually, there is a problem, Grace.' He motioned to the sofa and she hoped he might say the problem was with Tate. Perhaps Alistair had come back and found him dancing or even making out with Bebbie in front of potential clients. She sat and tried to match Alistair's concerned expression.

'The thing is, Grace, the problem I'm talking about is how sharp I was with you this morning. Over the kettle. And then I left you to train Tate.'

She conquered her disappointment that Tate was not on his way out of the company to tell him it didn't matter.

'No, hear me out,' he insisted. 'I realise it was hard for you being thrown together with Tate like that. After all, you didn't make it to the pub on Friday so this morning it must have been like jumping right in with a virtual stranger and showing him what's what. And then, to top it all, Emma rang and told me you have your dad staying.

Which made me feel even worse about being sharp with you. Now, I don't want to pry, but I do want you to know I'm here for you. I'm here, and Emma's here.' He seemed as if he were going to give her a consoling pat on the knee, thought better of it and brought his hand to rest on the table. It looked beached and awkward and he obviously felt that too, as he moved it again. 'So, don't worry about finishing off anything else on your desk, you just take your time with your mother . . .'

Grace did a mental backtrack over those last words because she had been barely concentrating, thinking instead about how kind Alistair could be when he wasn't in blustering boss mode.

'I'm sorry? Take time with what?'

'Your mother.' Alistair nodded towards her office and Grace realised what Bernice's mime had meant.

'Felicity!' she said, leaping to her feet. 'Felicity is here?'

Alistair gave her a reassuring smile. 'It's all right, Tate's looking after her.'

In her head, even as she launched herself at her office door, Grace could hear herself screaming, *Noooooooooooooooooo!*

CHAPTER 15

They both looked up as she came in, Tate sitting on his new-found treasure from the skip and her mother next to him, in the easy chair. Between them was the small table holding the tea and coffee things, moved from its usual position against the wall. With Tate in his billowing shirt and eye make-up and her mother in her usual boho get-up, she felt as if she'd walked in on Lord Byron and Lady Caroline Lamb having a tea party and a cosy chat.

Grace didn't begrudge them the tea, or the fact that the office had been rearranged, but she did very much mind the chat. While others swore by free-range meat, her mother was addicted to free-range conversation: she roamed at will, regardless of taboo or sensitivity. Nothing was off limits. Grace tried to read the expression on Tate's face, hoping it might indicate what her mother had been saying. Apart from looking dazed, which was usual on first meeting Felicity, the message she was getting back from his green eyes was, *You a foundling, Gracie? 'Cos this sure as hell isn't the mother I'd have paired you with.*

'Here she is, my gorgeous Grace,' her mother said, struggling up from her chair, and whereas Grace had been on a state of high alert before, she now went straight to Defcon 1. The last thing her mother had done was slam down the phone on her, so either this show of affection meant Felicity was feeling guilty (oh God, what had she been telling Tate?) or she wanted something.

Grace only got out, 'Mum, how long have—' before she was swaddled in her mother's arms and engulfed by the smell of patchouli oil. And, oh no, it was one of those days when Felicity had not bothered with a bra. Grace tried to ignore her mother's unfettered breasts squashing up against her own. Over her mother's shoulder she saw Tate grin.

Grace waited until her mother's grip lessened, having learned years ago that struggling to escape only made her hold on tighter.

'You're looking well, Grace.' Her mother had brought out the soft voice she used in front of young men. 'I've been talking to Tate . . . just chatting, till you came back. You didn't mention you had someone new here. He's been making me feel very welcome.'

'How kind of you, Tate.' Grace talked without taking her eyes off her mother. She was pleased to see that Felicity was aware she was being scrutinised and was now starting to fret at the dangling ties on her peasant blouse.

'No sweat. I've enjoyed it,' Tate said, trying, half-heartedly, to maintain a straight face. 'Felicity's great, we've had a ball, haven't we? She's read my palm. Checked my aura. You name it.'

Felicity did something with her head and her laugh that combined the very worst features of a simper and a flirt.

'Lovely.' Grace meant exactly the opposite. 'So glad you hit it off. But if you'll just excuse us,' she caught hold of her mother's arm, 'I need to show my mother something in . . . in . . . the toilet.' Grace knew how weird that must sound, but having discounted hauling Felicity to reception because Tate would be able to eavesdrop, or the kitchen because it was likely Alistair's door was locked and the route blocked, it was the only place left to interrogate her mother.

'In the toilet, Grace? You've not had that problem . . .' her mother did not get the chance to finish as Grace hustled her from the room and along the narrow corridor.

There was too much of her mother and too little toilet cubicle for either of them to fit in comfortably, but Grace had the shoehorn of determination on her side.

'Right,' she said, when she had managed to get the door shut and locked, 'I am going to ask you this and you had better give me an honest answer: what have you told him, Tate?'

'Nothing, love, nothing. Like I said, we've just been chatting. He seems nice – different. What is he? Twenty-two, twenty-three? I like what he's done with his eyes . . .' Her mother trailed off and was trying to look anywhere but at her. In such a small space she soon ran out of possibilities.

'Mu-um . . .'

'Honest, Grace, I've said nothing wrong. I've done nothing wrong.'

'You haven't mentioned Bill . . . or Spain?'

'Not a whisper, although why you're ashamed of all that, I don't . . .' Felicity obviously decided not to chance her luck and veered off to, 'Honestly, Grace, all I said was that you've always been the brainy one of the family. I told him how well you did up in Edinburgh.'

Grace recognised attention-diverting flattery when she heard it, but Felicity seemed earnest enough and a touch scared. That realisation, now her initial panic was subsiding, made Grace feel slightly ashamed of herself. She regarded her mother in all her shabby glory – her hair in need of a bit less henna and a bit more styling – and wondered whether to give her the benefit of the doubt.

'You're sure, Mum? Nothing about what I did before

university? You're not just telling me what I want to hear?'

There was a hesitation before Felicity said, 'I mentioned your sisters, just a bit. Now, don't give me that look. What harm can that do?'

Grace wanted to say, *It's another door you've opened which someone like Tate will lean against*, but she doubted Felicity, who was very much of the fling-every-door-open persuasion, would understand.

'All right, Mum. All right.' Grace let her escape out of the cubicle, despite knowing that a released Felicity would be free to feel aggrieved. Grace could see it, even in the way she was smoothing out her skirt, if it were possible to smooth out pre-wrinkled cheesecloth.

'Not a very nice way to greet your Mum,' Felicity said, 'imprisoning her in a toilet. Not that there's a lot more room out here in this corridor.'

'I'm sorry . . . it was a surprise to find you here.'

'Well, I'm allowed to visit, aren't I? Or has your father poisoned your mind against me?'

'Stop being overdramatic, Mum.' Grace folded her arms, wondering if she looked like a teacher again. 'And, as you've brought up the subject of Dad, perhaps now you'd like to tell me what's going on between the two of you? I'm presuming that's the purpose of the visit? To win me over with your side of the story?'

'No. I told you on the phone, I've got nothing to say. He's the one who should be talking.' Maternal arms were also folded.

'Well, someone needs to say something. This is ridiculous. You know this is ridiculous. At some point, one of you will have to come clean.' Grace let her mind clear. 'So, what exactly have you come here for then?'

'Some help.'

'With?'

Her mother was looking evasive again. 'Can we go back to your office first?'

'No. Tell me here, without the audience.'

Felicity suddenly placed her hand on one of the walls and closed her eyes. 'You know what?' she said. 'I'm feeling a bit faint. Yeah, a bit woozy.'

Grace bit back the urge to say, 'Come off it, Mum.'

The pattern of communication between her and her mother was well established these days. Grace would make some kind of headway, gain the upper hand and then Felicity would slap down the playing-for-sympathy card. If Grace was feeling brave, she would call her bluff, but today, the prospect of having to haul her unconscious mother back along the corridor and into the office in front of Tate made her uncross her arms and say, 'All right, come and sit down. Have a cup of tea. I suppose if I'm actually in the room with you, you can't say anything to embarrass me too much.'

'Charming.' Felicity's wall-leaning and puffing subsided and Grace steeled herself to face Tate and that amused expression of his.

He was sitting in her seat, looking at the computer screen.

'Just checking on how many more reservations I've got,' he said cheerily. 'Yup, two more victims. So, how did it go? Show your mother that rash?'

Grace's laugh in response to that was a false one; her mother's sounded genuine. If Grace hated an audience, Felicity revelled in one.

Tate was up and out of her chair. 'Take a seat – warmed it up for you. Another tea, Fliss? Gracie? Should be plenty of water in the kettle.'

Felicity handed him her cup with a look from under her eyelashes. 'Do all American men have nice manners like you, Tate?'

Her mother seemed to be playing the part of an English woman who had never met a real live American man before. Possibly she was in some time warp involving the Second World War, a brave nurse and some wounded American fly boy.

'No, ma'am, we don't. But us men from the eastern seaboard, well, we're a breed apart.'

Great. Tate was joining in the fantasy. Any moment now they'd start singing a duet of that song that goes 'You say tom-a-toes, I say tom-ar-toes . . .'

'So, Mum, now you're feeling better,' Grace said, sitting down and giving her mother a look that brought her back to the twenty-first century, 'what can I help you with?'

'That's it, that's my Grace,' Felicity said, chuckling coquettishly. 'No small talk, no messing about, just straight to business. Oh, she keeps us all right, does Grace.'

Tate nodded. 'I'm getting that idea.' He bent down to switch on the kettle, which, now that the table had been moved, was sitting on the floor.

Grace saw her mother give his backside an appraising look and she was still looking as he straightened up and waited for the kettle to boil.

'Mum!'

'What?'

'You were about to tell me how I can help you?'

Felicity tore her gaze from Tate's backside. 'I was? Yes, I was. Yes. Well, I need to know the ins and outs of starting a business from home. What do I need to do?'

'A business? What kind of business?'

There was a hint of defiance in the tilt of her mother's chin, but her fingers were once again straying towards the ties on her blouse. Her bangles slid, rattling, towards the crook of her arm. 'Readings,' she said. 'You know, palms, auras. The cards. And classes, small ones, for yoga, meditation . . . and other stuff.'

Grace checked on Tate. He was still watching the kettle.

'Other stuff?' she mouthed at her mother. The stuff she had mentioned was bad enough – the constant companions of her childhood and teenage years; the things that had helped make her who she used to be.

The defiance in her mother's chin had obviously spread to her mouth. 'Grace doesn't believe in mysticism, Tate. In harnessing the power of the universe, anything like that. Not like her sisters.'

'Yeah? Well ain't that a surprise?' Tate said to the kettle and Grace tried to fire another warning shot across her mother's bows with a particularly ferocious glare. She got a look back that made her wonder who was the child and who the mother.

'What other stuff?' Grace repeated, out loud this time, and had to wait for a reply while her mother watched Tate bend down again, switch off the kettle and carry it over to the table. He was standing putting the teabags in the teapot, half obscuring her mother, when Grace heard her say, 'Massage and reflexology.'

Tate did a good job of not missing a beat but she saw his shoulders give one hike up and then down as if he were laughing. Grace was glad he found it funny. She concentrated on watching the steam rise from the water being poured from kettle to pot before choosing her words very carefully.

'Massage and reflexology? You're practising those? Is this something new?'

'No and yes.' Tate was returning the kettle to the floor and it was only when Felicity had got watching that out of her system that she elaborated: 'No, I don't do it, and yes, it is new. My partner's going to do it. Oh, thank you, love.' She simpered up at Tate as he handed her a cup of tea.

Partner? Not in a million years could that mean her father. The only way he would lay his hands on anyone he didn't know was to frisk them. *Partner?* Ah, she had it. 'Is this Maureen, the one with the mobile nail service? She does a bit of massage, doesn't she?'

'No. Not Maureen. It's a man called Jay. Jay Houghton.'

The name arrived at the same time as the cup of tea which Tate was holding out towards her, and despite having her fingers round the handle, she seemed unable to grip. Obviously aware of this, he continued to stand there looking down at her as she let that name wander round her brain, zap across a few synapses and come up with a face. A face attached to a guy who was all pecs and flash. Didn't he work in that gym by the station? There was a Nikki Houghton too, from school. His sister. Grace thought she remembered something about shoplifting. Or was Nikki the mother?

'Jay Houghton,' she said, and found herself looking into green cat-like eyes, uncomprehending but amused nonetheless. A cat picking up a scent of something.

'You gonna take this tea?' he said. 'Or shall I just keep holding it and you can bend forward and slurp? See you got your mouth open ready.'

She closed her mouth, took the tea and opened her mouth again. 'I think there's something else I need to show you in the toilet, Mum,' she said, putting down her cup without spilling anything and getting up without appearing to rush.

But her mother was shaking her head, feet in her pointy boots still resolutely planted on the floor. One hand plonked her cup on the small table. Grace saw tea lap over the side of it and splash on to the wood.

'Not going,' she said, her telephone voice replaced by that of a truculent toddler.

'I see. Well then, Tate, would you mind giving my mother and me a few minutes alone?'

Tate shrugged. 'Sure.'

'No you don't, Grace Surtees,' her mother said, struggling to her feet now, bangles rattling. 'You stay right here, Tate.

Go on, Grace, say what's on your mind. Attack me, even though you know how sensitive I am. Even though I've brought you up not to be small-minded. Narrow. God knows I tried hard enough to make you a free spirit like your sisters. But if all you can say is, "Isn't Jay young?" Or, "Aren't you old enough to be his mother?" Or even, "Who's he been practising his massage on then, Felicity?" Well, don't bother. It's a business arrangement. That's all.'

Tate had seemed unsure at the start of that speech whether to stay or go, but now he was sitting on his chair and, as her mother stopped speaking, he swivelled his seat to face Grace, looking as if he were in ringside position for whatever she had to say next. He had his eyebrows raised expectantly.

All the things that Grace had been going to lob at her mother died in her mouth. She was not going to provide Tate with any more entertainment today. 'Don't be silly, Mum,' she said reasonably. 'I just thought you'd like to discuss business in private, but if you're happy to do it here . . . Let's see . . . So first, I'd advise you to go and see a small business adviser – they'll be more up to speed with everything than me. If you want a bank loan, say for equipment such as massage couches or to cover your increased fuel bills, you'll need a business plan – projected costs, earnings, that kind of thing.' She sensed Tate was watching her closely. 'It might also be an idea to consult a solicitor about getting your partnership set up legally, sorting out how capital investments, expenses, profits and so on are divided. Then, of course, you'll need to ask the council whether you have to have any kind of permission to operate a business from a domestic dwelling. Oh, and think about your tax position; I'm sure the accountants near the library would be happy to help. Plus there's stuff like insurance, safety regulations, etc. etc.'

She finished with a beatific smile, fuelled entirely by willpower.

Her mother's expression had become more and more disappointed as Grace had been talking and now she had the appearance of a knight who had strapped on armour and girded his loins for a fight, only to be told that the dragon had turned out to be a pacifist.

'So, was there anything else?' Grace asked, chancing lifting her cup of tea to her mouth. Her hand was as steady as Tate's gaze.

'No,' Felicity said, looking confused now as well as thwarted. 'No, that's . . . that's helpful Grace. I knew you'd understand where to start. Uh, I'll have a look into that adviser bloke. Yes. So . . .' Felicity was gathering up her bag as if she had no game plan left and the only thing to do now was bail out. She looked theatrically at her watch.

'I . . . I'd better be off. I said I'd meet Jay later to . . . discuss plans.'

'I'll see you to the door.' Grace put her cup down and helped her mother retrieve her cape from the coat hook, a cape which had been in and out of fashion at least twice since Felicity had first bought it. Grace even held her mother's bag while she struggled into the orange and green tartan wigwam.

'Goodbye, Tate,' her mother said, and he gave her a thumbs-up and a wink, which she took with a slightly martyred air, as if it were her due.

They were only just outside the black door, still on the landing, when Grace let her have it: 'Mum, you should be very careful with Jay Houghton. Going into business with him.'

Her mother turned on her, immediately powered back up into righteous indignation mode. 'Oh, I see. Got me outside to say that, did you?' And why should I be careful, Grace? Huh? Huh? He's a fully qualified fitness instructor. And he's got certificates for massage courses. Reflexology courses. So spit it out, girl, what are you getting at?'

Felicity's hands were on her hips, which made it look as if someone had pitched the wigwam and balanced her head on top of it.

'I'm not getting at anything,' Grace said, trying to soothe

her mother by dropping her own voice. 'It's simply that you can be impetuous and Jay can be charming. It's not a good combination for making objective business decisions. I think you need to take a step back.'

Felicity took a step forward. 'You know what, Grace? I could have guessed what your attitude would be. And know what else? I can guess what your sisters will say. *They* will wish me well.' She turned and started walking down the next set of stairs, a constant stream of talk coming back at Grace, most of it to do with her negative energies. Grace was rounded on again as they reached the bottom of the staircase.

'Your aura. It's stinking black – you know that, don't you?'

Grace didn't answer and did her best to look bored, but her mother's finger was jabbing at a place where Felicity believed her aura should be. 'You can't go against your true self. You're a child of nature, not commerce. You've never let your heart open up again after Bill, that's the trouble. You've just bound it up tight. You'll do yourself damage. It'll burst out one day, your heart.'

'I think biology is a lot more complex than that, Mum.'

Felicity shook her head as if she couldn't even put into words how she was feeling, and Grace considered taking advantage of this pause to get her mother out of the building. Too late, Felicity was off again.

'You know who he reminds me of?' she said with a sly look back up the stairs.

'Mark's home this weekend,' Grace said coolly. 'Home and a lot put out that Dad – you remember Dad? – that Dad is living in my flat. Still, every cloud . . . we're going to a good hotel to make up for it.'

'How long's he back for this time?' Felicity said, hitching her bag up her arm and reordering her bangles. She had the stroppy look on her face that she always had when Mark was discussed.

'Just Friday and Saturday night here, plus a stopover in Birmingham to see friends. Then he's off again. Kazakhstan, if you're interested.'

There was a sulky set to Felicity's mouth as she moved along the hall. She didn't even return the wave Bernice gave her as she walked past Far & Away's door. Grace knew this meant that she was saving herself for one last grenade that she could chuck to re-establish that she knew the ways of the universe better than anyone.

Sure enough, prior to stepping out into the street, her mother paused with one hand on the door, rearranged herself and her cape and said, 'He's not one of us, that Mark. His aura's rotten too – that's what you get from messing about with Mother Earth; drilling away at her skin. And you . . .' She pointed back up the stairs and dispensed the kind of knowing look that suggested she had a direct line to some ancient wisdom, 'you're in trouble, my girl.'

'I very much doubt that,' Grace replied, hoping her mother couldn't hear the rapid beat of her heart running under the words, but her mother was gone.

Grace walked slowly back up the stairs, trying not to think about what her mother had just said, but about Jay Houghton and the mad idea for a business. Well, at least she now knew why her father had got into an almighty huff.

As she pushed open the door to Picture London, Grace could have been forgiven for thinking she'd walked into a rerun of events from that morning: there was Tate lying full length on the sofa, his hands behind his head and his feet in those boots, hanging over the end of the sofa cushions.

'Now, that is one interesting mom,' he said as she passed him. He opened his eyes. 'And you're one of four sisters, huh? So, let me see if I've got this right . . . Aurillia, Zinovia True and Serafina. Pretty exotic names.' He lifted his head. 'What happened to you? Just the one name, the one syllable?'

'Sorry. I think my parents ran out of ideas.'

'You sure? I mean, you don't have some exotic name you're hiding away?'

'No, I'm just plain and simple Grace.'

He laid his head back down and did a movement that suggested he was sorting out some kinks in his backbone and Grace was glad he had a big shirt on and not a T-shirt that would have ridden up to reveal his stomach, which she suspected was tanned and flat and . . .

She concentrated extra hard on being dull and not thinking about his skin.

'Plain and simple?' he said, turning his head to look at her. 'Don't think so. Unless they mean something different in the UK. Do they mean something different?'

A flash of need ripped through Grace – she had the urge to hitch up her skirt, sit astride him on the sofa and take his face between her hands and kiss it roughly.

'I think I can hear my phone ringing,' she said, moving away quickly, and he laughed and said, 'You got dog hearing?' but let her go.

She went back into the office, automatically sitting at her desk and sipping at her tea before she registered it was cold. Her hand wasn't as steady as it had been when she was drinking it before. She wondered if Tate still had his eyes open in reception, if his head was still turned.

No, no, no. She had to stop wondering anything about Tate. Felicity's visit had disturbed her more than she'd imagined, made her lower her guard so that all kinds of things had come out to ambush her. Not good enough, Grace. Must try harder.

She scrolled through her emails, hoping there was enough potential irritation there to distract her – oh yes, three from her sisters, no doubt replying to her mother's earlier plea for sympathy. In their various locations around the world they always seemed a step behind. They were still dealing with their father relocating to Grace's flat, while she was having to get used to the Jay Houghton development.

Tell Dad not to adhere so strongly to patriarchal dictates, was one of the choicer lines from Aurillia's email. Zinovia True, who seemed to be going under the name of Zino T. this week, advised her mother and father to seek counselling to work through the issues they'd been sublimating for years. Serafina told them to try rebirthing. In front of an audience.

She heard Tate get up off the sofa and wanted to curl up in a ball to keep everything safe and out of his reach. She read Serafina's email again, slowly, word by word. Tate ambled in, yawning. 'You want the table moved back?'

'I'll do it. You can go if you want.' *Please. Go.*

'Hey, I can move a table. Anyways, I have a mom too, and she's red hot on tidying up.' Grace didn't look at him as he yawned and stretched, or when he bent to pick up the table, or put it back down by the wall. She didn't even look in his direction when he had to bend again to retrieve the kettle. It was only when he laughed that she couldn't stop herself from seeing what was so funny.

'Bet you were worried that you were gonna come back this afternoon and find reception in a big old mess?'

'Not at all.'

He glanced up at her to deliver his disbelieving look. It made her go back to her email.

'So, I'm out of here.' He put on his great big coat and picked up the dirty mugs, looping them on the fingers of one hand. 'Just take these into the kitchen, give 'em a rinse, say night to Al.'

He didn't need to: they both heard Alistair's door open and he appeared, looking into the room first, Grace presumed, to see if Felicity had gone.

'Mother all right?' he asked.

She nodded.

'Hell of a woman,' Tate said.

Alistair didn't comment on that; he had suddenly noticed Tate's taped masterpiece.

'Found it in a dumpster,' Tate said proudly. 'Think it looks kind of edgy . . . real.'

'Yes, very good, very good. A companion piece to the . . . uh . . . the Chinese thing,' Alistair gushed, but to Grace his body language was shrieking 'there's a mouldy, horrible chair in here. Please, God, don't let any clients sit on it.'

She momentarily forgot her pledge to be non-confrontational. 'It certainly intrigued the Austrian couple who were in earlier. Especially when it stuck to the woman's skirt.' The laugh she put at the end of the sentence got a boost when she saw Alistair frown and then died when Tate tilted his head and his green eyes flared and then narrowed.

'You told Gracie about tomorrow, Alistair?' he said as if relishing every word, and Alistair leaped out of his contemplation of the hideous monstrosity of a chair to say enthusiastically, 'No, slipped my mind. Now Grace . . .' His expression suggested he was about to tell her something wonderful, which gave Grace enough warning to maintain an absolutely neutral face. 'Tate and I thought it would be a good idea if we all accompanied him to a few of the studios on his list tomorrow afternoon. Maybe a gallery as well? Just so that we can all see what he's going to do with the clients. Get a bit of cross-fertilisation going in the company.'

Grace thought that sounded a bit sexual, and the way Tate was now looking at her suggested he did too. She felt hot, as if the sun were shining directly on her.

'You haven't got anything on after lunch, have you, Grace?' Alistair hurtled on.

'If she hasn't it'll sure make that cross-fertilisation easier.' Tate winked at her, but the joke went over Alistair's head.

'So,' he said, nodding earnestly, 'if you've got nothing on, Grace, we can all have a good run at it.'

Tate burst out laughing. 'Boy, now I'm looking forward to it even more.'

'I'm available all afternoon,' Grace said, not quite managing to choose words that were innuendo-free.

'Excellent. Gilbert's coming along too.' Alistair did one of his strange arm swings. 'I personally can't wait. Could do with getting in touch with the . . . the street. Excited too, Grace?'

Tate was watching her again.

'Very,' she enthused to a bit of wall between him and Alistair.

'Perfect. So if that's settled, I'll see you tomorrow, Tate. Oh, and give me those cups; save you having to tramp through my office to the kitchen.'

Grace saw the flash of a silver ring as Tate unhooked the cups from his fingers.

'No need for you to stay late,' Alistair called back to Grace as he went out. When he got back to his office, they both heard him lock his door.

'What's he got in there?' Tate asked. 'Weapons-grade plutonium?'

She stayed silent.

'Locked doors, locked doors,' Tate went on as if musing to himself. 'Lot of them in this office.' He was looking directly at her again.

She blanked him.

He came nearer. 'So, perfect end to your day, finding out about the tour tomorrow?'

'Not at all. Looking forward to it.'

'Really? Would have thought it was just what you needed – more time in the company of . . . how did you describe me to Gilbert? An obnoxious, opinionated American?'

'Don't be silly.'

'So I'm silly as well?'

She knew he was playing with her.

'No, no, that's not what I meant. What I meant was, I thought you were those things before I knew you.'

'And now you know me you don't think I'm any of those things?'

'No, of course not.'

'What am I now then?'

'What?'

'How would you describe me now?'

She swallowed. 'Very nice.'

He burst out laughing. 'Jeez, Gracie, try and hold yourself

back, will you? "Very nice" – that one of those Brit-speak things that means the opposite?'

She left a gap that was just a beat too long before saying, 'I'm sure I'll really enjoy your tour . . .'

'Planning to fall asleep, get your own back?'

'No.'

'I would if I were you.'

'I'm not that immature.'

There, he'd got what he wanted: she'd shown him she had claws. He was now sitting on the edge of her desk. 'OK,' he said, counting off on his fingers. 'So now I'm obnoxious, opinionated, silly and immature? I swear, Gracie, you've got the best way of insulting people. So polite.'

'I didn't mean it like—'

He waved his hand. 'Don't worry. I'm all of those things. And more, probably. So, Gracie . . .'

'It's Grace,' she said flatly. 'One syllable, remember? We discussed that earlier?'

He nodded. 'Oh, yeah. Grace.'

His tone suggested he didn't believe it was her real name. She felt a sense of unease twist and turn in her stomach and concentrated harder on breathing and moving slowly and not, whatever she did, showing her disquiet. She needed him to go.

'I'll be heading home in a minute,' she said, brightly. 'Are you off anywhere nice?'

'Trying to get me to leave?' he asked, and before she could deny it, he was standing up. 'OK, OK, I get the hint. Stop asking me questions. Stop sitting on my desk. I'm a busy woman.' He didn't appear to be put out about it: he still had a faintly amused expression on his face. 'I'll see you tomorrow then,' he called back as he went through reception. She heard the outside door open and close.

'Oh, give me strength,' she said out loud to the empty office as she crossed her arms, pitched forward and rested her head on the desk. She was going to close her eyes, but she caught sight of his horrible chair and suddenly she felt as if she wanted to do something vaguely wrong, something against her own rules. Take a bit of a potshot at Tate bloody Jefferson.

She got up and sat in Tate's chair, and with a deft move of her legs scooted it towards the wall with a thump. She laughed and propelled it towards the opposite wall. Another thump. She stopped to listen – no sound from Alistair's office and if he did decide to come out, she'd hear him unlock his door. She wiggled her hips and the chair went first one way and then the other. It reminded her of the way she used to dance on the table in that bar, invariably cracking her head on the light as the evening wore on. She did a bit more scooting and bumped into the filing cabinet and the wall again and then she pirouetted round one way, braced her legs and stopped. Something about the movement reminded her of a gunfight, that moment when the pacing away has to end and the cowboy spins around to fire. She turned quickly again and drawled, 'Reach for the sky,' as, with a quick flick of her hands, each one in the shape of a gun, she executed a perfect mime of guns being drawn. 'My name's Tate, Tate Jefferson, the fastest artist in the West, here to stir up trouble and then hightail it out of town.' It made her laugh and seemed to take some of the sting out of all that piss-taking he'd done and the discontent at being roped into one of his bouncy, bouncy tours of cutting-edge art. It seemed to put him back where he needed to be – an overenthusiastic boy, as feckless as Jay Houghton.

She put her hands down again and pushed off even harder this time with her feet, making the chair do two whole revolutions before it came to a stop. It made her feel giddy and slightly light-headed and this time her laugh was louder. She flicked her hands up again. 'Hold steady there, pardner,' she drawled, 'I wanna peer at you with these green eyes of mine. Get right under your skin.' She made some shooting noises and spun the chair again and then nearly dislocated both her knees and her hips by slamming her feet on the ground as she caught a blurred vision of Tate standing in the doorway.

The chair came to a jarring halt and she realised she still had her hands in the shape of guns and dropped them like stones to her side.

She didn't know whether she was going to die of heart failure or a hernia and she wasn't actually sure she blurted out, 'I thought you'd gone,' but he was shaking his head and saying, 'Nope,' so she must have done.

There was no explanation from him about why, earlier, he had given her the impression that he'd left. Not even any pretence that he'd forgotten something and had to come back.

She wasn't sure what expression she had on her face – wild panic probably – but the one on his said, *Well, look at that huge slice of free spirit peeking through there. And hey, if you wanna play games, I'm up for it.*

'Enjoying yourself?' he said.

'Uh . . . yes. Just seeing how it moved, you know.' She got up unsteadily and gave the chair a pat. 'Yes, quite good. Handles really well.' All she needed was a pair of driving gloves to look a bigger prat.

The set of Tate's mouth suggested he wanted to lie on the floor and laugh out loud but was going to keep her guessing about how much he had seen and heard. She felt the flush of heat over her face that she knew meant her cheeks would be pink. Gun fighting, whirling round and round and mocking the way he spoke. Pretty damning. What had she said about getting under her skin?

He came over and patted the chair just as she had done and she took a surreptitious step away. She knew it hadn't gone unnoticed.

'Yeah, she does move like a dream,' he said. 'Not surprising really. Older models, well, more to them then these flashy new ones.' His hand was indicating her office chair but his eyes were on her and there was enough seriousness in them to make her unsure about the true meaning of his words. She thought back to wanting to kiss his face. Had he sensed that too?

And then he was turning away. 'I'm really going this time,' he said and that was it. No other smart comments; just a 'Night, Gracie,' when he headed out of the office again.

'It's Grace,' she said after checking he really had gone this time. 'Grace. One syllable. Easy. Like Tate.' She thought about that and studied the chair. 'No. Not so easy. It's still only Monday. One day of him and I'm starting to lose it.'

That made her sit down in the chair again, but this time there was no spinning, or laughing or mock gun fights. She stayed absolutely still and tried to get the logical, ordered side of her brain to put in an appearance and to stop thinking about those green eyes and that silver ring, which she knew were already breaking through her defences.

CHAPTER 16

'So, are those part of your tour, dear boy?' Gilbert asked the following afternoon, indicating the graffiti along the side of the warehouse, and Grace tucked her hands further into the pockets of her coat and looked at her feet so that Tate wouldn't see her smile.

'Funny, funny,' Tate said, punching Gilbert softly on the arm before reaching out and pressing a bell – one of about eight on the wall next to the heavy iron door. Someone had written *Artists are puffs* on it and Alistair, clutching his briefcase, tutted and said, 'Philistines. No wonder they can't spell.'

There was the sound of something grating against the other side of the door before it was pulled back. The woman standing there did not have the asymmetrical fringe Gilbert swore all modern female artists had, but it was cut very high, making her look as if she were permanently surprised. She wore pale grey, draped clothing with a paint-smeared baggy shirt over the top.

'Tate,' she said, opening her arms wide to receive him.

Introductions were made and the woman led them up an industrial-looking metal staircase to her studio.

'Shawna does these amazing collages,' Tate said, 'real deconstructions of the alienating nature of post-boom, post-bust urban culture.'

'Oh goody,' Gilbert groaned, but Grace noticed he was doing it quietly so that Tate wouldn't hear.

They were in a huge space with metal beams and exposed London brick and leaning against some of the walls were large canvases of varying shades of grey. From the doorway they seemed as if they were just splodges of colour, but up close you could see that each canvas was covered with tiny bits of paper, each with its own grey image on it – here a vandalised sign, there a broken window or a single glove stuck on a railing.

'If there were handcuffs and some rope, she could call it *50 Shades of Grey*,' Grace whispered to Gilbert and he gave her a look as if he had no idea what she was talking about.

She made an effort to pay attention to Tate as he said, 'See, some of the images are found, some are photographs and some Shawna draws herself. Brought together like this, they have a more profound effect than if you viewed them alone. But, hey, let Shawna take you through the artistic impetus behind her work.'

'We're usually blind to the decay in our society.' Shawna's seriousness was the kind that made you want to giggle despite your better instincts. 'We see it so often – the boarded-up shops, the litter . . . Here I'm trying to make the decay the absolute focus, not something you can ignore. To raise it to an art form in itself.'

They all nodded as if they agreed, except for Alistair who was simply repeating, 'Marvellous, marvellous,' at every opportunity. He had done the same in the other studio they'd visited earlier, the one where Gnat (multiple piercings, skinny arms, indeterminate sex) rolled an assortment of prosthetic limbs through paint and then applied them to canvases. Gnat said that explaining what creative impulses lay behind this was 'an outdated, hierarchical, join-the-dots way of viewing art.' Tate had simply clapped and encouraged Gnat to expand on that approach. So Gnat had said the canvases spoke for themselves. Or, did they have to speak at all? Did art really have to have meaning? And anyway, how could he give them his take on the meaning when they were all individuals forming their own subjective conclusions? A dramatic pause. What was meaning anyway?

Grace had been unable to look at Gilbert during this lecture for fear that they would set each other off. There was an almost irresistible impulse to ask Gnat whether the price tags on his work had any meaning either.

Shawna continued to talk them through her canvases, Tate every now and again interjecting to point out something they might like to consider, such as what effect the different greys had and why this particular canvas they were looking at now, with objects rather than images, was probably producing a different emotion. Grace contemplated the discarded burger boxes, the lace from a trainer, the bits of plastic with worn lettering and the shards of glass, all painted zinc grey, and didn't quite know what emotion she was meant to feel towards any of it.

She had started off feeling jittery, expecting all kinds of memories to begin whirling around in her brain with each sniff of paint, each view of a canvas, but what she was seeing was so different from Bill's work, nothing seemed to be happening. Except she felt uneasy every time Tate caught her eye, remembering the chair incident. He made no attempt to bring it up, which spooked her even more. God, he was good at this unsettling thing.

His enthusiasm for all this . . . this stuff was unsettling her too. It was not the tinny falseness of Alistair's enthusiasm, but the sparkly, bright kind that lit up your eyes and had you bounding around. She supposed it was the same enthusiasm that had him retrieving tat from skips.

He knew his subject too; she'd studied enough modules

on conceptual and figurative art, absurdism and all the other isms to know that.

Grace focused again on Shawna, who was now showing them how she selected her images. They trooped along to a corner of the studio that reeked of chemicals. They stood and listened, they learned about techniques for distorting and colouring photo images, and they peered at a half-completed work. After a few more pleasantries, more gushing from Alistair, they were off, heading up another flight of stairs.

'I really have to show you these next guys,' Tate said, shepherding them along. 'They will blow your mind.'

'I hope they do blow my mind,' Gilbert whispered to Grace, 'because after that last place, I'm primed to cut my wrists.'

This time it was a man who opened the door, no older than Grace with jet-black hair that came to a point in the middle of his forehead and echoed the shape of his goatee beard. He was dressed in a black boiler suit. A black boiler suit that was pristine and had sharp creases in the legs as if it had been ironed very precisely.

'Tate, my man,' he said, and again Tate was received into wide-flung arms. It was beginning to grate on her how popular he seemed to be. She reasoned that it was because he was going to bring potential business to the studios.

She thought back to Bill. Always a bit of an edge to people's worship of him, as if they were scared he would take a chunk out of them verbally if he was bored. Or drunk. Or just 'being Bill'. *You can't be a real artist and have friends.* That was a Billism. *Everyone is a drain on your creativity in the end.* That was another.

Now Tate and the guy in the black boiler suit were bumping their fists together and laughing and Grace was curling her lip at that until she got right inside the studio and did have her mind blown slightly off track. It was filled with sculptures, and when she looked closely they were made of paper, great chunks of it. It was as if someone had taken the biggest phone books in existence and cut and shaped them as easily as blocks of cheese. There were nudes made from pages of porn magazines; fat bankers made from paper money; a nun made from a bible. Against one wall, another guy was leaning over a stack of old books with the covers removed and was cutting into them with an electric knife. He turned it off and lifted up his safety goggles when he saw them. He was as scruffy as the first man was neat, and his face, except where his goggles had been, was splattered with paper dust.

'Yo,' he said.

'Mi-keeee,' Tate replied. There was another series of those strange hand bumping and grasping rituals in which Tate excelled, before Grace, Gilbert and Alistair found themselves listening to Mike tell them how the whole artistic process was about taking things from one state to another, reversing the process that had begun by taking a solid tree and making it into fragile paper.

'It's a kind of rebirth,' he said, picking bits of paper dust from under his nails. 'We're allowing the corporality of the tree to have a second chance – it's a metaphor for the human condition really.'

'I liked those sculptures,' Grace whispered to Gilbert when they were leaving.

'Yes. But are they art?'

'There's more skill in them than the collages and the—'

'Do not mention Gnat and those limbs, I will be having nightmares as it is.'

Grace laughed which made Tate turn and, walking backwards, shout, 'You having fun there? Still awake, Gracie?'

'She's loving it, dear boy. We both are,' Gilbert shouted back, which saved Grace the bother of having to make something up. Tate gave her a look she didn't quite catch and turned back around and carried on talking to Alistair. Tate was leading the way at a gallop and Grace watched him talking, hands describing what he was saying, making points with his fingers.

'Tate's pretty impressive, isn't he?' Gilbert said, and

Grace wondered if that was his reason for coming on this tour when he obviously had no intention of viewing anything he saw without his sixteenth-century blinkers on.

She watched Tate again. She had been wondering what he would turn up wearing today – western garb, complete with chaps and a Stetson just to embarrass her? In fact, he was wearing a suit, tweed, with a matching waistcoat, and he'd teamed it with a collarless shirt and a scarf so that he might have been an extra from a Dickens' crowd scene, except he was also wearing a grey wool beanie, his blond hair just poking out from underneath it. It made his eyes look even greener.

He still had the biker boots on, and Grace wondered if they were his only footwear.

They arrived at the gallery and Gilbert groaned. 'I hate this place – saw it on the television when it first opened. It's what happens when limitless money meets limited taste.'

'Shh,' Grace said as they walked past the staff in their regulation black – black trousers, black T-shirts, black looks.

Tate led them through a run of high-ceilinged, white-walled, echoing rooms. They went past stoats preserved in plastic, pairs of crutches tied up with barbed wire, a piano made entirely from mouldering bread. There were canvases with just one word on them, canvases with nothing on them, canvases that had been ripped apart. As they went, Tate talked about what the artists were perhaps trying to express, how they fitted into current art movements and trends. They stood in the dark and watched a video of men getting on and off a fishing boat over and over again and another video of a woman peeling an onion and the onion crying. They stood next to a huge computer screen while an artist in Hamburg transmitted a thick red line and other artists around the world incorporated it into their own work on smart phones and tablets.

In a room displaying only a very small piece of curved metal with a black-and-white picture of an eye on it, Gilbert stood in front of the explanation on the wall and shook his head.

'Something up, Gilb?' Tate asked.

Gilbert gave the sculpture a jaded look. 'I just have a theory that a work of art should speak to you without needing a screed of explanation. I tend to think, dear boy, the longer the explanation, the poorer the piece of art.'

Tate screwed up his face. 'We-ell . . . depends what you think art is.' He put his arm round Gilbert's shoulders. 'Anyway, Gilb, your Titians: don't you explain them, set them in context? It all helps enrich the experience.'

'Yes, but it's an add-on with the *Great* Artists.' Only a

person with impaired hearing would have missed Gilbert's dig at the less great. 'I mean, even if I said nothing to my clients, they could still see the skill involved and know what the painter was getting at. But what on earth is this saying to me? "I am a piece of metal with an eye on it"?'

'Or is it saying, "I am an eye with a piece of metal *under* me"?' Tate shot back before peeling away from Gilbert, laughing. 'Just keep an open mind, eh, Gilb? Being frustrated, angry, irritated – they're all valid responses to any piece of art. It's even allowed to make you laugh.'

Grace wished Tate had been grudging or snarky. There was too much generosity in the way he listened to other people's views.

'I think it's marvellous,' Alistair cut in. 'Stark, concise . . . the inanimate, plus an inanimate image of the animate. Marvellous.' He nodded earnestly and took himself and his briefcase off to look at a fish made of shoes. Tate followed him, but Gilbert and Grace hung back.

'Talking of things that frustrate, anger and irritate, and rarely make me laugh,' Gilbert said, 'does Alistair keep having to prove how much he is "up with" the modern art world?'

'I think the expression is "down with".'

Gilbert flapped a hand. 'Is it too much to hope that

there's a coffee shop? I mean Tate's doing a wonderful job, but really, there's only so much of this I can take.'

'Go on,' Grace said, 'I'll cover for you.'

She watched Gilbert cut back through the room, giving the piece of metal and the eye a wide berth as if it might somehow infect his artistic sensibilities if he got too close. He turned and waved before he left the room, every bit a naughty schoolboy playing truant from a school trip. She wandered slowly after Tate and Alistair, but they seemed rooted in front of the fish sculpture, Tate's hands swooping up and back to describe something and Alistair responding with a volley of nods. At one point Tate stretched up his arms and put the palms of his hands together as if describing some kind of bridge and Grace stood watching him before realising that her attention had gone from his hands to his backside. She turned away and headed into another room. Safer to go off-piste as Gilbert had done.

She stopped in front of a poster advertising a Bollywood film, upon which the artist had stuck thousands and thousands of pieces of rice painted in jewelled colours. She was surprised at how much she liked it.

She stopped in front of another poster and then another. Yes, these were lovely; perhaps they didn't call out to her like a Monet or a Van Gogh, but there was something in them that touched her. She read the dense blurb about the artist and drifted through to another room, not really caring now if Alistair and Tate had noticed she was missing. She sat on a bench and did some people-watching – noting the ones who just skimmed through each room, and the ones who stood and stared. The ones who, like her, seemed glad of a sit-down. Some students were taking photos and others were sitting, cross-legged, sketching a long canvas dotted with splashes of colour. Nobody seemed to be giving tours, except for Tate. She wondered if Alistair had dislocated his neck yet from all that nodding. She wondered if Tate had lowered his arms.

In front of her was a sculpture of a huge white clam on a stark black plinth and the more Grace studied it, the more it reminded her of her father the night before when she had tried to get him to open up about her mother.

The conversation had not started well, mainly as Grace had come home to find more areas of her flat experiencing their own personal crime wave. Her father was in the kitchen 'working on a spate of post office raids in Surrey'; every surface was covered in paper and books. There were files open on the floor too and the phone was on the table. She knew if she touched it, the thing would be red hot. Her father had a number of pals who were also interested in crime, two of them being ex-policemen, and they were often on the phone to each other swapping theories and snippets of information. That they called themselves the Newham Gang showed that at least they had a sense of humour about their obsession.

'I see you've been unpacking,' Grace had said, looking back through the kitchen door at the books and magazines that were now out of their boxes in the hall and arranged in piles that obviously meant something to her father but just screamed mess to her.

Over supper, Grace had broached the subject of her mother's visit to the office and, in response, got a grunt and a request to pass the salt. When she tiptoed up to and delicately mentioned Felicity's plans to set up a business, her father began viciously to cut up his lasagne, but said nothing.

'Is it the idea of starting a business that's rattled you, Dad?' She had used her kindest voice, her softest tone.

He had said, 'No, it might be a goer. God knows there are enough mugs about,' and clammed up again.

Feeling like a dentist trying not to touch a nerve, Grace probed further, suggesting it was perhaps, then, the person her mother intended as a business partner that was unsettling? Grace had been unable to say Jay Houghton's name but her father had spat it out as soon as she'd stopped talking and vehemently used the word 'waster' to describe Jay, Jay's father and possibly Jay's father's father. 'He comes from a long line of wasters,' he summed up, doing horrible things to his salad with his fork. 'None of them has ever worked up a sweat at anything.'

Grace did not point out that as a fitness trainer Jay probably worked up quite a lot of sweat.

'He's not just a waster, Grace; he's a looker and a charmer too. And your mother, she gets passionate about things.' He indicated his papers and files. 'God knows I don't mind that. How could I when she's never complained about my hobby? And I've never minded when she latches on to someone and thinks the sun shines out of their backside for a while.' He brought his hand down flat on the table. 'But there are passions and there are *passions*.'

There was no further opportunity for discussion as her father took himself off for a bath. He had seemed so folded in on himself, so hurt, that she didn't broach the subject of tidying away his stuff in the kitchen.

Grace gave the clam another look as if she could work out how to get it to spring open and so use that knowledge in any further conversations with her dad. Had Felicity actually done anything specific to make her father jealous? Or was it a general grouchy, jealous feeling he was nursing?

None the wiser, she thought she'd better make an effort to rejoin Tate and Alistair. She began retracing the route she had taken, but there were no Bollywood posters in the room she entered, or the next one, and she was just turning around again when she stopped. The painting in front of her could have been a window, so clearly did it make her feel as if she were looking out on to the beach in San Sebastián. It was late; the families and the groups of girls flirting with the lads playing volleyball had gone home and, in the dipping sun, the beach was a red gash of paint and sand mixed and swirled and flung on to the canvas. The sky was blue-black as if a storm were coming; lines had been gouged in the paint by what Grace knew were fingernails. Two figures were running on the sand, their bodies twisted and stretched but still recognisably human. Grace could smell the sea, feel the sun on her skin. There was the sound of the waves, the seabirds getting noisier and noisier. She wiggled her toes – her shoes were gone and her toes were caked with sand. God, how she'd loved the fact that she could go days without having to wear any shoes, nothing between her and feeling life beneath her feet.

The gallery was falling away around her, the people like shadows, less real than the ones in the painting. She needed to move, get to a bench or against a wall. Where was the air in this gallery? There was no air. What the hell was the painting doing here?

'Yay, got you.' It was Tate's voice right next to her. 'Nice try, Gracie . . . nearly escaped, nearly made it to the main exit, but I tracked you down. Guess Gilbert's already gone over the wall, huh?' There was a laugh. Was it from him or the painting? 'Well, old Gilb's out of luck: Al's gone off to find him and drag him back . . .' She sensed he was looking at her more intently now and she tried, really tried to breathe and be bland and hope he didn't notice the sand on her feet and her wet hair and, God, why was it so suffocating in here?

'OK, what's got you so fascinated?' Tate was saying, 'Ah, nice one: a Bill Jackson. Well, look at that.' She saw him lean in for a closer inspection. 'Early one, I'd say.' He was walking to the label on the wall. 'Yup. Kindly loaned by the Scottish National Gallery of Modern Art. Painted during the summer of 2004 in Spain and conveys a particularly turbulent time in the artist's life.' She sensed he was back at her side. 'Turbulent? No kidding. Looks like him and the paint had a fight. The energy in that sky! Seen some of his more recent ones in New York. Nothing like this. This is wild. Apocalyptic.'

'It's very rare.' Had Grace said that? No, it was a woman, in black, with something written on her T-shirt. Grace registered that she was from the gallery and with that understanding the sand round her feet was disappearing, going back into the painting. She was standing by Tate, this woman, and he was no longer looking at Grace but at her. It was going to be all right; the window was closing, the noises fading. She chanced glancing down at her own feet again and saw the shine of her shoes. Her skin was cooling. 'Sorry to interrupt,' the woman was saying, 'I heard you talking about this painting. It's from Jackson's time in Spain, of course – San Sebastián. As you can see, we only have it on loan from the National Gallery in Edinburgh; they bought it a few years ago from a private collector. We're thrilled to have it here . . . it's possibly the only one remaining from that period of his artistic development. You probably know the story – destroyed the rest, burned them when he left Spain.'

Tate was nodding and as neither he nor the woman was looking in her direction, Grace fought to put the new version of herself back in charge and push Spain and Bill back down the years, away from the present.

She noticed for the first time that Tate no longer had his hat on. It was rolled up into itself like a soft grey ball and he was passing it from one hand to the other, back and forth, back and forth. His blond hair against the blue black of the sky made her want to turn away and run back through the rooms.

'Jeez, imagine burning all your work,' he said to Grace, still balling up his hat, and she realised it was because that thought really disturbed him.

She wondered if it would look weird if she went to sit down. She decided it would.

The woman was rattling on again, a smug look on her face. 'Of course, those of us in the know feel that Jackson didn't actually destroy his earlier paintings. We think he's holding on to them until his star rises even further. He's very collectable, you see, and the longer he keeps them off the market, the higher the prices will go.'

The woman gave the impression that she would like to go on proving to them how knowledgeable she was, but a couple were approaching, obviously intent on talking to her.

'You all right? Tate asked when the woman had left them. He was frowning. 'Look a bit clammy there. Wanna sit?'

'We should go and find Alistair.'

'He can wait. You sure you're OK?'

She nodded and he gave her and the painting another quick check. 'Think the woman was right, that he has kept them? I mean, everyone knows he's a nut job, but burning your own paintings. What a fucking waste. Just think if they were all as stunning as this one. A crime.' He shook his head as if it were unfathomable to him.

'Where did you say we're meant to meet Alistair?' Grace asked, already starting to move. She did not want to look at his sad face one moment longer.

'I didn't, but I guess the lobby's a good place.' He seemed loath to leave the painting, as if he feared someone would sneak up with a match the moment his back was turned. She was still walking, with no idea if it was the right direction, and suddenly she felt Tate next to her.

'It's this way,' he said, indicating the route with a nod of his head, and they retraced their earlier steps, Grace feeling calmer the more distance she put between herself and the picture and thankful that Tate seemed more concerned about unballing his hat and pulling it back on his head than talking to her. He'd noticed she had been rattled by Bill's painting, she was sure of that, but maybe his dismay at hearing about the burned paintings had wiped it from his mind. Now his hat was back on his head, he was giving every impression that there were no thoughts at all in his brain. Watching him bounding along, looking from left to right trying to spot Alistair and Gilbert, he was like an overenthusiastic golden retriever. In a suit. She wondered if he'd be as enthusiastic about everything when he was a bit older and wiser, when life had kicked him around a bit. He suddenly stopped and she had to halt and do a sidestep to avoid treading on the back of one of his boots.

'So, out of everything you've seen today, Gracie, what did you like the best?' he asked. 'I mean, I'm guessing it's not all new to you – must have seen a lot of good modern stuff when you were in Edinburgh – but you're hard to read.' He gave her one of his sidelong glances, that flash of green putting her back on her guard.

'I liked the paper sculptures a great deal.' She pretended she was also looking for Alistair and Gilbert. 'And those Bollywood posters back there. Really clever.'

'You sure? That's all? Not that Bill Jackson? 'Cos I thought if I hadn't happened along, you might still be standing there gawping at it?'

She frowned. 'Well, I was . . . intrigued . . . by how he'd managed to make it so over the top; you know, dark sky, blood-red beach, all that angst. Oh look, there they are . . .' Alistair and Gilbert came into view and she gave them a wave, even though she felt like running towards them and possibly hugging them. 'To tell you the truth,' she added, feeling bolder now escape was at hand, 'it actually made me feel a bit queasy – too much going on in it.'

She didn't know whether she'd gone too far with her explanation and she didn't wait around to find out if he believed it. She was advancing on Alistair and Gilbert.

On the way out, the know-it-all attendant passed them and gave Grace a patronising smile, and Grace would very much like to have said to her, *You really, really don't know what the hell you're talking about. Bill Jackson's early works did end up on the fire. All except the three sealed up in bubble wrap under my bed, the two I sold to a guy in Houston and that one on your shiny white gallery wall.*

She did not say any of that, just arranged her face into a mask of serenity and passed out into the rapidly cooling autumn afternoon.

CHAPTER 17

Violet watched Gilbert and his lamb chop. He was pushing it towards the mound of mashed potato at the edge of the plate. He swirled it around in the gravy. Now the chop was let alone for a while as he speared some peas with the prongs of his fork. She didn't like the look he gave them before he brought his teeth together around the fork and scraped the peas into his mouth.

The chop got another trip through the gravy.

'You're playing with your food,' she said.

He did not reply, although she was certain he had heard her. Or perhaps he hadn't – those mice were particularly verbal this evening, taunting her that the traps were still primed, still empty.

Gilbert put down his knife and fork on his plate and Violet said, 'On the hour, Gilbert. Please!'

He gave her one of his looks but reached out and reposi-tioned the fork so that it was no longer lying at about ten to the knife's twelve but right up hard against it. She didn't care for the smile he gave her afterwards. It was the one he had given Mother when humouring her.

'You didn't like your chop?' she asked.

'Not today.'

'But we always have a lamb chop on Tuesday.'

She thought that Gilbert was going to ignore her again. He was studying his plate.

'Yes, we do, don't we?' he said, eventually. 'Every. Single. Tuesday.'

Later he went out to the back garden to smoke and didn't change out of his slippers. She watched him in the security light, making sure she stood back far enough so that he would not see her.

'He's in a funny mood,' the mice said, and she had to agree with them. Restless. A bad evening. New people coming out of his mouth and into the house. Not just this Tate, but other names too.

Corinne. Jo. Someone called Baby? Bebbie? An infantile name.

Three women. Or was Joe a man? She couldn't remember. Definitely two women. Young ones.

And there was a woman called Shawna – she was an artist. Still a woman, though.

She watched Gilbert smoking and even the way he was doing that seemed wrong, as if he couldn't really be bothered.

She had been looking forward to cutting a swathe through Shanghai this evening, making headway with the Bund and Yuyuan Gardens, but how could she settle down to it now?

'You were going to talk to Grace,' the mice said. 'Better get a move on, before it's too late.'

'Yes,' she agreed, 'not that it's any of your business. Your business is to throw yourself on those traps.'

She waited until Gilbert had finished his smoke before she went to the back door.

'Grace,' she said, 'it's been a long time since I saw her. Would you like to invite her to tea? One day after she finishes work, perhaps?' She saw him trying to work out what this invitation meant. She was ready for him. 'You're very dull company at the moment.' She returned to the kitchen, then turned round again. 'You don't have to be here . . . when she visits. You could go out. You'd like that, wouldn't you?'

Back inside the kitchen she watched Gilbert flick the end of his cigar thing over the back wall. She'd told him about that before.

CHAPTER 18

Grace knew that Tate's first tour had been a success because he'd brought a large part of his group back with him and they were now out in reception talking about it. This was a slight improvement on the situation an hour earlier when they had been milling around her computer while Tate showed them some 'really cool things happening in digital art'.

And a huge, huge improvement on when she'd come in that morning to a strong smell of paint, the source of which was her office, where the Chinese lady had been relegated to one corner and the wall with the windows in it painted scarlet. Various sized rocks and bits of wood were leaning against the wall, some of which were painted gold and formed small cairns. A large question mark, also in gold, was painted on the wall and Grace felt that it mirrored the one filling her own head . . . well, the space that wasn't filled with the words *What a pile of rubbish*. As she was thinking that, one of the cairns collapsed, and as she picked up the loose bits of rock and piled them back up, she got gold paint on her fingers.

When she went to the toilet to try to wash off the paint there was a rubber glove over the handle with chopsticks skewered through it. She wondered, if she took it off the handle and blew it up, would it stay inflated long enough to hit Tate around the head with it? She tried to go through Alistair's office to retrieve her grout-cleaning toothbrush so she could scrub at the gold paint on her hands, but his office was locked.

'Of course it sodding well is. Bastardy, bastard, bastard,' she shouted, before remembering that she didn't swear and she didn't shout and she had a nailbrush in her own desk.

Tate seemed to think no explanation was needed for the artwork when he arrived, and since then Grace had been on barista duty again, her pleasant demeanour never wavering, even when a Goth girl and an austere Belgian couple requested decaf. Alistair had appeared and seemed delighted with the fact that the office had been invaded, presumably because it made him feel 'hip with the happening' or whatever mangled reading he was putting on it. Although Grace could see he wasn't so overwhelmed with the wall and the rocks. He spent a few minutes weaving among the group to shake hands and ask them where they had come from as if he were suddenly a member of the royal family. Everything was again 'Marvellous, marvellous,' and while not exactly slapping Tate on the back, Alistair touched his arm in a gesture that suggested he was congratulating him. It was at that point that Grace discovered how hard it was to smile when your lips wanted to curl downwards. She found it even harder when soon afterwards Alistair disappeared into his office, only to emerge again clutching his briefcase and saying he was off to a meeting. He gabbled something about a London tourism committee, which was news to Grace. When she passed through his office to fill the kettle, she saw he had cleared a space for the secure cabinet.

With the sound of more people arriving, Grace returned to reception to see Corinne, Joe and Bebbie. They laid claim to the sofa and the pastry and croissant eating session was repeated. Joe, still largely monosyllabic, went out for extra supplies for the people from the art tour. Music was put on again. Someone had a guitar, not electric thankfully, and started to play, trying to keep time with the music playing on the laptop.

Grace made more coffee and returned to Alistair's office, trying to block out the discussions about the 'death of figurative art' and who in the art world had or had not 'sold out'. Unwilling to overhear which artists they might mention, she went to the kitchen and cleaned the grout between the tiles with her nailbrush and the toothbrush. In a small act of rebellion she also turned the cut-out of the Chinese lady upside down so she stood on her head, or where it would have been had she had one, and wrote on a Post-it note, *Some people have no idea which way is up.*

Part of her bad mood, she knew, was down to jealousy. Her tour of 'The Nation's Best-Loved Paintings' in the National Gallery that morning had not been as successful as Tate's. Even before it started she had felt uneasy: Mr and Mrs Baldridge would again be part of her group and, so it appeared, would Monsieur Laurent. Tate must have booked him in. Memories of the currents of tension that had run between the Americans and the laconic Monsieur the first time had resurfaced as Grace walked along St Martin's Lane towards her 10 a.m. start, but for the first hour and a half of the tour, history had not repeated itself. The other members of the group were a very quiet couple from Scotland and a Russian man who spoke excellent English. Mr Laurent was listening in his usual laid-back way and the Baldridges weren't complaining about anything. There was even a bit of bonding between the two men over the shared reminiscence of that 'goddam awful blond kook from the last tour'.

This all changed when they gathered in front of Goya's portrait of the Duke of Wellington. Mr Laurent sighed in a way that suggested he found the subject of Waterloo and Wellington's victory over Napoleon deeply, deeply boring. At which point Mr Baldridge, with an overfamiliar nudge to his arm, had said, 'Yup, that guy sure gave you a whipping.'

Grace had hurried everyone along to the next painting, talking all the while, but Mr Laurent's body language suggested he was seething.

Grace thought of the paintings ahead, trying to anticipate any other potential flashpoints: Constable's *The Haywain* and Stubbs's *Whistlejacket*. Surely no one could get into a fight over a pastoral scene and a horse? And the painting after that? Oh no. Turner's *The Fighting Temeraire*. Could she miss it out? Unlikely: it was on the publicity leaflet and they would walk right by it. She decided she'd simply elaborate on how Turner's masterful brushwork in sky and sea invoked a sense of impending loss as the old ship was towed away. She would forget entirely about the battles it had fought.

'Painted when Turner was in his sixties,' she began, feeling a chill skim up her neck as Mr Baldridge opened his mouth.

'Hey,' he said, delivering another nudge to Monsieur

Laurent, 'I know this one . . . this is the ship that helped whop your ass at Trafalgar.'

'If we could just return to the painting,' Grace said, seeing Mr Laurent squaring up to Mr Baldridge. 'The feeling here is of an age that is passing—'

'I 'ave 'ad enough of you, you odious fat man.' Monsieur Laurent's verdict was accompanied by a pointing finger that seemed to stir Mrs Baldridge into life.

'Don't you raa-ise your voice to myyyy husband. And he is *not* fat. He is manly.'

'The ship was being towed—'

'I will raise my voice to whom I like,' Monsieur Laurent snapped. 'Your 'usband is deliberately trying to provoke me. Because. I. Am. French.'

'Yeah, well, the truth hurts,' Mr Baldridge said.

'. . . was being towed to scrapyards at—'

'Truth?' Mr Laurent cocked his head.

'Trafalgar, Waterloo. Ten years between 'em but yah got yer ass kicked both times.' He smirked towards his wife. 'Nothing changes, huh? Last time you had to get us to come bail you out—'

'Mr Baldridge, I cannot talk at the same time as you,' Grace said in her sharpest voice, 'which is a great, great pity as the rest of the group would like to hear about this painting. And, Monsieur Laurent, can I just ask you to please move to the other side of the group where you might be more comfortable.' Grace stood her ground, knowing as she did that either Mr Baldridge or Monsieur Laurent might protest. When they both did, she repeated her request and suggested that if they didn't wish to comply, they should leave now; this was, after all, the last painting on the tour.

Nobody left, but a nasty, clotted atmosphere hung over the group as Grace battled on with Turner, and when she wound up the tour, those who had behaved seemed eager to get away and those who hadn't engineered showy, huffy departures. Grace felt a sense of failure churn through her stomach. How had she let this happen? Things were starting to slide, she could feel it.

Even a visit to see Samuel stationed in 'Dutch Painting 1660–1800' didn't cheer her much. She had hoped to drop Gilbert into the conversation to see if she was right about how Samuel felt towards him, but the poor guy had been surrounded by a group of schoolchildren, his grey uniform disappearing among a blur of bright clothes, and Grace only got a raised hand in greeting before his attention was grabbed away again.

Grace decided to stop thinking back over her tour, rinsed off the nailbrush and the toothbrush in the kitchen sink and returned to her office through the people and the mess in reception. Tate was helping the Goth girl balance on Joe's shoulders and someone else was taking photos. She laughed long enough to get through the door and to her chair, stepping over some more rocks that had dislodged themselves from a cairn.

She logged into her email account. No further correspondence from her sisters, which suggested that Felicity had not yet told them about her business plans or Jay Houghton. Typical Felicity – she was leaving it to Grace to broach the subject, which meant it was Grace who would suffer the flak if she didn't get the wording just right. She tried to think how she'd phrase that particular email but was finding it impossible not to get distracted by the noise coming from reception and the knowledge that it would now have descended even further into a quagmire of crumbs, empty paper bags and dirty cups. And she would most definitely not take any notice of Tate who kept calling out to her to 'come and kick back and join in'.

Here he was again, but this time heading for the kettle, Bebbie following. As he spooned more coffee into his cup and flicked on the kettle, Bebbie wrapped her arms around him, resting her head against his back. Grace imagined how uncomfortable that must be – today Tate had on jeans and a T-shirt plus a black leather jacket, scuffed as badly as his boots and with a pattern of tiny studs across the shoulders. There had been a number of these hugs from

Bebbie and a range of other signs of intimacy – a hand on Tate's arm; reaching out and running her fingers down his thigh. At first Grace had taken them as lavish signals from Bebbie that Tate was her man and she was his woman, but now she wasn't so sure. There was something needy about Bebbie's movements and a touch of indifference in the way Tate reacted to them. The kettle hadn't even boiled when Grace heard Tate say, 'Bebbie, honey, I need to get that,' and flex his shoulders as if he wanted to underline his desire to be free of her.

Bebbie released Tate and moved to his side. Her hand reached out for the milk, presumably to add to his coffee.

'I got it,' he said, picking up the carton himself. 'You wanna check and see if anyone else needs a refill?'

Grace made sure she did not look up as Bebbie walked by her desk, but she could almost smell the frustration and confusion coming off her.

'Sure you don't want a coffee?' Tate asked, holding out his cup to Grace.

She shook her head.

'Anything to eat?'

'No.'

'Like a spin in my chair?'

'Thank you. No. I'm quite comfortable here.'

'Don't look comfortable. Look kinda under siege. Want me to take all those rocks and stones and build a wall around you?'

'Not at all. Nice to have some life around the place.'

'I'll get Joe to bring in his electric guitar next time then.'

She did an approximation of a giggle and he watched her and twisted his mouth. It was a movement that made it clear he knew there was nothing real about the sound she'd just made.

He strolled over and perched on the desk, still holding his coffee cup. 'Sure you don't want me to build a wall round you?' He dropped his voice. 'Keep you safe?'

'Safe? No, and by the way, it's lovely, your . . . installation.'

He grinned. 'Really? You like it?'

'It's . . . intriguing.

He slapped his leg and hooted with laughter. The genuine kind. 'Intriguing is good, Gracie. So, whaddya think it means?'

'Does it have to mean anything?'

He put his cup down. 'Nope. But in this case it does. It's kind of a metaphor for our relationship.'

Grace didn't like the way he was looking at her now. Too much warmth. Too close.

'I see.'

He raised his eyebrows. 'You *see* as in you understand, or you *see* as in "oh no, what's he gonna say now?"'

She couldn't stop herself from smiling at that and she received a smile back from him that made some long-dormant nerve endings perk up.

'I should really be getting on with—'

'These,' he nodded at the nearest cairn, 'these little mountains represent an uphill struggle.'

'Fascinating,' she said matter-of-factly. 'Now, if you'll just—'

''Cos that's how it feels with you, Gracie. Even having a conversation is an uphill struggle. But maybe it will get better because, see, every now and again, the rocks in these little mountains move of their own accord. Someone slams a door downstairs, a floorboard settles and down come a few more.'

'That's very Zen,' she said, choosing her words carefully. 'But what happens if someone keeps putting the rocks back on the piles?'

Why had she said the very thing that would make him come forward instead of backing off? Immediately she felt him take her hand.

'Yeah, I noticed that, Gracie,' he said, a wry expression making his eyes seem full of light. He rubbed one of her fingers. 'You've been caught red-handed messing with the artwork. I'm guessing you got gold paint on your fingers and tried to scrub it off.' He made a regretful little noise. 'Looks sore. Use the toothbrush in the kitchen?'

'Nailbrush in my drawer.' She hadn't meant to say that.

'Thorough,' he said, his mouth curving up into one of those fond smiles that told her that was a compliment.

She was aware of how his thigh was only inches from her other hand and how he might as well have had a sign on his body saying, *Do Not Touch. Danger of Burning.* Or maybe it should read, *Crashing and Burning.*

He was still gently rubbing her fingers, but it was beginning to feel increasingly like a caress and her heart was throwing itself against her ribcage. She wished he'd let her hand go, but seemed unable to move any part of her body to make that happen. Now he was looking at her fingers as if they were the most miraculous things he'd ever seen, and she suddenly became terrified that he might lift her hand to his lips and kiss the sore patches, and she feared if he did that the rocks on those small mountains would all fall at once and possibly the windows would crack and a huge great dark gust of wind would blow into the office, whirling everyone and everything around like a scene out of *The Wizard of Oz* . . .

Except none of those things happened because he was lowering her hand and looking towards the door, and as

Grace saw it open, Bebbie appeared carrying in some cups. Grace put both her hands on her keyboard and typed *Tohgjskt hsuddu* and tried not to think of that stabbingly regretful look Tate had given her just before he let her hand go.

The expression on Bebbie's face suggested she was not happy with Tate sitting on Grace's desk and not particularly happy that Grace knew how to breathe either.

'Three more coffees,' she said to Grace, peevishly plonking the cups down on the desk next to her arm. Bebbie's hand then went to Tate's thigh and gave it a rub.

'Come on, Tate, we're just discussing the Hockney retrospective. We need you.'

With enough allure lavished on every word to power a small massage parlour, Bebbie's inference was clear: I *need you Tate and later I'll show you just how much . . . so stop wasting time in here and let Miss Boring make the coffee.*

Somehow the coffee cups that had been on Grace's desk were now on the floor. Grace resisted the urge to rub her elbow.

'There's a slight tilt on this desk,' she said. 'Should have warned you.'

She was going to stand up, but Tate beat her to it. He held his own cup of coffee out for her to take. 'Better keep a grip on that, Gracie, don't want that sliding about too. First my chair, now the cups.' She had no choice but to take the cup from him, although it looked as if Bebbie would have fought her for it, and then he was bending down, picking up the ones on the floor.

'You go on out, Bebbie,' he said. 'Just gonna get those coffees.' He soon had his back to Bebbie again, busy over at the coffee jar.

Grace made an effort at least to look as if she were composing an email in a vain attempt to avoid thinking about what he'd just said and done and what she'd just felt, and how the thing with the cups was exactly what she'd been afraid of – a lapse into her old ways, a flash of rebellion.

Looking at her email also meant she didn't have to watch the embarrassing sight of Bebbie still loitering in the room. She could hear her, though, advancing on Tate again, picking up his cup, offering to carry one of the other ones. Grace did a quick check despite intending not to. Yes, Bebbie was lavishing all kinds of doe-eyed looks on him.

When they both finally left the room, Grace felt as if a boulder had been lifted off the top of her head. Or a small cairn. She looked at them and grimaced.

She wanted to close the door on all that life in reception, but knew it would appear too antisocial. She thought back to that awkward scene over the coffee-making and wondered whether this kettle wasn't turning into some kind of magnet for tension and uncertainty, even if, unlike its predecessor, it didn't fuse all the lights. She remembered the way she had misunderstood Alistair asking what she thought of it, and her mother watching Tate bending over it. And then, this morning, when she had arrived early to an empty office, she had found it still warm. Which could only mean that Alistair had been in earlier and disappeared out again. Particularly confusing behaviour as when he did appear later, just before Grace set off for her tour, he was chuntering on about how bad the trains had been that morning, that's why he was late. Lying, locking himself in his office, coming in early, not mentioning it – it all pointed to him doing something underhand.

And Grace was meeting Emma tomorrow with all those suspicions in her mind.

She turned back to her email:

Dear Aurillia, Zin and Serafina,

I am no nearer to finding out what caused Dad to leave home, but Mum popped in earlier in the week. She is planning on setting up a business from home – massage, reflexology, yoga, that kind of thing – and her partner in this business will be Jay Houghton.

I gave her some advice regarding loans, etc. Talked to Dad about it and he was not very forthcoming, but did give me the impression that . . .

Grace hesitated. If she wrote something like *he is afraid Mum is not being objective*, it would elicit a three-pronged lecture from her sisters, who had largely cast objectivity aside to make all their major life decisions based on listening to their inner voice. She settled for *he is afraid Mum is not considering all the implications* and, after adding a few more lines enquiring after Zin's partners and Serafina's children, sent it. Out there in California and India and the Philippines, she hoped alarm bells would start to ring without her forcibly having had to press the button. Then again, she might just get the usual deluge of huggy-feely claptrap back. Well, that got you nowhere. Actually it did – it was the kind of thing that made you stumble into situations that ripped your heart out of your chest and turned you into something scummy and flaky until you damaged everything around you, including yourself.

She wrote another quick email asking them to reply as soon as possible because she knew that would annoy them, and jabbed at the 'Send' button as if she wished it actual harm.

All of this could have been avoided if Felicity would accept that she was no longer the captivating wild child of her youth but, in fact, a grandmother. Please, God, let this whole thing be a storm in a teacup, one of Felicity's habitual infatuations that blew itself out after a welter of flirting, inappropriate hugging and not much else. As all four sisters agreed, these things were largely done to reignite their father's interest. But him being reignited usually took the form of a mini-break in the New Forest, not this latest crisis.

Grace heard the outer door open and close a few times and each time the noise of music and chatter in reception lessened. Soon it had died away altogether. Where was Tate? She went out to find him asleep on the sofa, surrounded by all the mess he had helped create.

She remembered another room with plates of dried-out food balanced on top of tubes of paint. Glasses with the dregs of red wine still in them. Cigarette butts in ashtrays, each tipped with a kiss of that pink lipstick she used to wear. All that mess, and another blond guy right at the centre of it.

'Penny for them,' Tate said, still with his eyes closed, and she scuttled back to her office wondering how long he'd been watching her and just what her face had been doing.

Her bottom had only just connected with the seat when, in quick succession, she took a phone call from her father and one from her mother. Her father wanted to know if he could have the Newham Gang round, just for a couple of hours, and did she have any superglue? He'd had a small incident with one of her kitchen chairs but he was optimistic that with a dab of glue it would be as right as rain.

She said yes to the Newham Gang and no to the superglue.

Her mother wanted to know whom she should talk to at the council about running a business from home, and when Grace said it would probably be the planning officer but shouldn't Jay be helping with some of this stuff, her mother accused her of being 'snippy' and said she was going to send her a crystal which she should put on her forehead at night to redress her negative impulses. Felicity then showed a few of her own by putting the phone down in the middle of Grace trying to tell her she'd emailed her other daughters.

When the phone rang again, Grace snatched it up ready to begin Part II of Grace versus Felicity, only to hear Gilbert's voice.

'First thing, dear girl: Vi would like you to come to tea. Yes, I know, bolt from the blue and she's up to something, but if you could oblige ... And second thing, fancy running away? I'm in the vicinity, haven't had my lunch yet so was going to go to Acar's. Come join me, Grace, hmm? I would drop by and scoop you up but Bernice the beast may see me. Come on Grace, what do you say?'

'Yes to Violet, I'd love to see her, though it'll have to be after the weekend and . . . just a minute,' Grace put down the phone and quietly closed the door before talking to Gilbert again. 'I think I could slip away to Acar's too. Fifteen to twenty minutes, I'll be there. Why not?'

Why not indeed? Hadn't she just spent her lunch break babysitting Tate and his tour? Now he could look after the office for a while.

She turned on the answering machine and gathered up her coat. She'd need to make it clear to Tate that he couldn't go out and leave the office unlocked. And remind him that that cabinet might come today. But what if he were fast asleep?

He wasn't. He wasn't even there. Neither was any of the mess.

She did a quick check to see if he'd just thrown everything behind the sofa, feeling pretty stupid even while doing it.

'Tate?' she said quietly, and then went to Alistair's room and through to the kitchen. She opened the bin and saw the bags and plates and bits of pastry.

She went back to reception and examined the carpet. It was free of all but the smallest crumbs and the table was wet as if he'd wiped it with a cloth.

How had he done that so quickly and where had he gone now?

She locked up behind her and went down the stairs, leaving the key with Bernice just in case the cabinet arrived while she was out, and as she walked towards Acar's she gave herself a good talking-to. Tate had just been winding her up with all that stuff about rocks and that hand-holding. Now her father had put superglue in her mind, she made a mental note to buy some after lunch and glue all those ruddy rocks into one great big immovable pile several feet high.

CHAPTER 19

Gilbert was sitting outside at Acar's, chewing his way robustly through lamb *güveç* when Grace arrived. There was a large glass of red wine in front of him, plus a bottle of lager, half-drunk by the looks of it.

'Mixing your drinks?' she said, sitting down and wishing that they could go inside today. She rearranged her scarf so there were no bits of bare neck exposed and thought she might join Gilbert in choosing something hot to eat. She had just picked up the menu when there was a huge guffaw of laughter from one of the other tables and she turned to see a group of men huddled around a backgammon board. Nothing unusual about that, except that Tate was with them and, as she watched, he stood up and rubbed his hand back and forth over his mouth. She caught a glimpse of his smile.

'Yeah, well done, Ekrem,' he said, putting his hand in the pockets of his jacket. 'Cleaned me out again.' There was more laughter as Tate dramatically pulled at the linings of his pockets.

'Dear boy,' Gilbert said. 'I've told him before that they'll beat him every time, but he's a tryer.' Grace turned to see Gilbert raising his glass of wine in Tate's direction in a kind of salute, leaving her to pick over the three pieces of information she had gleaned from that statement:

1. Gilbert had brought Tate to Acar's before.

2. Tate had already bonded with men who, despite her years of coming to Acar's, had only ever regarded her as if she were a unicorn.

3. Tate was persistent.

Well, she'd actually known that last fact already.

'I didn't expect to see Tate,' she said nonchalantly, over the sound of a lot of bonding from the backgammon table. 'You didn't mention it on the phone.'

'No, that's because Tate said you probably wouldn't come if you knew he was going to be here. Ah . . .' Gilbert was looking over her shoulder, which alerted her to the fact that Tate must be on the move. She steeled herself against his arrival.

How had things changed so drastically and so quickly? This used to be her and Gilbert's place. Six days, that's all it had been since they were last here discussing Violet.

Well, that was Pre-Tate. Never mind, never mind, soon it would be Post-Tate.

She simply had to survive Present-Tate.

When Tate came back to their table she gave him a smile designed to suggest that she had no lingering memory of him holding her hand.

He got the message; she saw him getting the message and she saw him swallow it down as he reached for his bottle of lager and took a sip from it.

'Leave reception tidy enough for you?' he said with a sideways shift of his eyes.

'Yes. Thank you.'

'Bet you thought I'd stuffed it all down the back of the sofa?'

She thought of the way she had checked to see if he'd done that. 'No, of course not. But you did it all very quietly, never heard a thing.'

He was staring at the label on the lager bottle. 'Nope, wanted it to be a nice surprise for you. Bit like turning up here and finding me, eh?'

'Yes,' she said. 'Lovely.'

'I'm sure. So, gonna have something to drink?' Tate was looking around, she presumed for Hakan. 'I'm guessing it'll be a lemonade or Coke or something?' He was fitting another piece to her jigsaw.

'Paragon of virtue is our Grace,' Gilbert replied, and although he said it with a grin in her direction, it felt like another betrayal on top of the one she felt he'd committed by inviting Tate along.

A worse thought hit her: Gilbert had invited Tate first. What if inviting her had simply been an afterthought?

'You know that really friendly, tall attendant at the National?' she said. 'The one with the lovely lilting accent.'

'Samuel?' Gilbert frowned.

'Well, have you ever talked to him? He seems—'

She stopped as Hakan came to the table bearing a bowl of olives balanced on an ashtray. 'So, Tate my man,' he said, 'you know Chicago, yeah? 'Cos Mum's been giving Dad all that . . .' Hakan made an opening and closing duck's bill with his free hand. 'Wants to go out there for a holiday, yeah? You talk to him about it sometime?' Hakan put the olives and the ashtray on the table. 'Hey, Grace, what'll it be?'

'Just a lemonade, please.'

'Nothing to eat?'

'No thanks, Hakan.' She felt stupidly self-conscious about eating in front of Tate, as if it were too intimate.

'I'll have another lager,' Tate said, putting the empty bottle on Hakan's tray. 'And Gilb, another wine?'

Gilbert shook his head vehemently before screwing up his eyes and saying, 'Well, just a small one, Hakan.'

'So, Gilbert, about Samuel,' Grace began again, 'have you had the chance to talk to him at all recently?'

'No, other than the odd "hello" and "goodbye". Smiles a lot, doesn't he?'

There was something so dismissive about Gilbert's verdict that Grace felt rebuffed too and she sat back and pulled her coat around herself. It was an action she saw Tate had registered and she wondered what meaning he had assigned to it. He was explaining something about Chicago to Gilbert, but she sensed his attention was on her. She concentrated on the noise of London in the background. The Christmas decorations were going up out on the main road, the nights were drawing in . . . it would be a hop, skip and a jump before Christmas was upon them. She could smell it.

He'll be gone not long after that, she comforted herself.

Hakan delivered the drinks and she sipped at her lemonade and eyed the remaining food on Gilbert's plate with envy. She should order something, but she imagined Tate watching her mouth and felt vulnerable. Oh God, he was watching her mouth now and she had to force herself not to put down her lemonade.

'I was thinking of growing a goatee,' she suddenly heard Gilbert say. He was tilting his chin this way and that. 'What do you think?'

Where had this idea come from? The tour yesterday?

Another disturbing new development to chalk up to Tate.

'Go for it, Gilb,' Tate said, 'you only live once. It'll suit you. Make you look . . . louche.'

'Louche?' Gilbert seemed pleased and took out his pack of cigars and proffered it to Tate.

'Stick to cigarettes, thanks.' Tate got out a packet, put a cigarette to his lips and leaned forward over the flame Gilbert was holding out to light it. Grace watched the tip of the cigarette glow orange and Tate pulled back from the flame and turned his head to look at her.

'I think I ought to be getting back,' she said, making to stand up, but Gilbert wouldn't hear of it.

'No, no, Grace,' he said, laying his hand over hers. 'You've barely had half an hour. Anyway, I've been most rude. I haven't asked you how your father is. Still with you?'

She sat back in her seat again, feeling more and more unsettled by Tate's presence. The way he was looking at her. Smoking and looking.

'Afraid so,' she said. 'I was hoping he'd be gone before . . . before the weekend.'

'You mean before Mark arrives?' Gilbert corrected her happily.

'Mark?' Tate asked.

'Grace's boyfriend. Works away. Seismologist for an oil company. Works all over, doesn't he, Grace?

She nodded, wishing Gilbert would be quiet now. She just knew Tate was building up to say something smart and she didn't want him trying to burrow into that part of her life.

She saw him take a drag on his cigarette, tilt his head right back and exhale a thin, rapid plume of smoke. 'Been going out long?'

'About a year.'

'Well, it's a calendar year,' Gilbert said as if thinking it through, 'but if you added up the *actual* time you spent together, it would probably only be a few months, wouldn't it?'

'How long's he back for now?' Tate asked, looking at the end of his cigarette as if it were fascinating.

'Just until Sunday afternoon in London. Then he's seeing some friends in Birmingham. I might catch up with him again for a couple of hours before he heads out of London later in the week. Maybe not.'

'Well, don't get too excited there, Gracie.'

There it was: the something smart. She didn't respond and concentrated on imagining what the Christmas decorations in Oxford Street would look like this year.

'Leave Grace alone,' Gilbert was saying. 'She is *quite* happy with a long-distance relationship. Before Mark there was David and he worked for a charity out in Botswana.'

Grace wondered if it would look strange to take her scarf off and gag Gilbert with it.

'Ah, pattern emerging.' Tate was nodding in a worrying way that suggested he had made another piece of the Grace puzzle fit. He took one last draw on his cigarette before stubbing it out in the ashtray.

Grace thought about the leaves falling in Green Park – would there be enough for a bonfire? Could she already smell bonfire smoke? *No. Don't think about bonfires. See, that's what Tate did: got you so riled you started thinking . . .*

'Pattern?' she snapped.

'Yeah, you know, not wanting to get too serious, keeping 'em at arm's length.'

'Why can't the pattern be that I like men who go off and do their own thing, but come back to me whenever possible?'

'What? When they can fit you in around visiting their friends?'

Grace wished he'd choke on that laugh of his and felt the indignation rise in her chest, before it spread outwards so rapidly that she had to take her hand off her lemonade glass for fear she would pick it up and chuck its contents over him. It was only because she knew it would be further evidence that he had got to her that she was able instead to force herself to say evenly, 'Well, we can't all want the same things out of a relationship. And I'm very happy with Mark and what we have. Just as I'm very sure you're *very* happy with Bebbie and what you have.'

She wished she could have reeled that last barb back in, but it was too late. Tate was leaning back, stretching out his legs. Cats scrunched themselves up to pounce, but his way of doing it seemed more disconcerting.

'So, these sisters of yours,' he said slowly, 'what was it Fliss said they all did?'

She had expected more jibes about Mark. What trap was he laying now? And was he incapable of saying anyone's name correctly?

'Aurillia is a life coach and yoga teacher in an ashram—'

'In California,' Gilbert supplied.

'Zin, well, she's . . .'

'A poet. Lives with two other poets on a houseboat in India.' Gilbert put on a scandalised voice. 'Both men. A *ménage à trois*.'

'Must be a big houseboat,' Tate said, with a wry grin. 'And the other one: Serafina?'

'She's part of a theatre troupe.'

'Mime,' Gilbert mimed, then added, 'all women.'

'Well, there's only so much mime a man can take,' Tate agreed.

'In the Philippines at the moment, aren't they, Grace?'

She said they were.

'Pretty exotic lifestyles there, Gracie,' Tate said plucking up an olive and popping it in his mouth. She waited while he chewed, now knowing where this was going. 'Exotic names, exotic jobs, exotic lifestyles.' He shook his head as if bemused. 'And you work for a company doing art tours, live in the city you were born in, have a boyfriend you don't see a lot.' A pause. 'You adopted?'

'No, just different,' she said over Gilbert's traitorous laugh. She tried to underline her nonchalance by reaching out for an olive, but Tate picked up the bowl and held it just out of reach and she felt too exposed to lean any further towards him.

'You didn't look so different on that beach,' he said straight to her face. A simple statement, a matter-of-fact delivery, but she felt as if she could have tipped right off her chair and sprawled across the table.

'Beach?' she blurted, hearing the word screech up at the end. But at least she didn't add, *What bloody beach, what the hell has Felicity shown you? Told you? Done?*

She was so close to Tate at that moment and, like a pulse running between them, she could feel his urge to open her up and get to the heart of who she was. She saw him put the olive bowl back down on the table and imagined him reaching out and putting his hands on her shoulders and pulling her into him, stroking her hair, murmuring that she should tell him everything, get it all out, it was all right. She remembered how he had got Bernice to unfold for him until she'd seemed drugged. A charmer. Another charmer, this time with disturbing green eyes and a backside just crying out for her to place her hands upon it.

'I'm not sure I know what you mean,' she said, sitting back but still imagining his hands on her shoulders, her hands on his backside.

'The beach,' he repeated. 'Fliss showed me a photo of you and your sisters messing about on the sand. You must have been about sixteen. All looked like peas in a pod to me – all that wild hair.' He let her stew a bit before saying pointedly, 'What beach did you think I meant, Gracie?'

She was going to kill her mother. Kill her and sprinkle her ashes somewhere she'd hate, like between the pages of a dull and dusty annual report or, even better, Mark's suitcase.

'Grace had wild hair?' Gilbert said, finally, finally doing something useful and breaking the tension. 'I've never known anyone with hair as neat as Grace's.'

'Should have seen it, Gilb. Wild, long . . .' Tate grinned. 'Blonde as mine.'

She prised his hands from her shoulders, her hands from his backside. 'It got darker as I got older,' she said, as if the topic bored her. 'It became mousy, so I went even darker. I like the colour. I like it shorter and—'

'Under control.' Tate popped another olive into his mouth. 'Dye your eyebrows too?' he said after chewing it.

'Where did you say your tour was this afternoon?' she asked Gilbert.

'Oh bugger.' He was scrabbling for his watch. 'Forgot about that. Better head off soon. Ten people to show around St Paul's.' He drained his wine and waved Hakan over, and when the bill was paid and they were all standing up to go, Grace made her apologies, saying she'd just remembered she had to rush and get something for her father, some crime magazine from the bookshop in the other direction. She'd see them, well, whenever they next popped into the office.

She caught the sceptical look Tate gave her as she briskly walked away, and once she was out of sight, she doubled back and cut down a different street. She snatched a glimpse of the two of them ambling along, Tate enthusing again, unwittingly forcing passers-by to step out of his way. All that burning energy.

Back at the office she made a detour into Far & Away. Bernice was alone and when Grace asked after Esther, it opened a floodgate of moaning. Esther had announced that she was off to Peru on an organised tour; she wasn't going to let her dream die. Bernice had helped her book it. Today she was taking a few hours out to go shopping for clothes. She'd be back soon, but even when she was in the office, she was worse than useless – either messing with her hair in the toilet or on the internet doing research.

'And I don't know what I'm supposed to do when she does go,' Bernice said, slamming down a brochure. 'I'm goin' to have to get Sol in to help a couple of days a week. I've had enough, I tell you. Soon as she's back today, I'm giving myself an early finish. Rest while I get the chance. So say thanks very much to Blond Boy for putting ideas in her head.' There was a sharp laugh. 'Mind you, I'd be worried if I was him. Still waters, that Esther. She's caught him twice already when he's come down to nip out for a smoke. On him like a rash: "Oh Tate, can you advise me about hotels?" or "How hot will it be when I get to Machu Picchu?"' Bernice's impersonation of Esther's rarely heard voice was spot on, but Bernice reverted to herself to say cynically, 'Like she doesn't know all that working here. Ask me, she's more interested in how hot he is than Peru. She'll be cramming him in her suitcase. You should see the way he leapt back up the stairs when she let him go. What do you think of these tie-backs?'

Once Grace had got over the whiplash effect of going from lovesick Esther to haberdashery, she gave her opinion on the tie-backs, sympathised with Bernice's impending staff shortage and laughed inwardly at Tate scampering up the stairs like some kind of blushing virgin. Gilbert running away from Bernice, Tate running away from Esther.

She shrugged off the voice that asked her who she was running from and spent a while longer with Bernice, happy to bury herself in home improvements before steeling herself to climb the stairs.

'You've had a delivery,' was Bernice's parting shot. 'Some kind of cabinet.'

Alistair was playing with it when she arrived and showed her what it did, which largely seemed to consist of lock and unlock.

'Just what we need,' he enthused. 'Anything sensitive can be put in here and that should cover us.'

Grace felt that he looked strung out again, not the manic kind that usually presaged a period of planting himself in her office and getting hysterical, but something less readable. He hadn't even grumbled that she'd left the office unattended. He shepherded her out after a few minutes and almost immediately after appeared in her office in his coat.

'Heading home,' he said, 'planning to take Emma out for an early supper somewhere nice. In fact, don't stay too late yourself, Grace. I've checked the phone messages, there's nothing that won't wait. Get yourself home soon; see if you can sort out your father.'

He did not have his briefcase with him and when he had gone, she went to his office and found the door unlocked, his briefcase abandoned under his desk. She picked it up and shook it, guessing it would be empty.

'Think he's hiding something?' Tate said from the door, making her jump. 'Playing around maybe?' He came into the room. 'Keeping the evidence in that baby?' He patted the cabinet.

'Not at all. I think he's keeping in it what he says he's keeping in it. And . . . was there something you wanted? I didn't know you were coming back?'

'Bet you didn't,' he said and wandered out of the room again.

Damn. She went to her office and there he was, sitting on his stupid chair. As soon as she turned on her computer, he scooted over so that he was sitting next to her.

'You gonna be long? I wanna see how many reservations I've got for my next tour.'

'No, of course not. I just need to check my emails.'

He didn't budge.

'Um, could you just give me a bit of privacy?'

'Oh, those kind of emails, huh? Lovey-dovey stuff from Martin.'

'Mark.'

'Right.' He rolled away before getting up and heading for reception. She heard him lie down on the sofa. 'Give me a call when you've finished with the porn,' he shouted.

She jabbed at her keyboard and arrived at her inbox. Three emails. Three sisters. She opened Aurillia's:

I've rung Mum and she's very upset. Says she thinks you and Dad are suggesting her and Jay are lovers, whereas she just wants to run a business. Really, Grace, how can you hope to understand Mum these days when you don't even understand yourself any more? We do a fantastic course on refinding yourself (only £1569 inc. accommodation). Give it some thought.

Zin's said:

Grace, I really think your negative experience has made you distrustful of what can be a liberating attitude to life – one which Mum may be on the cusp of exploring. Two men can work . . . look at me!!!! I will try to ring Dad. I have a poem that may help.

Serafina's was as self-absorbed as the others:

Sorry, but have you any idea what real problems look like?
There are women out here who've never even experienced
theatre before. You have no idea what a struggle it is to
educate them in the arts. All power to Mum. Stop being so
negative, Grace . . . sisterhood is for mothers too.

No surprise there then. And no help. The only bit of light
relief was imagining her father holding the phone and
listening to one of Zin's interminable poems.

She saw Tate a second or two before his seat bumped
against hers again.

'Come on, Gracie, you'll go blind. Save all that sex talk
for the weekend. He's a seismologist; you know he'll make
the earth move for you.' He gave her chair a further push
with his hands so that she rolled away into dead space.
That was the moment when Grace feared something
might explode in her skull if she did not get away from
him.

'Ooh, look,' he said, tapping the screen. 'My next tour
is full up and . . . let's see . . . how's yours going?' He made
a regretful face. 'Still a few short there, Gracie.'

'I'm going now,' she said. 'So you'll need to go too as I
have to lock up.' She did a quick tour of the office, left a
note for the cleaner to give the toilet a good going over,
checked all the taps were off, all the plugs out. He was

waiting for her in reception. She'd need to shake him off when they got outside; she wouldn't even bother with an excuse this time. There was a large pit waiting for her if she wasn't careful: a large pit with a sharp spike at the bottom.

Her mobile rang, which was perfect timing; it meant she didn't even have to talk to him as they went down the stairs.

It was Emma, but Grace could barely hear her over the noise in the background.

'You'll have to speak up,' she said.

Emma's voice came through louder. 'Still on for tomorrow?'

'Of course. Straight from work. But where are you now? It sounds like a rugby match.'

'Close. It's Brent Cross shopping centre,' Emma sounded weary. 'Need to buy a birthday present and decided I might as well have a mooch round here for a few hours. Poor Alistair's got another one of his tourism meetings till really late this evening – he says they're going to be a regular Wednesday night thing – so I'm going to head back in a minute. Have an evening in on my own with a takeaway, watching a weepie.'

'Everything all right?' Tate asked, watching as Grace put

the phone back in her bag. 'That was Al's Emma, wasn't it?'

'Everything's fine. Sorry, can't stop. Need to go—'

'Back to the office.'

'What?' She had stopped walking.

'Weren't you gonna say you needed to go back to the office? Get that magazine you bought for your dad? Must have left it up there 'cos I didn't see it in your handbag.'

'Uh, they'd sold out.'

'No kiddin'?'

His face told her he knew she was floundering as clearly as if he'd written it on a note and Sellotaped it to his forehead. Her irritation at that put words into her mouth that she didn't know were coming.

'Actually, Tate,' she said, '"kidding" ends with a "g" not an "n".'

'Yeah,' he said, moving closer to her, 'and "lying" starts with a great big "L".'

'I do have to go now,' she said quickly, thinking that what he'd said was bloody clever and figuring out at last why his eyes were so disconcerting: they should be blue. With that face and that hair they should be sunny blue, the kind of eyes surfers had. Green ones made him into something else. But what?

She had got right to the bottom step when she felt a tug

on the strap of her handbag. She was on alert; that strap had misbehaved before.

'Hang on there, pardner,' he said in a pronounced drawl, and she wondered whether he was going to bring up the mock gunfight on the chair thing. Or was it a new test coming? He'd been circling her all day, making inroads with holding her hand and that 'uphill' stuff, then again at Acar's. He was slowly sweeping away the sand to see what lay beneath.

It was gloomy in this part of the hallway, although further along was a rectangle of light shining through Far & Away's glass door. Grace felt that if she could reach that light everything would be fine. She stepped down into the hallway, but all that happened was that, still holding the strap of her bag, he followed her and, with a nifty bit of footwork, ended up in front of her. So there they were, just a few inches apart and with the gloom seeming to thicken with every second.

'What can I help you with?' she said, her stomach feeling as if she were in a car that had just executed a really sharp turn. He didn't speak straight away; there was just the gloom and the closeness of him and she tried not to look at his eyes or his mouth.

'It's what I can help you with, Gracie,' he said, inclining his head towards her. 'I can stop you killing yourself with all this nicey-nicey.'

'I'm sorry?'

'There you go again.'

'I'm not sure what you mean—'

'Oh, come on, Gracie,' he said with the kind of sigh someone gives when they had hoped the other person would see sense. Grace's stomach now felt as if it were planning to fold itself into something smaller. 'See, I know I'm bugging the hell out of you. In fact, I'm doing it more and more, just on purpose, to see what happens. I'm doing it so much I'm even gettin' annoyed with myself. Yet there you are, just keeping right on bustin' a gut to prove everything's fine. Why would that be, Gracie?'

'That's just how I am. Unfailingly polite.'

'Yeah? Really? God's honest truth? Even when you're doing the mime for a dickhead, in the dark? Learn that one from Serafina and her troupe out in the Philippines?'

The urge to check and see what his face was doing was too much. A quick glance at those green eyes made her stomach give up folding and start scrunching. It was a bad look he was giving her, a very bad look indeed. As if he understood the real her.

'Jeez, Gracie, when I held your hand . . .' he said softly and took in a deep breath, letting it out again without speaking.

'I really do have to go.'

'What happened, Gracie?' he said suddenly, touching her arm.

'Um . . . what happened when?'

'Between that photo and now? What happened to that girl?'

'She grew up,' she said steadily, despite the thrumming in her throat that she swore should have made her voice tremble.

He nodded as if thinking about that. 'Maybe,' he said finally, 'or maybe she closed down. Someone hurt you, Gracie?'

She was glad it was too dark to really see his face because that meant he couldn't see hers either, but now the silence between them seemed loaded and as it continued, it weighed heavier and heavier on Grace until she just had to speak.

'It was thirteen years ago,' she said. 'I expect you've changed a lot since you were sixteen.'

His laugh came to her out of the gloom. 'Yeah, I've got more childish.'

That laugh wrapped itself around Grace and she felt a skittering of something across those dormant nerve endings, closely followed by her brain telling her to get a grip and then, unbelievably, he was walking away from her.

She had expected him to press home his advantage, niggle further. Ah, here it came – he was stopping.

'OK, OK,' he said, 'I guess you're not going to tell me a thing about yourself, so I'll just tell you something about me . . .' He was speaking into the gloom without turning to face her and she realised that he hadn't been walking away from her, but towards the comfort of saying something serious in the dark. For the first time since he had exploded into her life like a paintball, she saw there was vulnerability under all that swagger and self-belief.

'You were wrong at Acar's,' he said. 'I'm not *very* happy with Bebbie. Haven't been for a long time. Keep trying to tell her – won't listen.'

She didn't want that information from him, was determined to kick away the bridge he was trying to build between them by giving it to her.

He had reached that patch of light and just at the edge of her consciousness she became aware of sounds on the other side of that glass door and of the conversation she'd had earlier with Bernice. As he moved on, the door of Far & Away sprung open and there was Esther.

'It *is* you,' she said in that washed-out voice of hers. 'You couldn't just spare me a few minutes? There's something I don't understand about access to the actual Machu Picchu site.'

Grace feared that if Esther kept running her tongue along her bottom lip like that, she'd need a lot of lip salve to put it right.

'Well, I'm kinda in a hurry . . .' Tate began and again Grace saw what he looked like when he was unsure of himself. He seemed so young. He was looking past Esther into her office and it was obvious that he understood Bernice was not there. 'Yeah, kinda in a hurry,' he repeated. 'I'm meeting these friends down the road, I should go or they'll wonder where—'

'In the White Hart?' Grace stepped forward. It was a name she'd heard Joe and Corinne mention as a place they liked to go.

The way that Tate said, 'Ye-ah,' suggested he knew what she was about to do.

'That's no problem then,' she continued heartily. 'I go right by there on my way home. I'll just tell them you're going to be what, quarter of an hour, half an hour, late, Tate? Don't worry, you just toddle off and help Esther. Take your time.'

Tate's forlorn expression as he walked into the room ahead of Esther kept Grace feeling buoyant all the way to the street door, until the reality of what she'd done kicked in. Now he'd know he'd got to her with that conversation in the gloom.

As she pushed open the door, she thought of how he was doing the same to her and how she couldn't trust herself not to let him come right in.

CHAPTER 20

Alistair turned on the heater in his office and pressed himself against it until he felt less chilled. The building was cold and empty; he'd waited a full half hour after he'd calculated that everyone would have gone home – even that miserable bugger of an ex-father-in-law on the top floor.

Still, the coast was definitely clear now. He took out his key and unlocked the cabinet, removing the tea lights he'd bought earlier. Once he'd placed them around the office and lit them he turned out the main light, leaving on just the desk lamp. Much better. A softer atmosphere. It might be an office, but it didn't have to look like one. He went back to the cabinet and got out the earrings, his mouth drying. But it was the shoes that made his pulse really race. Bought this afternoon, more than he'd ever paid for any shoes for anyone, he lifted them out of their box one by one and put them on the desk. Not too high, not too pointed. Stylish, like she was. He couldn't wait to see her walk in them. She had a way of swinging her hips that . . . well . . . that did it for him.

He turned one of the shoes over and peeled off the price sticker, wondering how he could hide spending that amount of money from Emma. Could he say he'd got out some cash and lost it? Might work. He'd lost money before. Add it to the blouse, though, and it was all starting to mount up.

The shoe felt light in his hand. So light yet so expensive. He lifted it up and studied it as if her foot were already in it.

Hang the expense. She'd be here soon.

CHAPTER 21

It was the question Grace had been dreading since she had walked into the pizza restaurant, and despite having run through various answers in her head all day and settled on the exact words she wanted to use, she still wasn't sure she was going to get the tone right.

The pause between the end of Emma's question and where the start of Grace's reply should be was lengthening.

Grace went for the 'concerned but confused' approach.

'Alistair acting weird? No, I haven't noticed. Is he? In what way?'

Emma poked a piece of discarded pizza crust with her finger and Grace wondered upon which of the many ways in which Alistair was acting weird Emma would elaborate. Staying late for meetings that did not exist? Clutching his briefcase as if it contained his internal organs? Or that morning's absolutely priceless performance when he had obviously remembered that Grace was meeting Emma later on and that his story about taking his wife out for an early meal the night before might be exposed as a lie. He had tied himself in knots relating to Grace how after he'd left work he'd been halfway to Waterloo when he'd got a call telling him there was an emergency meeting of the tourism committee and so he had had to remain in town.

That was weird enough – what counted as an emergency in the world of tourism? Everything in Madame Tussauds melting? The London Eye spinning off down the Thames? But then it got weirder when he had shouted at Grace for not putting her evening out with Emma in his desk diary in the first place. She presumed that was because, if she had, he wouldn't have thought up a lie that involved his wife in the first place.

At any point Grace could have blown him out of the water by relating the conversation she'd had with Emma on the phone from Brent Cross, but she was afraid he'd have a seizure right there on the spot.

Grace looked uneasily at the only part of Emma she could see at the moment: the top of her head bowed over her plate. Her straight hair hung in two neat sheets and almost touched the crust of pizza she'd left. Impossible to see what her face was doing.

She hadn't seemed that upset when they'd met, nor during the pizza-eating part of the evening, but now, on her third glass of wine, it was obviously all going to come out – whatever 'all' was. And as Emma's friend and Alistair's employee, Grace did not know how to play this. That Alistair was lying to Emma was obvious; why he was doing it was not. Although Grace had to agree with Gilbert and Tate that it probably involved another woman.

If Emma asked her if she had any suspicions about an affair, she was damned whatever she replied. Pour cold water on the idea and it later turned out to be true, and she'd lose Emma as a friend. Give the slightest hint that she suspected Alistair might be playing away and she'd be clutching her P45 by the end of the week.

What was she doing thinking of herself in all this? She should be thinking of Emma. She was a friend who, until Grace had introduced her to Alistair, had been remarkably easy company. Grace had met her at a Pilates class when she had returned to London from university and she had not only been friendly but had fulfilled two requirements that Grace had of any new friends these days: she hadn't asked too many questions and she'd talked about herself a lot. While this often made for dull conversation, it did have the advantage that you knew you could relax and kick back because Emma wasn't going to say, 'So, what did you do after you left school?' She'd be too busy saying, 'This is what I did.'

Emma's preoccupation with 'I' had become 'we' when she and Alistair had married, barely six months after meeting. Emma was one of those wives whose likes and dislikes seemed to be subsumed under her husband's. Now she would talk about films 'we' liked or meals 'we' enjoyed, as if they shared the same brain and taste buds as well as the same surname. It grated a bit on Grace, especially when Alistair was held up as being a complete paragon, but there was also something quite touching about Emma's belief in him and, up until now, he'd seemed besotted with her too. This was all so sad. She was tempted to get up from her seat to go and sit next to Emma and put her arm around her.

Emma still had her head bowed and Grace wondered how to distract her. They'd exhausted talking about the women in Emma's office, who seemed to be either macrobiotic, bulimic or catatonic. They'd talked about Mark too, Emma making unsubtle suggestions that it might be time for Grace and him to get serious. They'd also 'done' Grace's family problems, although Grace had edited the story and added more humour to it than she actually felt. They'd even done a quick tour around Tate, during which Grace had regurgitated the normal platitudes. She had been able to be dispassionate about him tonight having had a Tate-free day while he was off doing whatever he did when he wasn't leading a tour or bugging the life out of her. To sit in her office without him either zooming around on his chair, flaked out on the sofa or holding impromptu coffee and jamming parties in reception had felt like a holiday.

She had even been able to resist the urge to superglue all the rocks back in place, although any new ones that wobbled free she had rounded up and chucked in the bin on the grounds they were a threat to health and safety.

'It's just Alistair seems . . . a bit jittery,' Emma said, suddenly raising her head.

Grace was relieved to see she did not look as if she were on the verge of tears. If anything, her expression mirrored Grace's earlier perplexed one. There was a group of vertical lines between Emma's eyebrows. 'It's almost as if he's on edge all the time, very volatile,' she explained. 'I think he's taken on too much. You know, with these extra meetings, hiring Tate. He's so tired when he does get home too.' She glanced at Grace and away again. 'And then there's the money.'

Grace stayed quiet. Money and sex were two aspects of Alistair and Emma's private life that she didn't want to hear about.

'He's going through quite a bit. I do the accounts, you see; he's hopeless with money. Well, I don't need to tell you that . . . And he's taking out a lot of cash, but I can't seem to see what he's spent it on. He tried to tell me he'd lost some of it, but he was lying, I could tell. Hiding something. You don't think—'

A sudden need to calm Emma and make the conversation go away caused Grace to blurt, 'I think perhaps . . . perhaps he's saving up for something special for you for Christmas. Wants it to be a secret.'

Emma had large, quite beautiful eyes and Grace saw the worry seep slowly away to be replaced by what might be a willingness to believe Grace's theory. It made her feel simultaneously pleased and cheap.

'He could be, couldn't he?' Emma said, raising both hands quickly to scoop and push her sheets of hair behind her ears. 'I'd never thought of that. You know, I did tell him I'd like one of those benches for the garden, the kind that go around the base of a tree? Perhaps it's that . . . they're really expensive.'

Grace pictured the locked cabinet: nope, it wasn't big enough for a bench that would fit around a tree. Emma was wrinkling her nose and making an 'ahh' sound. No doubt she was already picturing Alistair and her on Christmas morning cosied up on their special bench. Emma's hope now had a momentum all of its own.

'The more I think about it,' she said, a flush on her cheeks, 'the more I think you might be right. Maybe the grouchiness, the mood swings, it's just the wear and tear of commuting and running a business. We find it tough, very competitive.' She giggled. 'But in all other areas, we couldn't be happier. Even when he's terribly tense, I can relax him.' She dropped her voice, looked like she had the biggest secret in the world to tell. 'The sex is still amazingly satisfying. He's very demanding. Very imaginative.'

'Oh good,' Grace said softly and refilled Emma's glass. If only she still drank herself, it might take the edge off the picture of Alistair performing his marital duties that she now had thrusting away in her head.

Alistair had the television switched on, but he wasn't really watching it or listening to it. All of his attention was on the mobile phone on the sofa cushion next to him. Shiny black against the red velour, it was like some hard-backed insect. Menacing.

When Emma rang to say she was on the train, he'd know from the sound of her voice. Just know.

Why hadn't he told Emma and Grace the same story about last night's meeting? All they had to do was compare notes and his lie would be found out. Either the meeting was a planned one as he'd told Emma, or it was an emergency as he'd told Grace. It couldn't be both. And what the hell would constitute an emergency in tourism? Not enough street performers for Covent Garden? The royal family being replaced by the Muppets?

She'd have called straight away if she'd been suspicious about something, wouldn't she?

He looked at his watch, not registering what the time was, in the same way he hadn't registered it when he'd tipped his wrist before.

Why did she have to be meeting Grace today when that conversation they'd had about money over breakfast would still be fresh in her mind? He could tell she hadn't bought that story about losing the money near the cashpoint.

Perhaps they wouldn't talk about him.

No, women talked about everything.

The phone rang and he snatched it up.

'I know what you're up toooooo,' Emma said into his ear and he was up and off the sofa heading he didn't know where, until he registered that she sounded, (a) drunk and, (b) happy.

'Are you a bit tipsy?' he asked breathlessly.

'A teensy bit. But I'm on the train safely. Safe. And. Sound. Gets in at eleven. And you . . . you're a bad, bad man, but a lovely one too.'

His mind came back from the precipice. 'I am . . . I mean, yes, I am, but why?'

'Shh. It's a secret, but it makes me love you more and

let's just say Christmas can't come quickly enough for this happy bunny.' There was a clunk where she had obviously dropped the phone and then it was picked back up and she said, 'Oops,' before all went quiet.

Alistair sat back down on the sofa. Was he feeling relieved or even more of a bastard? No, definitely relieved – he was going to live to fight another day. Grace hadn't dropped him in it. Good old Grace. He remembered how he'd shouted at her that morning and screwed up his face. That had to stop.

But what had that Christmas comment meant? Was she planning a trip away for them?

He went to fetch his car keys. Probably find out on the drive home – she was hopeless at keeping secrets.

That was *his* speciality.

CHAPTER 22

One-hundred-and-eighty-thread Egyptian cotton. Twenty-four-hour room service. Grace welcomed the solidity of numbers – you could count on them to be exactly as they promised. Do what you expected.

Like Mark. She turned her head on the smooth, cool pillowcase and watched him perusing the menu. Suntanned. Solid. Here when you wanted him, gone when you didn't.

His brown hair was lighter than she remembered, but otherwise, he was a surprise-free zone.

Even down to the sex. Energetic, satisfying, but like having a good workout rather than someone throwing you over a cliff with both hands still clamped around your heart.

'What do you fancy?' he said without looking up.

'Soda water. And a Caesar salad.'

'Nothing else? No bread? Don't want you wasting away.'

He glanced up, a hint of teasing about the eyes. But only

a hint: Mark's face, with its dark brows and straight nose, easily conveyed earnestness. It was an eminently straightforward face with nothing unsettling in it.

'I'm fine. So . . . what are you having?'

'Merlot, steak sandwich and chips.'

Of course he was.

She saw him put down the menu, felt his hand slide its way between her legs.

'You first,' he said, moving nearer, hand probing deeper. 'You first and then food.'

That wasn't a surprise either.

Grace was drinking her soda water in the bath later, her back against Mark's chest, when he said, 'This still working for you?'

She wondered what he was really asking, but nodded, before adding, 'I mean, of course it would be good to see more of you.'

His chest moved as he laughed. 'There's not much more of me to see.'

'You know what I mean. And why are you asking anyway? Don't I seem happy?'

She saw his glass go past her head en route to his mouth and thought how weird it was having a conversation where both of the participants this time were talking to the taps.

Perhaps in a moment he'd put his mouth against her hair, talk into it.

Probably not.

'I just don't want you to think I'm taking you for granted, that's all,' he said when the glass, slightly emptier, had been lowered again. 'I don't expect you to sit around just waiting for the times we meet up again. I like it that you do, but I don't *expect* it.'

She turned round, making the water run and splash up the side of the bath. 'Everything's fine, Mark. Absolutely fine.' She put her hand on his thigh, registering how attractive he was when wet.

'It is, isn't it?' he said, transferring his wine glass to his other hand. 'I mean, in a couple of years' time, you know, when I stop travelling so much, maybe then . . .' She moved her hand over him, feeling how he had already hardened under the water, and he didn't finish talking, simply leaned over the side of the bath and put his glass on the floor.

'Yes, maybe in a couple of years . . .' she said just before he sat back up straight and reached for her. Chest to chest this time. Mouth on mouth. No room for talk.

Grace took a taxi back from the hotel late on Sunday afternoon, Mark's goodbye kisses still on her lips. London was spread out around her: a swirl of twinkling lights, silent parks, snatched views into shops and homes. This was one of those taxi rides where she felt everything was laid on purely for her pleasure – a stage set to entertain her eyes alone. She relaxed back into the seat. Two days seemed to have taken years off her shoulders. She thought of her father in her flat and there was no tightening of her chest. This week she would finally get him and her mother together and make them talk it through.

She thought of Tate. What a boy compared with Mark.

As the taxi headed over Putney Bridge, the Thames dark beneath them, all the things that had been bubbling away, threatening to boil over, seemed unimportant, like shadows on the edge of this glittering evening.

She walked along the path to the front door and opened it; almost felt she was gliding inside. Monday tomorrow – the dental surgery would be open again. She'd have to catch them to explain about the chipped paint, ask them about their holiday. She went through the fire door and up the stairs, a part of her brain telling her that she was smelling paint again and also, this time, something that made her think 'white spirit', and as she unlocked her own front door and pushed it open she saw her father running down the stairs towards her with a rag in his hand.

'Now, Grace, it's not as bad as it looks,' he said, while his face suggested it was almost certainly worse. Still in five-star hotel mode, Grace was slow to register that Nadim was standing further up the stairs with a bottle in his hand and another rag. If possible, the expression on his face was worse than the one on her father's. She wondered what was in the bottle as Nadim didn't drink and then the earlier message to her brain about paint and white spirit collided with all the other information with which she was being bombarded and she lowered her eyes to the carpet.

'Oh my God,' she said.

'It'll come good,' Nadim assured her, getting down on his knees and rubbing at the carpet, which from the top step to the very bottom one was splashed with green paint, the pile slicked with it in some places and in others, where she presumed white spirit had been applied, rubbed into a wet, green, matted mess. On the buttercream-coloured wallpaper up both sides of the stairs, and on the paintwork, were splashes, dribbles and smears of green.

Her father was jabbering. 'I knew they'd be back tomorrow, see, the dentists, and I thought I'd just touch up that bit of paint I damaged. Well, couldn't get the lid off downstairs so I brought it up to get one of the knives in the kitchen to prise it off and . . .'

He really didn't need to say any more. Grace guessed he'd dropped the tin on the top step.

'I'll pay for everything,' he added.

'Be fine, Grace, just need to get it treated before it dries,' Nadim assured her again. He was still trying to rub the carpet but she could see his heart wasn't in it. The fumes of the white spirit and the paint were making her eyes water and she wondered how long these two had been breathing it in.

'I'm going to open some doors and windows, let out these fumes,' she said, feeling nothing. There was paint on her stairs. They were cleaning it. That was all.

She wedged open her front door and went downstairs to do the same to the others. Her father followed her.

'Grace—'

'Please, Dad. Just say nothing.'

Back up in her flat, she picked her way carefully over the ruined carpet and in the kitchen found the work surfaces were not only covered with various sheaves of paper and plans, but dirty plates, glasses and coffee cups.

Her father was behind her again. 'I was going to get this all cleared up before you came back.' He made an ineffectual attempt to move things about. 'Only what with the paint . . .'

'The Newham Gang have been round again, have they?'

She didn't wait for his reply but turned and went back to the top of the stairs.

'Leave it now, Nadim,' she called to him. 'Go on home. Thank you for all you've done.'

Nadim didn't even protest; he was down the stairs and out the door before Grace had reached her sitting room. More chaos. Bathroom? She turned round quickly and retreated. Pointless going to her bedroom, it wasn't even hers any more.

'Grace, love . . . it'll only take a few minutes to tidy . . . apart from the carpet. I can—'

The storm started to break in her without her knowing it was coming.

'Dad, I can't keep on living like this. You and Mum know I can't handle chaos and mess, but you keep dragging me back into it. You and Mum – your stubbornness and her stupidity. This has to stop, Dad.' She turned on him and saw how he was shrinking away from her. 'Tomorrow, after work, you are coming with me to Newham and we are sorting this out. I don't care what's going on . . . it ends tomorrow and you go back home.'

'No. Can't.' He was shaking his head.

'You're not listening to me, Dad. I am losing it here. I have no bedroom. I'm not getting any sleep. I can't use my own kitchen, it's so messy. You're taking over the whole flat. I need peace and quiet at home, I need order – things are very . . . very . . . difficult at work.' Her voice was getting louder and louder, she pulled it back. 'This isn't me asking, this is me telling. You and her, tomorrow. Talking.'

He shook his head again and it made her want to wound him to get him to listen. More disconcertingly, though, she had a craving for the contents of that biscuit tin in the kitchen and that realisation made her even harder on him.

'Don't keep saying "no", shaking your head. We're getting this sorted. Stand there now and tell me, tell me what she's done this time that's so bad you can't forgive her. Come on.' She pointed to the stairs. 'Don't you think you owe me that?'

No response.

'Tell me now, Dad, or I'll get Nadim back to ask him if you can go and stay there. I will throw you out, Dad, honestly I will—'

'I caught them,' her father said softly, his head right down. 'In our bedroom. She had her . . . her bra off, he was . . .' He ground to a halt and suddenly she didn't want to wound him – she wanted to tell him it was all right, he didn't have to say any more.

When he looked at her his eyes were brimming with tears. 'She said he was practising his massage on her but he wasn't, Grace. She was lying on her back.' She saw him swallow. 'I've tried to put a brave face on it, but everyone's got their tipping point, haven't they? There's only so much provocation a person can take.'

CHAPTER 23

Grace found a large note from Tate when she arrived at the office on Monday. It was so large it covered the entire surface of her desk and he'd decorated it with all kinds of curling tendrils and squiggles. It was beautiful, except for the message in large black letters in the middle. *I. O. U, Gracie*, it said, *Big Time.*

'You been lending Tate money?' Alistair asked.

Grace felt uneasy, knowing that Tate was going to get her back for the Esther incident, but there were so many other emotions she was experiencing at that moment, uneasy was going to have to take a ticket and join the back of the queue.

Shock at her father's outburst had been followed by confusion, anger and then weariness. The anger was directed towards her mother; the weariness was a result of sitting for a couple of hours with her father on the sofa last night with her arm round his shoulders. He hadn't wanted to talk about it any more and she didn't want to make him. When he'd limped off to bed, she had stayed up cleaning the flat, although the stairs were a job too far, even for her. She left all the windows open, shut the doors and decided to worry about it later.

Her weekend with Mark now seemed years ago, and apart from the first twinges of what might be cystitis, she had nothing to show for it. All traces of well-being, of having recharged her batteries to be able to withstand what else might come her way, had been replaced by an image of her mother lying naked on a bed with Jay Houghton massaging her breasts.

Grace filled up her cup with hot water from the kettle and thought again of her poor father and how bony his shoulders had felt under her arm last night. She was intending to ring him to see how he was this morning, but she appeared to be ringing her mother.

'How could you?' she said as soon as Felicity answered, which wasn't the non-confrontational start she'd had planned either. 'How could you do that to Dad? I mean, God knows I never understood you as a couple, but in your own weird way you've always worked.'

'Now look—'

'No, don't you speak. Don't you say anything at all. You just bloody well listen to me. Were you or were you not lying half-naked on a bed with Jay Houghton and letting him . . . letting him . . . ?'

'Letting him what? Go on, spit out whatever filth that man has told you. Wait till I tell your sisters about—'

'He's not *that man* – he's my dad and your husband, a husband who has put up with a lot from you over the years, not least your addiction to flirting. But he's right – this has crossed the line, Mum.'

'Oh, and he's been a saint, has he? Haven't I had to put up with all that crime stuff and those stupid friends of his? Him acting like he's Gene Hunt and Sherlock Holmes all rolled into one.'

'Whatever he's done, it hasn't involved lying on a bed and letting another man play with his breasts . . .'

Grace stopped talking, aware that Alistair was back in the office.

'Uh, I heard shouting,' he said, not taking his eyes off the phone. 'It's not a client, is it?'

Had she been shouting?

'My mother. It's a long story, Alistair.'

He nodded as if his life were full of long stories and backed out of the room, closing the door behind him.

He needn't have bothered – when Grace held the phone back up to her ear it was silent.

Grace left early to get to the Paddwick Gallery, knowing

she was avoiding Tate and anyone else who might pop into the office. The only person she really wanted to speak to today was hundreds of years old and holding a baby, but when she arrived in front of the icon, there were too many people around. She had to settle for willing her thoughts to transmit themselves from her flesh-and-bone head to the painted one. She started to feel calmer.

She was certainly calmer than Norman, whom she passed on the way back downstairs to meet her group. Sitting by *Lady in a Robe*, he was jouncing his leg up and down as he told her that Ludmilla didn't like the necklace he'd bought her for her birthday; said it was 'cheap'.

'It wasn't, Grace.' He looked gutted and filleted. 'I got it in Bond Street. Well, one of the roads off Bond Street.'

'I'm sorry, Norman.'

'S'all right. She's hard to please. Has high standards. Likes the best of everything.'

Grace regarded the balding Norman in his slightly too tight grey uniform and doubted if that were strictly true. She made her way to the meeting point next to Lilly on the ticket desk.

'All right, Grace?' Lilly said looking even more painted than usual. 'See Norman while you were up there?' She clicked her tongue. 'He wants to ditch that wife, get himself a new model.'

Grace was wondering whether Lilly might like to be considered for that role because there always seemed to be a hint of petulance whenever she was discussing Norman's wife and a lot more appearance primping, but got no further with this reasoning as she had just glimpsed a mop of blond hair through the glass of the door. Her panic subsided as she saw it belonged to the teenage son of the Dutch family she was taking round the gallery today. All five of them towered over her, were polite, ridiculously healthy looking and spoke perfect English. Grace hoisted on her professional persona and set off up the stairs with them, and as she settled into her tour she started to enjoy it, despite her mother, despite Tate, despite her flat-wrecking father. The de Janvers were knowledgeable and interested and nodded in all the right places.

A Bar at the Folies Bergère,' she said, stopping in front of the painting and falling silent just long enough for them to take stock of it. She turned back to them and what she was going to say next disappeared from her brain. Either the de Janvers now had another blond son or Tate Jefferson had joined them. Today he had on the same pinstriped trousers he'd worn the day Grace first saw him but this time with the addition of a red T-shirt with a silver skull on it.

'Hi,' he said to the de Janvers. 'Don't mind me. Just

here for training purposes. Keeping an eye on the new girl. Carry on, Gracie,' he added with a cheerful wave of his hand.

And then he did absolutely nothing. No smart asides, no yawning or wandering about. No examining his finger nails. He just stood there, arms crossed, chin slightly down, watching her. She'd never seen him stay still for so long and it absolutely, utterly, spooked her out.

She fumbled her way through Manet's motivation, making such a stop–start hash of the whole thing that it would have seemed quite believable to the de Janvers that she was a beginner.

She tried not to look at Tate, but was repeatedly drawn to his eyes. She turned away and could feel his gaze like a hand on her hair, her neck, her back. Her mouth was growing dry. They moved to the next painting and he followed, but this time he tilted his head slightly as he stood and frowned. That tripped her up again, made her wonder what he was thinking when she should have concentrated on what she was saying.

As they moved on again, she hung back and got close to him.

'Stop it,' she said.

'Stop what?' He shrugged, all innocence. 'Standing here and listening? What's the problem? It's a free country isn't it?' He patted her on the arm. 'Now, don't be nervous, you're doing OK . . . for a beginner. Isn't she?'

The last question was aimed at the de Janvers family and they all said 'yes', except for one of the sons who did a turning 'so-so' motion with his hand.

Tate laughed. 'There you go. So, what's next?'

'You're going to leave. You're going to bugger off,' she said with as much force as she could get into a whisper and went back to stand in front of the group and talk about Van Gogh.

'Oh, and just a suggestion,' he called out, before she had even finished her first sentence, 'cut the swearing and smile now and again. The public like that. Lightens the whole thing up.'

The de Janvers nodded and she was thrown again. As the paintings passed and he kept watching, she felt the frustration and anger build in her. And, as they neared the halfway point of the tour, there was something else building in her that grew stronger every time she saw him watching her: the fear that he was peeling away everything and getting inside her, making her feel as exposed as if he'd just undressed her.

'Before we go upstairs,' she said hurriedly, 'we're going to take a detour—'

'Oh crap,' Tate said. 'Not the sad woman and the baby.'

When Grace could think about what happened next with any degree of objectivity, she pictured herself as a firework, deceptively harmless-looking and with a very long fuse, but finally exploding as gunpowder met flame.

'Don't you dare start on her. You leave her alone,' she heard herself shout, registering that this was the second time she had raised her voice that day. She also registered that the de Janvers were staring at her, several other people in the gallery had turned to look and Tate was now right in front of her.

'Hey, keep a lid on it,' he said. 'You go see sad lady if you like. I just feel you've bored these nice people enough.'

'Stop it,' she snapped. 'You've made your point; you've paid me back for Esther. But leave the icon alone.'

He shook his head, widened his eyes. 'Paid you back? You're joking. You, Miss Nicey-Nicey, left me to Esther for a friggin' hour. I had to hear every one of her travel plans, including flight times. I thought I was gonna be there all night.'

'Well, that's what you get when you stir people up, go out of your way to show them what a free spirit you are and how they ought to be one too.'

Grace sensed that he was actually getting annoyed now – his eyes were stormy green. He took a step closer. She stood her ground. 'Oh, that's what I'm doing, am I?' he said. 'Not just being friendly? You see, maybe you don't recognise "friendly". You with all your rules, looking down your English nose at me. "Don't breathe my air, Tate."'

'You're a stirrer – a great big spoon on legs. You're stirring up all kinds of people: Esther, Alistair . . .' She stopped herself from saying Gilbert.

'You sure they're the only ones? 'Cos know what? You're looking pretty stirred up yourself. Touch of the real Gracie slipping out from under all that ice, huh?' He stopped talking and suddenly his expression cleared and he clicked his fingers and pointed at her, 'That's it, that's who you've been reminding me of. Yup, got it now: George.'

She was confused enough about what he meant to stop talking, and during that lull she saw Norman look into the room. The way he was frowning and the realisation that more and more people were watching them made her lower her voice. If they weren't careful, they were going to get thrown out.

'I do not know a George,' she said quietly but with feeling. 'I have no interest in a George. Now please, go away.' She turned to the de Janvers. 'I'm sorry.' She straightened her jacket and pulled back her shoulders. 'I'm sorry . . . let's—'

There was a tap on her shoulder and Tate's mouth was close to her ear. She remembered the time he'd blown on it, in the dark.

'George is my cousin. He's an actor, Gracie. Hell of a lot of enthusiasm, but he stinks. Always seems as if he's just playing at being someone else. You're better than him, but you're still not quite good enough. Cracks appearing, Gracie. Cracks definitely appearing.'

'Well, let's hope you fall down one of them and disappear. And let's hope you do it before you inflict your wonderful video installation on the world. God, the old masters must be quaking in their frames.' She stepped away from him. 'So, if you'll just follow me . . .' She started shepherding the de Janvers towards the door. She checked to see if Norman was still looking at them but he wasn't there any more, and then very distinctly she heard two loud clunks as if someone were throwing heavy things to the floor. There was a hissing noise, a weird sound that she couldn't place, but as she strained to listen, all at once it was as if someone had taken a fistful of pepper and rubbed it into her eyes and onto the lining of her mouth and throat. She felt tears spring up and as she tried to rub whatever it was away, they streamed between her fingers and down her cheeks. Her nose was running too – it was unstoppable – and her throat felt as if it were swelling so much that she struggled to breathe. She began to panic. She was aware of attendants running towards and past her; she caught a glimpse of Lilly tanking up the stairs, her arm held over her nose and mouth, and of the de Janvers coughing and flailing around and trying to help each other to the door. Now a hand was on her arm, pulling at her, and she heard Tate's muffled voice saying, 'Come on, get moving, we've gotta get some fresh air,' before everything disappeared under the jarring, screaming noise of the gallery's alarms. It was hard to know if it was her ears, her eyes or her chest that hurt the most as she was stumbling after Tate, his hand locked round her wrist, bumping into people and coughing, slipping on the stairs, joining the mass of bodies trying to get to the door, and then they were out in the fresh air, gulping in great lungfuls of it.

'Stay here,' Tate said to her as she tried to open her eyes. 'Don't move.' Still struggling to breathe normally, she attempted to peer around to see if, among all the other people bending forward with their hands braced on their knees or sitting with the heels of their hands over their eyes, she could see the de Janvers. She couldn't, but felt strangely dislocated from that as if this were all happening on a screen in front of her. The gallery alarm was still ringing out and now there were sirens added to it. Police cars were arriving in the courtyard.

Tate was back. 'Hold out your hands,' he ordered and when she didn't, she felt him take hold of her wrist again. 'Cup your hands – I'm gonna pour some water in them.

Give them a wash and then I'll give you some more; you need to bathe your eyes. Tear gas, nasty stuff.'

'How do you know?' she said, fumbling around to do what she was told.

He snorted. 'Friend of mine did a "happening" with it once. Let a canister off in a huge multi-storey car park; thought it would just make people cry a bit. Wanted to show how the world's love of the combustion engine was really a source of sorrow, that kind of crap. Big mistake. Still getting the ass sued off him.'

Bit by bit, she was able to open her eyes properly and keep them open, and she saw him bathing his too, his eyelids looking puffy and his nose red. She saw him take a drink of water, slosh it around his mouth and spit it on to the cobbles. She did the same and he smiled at her.

'Looks funny, seeing you spit.'

Now, when she felt grateful to him, when they were bonding over what had happened to them, this was when she had to be careful.

'I ought to find the de Janvers,' she said, although she dreaded the thought of standing up and walking.

'No need. They're out on the street, sitting on the kerb. They're safe; saw them when I went to get the water.'

It felt hard to say 'thank you' to him, but she did.

'That's OK.' He smiled at her again, a self-conscious one

this time it seemed to Grace, and they didn't say anything for a while, both of them watching the people still coming out of the gallery and the police going in. The crowd had grown bigger: some people standing around and talking, high on adrenalin, some still dabbing and wiping and sitting propped against bollards and walls. A few were on their mobiles and Grace wondered if it was loved ones they were texting or just splurging their experience on Twitter.

She still felt removed from it all, confused about what had just happened, and she guessed Tate was too because he called over to a couple of men in suits who were standing nearby, 'Any idea what's happening?'

'We think,' the elder one said, 'someone's tried to steal something.' His companion nodded. 'Won't have got anywhere, security's so tight. Even if they got something off the wall, they won't get it out.' He was indicating the number of police cars and, as if to underline the fact that no one was going anywhere, Grace saw that the gateway leading out to the Strand was full of men and women in uniforms. She turned to the other exits. Same.

'They'll be wanting to take witness statements, I suppose,' Grace said, a piece of information she'd picked up from years spent listening to her father.

She was right – they did – and it was when a policewoman came round to take their names and contact details that Grace found out the man in the suit was wrong. 'They' had managed to get something off the wall, and get it out of the building. Or maybe 'they'd' hidden it somewhere in the building. Whatever: it was missing.

'What was it?' Grace asked, suddenly not looking at things happening on a screen, but knowing she was right there on the cobbles, her eyes stinging, her nose running and water all down her jacket.

'I'm afraid I can't tell you that,' the policewoman said.

She didn't need to be told. Grace just knew it would be the icon.

CHAPTER 24

Violet felt that the least your guest could do when you had spent six days cleaning the house, making sandwiches and cakes, rinsing cups and saucers and plates, shining the cutlery, putting down fresh paper on the route from the front door to the sitting room and to the downstairs toilet . . . the least your guest could do was sing for her supper. By that she supposed she meant be lively and talk a lot, particularly about what Violet wanted to talk about. Although, now Violet thought about it further, 'singing for your supper' was an expression her mother had used and she wasn't completely sure it *was* about being lively and talking a lot; it might actually involve singing.

Anyway, Grace could certainly be a lot more forthcoming and not sit there like a wet weekend – another of her mother's expressions, which seemed to apply in this case even though it was Tuesday. Violet supposed she ought to be more sympathetic and perhaps more grateful: Grace could very well have postponed her visit after the upset yesterday. But my goodness, she was being irritating.

Violet was eager to get on to the subject of Tate and when Grace wasn't just staring at the rug, she was chewing unenthusiastically on an egg and cress sandwich and not being particularly careful about how many crumbs she dropped on her plate. Violet was pleased to see that Grace was at least trying to keep both of her feet neatly on their allotted pieces of paper.

Yes, Grace was definitely looking peaky. Slightly bloodshot eyes. Still neat, though. Neat hair, neat clothes, neat nails. Very glossy hair. Gilbert said she was neat at work as well, and very, very organised. He liked her a lot, said she was good-looking. Well, that was allowed because it was obvious that Grace wasn't Gilbert's type. But what about those other women Tate had brought into Gilbert's life?

'It was just so quick . . . so brutal,' Grace said suddenly, and Violet forced herself to agree: 'Awful, awful,' but made sure she added, 'that's what I said to Gilbert when he told me *all* about it.' She hoped that conveyed to Grace that she felt there was nothing left to be said on this subject. She'd heard more than enough. Gilbert hadn't stopped going on about it when he came home from work last night, and he'd rung again today, just to keep her up to date – how the police had been to the office to take statements from Tate and Grace, how the Russian picture of Ivon someone was still missing and how people were whispering that it must have been an inside job, despite the gallery having been searched right down to the baby-changing room.

There had been lots of other snippets and details but Violet had a hazy recollection of them. Tear gas was one and a thing called liquid plastic, which had been painted over some of the cameras inside and outside the gallery so they weren't actually recording anything.

'Did Gilbert tell you that Tate and I were having an argument when it happened?' Grace said. Violet felt her interest peak.

'Tate?'

Grace nodded. 'Yes, and the Dutch family have complained, asked for a refund, and Alistair is angry because he thinks it's unprofessional and people might start wondering if we were causing a diversion.'

'Were you?'

'No. Of course not.' Grace appeared affronted, but then seemed to lapse back into misery. 'It's awful. I've never, ever had someone complain before and they had every right. I really let him get to me.'

Violet sat forward. 'Ah, Tate. Gilbert . . . well, Gilbert seems to think he's nice. "A breath of fresh air" I think he called him.'

Grace definitely didn't care for Tate, even the way she took a bite of her sandwich suggested that. She didn't need to be quite so wild, though – a bit of egg had fallen back on to her plate.

Violet considered getting the dustpan and brush out, but decided that would interrupt the flow of conversation.

'In fact, Gilbert talks about Tate quite a bit.' Violet let that sit for a while. 'And someone called . . . Baby.'

'Bebbie.'

'Hmm. Yes, an unusual name. I can't quite picture what a woman with that kind of name would look like.'

Grace screwed her mouth up, which was not attractive.

'She's quite stunning: long legs, long hair. Arty type, you know.'

Violet didn't, but she did know danger when she heard it described to her. She looked around her sitting room, imagining what a long-limbed, long-haired arty woman would do to it. Would do to Gilbert. It was no good; she couldn't go on inching her way forward like this. She put down her plate.

'Is she someone Gilbert might like?' she said, knowing her voice had wavered as she'd asked the question.

She saw Grace's expression change as if something had

just broken above her mind and the noise had made her wake up. Her face looked like those idiots from social services; she was leaning forward. Did she still have her feet on the paper? Just.

'Are you worried about something, Violet? Is that why you wanted to see me?'

Violet nodded at the relief of being understood. 'Yes, and please, Grace, not a word to Gilbert . . . but this Tate, he seems to be bringing in all these women and Gilbert . . . well, Gilbert . . . he likes beautiful things.'

Violet feared that Grace was going to try to reach out for her hand, but she must have thought better of it.

'Violet,' she said, and her tone was gentle, a nice gentle, not that horrible patting-on-the-head gentle, 'Bebbie is no threat to you. She was Tate's girlfriend; not so sure she is now. Don't expect she'll be around much.'

'And Corinne? And Jo?'

'Joe is actually a man. He and Corinne are together, I think.'

Violet was daring to hope. 'And Shawna?'

Grace frowned and then her expression straightened itself out. 'Oh, Shawna! Well, she's just an artist we met. She doesn't come to the office.'

'But Gilbert might still like her.'

Violet couldn't work out what Grace was doing with her

face now. There was obviously some kind of fight going on in her brain. Maybe she was hearing voices. Couldn't be the mice, they were quiet at the moment. But they'd be back. They'd come sniffing after those sandwiches.

'Violet,' Grace said finally, 'I can promise you, absolutely, that Gilbert is not going to be interested in any woman who Tate introduces him to.'

'Promise? Absolutely?' Violet said. 'Is that possible? He's . . . he seems unsettled, not himself. Complains a lot. About food – that we have chops on a Tuesday, that kind of thing – and I thought maybe there's a woman, and you know how women are, making you discontented with what you've got, getting you to spend money on them, dragging you away from what you've always . . .'

She stopped because Grace was looking at her in 'that' way and Violet realised she was clasping and clawing at her own hands.

She remembered what Gilbert said about focusing on something in the room and calming herself.

When she felt she was calm enough, which was sometimes before other people thought she was, she tried again.

'You're certain . . . about the women?'

'Trust me. You don't have anything to fear from any woman.'

Violet liked the way Grace was so definite about that,

but not the way she'd shifted her gaze away before she'd finished talking.

Oh well, perhaps it was something to do with having sore eyes.

Violet unclenched her toes and let her legs relax. A feeling of ease spread slowly up her body.

'Thank you, Grace,' she said, 'you've put my mind at rest. Gilbert can be so evasive sometimes. I can always depend on you to tell me the truth.'

Grace made a funny noise at that, like she had a sore throat as well as sore eyes. And then she sat there, not eating or drinking anything and, if possible, looking even more miserable until Violet was half hoping that the mice might put in an appearance just to add a bit of life to the proceedings.

CHAPTER 25

The phone on her desk rang.

'I'm not speaking to you,' Felicity said. 'I'm only calling to see you're all right.'

'Even by your standards, Mum, that sentence is gibberish.'

'And I'm not listening to you either, so don't be snitty with me. Well . . . are you all right? You were in that gallery, weren't you, when it was robbed?'

'How do you know that?'

'Your father left a message. So, are you all right? You don't sound all right.'

'I'm all right.'

'You're not all right, are you? I can hear it in your voice.'

'You said you weren't listening to me.'

The line went dead and Grace knew that wasn't the way to handle her mother if she was ever going to broker some kind of reconciliation between her parents.

Her father. She was surprised he'd had either the time

or the inclination to ring her mother. He'd practically been dancing around the flat on Monday evening when she came home, bleary-eyed and dishevelled. For him, this robbery was the payback for all of those years of preparation, all that crime-watching and analysing – and, added jackpot, now he had an eyewitness he could question any time he chose. New files and plans and graphs had materialised to colonise her worktops by the time she'd left for work the next day, and after returning from Violet's last night she'd had to face interrogation in the sitting room by the Newham Gang – her on a stool from the kitchen, them lounging around on the sofa and easy chairs.

They seemed particularly interested in pinpointing where each of the gallery attendants had been at the time of the robbery, something Grace had no way of knowing, but which didn't stop them repeatedly asking her. This led her to conclude that they had joined the ranks of people who felt it must have been an inside job, or at least carried out with some inside help. When she let slip that Norman had appeared and then disappeared again, Nadim became thoughtful and said, 'Is he the one with the Russian wife?' which set off a lot of meaningful nods from the others and much discussion about the black market for icons. Unable to bear any more of it, Grace had left the room, reasoning that it was going to be hard to lie down on the sofa with two ex-policemen still sitting on it. She wanted to detour via the kitchen, just to have a look at the contents of her biscuit tin, but forced herself to go and lie on her bed instead, pushing aside her father's papers to do so and trying to ignore the smell of white spirit and paint that still lingered in the flat. While her father and his mates were sifting through facts and figures and psychological profiling, all she kept seeing was the icon shoved in a lock-up garage somewhere or just about to disappear into some private collection.

Grace stopped thinking about her father's interrogation techniques and returned to the present moment and her office. She was still holding the phone even though her mother was long gone. She put it down on the desk and hoped that it would ring again and it would be Mark. She debated calling his mobile. He'd contacted her when he'd seen the robbery on the news, not sure if she'd been in it or not. Then he'd made all the right sympathetic noises, even sent her some flowers. She looked at them now in their glass vase on her desk: white roses, long-stemmed. He said he'd make a real effort to grab that couple of hours with her before he flew off again this evening. She could just ring him and see if it was still on.

Alistair came in as she was dialling the number, so she stopped and put the phone down. Ignoring Alistair just at this moment wasn't a good idea. He was still put out with her for arguing with Tate in front of clients.

'The Paddwick won't reopen again until tomorrow,' he said. 'Just been talking to the director. He sounds gutted, I can tell you. I apologised for . . . any upset you might have caused beforehand. I don't think he was really listening.'

'It wasn't just me, Alistair. Tate can be very—'

'You're my right-hand woman, Grace, we went over this yesterday. I expect better of you. The other galleries hear about it and they might think about restricting our access.'

She felt the injustice of what he was saying and he must have seen it.

'All right, all right, just be careful, hmm? Best behaviour when you get back in there.'

Grace didn't want to go back in there ever again. The embarrassment she could cope with; the empty room where the icon had been she could not.

Please let whoever had the icon be looking after it. Please don't let them have splintered the wood or scratched the gilding.

When she thought of that little foot in the blanket shoved somewhere unloved and unlooked at, it made her want to cry. No, not just cry – she wanted to beat her chest and wail. She should have kept more of an eye on it; when the tear gas started, she should have realised and run to it. Kept it safe. It was the least she could have done to make some kind of amends.

Alistair, perhaps spooked by her misery, had gone back to his office. Now she felt too upset to ring Mark. She would come across as needy.

This was Tate's fault. He'd caused it somehow just by existing. Since he'd arrived things had been going wrong – Grace's parents, Emma and Alistair, Gilbert and Violet, Esther . . . and now this. And she was letting them go wrong, letting things slip away from her.

Why hadn't they stolen Tate instead of the icon?

She back-pedalled on that as she remembered how he'd got her out of the gallery, how kind he'd been finding the water. She could feel his hand around her wrist again.

No, no, no. Stop thinking about that. And about yester-day – how before the police had been to the office, after the police had been, he'd been acting as if this shared experience had created some bond between them. Kept asking her if she was all right. Telling her not to worry, the icon would be found.

Getting back in control, especially of any feelings for him, was even more important now than ever. She must keep her back turned on all this. Keep the lid on that tin.

She'd been distracted by him and whoosh . . . she'd begun to slide towards that pit.

The phone rang again.

'Aurillia,' she said when she recognised the voice. 'What are you doing? What time is it over there?'

'Early, very early, but as you haven't answered my latest email, or Zin and Serafina's, how else are we going to communicate with you?' There was an aggrieved whine under the drawl which Aurillia had affected despite only having been in America a couple of years. 'Think of this as an intervention.'

'A what?'

'Mum has been on the phone saying you've actually accused her of having sex with Jay. Is that right?'

'Not exactly. Dad—'

'Don't hide behind Dad on this. Look, you really need to start chilling – about this, about everything – or you'll have some kind of breakdown. The body is only the mind's carrier. Mum swears that Jay Houghton and she just have a business arrangement, not that she really needs to explain anything to us anyway – a woman is in charge of her own body. So, the question is, why have you purposely chosen to disbelieve her? You wanna' think about that—'

'No, I don't,' Grace said firmly, 'this is not about me. This is about our mother and our father and how the latter feels the former has had some kind of sexual encounter – I did not say "sex"– with Jay Houghton. Now, you can empathise and sympathise with Mum all you like, but it is Dad who needs to be made to feel better.'

'I have tried to talk to him,' Aurillia said in a sulky voice.

'Really, or have you talked at him?'

'You're very aggressive this morning. Why are you so aggressive?'

'Well, perhaps because I have been in a robbery, been tear-gassed, if there is such an expression, and one of my favourite paintings in the whole world has been stolen. Yes, that will be it. I don't suppose Mum mentioned that?'

There was a beat of silence and then Aurillia said, 'A robbery. My God, you're probably suffering from post-traumatic stress . . . you need to go lie on the floor. No, wait, we do courses to help you deal with the feeling of helplessness and deep-seated pain that can arise from one of these incidents. You ought to think about it.'

It was with supreme self-restraint that Grace did not shout, *Oh, bugger off!* down the phone. 'Thank you, I will consider it,' she said instead. 'In the meantime, if the coven could get its act together, if the three of you could try to make Dad feel better about this, I'd be grateful. Was that all? Good.'

Grace was rather pleased with her measured response to such provocation and with equal delicacy opened up her email account and zapped every one of her sisters' latest emails without reading them.

The phone rang again. It was her dad.

'Can you remember? Were the blinds fully up or halfway down in the room you were in when the robbery started?'

'If I tell you, will you listen to what I have to say first?'

'Uh . . . ye-es.'

'Right. You had better brace yourself as it is likely that today you will have phone calls and emails from Zin, Aurillia and Serafina. We are all getting weary of being ping-ponged back and forth between you and Mum. At some point you have to talk about this to Mum, face-to-face. So . . . blinds? All the way up. Goodbye.'

She contemplated ringing Mark. No, he'd come to her if he could.

The phone rang again. Bernice.

'You couldn't come down for a few minutes, could you? Esther's not in till later.'

That was intriguing enough to get her down the stairs.

After some initial fussing around her to make sure she was not suffering any long-term effects from the robbery – Grace avoided looking Bernice in the eye when she said, 'No' – and a bit of news about how the garden overhaul was going now the house was finished, Bernice jabbed her thumb towards Esther's desk.

'She's up to something,' she said. 'See, that's the trouble when she gets ideas in her head. And . . .' she seemed to be considering whether to go on or not. She lowered her voice. 'Look, Esther is family and she's not had an easy life, but she gets fixations, you know. Goes for years placid as anything, then gets . . . focused on things . . . on people.' Bernice's look suggested she was trying to tell Grace something without actually saying it.

'Do you mean people, or do you mean men?' Grace asked.

'I mean men, Grace. A few years back this guy, local driving instructor, persuaded her she needed to learn to drive; it would give her some freedom, no need to wait for buses, blah de blah. Anyway, he starts teaching her and she's getting along fine, but I can tell . . .' Bernice didn't actually tap her nose but the inference was there in the tip of her head. 'I can tell she's getting a bit fonder of the guy than the driving. He rings me up one day. She's sitting in a car outside his house and every time he goes out she's on him . . . not literally but, you know, questions about gear changes and the Highway Code. She's only gone and bought a car, got a friend to drive it there. His wife's getting jittery about the whole thing, he's getting jittery. Can I do something about it?'

'Could you?'

'Well, this was before Sol, so me and me Dad and brothers

went around and drove the car away with her in it and had a chat with her, you know, explained that it was too over the top. Off-putting. Of course she's upset, says she's in love with him and he's in love with her. My brothers are ready to go back round and punch the guy for leading her on, but then it becomes clear it's all in her head. He's just been teaching her to drive, been nice, chatty, kind.' Bernice grimaced. 'You might want to give Blond Boy the nod 'cos I'm reading the signs, Grace, reading the signs.'

Grace went back up to the office, the rational side of her brain planning how to tell Tate, the irrational side laughing its head off that Mr Free Spirit had started something that was going to come back and bite him on the bum. Probably literally in Esther's case.

She spent a few minutes getting to grips with the urgent stuff on her desk and on her computer, including sending a refund off, with a wince, to the de Janvers, but she couldn't really settle. She'd thought yesterday had been bad: a stream of people calling in to see what had happened – Joe and Corinne, the police – but this silence was worse. Too much space in which to worry about that tiny foot in that blanket. There was only one other place where she might feel at peace and gather some strength. She went through to Alistair and made up some reason for going out.

'Go on then, I'll man the fort. No, wait, before you head off, have you rung Tate with numbers for his tour yet? No. OK, leave that with me then. Well, go on, what are you waiting for? And don't be too long. I have a meeting later.'

Another phantom meeting. She agreed that she'd only be out a while and she was, just long enough to stand in the Shillingsworth and talk to the icon there. She told the mother about the other robbery, warned her to look after herself and the baby. Said, yet again, that she was sorry, so, so sorry.

On the way out she asked the girl on the front desk if they'd upped security at all and she just shrugged.

Despite that, she felt more grounded as she neared the office again, still sad but calmer, and she managed to laugh when she saw Gilbert skulking about outside. She guessed he was working out how to get inside without Bernice spotting him.

'Ah, Grace, dear girl,' he said holding out a hand to her which she took. 'Thank you for yesterday, with Violet. I don't suppose you're any the wiser about what she wanted?'

'No,' Grace lied. 'Come on, let's get you upstairs.' She made a big show of waving at Bernice as she passed the door, allowing Gilbert to sneak unseen behind her.

'So, you here for anything in particular?' she asked him when they reached the office.

'Just to make sure you're all right. Not just about the robbery but about Tate as well. I knew you two didn't see eye to eye, but this argument in the gallery . . .'

'It was about something and nothing,' she assured him, feeling ashamed for lying twice to Gilbert in such a short space of time. She moved the conversation along to other things and as they sat and chatted and Grace worked, it felt like the old days, the days before Tate.

Alistair came into the room at one point, gave a start when he saw Gilbert, and deposited a sheaf of papers on Grace's desk. 'When you've cleared up these bits and pieces, you can head off,' he said. 'Aren't you meant to be seeing Mark tonight?'

'Probably. I'm waiting for him to call.'

'Well, I'd head off early whether you hear from him or not. There's nothing that won't wait till tomorrow here and you ought to take it easy. You'll still be in shock.' Alistair was fiddling with his tie, scraping something off it with his nail. 'Besides, I'm off to a meeting myself in a minute, and I've absolutely no intention of coming back afterwards.'

'What meeting is that?' Gilbert asked.

Alistair stared at him. 'Subcommittee, looking into how we can capture more of the Asian market.'

'Has anyone suggested a big net?'

'No, definitely won't be back,' Alistair said, ignoring Gilbert. 'Might actually get to treat Emma to that meal.'

Grace presumed he must mean it this time, dangerous to use the same lie twice. But where was he off to now?

Gilbert must have been thinking the same because when Alistair had gone he said, 'Asian subcommittee meeting, my eye. He's off for a spot of afternoon sex. Here, look at this.' He was on his feet, rooting around in the filing cabinet. 'I put it away in here,' he explained, a furtive look to his blue eyes. 'It's the one place Alistair never looks.'

Gilbert pulled out a posh carrier bag, the kind made of stiff card and with cord handles. It was shocking pink and, in places, quite grubby.

'Found it in the kitchen bin last week,' he said, placing it on her desk.

'What were you doing in the bin? And why's it now in the filing cabinet?'

'It's evidence. Exhibit A. It says *Julietta's* on the side, see?'

'So, he's been buying Emma underwear. That's allowed.'

Gilbert shook his head. 'I saw him through the window, Grace. I was going to tap on it, really embarrass him. Childish, I know, but, heigh-ho, small pleasures. The thing is, dear girl, the stuff he was buying was . . . quite substantial.' Gilbert made a vague wafting motion towards his chest while scrunching up his face. 'I mean, I'm the last person who can profess to be an expert on . . . these *things*, but even I could tell it was the wrong size.' He leaned forward. 'It's all pointing one way. You were out with Emma last week – did she say anything?'

'Nothing at all. They seem very happy.'

Gilbert was obviously disappointed.

'I'll put that back in the bin, shall I?' she said, whisking the bag away from him. This was getting worse, hard for them all to ignore. Every time she remembered her conversation with Emma she felt awful. It wasn't a seat for the garden he was buying, it was expensive underwear and God knew what else. In the kitchen she pushed the bag right down to the bottom of the bin.

Gilbert read a magazine while she worked her way through the papers Alistair had left, checked on the next day's bookings and ran off some spreadsheets showing how many tours had been carried out that month, along with a breakdown of payments.

As the last spreadsheet churned out of the printer, Tate walked through the door. Today he had on a white T-shirt and a black waistcoat and black trousers with loads of zips. Over it all was his greatcoat, the collar up, and she felt the pull of that slide that had started when she first saw him.

'Yo,' he said, 'look what I've got.' From his coat he extracted a large stick. 'It's a rainmaker. Guys in that band that plays round by the tube let me have it.' He tipped it one way and then the next, and whatever was inside it did make a noise as if it were chucking it down with rain.

'Why did they give it to you?' Gilbert asked, leaping up and taking it from him.

'Helped them out – bit of a slow crowd, got them dancing.'

'Conga, was it?' Gilbert said, tipping the stick forwards and back and jiggling his hips.

'Something like.' Tate was looking at her. 'You want a go on it, Gracie?'

'No thanks.' She crossed her arms.

'OK, OK.' He stepped back to avoid a particularly enthusiastic shake Gilbert was giving the stick. 'So, how are you feeling?'

He was talking to her in the same concerned way as yesterday, suggesting that they had moved closer together out in that courtyard as he'd helped her rinse the tear gas from her eyes.

She was going to kick them apart again with a few well-aimed pieces of English politeness.

'Perfectly fine. Absolutely. Good night's sleep. Right as rain.'

'If you'll pardon the pun.' Gilbert shook the stick more violently.

'How about you? Are you well, Tate?' She gave him a toothy smile.

He wasn't looking kind any more, but mainly hurt, possibly disappointed, and there were definite overtones of being hacked off.

'So we're back to that again, are we?' he said, plonking himself down on her desk. 'Shields up, get back in your basket, Tate?'

'Now, now, children,' Gilbert said in the way that someone does when they know there is an argument in the offing. He stopped shaking the stick and laid it tentatively on Grace's desk.

The phone rang and Tate reached it before Grace could. 'Yeah, right here,' he said and passed it to her. 'It's Martin.'

'Mark,' she snapped, taking the phone from his hand. Gilbert got up and tactfully went out of the room, but Tate stayed put and just before she turned her back to him, she saw him move the vase of flowers towards the edge of the desk.

'Sorry, Grace,' Mark said, 'I was going to ring you earlier, but the day's just got away from me. I'm not going to be able to see you before I go – company's put me on an earlier flight. It's a pain. I'm really sorry, Grace. I wanted to see you, after Monday's upset, you know, but catching this flight's going to be tight as it is. I'm hacking towards Heathrow right now, and I've got to return the hire car . . .'

'It's OK, Mark. It can't be helped. Don't worry.'

'Look, it's not long till I'm back again. We'll have a rematch of last weekend. My treat.' A pause. 'I do . . . I do miss you, Grace, when I'm not with you.'

Grace hadn't even put the phone back down when Tate said forcefully, 'So, everything since the robbery just a mirage then? 'Cos I could have sworn we had a breakthrough. You shouting at me in the gallery, letting me help you, showing how upset you were about the icon. Real emotions, the real Gracie. And now, today, we're back to this.' He did an impersonation of her earlier toothy smile, which was at odds with how hard his eyes looked.

She didn't answer and he shook his head. 'Jeez, I don't get you at all. Next time perhaps I'll just leave you to flail around and stop breathing. Go for the easy life.' She could see his chest was rising and falling rapidly and then he tipped his head back as he did when he smoked, but this time it was just a breath he blew in the direction of the ceiling. 'OK, OK,' he said when he lowered his chin, 'It's as we were then. Me being a pain in the ass, you acting your butt off. But don't you ever get tired of this, Gracie?'

'It's Grace,' she said firmly, and in one sudden movement

he got off the desk and she had to grab the vase of flowers before they wobbled off the edge.

'You can come back in now, Gilb,' he shouted. 'The lovebirds have finished on the phone.' He gave the flowers a scathing look and walked over to the nearest pile of rocks and gave them a kick. Grace watched them scatter.

Gilbert didn't actually tiptoe into the room, but he moved tentatively, especially when he had to pick his way through the rocks. There was a quick check on both of them before he said, 'So, are you seeing Mark this evening, Grace? Everything . . . everything all right?'

'I'm not seeing him, but everything's fine.' She registered that she was still holding the vase and put it back in the middle of her desk. 'He's having to go back earlier than he thought.'

'That's a shame,' Gilbert said.

'No, not really.' Tate was looking at another of the pile of rocks as though he were going to kick that one too. 'See, that's how Gracie likes it. Nice and cool, so everything stays frozen in place.'

Gilbert regarded the flowers and the floor.

'I'd better go,' Grace said.

Tate jabbed at a runaway stone with the toe of his boot and then brought back his foot and aimed a kick that sent it spinning towards the skirting board and then away under her desk. It should have made him seem like a sulky boy, but it was too raw for that. 'Yeah, you run along,' he said, 'Just keep running, 'cos we gotta be going too.'

'*We*?' She looked at Gilbert.

He nodded. 'Yes, we're going to scout out some possible locations for Tate's filming. And Tate's going to introduce me to some more of his friends afterwards – other artists, musicians. We might go on to a club as well.' Gilbert had started his speech obviously worried about why Tate was kicking rocks around the office, but was now looking increasingly excited.

'Why don't you come along, Gracie?' Tate said, his tone dry. 'It'll be fun and we all know how much you enjoy fun, don't we?'

Gilbert was obviously not tuning into the negative body language both Grace and Tate were now displaying, or maybe he was trying to pour oil on troubled waters. 'Oh, yes, do come, Grace,' he said. 'It would be lovely to have your company. I can't remember the last time I went out on the town!'

Where Gilbert saw only enjoyment ahead, Grace saw danger. Or did she feel excluded again and jealous for something she didn't even want to be part of? Whatever her motive, she asked quite possibly the worst question she could.

'Does Violet know you're going out tonight, Gilbert?'

Gilbert's expression stiffened. 'Yes, she does. She's not my keeper, Grace. And I've told her to get used to me going out a lot more.' He actually sniffed. 'It's time I did some different things, and if you don't mind me saying, Tate is right: it will be fun and you might benefit from getting out of your rut once in a while too. Might stop you trying to organise other people's lives.' He was pointedly not looking at her. 'Now, if you'll excuse me, I need to go and freshen up.' He left the room in the direction of the toilet, bizarrely taking the rainmaker with him.

Grace felt as if she'd been slapped in the face. Tate's handiwork again.

She knew he was watching her as she cleared her stuff away, her throat feeling lumpy and thick. She should just leave without saying anything, but she thought once more of Gilbert out on the town. She raised her head and registered that Tate wasn't smiling.

'You will keep an eye on Gilbert, won't you?' she said. 'He's right, he doesn't go out much.'

He was looking at the rocks again but lifted his head long enough to say tersely, 'What, you think I'm gonna' pump him full of drink and drugs and let him walk home along the railroad tracks?'

'No, of course not. It's just he . . . he's . . .' She wanted to say, *he's getting really fond of you, I can tell, and it's going to end in tears*. 'He's quite a softie.' She didn't know what on earth she meant by that so she wasn't surprised to see the lacerating look Tate gave her.

'Gilb's a grown-up,' he said, pointing at the door through which Gilbert had gone. 'And you don't have to look after everyone like some freakin' mother hen. The world won't stop spinning if you take your eye off it. Things won't descend into chaos just because you're not there to keep everything under control.' He raised his chin. 'Why not just concentrate on keeping yourself buttoned up, huh? Leave other people to go grab hold of life if they want.'

She didn't rise to that, just left without even saying goodbye to Gilbert. It was only as she reached the bottom of the stairs that she realised she needed to lock up if Alistair wasn't coming back. Perhaps she should lock the pair of them in, which would keep Gilbert out of harm's way.

She pushed open the door to Far & Away.

'Still no Esther?' she asked.

'Been in for a bit and gone again. Off to the dentist's. Says she's having her teeth whitened.' Bernice's expression showed what she thought of that.

'Right, well . . . couldn't do me a favour, could you? Tate and Gilbert are still upstairs and Alistair isn't coming back.

Would you lock up for me when they've gone? I'll get the key back from you in the morning.'

Bernice held her hand out for the key and as Grace passed it over she saw there was a brochure about China on her desk. The hurt she felt at Gilbert's words, the way Tate was making her feel, the frustration with her family, suddenly a great messy plume of it escaped from under the lid she had forced on it. 'China,' she heard herself say, 'there's a coincidence. Gilbert's suddenly become quite interested in China and he'd love if you'd have a chat with him about it, but he's too shy to ask. Perhaps if you're not too busy . . . before he leaves this evening?'

Bernice was delighted. 'Course I can. Daft old devil, he only needed to ask. Let's see,' she was moving to the racks of brochures, gathering new ones into her arms. 'Yeah, here we go. And Sol's coming by in a minute – he's actually been to China. We'll both go and see him, we can lock up after.'

Grace left Bernice amassing more brochures and chattering away to herself, and outside in the street saw Sol heading her way. He had a long fencepost under his arm.

'Going jousting?' she said and Sol said gravely, 'No, it's a fencepost.' That was Sol: quiet, kind and completely humourless.

'See you,' she said and moved hurriedly along the street.

Another bit of rebellion, but this time for a good cause. And the lid was back on all that stuff with Tate, firmly back on, just like the lid on that biscuit tin.

Alistair stood on the other side of the street in a spot he was sure was out of sight if anyone looked out of the window of Far & Away or Picture London. It might still be possible to see him from the top floor, but his ex-father-in-law was away, would be away for two weeks. Something to do with an operation. Alistair hadn't asked any more details.

But something was wrong. The lights on the first floor should be off by now. Why was anyone still there? He'd told Grace to go home early. Bloody conscientious Grace.

This wasn't fair. He'd banked on this gap between Grace going home and him having to catch the train. Just an hour or two at tops, just long enough to see her again. He felt shivery and didn't know if it was from standing in the cold or sheer, bloody frustration. He glanced at his watch. If that light didn't go out in the next twenty minutes, it would be too late. Not enough time. She couldn't get herself there and then away again in that time. It would all be rushed. Tawdry.

He walked around the block for a while so people wouldn't see him loitering, but when he returned to his spot he knew it was no good. All he could do was go in, make some excuse about having to come back for some papers and stow his latest present for her in the cabinet. He took the box out of its carrier bag and placed it in his coat pocket. The carrier bag he scrunched up and put in the rubbish bin between the dry cleaner's and the bookie's. Just don't let Grace try to talk to him or he couldn't promise to be kind.

Crossing the street, he took his boiling frustration in through the main door.

CHAPTER 26

Grace was dreaming of phone calls. So many, all lined up behind each other – Mark, Aurillia, her mum, her dad. All wanting an answer.

She jolted awake. A phone *was* ringing. She reached out her hand for the bedside table but it wasn't there. More fully awake, she remembered she did not have a bedside table because she didn't have a bed. She got out from under her duvet on the sofa and fumbled around in the sitting room. Light on, eyes screwed up, she located her mobile.

'Gracie!' It was Tate's voice and she felt spooked enough hearing his voice so close when she was only wearing a large T-shirt and no knickers that she crossed her legs and held the phone away from her ear. She could still hear him. Maybe if she just cut him off . . .

Had he rung her up to shout at her about dropping Gilbert in it with Bernice? Gilbert. She saw the time on the phone. Half past one.

She put the phone back to her mouth. 'What's wrong? Is Gilbert all right?'

'Kind of. Got a bit of a situation here.' There was a cough and she could tell this was killing him. 'Gilb went for it big time. He's drunk quite a bit . . . I mean, even by British standards he's pretty full.'

'Where is he now?'

'He's lying on his side in his front yard . . . not unconscious,' he added quickly, 'just not able to get up. See, the thing is, his sister, Violet, she won't open the door and I've rung a couple of cabs, thought I could take him back to mine, but when they see him, man, they're not happy.' There was a pause. 'He's a bit of a mess.'

'Mess?'

Another cough. 'Vomit.'

'His own?'

'Course it's his own. What, you think I got him drunk and then vomited on him? Jeez, you're priceless, and you know what, he might not have started off at such a lick and kept right on throwing it down his throat if he hadn't had to put up with Bernice and Sol beforehand. They had him trapped in the corner. Only thing would have made it worse was if Esther had shown up. This a party trick of yours? Dropping me in it with Esther and now doing it with Gilbert and . . .' Grace could almost hear Tate's mind putting the brakes on as it pointed out to his mouth that Grace was their best hope of sorting this out. 'Look, scrub that. He got drunk on my watch, I'll put my hand up to it . . . But Gracie, it's freezing out here. I'm worried about him getting hypothermia.'

'Have you tried ringing Violet? She'll be too scared to open the door.'

'Tried it. Won't pick up. I was wondering . . . Gilb says she talks to you and listens to you. We need your help to get her to open up this door.'

'But you said I didn't have to look after everyone like some freakin' mother hen.'

There was a sigh. 'I did, didn't I?'

'And that the world wouldn't stop spinning if I took my eye off it.'

'Yeah, I said that too.'

Grace went for the triple. 'You assured me that things wouldn't descend into chaos just because I wasn't there to keep everything under control.'

'Remembered it word for word, huh? OK, OK. I was wrong, big time. We do need you.'

'I'll be there as soon as I can get a taxi. Make sure he's lying on his side. Tell Violet quietly through the letterbox that Grace is coming. Oh, and she'll need to put some paper down. Probably a lot of it. And try to keep Gilbert warm.'

'Thanks, Gracie. Appreciate it.'

'I'm doing this for Gilbert and Violet.'

'Kind of figured that,' he said morosely before Grace ended the call.

Violet had come to the bottom of the stairs once or twice but retreated again to the upstairs box room where she could look down on Gilbert lying in the flower bed. That lavender would never recover. The blond-haired man was on the telephone and it made the phone in the hall ring, which really wasn't nice. He kept looking up at the window and Violet kept ducking out of sight.

She needed to sit quietly and have a think about this. Her heart felt as if it would break a rib.

She wanted to let Gilbert in, but she didn't want that other one in. That Tate. She was sure that was who it was. Gilbert said he had blond hair and this man had blond hair. She scurried to her own bedroom before drifting back to the box room and peering out of the window again. Tate didn't have his coat on any more – it was draped over Gilbert – and Tate was blowing on his hands and then wrapping his arms around himself. Why did he have so many zips on his trousers?

She saw him kneel down and heard the letterbox clunk. Was he putting something through? She ran to the top of the stairs and bent down until she could see. No, nothing on the mat. He was saying something, but she couldn't make out what. Not speaking English. He was going on and on and it was getting inside her head, not making any sense. She put her hands over her ears. It was worse than the mice.

As the taxi drew up outside Gilbert and Violet's house, Grace caught a glimpse of Gilbert lying on his side in a bed of lavender. He was under Tate's coat and doing a strange bicycling action with his legs.

Tate was kneeling down talking into the letterbox and, as she paid the taxi, making a note to get the money back later, she saw him jerk his head back sharply from the letterbox.

'Holy crap,' he shouted as his hand came up to his mouth and he flung something down on the path. He staggered to his feet and stood, hand to his mouth again, looking at the letterbox.

As she walked up the path, she saw there was a stick with a claw-type mechanism lying near the door.

'Owwww,' Tate was saying, squeezing his eyes shut and then opening them. He moved his hand and she saw there was a red mark on his lip. The silver ring on his thumb shone in the light from the upstairs window and he touched his lip again tentatively. He looked frozen. 'Just attacked me with that,' he said, aiming his boot at the stick, and she found that idea so funny that she started to laugh and couldn't stop, even when she went over to Gilbert and put her hands on his legs to prevent him from cycling any further.

'Ohhhh, Grace,' Gilbert moaned and hid his face in the lavender.

'Soon have you in the warm, Gilbert,' she said, tucking Tate's coat round him more securely.

She left Gilbert and returned to the front door, but started laughing again when she saw the stick thing. She didn't even care that she might be giving too much of herself away with that laugh. She was tipping her head back, her hand over her mouth. When she'd got herself back under control, she picked up the stick and pictured Violet creeping up to the letterbox and managing to catch Tate's lip with it.

'Good shot,' she said. 'She's sixty and she gave you a thick lip.'

Tate rolled his eyes. 'Yeah, and thanks for suggesting that talking through the letterbox idea. Really worked out for me.'

'Big target to aim for, your mouth.'

'Yup, good one. Got any more? 'Cos I'm dying of laughter here. Think it might get me before the hypothermia.'

'Oh, come on, don't look so down in the mouth.' She started to laugh again and he shook his head and went to check on Gilbert.

Grace was getting cold herself now so did the special knock Violet had asked her to do when she visited and waited a few seconds. She put her mouth to the wood of the door.

'Violet, it's Grace. I know you're probably very upset by all this . . . commotion, but Gilbert needs to come in the warm or he's going to get ill. I promise you that I will keep an eye on Tate, but we will need him to help carry Gilbert into the house, so I can't send him away.' She waited and listened. 'Violet, I'm not going to say anything else. Just leave you to have a think about that. I'm going to post your stick back through the letterbox. I have my gloves on.'

She posted the stick back and heard noises on the other side of the door. A few minutes later and it opened a crack, then a little more.

'Would you like me to push the door open all the way now, Violet? Do it for you so you can just go away?'

There was a faint 'yes' and then, 'Make sure everyone stays on the paper.'

'I will.' Grace pushed the door open and saw the sheets of paper along the hall and up the stairs.

Tate managed to manoeuvre Gilbert into a sitting position

and then the two of them got him to his feet. He smelt hideous. Tate draped one of Gilbert's arms over his shoulder and Grace took the other one. Gilbert's head mainly lolled downwards except when he lifted it to go 'oomph' or 'ohhhh'. They shuffled him over the doorstep and into the hall and Tate kicked the door shut behind them.

Grace didn't much care for her head being in such close proximity to that blond one, but the smell of vomit and the strain of Gilbert's weight on her shoulder was more pressing.

'We'll take him up to the bathroom first. Is that all right, Violet?' she called and got a wobbly 'yes' back. The plan was going well; they'd even managed to turn so that, while Tate paid attention to Gilbert's legs, Grace went up a step and then another before Tate followed. But on the third step the jarring must have got to Gilbert because he threw up, heaving over and over again. And almost none of it went on the paper.

'What's happening?' Violet called.

Grace didn't want to answer because that meant breathing in the awful smell.

'Gilbert's hiccupping,' Tate said, 'but Gracie has got it all under control. You know Gracie,' and then they carried on hauling Gilbert up the stairs.

Violet sat in the kitchen holding on to the edge of the table and listening to people moving around upstairs. They were talking, running the water and flushing the toilet.

'Can I come into the kitchen?' she heard Grace ask from the doorway and when she said, 'Yes,' there Grace was. She didn't look very neat tonight. Her hair was all messed up and her face was shiny as if she'd been exercising.

'Would you mind if I got some hot water, Violet? I need to . . . wash my face. And freshen up a bit of the stairs.'

'Freshen up?' Violet felt as if she might need to get the paper bag out of the drawer and breathe into it.

'Just a few spots of mud that went from Gilbert's shoes on to the carpet. Soon lifted,' Grace said brightly and Violet considered that. Mud was a good dirt – smeary, but plants grew in it and it might be all right if there wasn't much. Grace seemed confident it would be easy to clean.

She put the kettle on and the immersion heater for later.

'You gave Tate quite a nip with your stick thing,' Grace said, nodding at it on the table.

Violet had forgotten that. 'Well, he wouldn't stop talking.' A sudden spike of fear shimmied up between her lungs. 'It wasn't a bad thing to do, was it, Grace?'

'No,' Grace said. 'I've often felt like doing it to him myself. I may have to buy something similar.'

Grace had sponged Gilbert down as well as she could and washed his hands and face, and she left the room while Tate undressed him as far as his underpants and got him into bed. Grace found a bowl in the bathroom and they put Gilbert on his side and the bowl on the floor by the bed. Working together like this made her think of Monday again – that companionship – so she went to clear up the mess on the stairs, quietly opening the front door and chucking the dirty water into the garden. She didn't give much for the chance of that lavender surviving now. She tried to smooth out the scuffed and grubby paper too, but the stuff up the stairs was as sorry-looking as the lavender.

Violet appeared in the hall just as Grace was finishing up and Grace registered for the first time that she was dressed. Had she been sitting up waiting for Gilbert to come home? Grace waited for some adverse reaction to the wet stain on the stair carpet and the lingering smell. Although if Violet really wanted to get upset about a stair carpet and a smell, she might like to pop round to Grace's flat.

Violet didn't say anything; she seemed to be listening to Tate upstairs. He was talking to Gilbert, saying, 'OK now, that's it, yup, better out than in,' which Grace took to mean Gilbert was throwing up again and Tate was holding the bowl.

'He's had too much to drink, hasn't he?' Violet said. 'My father used to do that. He'll hiccup for a while and then go to sleep. Tomorrow he will be very quiet.'

Grace thought about Gilbert's 'Highlights of the Renaissance Tour' the next day and wondered if Alistair would have to do it. Then Violet wrong-footed her completely.

'When Gilbert is asleep, you may bring Tate down. He must sit with his feet on the paper and . . . if he could remain silent. I . . . I do feel fairly anxious about his lip.'

Grace nodded but did not understand Violet's expression. It suggested that she was not particularly sorry about his lip but was occupied with some other idea that she wasn't sharing and which was making her do that horrible agitating thing with her hands.

He had lovely manners. Stayed silent to begin with and then simply said, 'Ma'am,' and tilted his head when she talked as if he was really listening to her. Very neat with his tea. Hair needed a good cut, however, and a severe brush. It had been quite amusing when she asked if he'd prefer coffee and he'd said, 'No, when in Rome.' He wasn't meant to talk, but by then she had got used to him and hadn't minded. Grace had given him an awfully strict look and that had been quite amusing too.

He would do. After all, how many real live Americans

did she have passing through the house these days? Any days? It had taken her a while to pluck up the courage, but when she asked him he told her like a shot: 'Rhode Island, ma'am,' he'd replied. She had left him in the sitting room while she went to fetch the right scrapbook.

He was looking at it now, saying such complimentary things. Telling her bits of extra information she didn't know.

She realised she hadn't said sorry about his lip. It was somewhat swollen. She offered him more tea instead. And really, it was his own fault. It would teach him not to talk through letterboxes.

Grace was not sure who had got the worst deal. She was wrapped in a blanket on a chair while Gilbert took in squeaky breaths and snorted them out again. Tate was downstairs with Violet, being force-fed tea and shown her scrapbook on Rhode Island.

Well, it had been Rhode Island when Grace had returned upstairs to watch over Gilbert, but Violet might have moved on by now.

She hoped so.

The thought of Tate sitting downstairs bored out of his mind but unable to show it made her smile. Although she should give him points for playing a blinder with Violet.

Who knew he could sit still and not yabber on so much, or be quite so deferential in the way he treated her? He got the tone exactly right. Grace shifted around in the chair to relieve the numbness spreading up one thigh. She remembered how Tate had been all 'ma'am' and polite with Felicity too. Must have taken a lot of self-control not to shrink back into the sofa when Violet advanced on him with that dustpan and brush, though. All she'd spotted was a nervous covering of his lip with his hand.

She was smiling again, but this time it seemed more like a sign of support and so she scotched it abruptly.

Yes, he obviously did have some manners hidden away in there. Bill wouldn't have been so polite. Never was. Not till the fag end of it all.

Grace looked around the bedroom. Framed prints of a couple of Titian's religious paintings; a shelf of hardback art books. A teak table with more art books. Drab walls, drab curtains, hideous bedcover. Like an old man's bedroom, or even a monastic cell. Poor Gilbert, where would he have been living if his mother hadn't died just when she had? Would Tony and he have lived in a flat? She saw him in a modern flat, with nice sleek pieces of furniture, his Titian prints next to Tony's Rothko ones.

She shifted again. Would Mark be in Kazakhstan already? She was too tired to work it out. More to the point, would she have liked him to have cut short his visit to his friends and rushed to her when he heard about the robbery? To have moved heaven and earth to see her before he left? She guessed if she had to think about that, as if answering a quiz, the answer must be no.

Gilbert was still rhythmically pulling in air and then snoring it out again. Would he be safe to leave yet? She could barely keep her eyes open. It wasn't physically possible that he had anything left in his stomach to bring up, not unless he was manufacturing the stuff in there somewhere.

She closed her eyes and opened them again to check on him. Still snoring.

If she didn't get up now, she'd fall asleep. But was it fair to leave Violet alone with Tate? Or did she mean Tate with Violet?

She heard a door open downstairs and the sound of Tate and Violet talking, their voices getting louder as if they were coming out into the hall. Violet was actually giggling.

'Goodnight,' Violet said and Grace heard footsteps on the stairs, the paper crinkling. The footsteps were too light to be Tate's and, sure enough, Violet soon appeared in the bedroom doorway.

'How is he?' she said, looking with distaste at Gilbert.

'Stabilised, I think, Violet.' Grace stood up slowly, her legs feeling stiff. 'I should probably head off now, leave you with him.'

Violet stepped back as if that thought physically hurt her. 'Leave me with him?' she said. 'No, I'm afraid not, Grace. I can't cope with anybody being ill. I mean, can you imagine if he woke up and instead of just doing that dreadful hiccupping he was actually sick?'

Grace did not have to imagine it; she could have drawn Violet some quite spectacular pictures from recent memory.

Violet was shaking her head particularly vehemently for someone who was meant to be delicate. 'Oh no, I need to go to bed if I'm to be strong enough to deal with him tomorrow.'

Grace tried not to look put out. 'Well, OK. You know best . . . but perhaps I could ask Tate to take over? I've got work tomorrow first thing and he hasn't so—'

'Dear me, no. No. No. No.' Violet was shaking her head and flapping her hands and Grace wasn't sure whether she was building up to something more unpleasant.

'No?'

'No.' Violet brought her hands together with a clap. 'I cannot be left alone with a strange man.'

'He's not strange . . . well, he's . . . I'm sure he'll be fine,

Violet. You've had a good chat with him downstairs, haven't you? And his manners . . . he has nice manners.'

Violet was obviously not listening and Grace did not like the way she was starting to claw at her own hands. 'It's all right, Violet,' she said quickly. 'I'll stay and keep an eye on Gilbert. I can go straight to work from here. You get some rest.'

Violet nodded, said a stiff, 'Goodnight, Gilbert,' and left. Grace sat back down and listened to her moving along the landing to the bathroom and then to her own bedroom. But she was also listening out for Tate, hoping that he was putting on his coat and getting ready to leave. What was it Violet had said? *I cannot be left alone with a strange man.* She was beginning to feel fairly jittery herself about that prospect. So jittery that she jumped when she heard footsteps on the stairs again, heavier this time, doing more damage to the poor paper.

Tate appeared in the doorway. He had his coat on.

'Just off?' she said.

'Off?' He came into the room and she nodded at his coat.

'No, come to take over with Gilb. You can head home. You'll get a couple hours' sleep if you're lucky. Think Vi will mind that I just turned the central heating back on?'

He seemed tired and subdued. There was no sign of the rock-kicking Tate. He lowered himself on to the edge of Gilbert's bed.

'How's he doing?'

'Been quiet for a while. Apart from the snoring. No more vomiting anyway.'

'Gonna feel like crap tomorrow.' With a movement that was almost tender, he rearranged the sheet and blanket around Gilbert's shoulders and Grace looked away. 'Should have known Gilb wouldn't have had a duvet,' he said, but when she expected him to laugh at the end of the sentence, he didn't.

She remained quiet and they sat there with only the noise of Gilbert's breathing between them and the light from the bedside table shining on them.

'You want me to call for a cab?' he said after a while, still looking at Gilbert.

'No. I'll stay for a bit longer.'

He raised his head and his expression brightened. 'You will? That's good of you, I mean, I don't expect—'

'Violet doesn't want me to go.' He looked quizzical and she took great pleasure in adding, 'She doesn't want to be left alone with a strange man.'

'Strange?' He rolled his eyes. 'She didn't think I was too strange to go through Rhode Island with her. And Maryland.

And Connecticut. And Vermont. Jeez, I thought we were gonna do the full fifty.'

'Plus Washington DC?'

'Yeah, smart ass, plus Washington D.C.' She realised that, unwittingly, she had come very close to flirting with him. She pretended that she needed to shift position in the chair and spent a bit of time flexing her foot and re-arranging her blanket.

Silence set in again, for a while, until she realised she hadn't told him it was pretty pointless them both staying. He simply replied, 'Doesn't seem right, leaving you here.'

'I'll be fine.'

'Yeah, I know, but I got Gilb into this state and you . . . well, you were the one told me to keep an eye on him. Poor Gilbert.'

'He'll be all right,' she said, trying to chivvy him out of an expression that was doing unfortunate things to her ability to resist looking at him. 'There's no lasting damage done.'

'I didn't mean just about tonight. I meant . . . about Violet. No idea about her.' He dropped his voice 'She's a sweetie, but boy . . .' He seemed unsure how to finish the sentence for a few moments until he added, 'She's complicated. Must be difficult for him?'

Grace made a neutral sounding noise, something between a 'we-ll' and an 'umm'.

'And you know anything about this Tony guy? Gilb mentioned him a lot, 'specially later on – well, while he could still speak. What's that all about?'

Grace tried the same neutral sound again and Tate watched her for a while. She expected that he was going to criticise her again for being too buttoned up, but he was smiling and she couldn't help looking into his eyes. Warm, reaching out for her.

'So . . . Tony?' he prompted.

'You'd have to ask Gilbert about that.'

He was still smiling. 'See, that's what I like about you, Gracie. You're still looking out for Gilb. Still watching his back. Covering his ass.'

Gilbert shifted in the bed and muttered something, and Grace had the impression it might have been 'if you'll pardon the pun.'

'Yeah. Loyalty's good,' Tate went on. 'And keeping a secret. Well,' he shot her a look, 'keeping other people's secrets.'

'There really is no need for you to stay any longer.'

He nodded slowly. 'Don't blame you for trying to get rid of me. Not gonna make you like me any better this, is it?'

When she didn't answer, he said, 'I'm taking that as a no,' and went quiet.

The longer they sat there, the silence around them, everything dark outside the pool of light, the more she felt the intimacy of this shared watch, as if they were parents caring for a sick child.

She was worrying away at this feeling when he surprised her by saying, 'Fliss, she reminds me of someone else.'

Grace tried to read his face. It looked innocent enough. 'Really?' she said, 'I thought she was a one-off.'

'Nope, got one just like her at home.' He looked slightly sheepish. 'My mom. Her and Fliss could have been separated at birth. My mom might even be more out there.'

Grace sifted through that new piece of information and decided that another noncommittal noise would be the safest response.

'Not gonna say anything, huh? Probably best – don't know what to say about her myself a lot of the time.' He was scrunching up strands of his hair with one hand as he talked. 'She's a free spirit, Mom.'

Despite determining not to ask any questions, Grace said, 'Is she an artist too?'

Tate's grin looked like an apology. 'Kind of. Bit like my cousin George . . . you remember, the actor? Mom tries hard, got the temperament, but . . . Parents, eh?' He stopped messing with his hair and did a theatrical palms-up shrug. 'What can you do?'

'And your dad?'

'My dad grows apples and pumpkins.'

She was so surprised that she couldn't immediately respond to that. She tried to imagine Tate surrounded by red, shiny apples and orange pumpkins but could only see him smashing them with a hammer and getting someone to film it.

'Sounds idyllic,' she said off the top of her head, but knew immediately that she'd caused him pain.

'Yeah, it was,' he said, looking sadly at Gilbert but, from the expression on his face, seeing something else entirely. 'Yeah, I remember it was. Still is, whenever I go back. See Dad. The rest of them. I mean, I don't see myself as an apple farmer, but maybe when I'm older. Bit of land . . .'

Grace realised she was now the one trying to fit the pieces together in the jigsaw. Then she reminded herself that she didn't care about Tate, his mother, his father or their bloody apples.

She heard Tate sigh. 'You're not gonna ask me what happened, are you? Is that 'cos you're being polite, being English? Or you're keeping me at arm's length again?' She opened her mouth to deny both, but he carried on, 'Mom hooked up with a younger guy when I was ten. Left my dad and took me off to Chicago along with her.' Tate regarded his boot. 'Her and Dad never had much in common, except us kids. Oh, and a love of nature . . . although he was always kind of taming it while she was trying to be at one with it.'

'Kids?'

'Yup. I'm the runt of the litter. Left my sisters and brothers behind on the farm.' When he saw Grace's shocked expression he shrugged. 'Says she could tell I was going to be an artist, not like the others who were gonna take after Dad. Says she was saving my spirit as much as hers.' He pulled a face. 'Drama junkie, Mom. Lovely, but a drama junkie.'

'But your father: he didn't just let her go, did he? With you?' They were questions Grace had to get out there, although she wasn't sure he would answer. He was sorting out Gilbert's bedding again, but with a smoothing sweep of his hand over the blanket, he said, matter-of-factly, 'Well, to be truthful I think it was a relief to him.'

'I can see he might have felt that about *her* leaving, if they had nothing left in common, but about *you*?'

'I was talking about me,' he said, not meeting her gaze. 'He didn't know what to do with me. I stood out. I was crap at sports. I answered him back. I was starting to wear weird clothes.' Tate stood up. 'Still, we get on OK now when I go visit. And, hey, my new dads were cool. All of them. No harm done. You wanna coffee?'

Why had he told her this? Was it another of his attempts to build a connection between the two of them that he could nip across? She couldn't decide – the way he was getting himself to the door, head down, not making a clean movement of opening it wider, didn't suggest that. It suggested he was embarrassed.

He stopped on the threshold and said, out to the landing, 'Just thought back over what I said . . . you know, I didn't mean Fliss was *exactly* like Mom. I don't want you to think I'm telling you she's gonna do something crazy with that James guy.'

'Jay.'

'Yeah, Jay.'

'Why did you tell me then?' It came out sharper than she intended, probably because she knew her mother had already done something crazy with Jay.

'Because I trust you,' he said, still not turning around.

'And you're hoping I'll do the same with you? Trust you back. Tell you something more about me?'

'Jeez,' he said softly, 'give me a break here, Gracie.' He turned to face her, his eyes and his hair, without the light on them, looking washed of any life. 'Look, I'm miles from home, it's the middle of the night, I've just got an old guy blitzed so bad he's chucked up everything he's ever eaten . . . I just felt the need, OK?'

He exited sharply after that, leaving her to try to think of nothing, but she kept imagining him as a boy, knowing that his dad wouldn't be coming to Chicago to get him back, having to get used to a new life and a new man. A few new men by the sound of it.

And what about his brothers and sisters? Did he miss them when he left? Did they miss him? And he still told people he was from Rhode Island. Not Chicago . . .

She brought her hand down on the arm of the chair. 'Damn, he's made me feel sorry for him now,' she said out loud, and Gilbert moved his head from left to right a few times and his eyelids fluttered before he went right under again.

She waited for Tate to come back upstairs with the coffee. And waited. Then she went downstairs and found him asleep on the sofa, his coat wrapped around him. Of course he'd be asleep on the sofa. She watched him from the doorway, saw how his chest rose and fell, and knew that if she had to draw a picture of the kind of man who she could fall for, it would be him. And if she had to draw a picture of the kind of man she should never fall for again, it would be him too.

It was the first time she had allowed herself to think that objectively and it hit her as if it was something physical. He was the edge and she was tumbling over it again.

Was all that brashness, all that confidence, something he'd hoisted on to himself when he was a boy?

When she went upstairs again, she left the door of Gilbert's room open and listened out for Tate's footsteps with a sense of anticipation. It was frightening, but hadn't it been inevitable, this pull towards him? It was going to end badly, she knew that, just as she had known that Gilbert's trip out on the town would end badly. But what could she do faced with that body and that enthusiasm, and now that hint that underneath there was more substance?

She registered that it was four o'clock in the morning, but the next time she was aware of being awake, it was six and she was feeling frowsy and crunched up, and if she didn't shift she was going to be late for work. Gilbert was on his side, still snoring.

She struggled to free herself from the blanket and saw a note fall from it to the carpet: *Money on side for the cab last night. Thanks again for coming to the rescue. More than I deserved. PS You ought to sleep more often. It suits you.*

She checked on Gilbert one last time before executing a quick and silent face wash in the bathroom, but this morning the tiles appeared too much like the ones in the bathroom in San Sebastián so she got out of there as quickly as she could. She tiptoed past Violet's bedroom door. Everything was still and neat, so unlike her own flat at the moment, but it felt dead too, the kind of place where the ticking of the clock was the most exciting thing that ever happened. Poor Gilbert. On duty here for the rest of Violet's life.

A board creaked under her foot.

'Goodbye, Grace,' Violet said from the darkness of her room. 'Please tell Tate, before he comes again, to get his hair cut.'

CHAPTER 27

Grace knew her descent down the slide had speeded up when, after going down her paint-splattered stairs on her way out to work, she found herself back in the kitchen moving the butter dish so that the china cow on top could see out of the window properly. Lining the cutlery up neatly, checking the plates were back in the cupboard in the right order, all those things she regularly did before going to work. But worrying whether a piece of china had a good view?

Definitely a bad sign, although perhaps she should cut herself some slack. She had barely slept, just had a shower in cold water as her father had used all the hot for his bath, and undergone another interrogation about the position of the blinds in the gallery as 'the gang' felt they could have been used to transmit a signal. A phone call from Serafina, during which her father just kept saying, 'Uh-hmm,' was the only reason she had managed to escape down the stairs at all.

And why was she bothering with what the cow could see anyway, when, knowing her father's clumsiness, it would soon be getting a better view of the inside of the bin? There it could make friends with the various glasses, bowls and plates he'd managed to smash over the past few days. She was not sure how he'd managed to work loose the hour hand on the clock; he'd said he was demonstrating how the icon robbery was a work of split-second timing. That the clock in her flat had now stopped seemed to underline that nothing would ever change from here on – she was stuck with her father forever.

At work, her office was beginning to look as messy as her flat. There were rocks scattered all across the floor and an assortment of plastic food had been arranged along the window sills – outsized prawns, bowls of noodles, a spring roll and some wontons. She assumed Tate had been through the bins of some Asian restaurant that had tired of displaying these solid representations of their fare in the window. Perhaps he had spent the time while Bernice and Sol were cornering Gilbert arranging them in a way that probably only made sense to him.

In the kitchen she had stepped back, surprised by a shape leaning against the cabinets, but when she turned on the light she saw that it was the rainmaker in a plastic poncho.

Alistair arrived, still in a rage about returning to the office the day before and finding she had given the key to Bernice to lock up. She suspected, however, that what he was really put out about was returning to the office to find people still in it. While he was haranguing her, he kept glancing at Tate's chair and the rocks, the scarlet wall and the plastic food, and she knew he was angry about those too, but wouldn't admit it.

She let him rage and bluster and wondered when would be a good time to tell him that Gilbert might not be able to do his tour today. Never, probably.

Her punishment seemed to be filing a load of crumpled bits of paper. Still, at least being busy might stop her falling asleep. Thinking about sleep allowed Tate and particularly that PS to slip into her mind. *You should sleep more. It suits you.* Had he sat and watched her before he went home? Her stomach did a shimmy at the idea. She tried to offset that by dwelling on how irresponsible he had been with Gilbert. Her stomach was still shimmying.

Forget last night, Grace. Read the signs. Dad decamping to your flat, Mum taking up with Jay, Gilbert getting drunk, the arty-fartification of the office. Things are slipping away from you.

She had barely smoothed out the first of the pieces of paper Alistair had given her when the phone rang and she heard the voice of a man whose vocal chords had been washed in vomit repeatedly the night before.

'How are you feeling, Gilbert?' she said softly.

'As if I have been exhumed,' he croaked back. 'I think, dear girl, you had better put me through to Alistair. I can barely raise my head, let alone do a tour. Oh, and Grace, thank you for coming round last night . . . so grateful and so . . . ashamed, after what I said to you in the office . . .'

She imagined him hunched over the phone with Violet listening in, even the sound of his own voice ricocheting through his head.

'Forget it, Gilbert, you've suffered enough.'

Alistair stalked back into Grace's office when he had talked to Gilbert, looking florid and sulky, and said he didn't suppose Grace could do Gilbert's tour for him? When she said she had one of her own at twelve and another at 3.30, he went back into his room, saying, 'Damn, damn, damn.' The outside door slamming a couple of minutes later was him leaving, she supposed. More weirdness.

Grace went back to smoothing and filing. If she got a move on and the phones didn't ring too much, she could get it done before she went out. She hauled out a file, put it all in order and started on another. Perhaps she wasn't sliding; if she hemmed herself in with enough routine and hard work she could hang on. If she didn't think about Tate, she could definitely win this battle.

She heard the outside door open and someone barge into reception and throw themselves on the sofa. There was sobbing, so it definitely wasn't Tate. She found her mother face down, her shoulders heaving. She was a small hillock of wobbly tweed.

'Graaaaaace,' she wailed, raising her chin off the sofa to do it. 'Graaaaace, Graaaccce, Graaaaace.'

Grace got down on her knees and patted her mother's back and the wailing gradually subsided into sniffing and the odd sob. Eventually Grace persuaded her mother to sit up. It was a mistake: now it was possible to see her face, bloated and ruddy, devoid of any of her usual make-up. Someone had put a hand-whisk in her hair and turned it to full power.

'Take some deep breaths,' Grace said, 'have a go at telling me what's wrong.'

'I . . . I . . .' Felicity was stuck in a cycle of gulps and juddering breaths that had to run its course before she could speak. Grace went to fetch some tissues from her bag. Eventually her mother managed to say, 'He's taken the money, Grace. Taken the money and buggered off.'

'Jay?'

Intense nodding. More sobbing.

'Taken? But how, Mum? Taken what? You haven't even applied for your bank loan—'

'I had savings,' her mother said tersely. 'I'm not a complete idiot. I've always had money for an emergency. Running-away money, just in case. A bit skimmed off the family allowance when you were all growing up, a couple of quid here and there. It's mounted up. I've been careful.' The thought of how careful she had once been obviously collided with the knowledge of how stupid she was now and produced a fresh bout of sobbing. It allowed Grace to go over what her mother had just said while fighting the urge to say, *I told you he was a bad bet.*

'How much, Mum?' she asked when Felicity's sobbing allowed it.

'Three thousand pounds.'

On further questioning, Grace discovered that Jay had not so much taken the money as been given it. They'd decided, or he had, that they needed to publicise the company, 'get a buzz going' before it opened. No good waiting for the loan application to be done. But Felicity hadn't seen him since he had gone off to talk to one of his mates about some cheap flyers. The mate hadn't seen him either. Neither had his mother. When Felicity had gone to the gym where he worked, the lad on the desk said he'd handed in his notice a couple of days before.

And so had the woman who ran the Zumba classes. Funny, that.

Recounting the story sent Felicity off again and Grace had to wait to say, 'It doesn't matter, Mum. I know losing the money is hard, but look at it this way: if the company had been up and running, he could have siphoned off more than a few thousand pounds. And think of what could have happened if it was a bank loan he was dipping into – you'd have been left to pay back the bank.'

Felicity was giving her eyes a good wipe and with one particularly ferocious one she turned on Grace. 'What, you think I'm crying about the money? That's typical of you Grace. It's this I'm crying about.' She thumped her chest and Grace stood up quickly. Was it the headlong rush upwards that made her feel dizzy or the understanding that whatever had happened with Jay was more serious than a bit of groping? That more than her mother's breasts had been involved? Yes, that was definitely her heart she'd thumped.

'So . . . what Dad saw – it was more than . . . ?' She couldn't bear to voice it.

'We never had sex: our relationship was purer than that.' Felicity was struggling up off the sofa. 'And what your Dad caught us doing . . . it was only that once. Jay worshipped me. Called me a goddess, a wise goddess.'

Grace was tempted to observe that letting a man feel your breasts in return for three thousand pounds was not the action of anyone with any kind of brain cells, but it was too cruel and her mother looked too crushed. Impossible to get through that thick shell of self-delusion anyway.

'Oh, Mum,' was her only comment, but after a cup of tea, during which neither of them spoke, she did say, more forcefully, 'I'm sorry about what happened, Mum, but I think you have to face facts: Jay's gone, the money's gone and if you're not careful, your marriage is going to be gone too.' She did not add that her dad, currently obsessed with the robbery, was giving every appearance of a man who had forgotten he had a wife.

Felicity took Grace's speech more or less on the chin, but there was more sobbing and eye-wiping and falling on Grace's neck before she headed home to 'realign her emotions'.

Grace went back to her filing, knowing for certain that some kind of domino effect was sending all the certainties of her life falling one after the other. Felicity had always been an outrageous flirt, always too touchy-feely, but was this her first outing into really being unfaithful with her heart as well as her body? Or had it happened before, and her dad just put up with it because it was the oil that greased the wheels of their marriage?

She should try to look on it as a timely example of the things that happened when you let passion run away with you. Not that she really needed a new lesson on that.

She heard a noise behind her and turned.

'Is Tate in yet?'

Seeing Esther in her office was like finding a jellyfish up a mountain. It just shouldn't happen. Grace wasn't even certain that Esther knew how to climb stairs.

'I'm afraid he isn't,' she said.

'When *will* he be in then?' Esther was almost truculent; that mouth was getting a lot of pulling about.

'Well, probably later, just to check on names and numbers for his tour.'

'How much later?'

'I don't know.'

'I'll wait then.' The mouth was pouting; the bottom was on Tate's chair.

'You'll wait? But doesn't Bernice need you downstairs?'

'Probably.' Esther folded her arms.

For once the kettle came to Grace's rescue and she used the need to fill it as an excuse to leave the room. In Alistair's office, she phoned Bernice.

'How does she look?' Bernice said.

'Dug in.'

'I'll be right up.'

Grace feared that there might be a bit of a scene when Bernice came to round up Esther, but Bernice did it very well, bustling up with a brochure, saying she couldn't understand the surcharges and Esther had a better brain for these things than her.

Esther unpeeled herself from Tate's chair, but as she left she reached into her pocket and got out a long white envelope. She put it on Grace's desk.

'Give this to Tate,' she said.

Grace eyed the envelope with unease and then tried to ignore it. She should get back to worrying about Felicity. She didn't look anywhere near to throwing herself on her husband's mercy. What to do? She was sure if she opened up her emails there would be another battalion of crap from her sisters, one step behind as usual and some way off the shores of planet normal. She ought to tell them this latest development, but her hands did not go to her keyboard.

A month ago, perhaps, she would have worked out a sensible, objective solution. Now, her head seemed too full of everything else to cut a way through. She heard the main door open and close and sensed it was Tate before he appeared. Suddenly she didn't know how to be with him, how to act or what to say.

'Hi,' she tried.

'Yeah, hi,' he said back. He went to his chair and pushed it towards her desk, but he didn't bring it round and bump into her this time.

'Bit of a night last night, huh?' he said gently. 'I'm really sorry, you know, for the whole calling-you-out thing.' She wondered if he was going to put his hand on her arm or touch her in some way. She sensed he wanted to and she wondered what she would do if he did.

'Forget it,' she said.

He was pressing his lips together as if thinking about what to say next.

'I . . . I rang Gilb just now.' He screwed up his eyes. 'Didn't sound so good. You heard from him?'

'Yes. Alistair's doing his tour. I don't think Gilbert told him it was a hangover, so you might not want to mention it if your paths cross at any point today.'

He didn't answer. There was still a dark red mark on his top lip. She saw him rest his elbows on the desk, lower his head to his hands and then rub them up and down his face as if he was exhausted. Had he got any sleep before work at all?

He raised his head. 'Al's pretty hacked off, right? You get it in the neck?'

She wanted to lean across and gently touch the red mark

on his lip. What would it feel like? What would his lips feel like? She stopped looking at his lips and looked at his eyes instead.

'Alistair's permanently hacked off these days. Don't worry. I'll . . . I'll just run off a list of the clients on your tour this afternoon.' She was operating on autopilot now, a last desperate attempt to put normality and order between the two of them.

He nodded, said 'thanks' and rubbed his face one more time before removing his elbows from her desk and sitting back. Was he letting her take her time? Come to him?

They both watched the sheet of names chug out of the printer and when it had stopped, he gave her one of his megawatt smiles and said, 'Safe pair of hands, Gracie.'

She sat quietly, not knowing what to do with those hands, while he sat and studied the names on the paper, and then slowly he leaned forward. She knew this time he was going to take her hand and something about his mouth told her he was going to put it to his lips. He was going to go for it this time and if she hadn't seen that flash of silver on his thumb just as he started to move, she would have lost it then, thrown everything up in the air and waited for lightening to strike again. But once she'd seen it, something in her brain hit reverse and she remembered the envelope on the desk.

'This is for you,' she said, picking it up and holding it out so that his hand collided with it.

'Love letter?' he said with a shy smile and took it from her.

'It's from Esther.' It was as if she'd thrown a cup of cold water in his face.

'Esther,' he repeated. He turned the envelope over and over before ripping it open. Grace tried not to watch, but her curiosity won out.

'Jeez, Esther,' he said, pulling out a paper wallet. He scrunched the torn envelope up with one hand and dropped it on the desk, opening the wallet as if it might explode. He extracted what was obviously a plane ticket and made a groaning noise. The ticket went on the desk and his head went in his hands again, his fingers covering his eyes. 'Esther, Esther, Esther,' he was saying softly.

Grace picked up the ticket. *London Heathrow to Jorge Chávez International Airport, Lima.*

'Oh God. She must have gone to a different travel agent's to organise this for you.' She put the ticket back in the wallet. It was another sign of chaos. 'You need to talk to her. Bernice says she's . . . well, she forms attachments. She's done it before.' He dropped his hands from his eyes and stared at her as if that were the worst news she could have given him.

'You always known that?' he asked.

'Only found out yesterday.'

'The day I told you to stop clucking over everyone like a mother hen?' He seemed angry with himself.

'Well, yes . . .'

His response was a wry, sour noise. 'Me and my big mouth.' When Esther had cornered him before, he had seemed younger, more vulnerable. Now he looked ancient.

'Gotta learn to keep it shut. But hell, I don't get it. I mean, I never did anything to make her think . . . I was just being friendly, waking her up a bit.' He stared sadly at the ticket. 'How much has she spent on this?'

He seemed to have retreated inside himself and Grace did not know what she wanted to say to him or do for him, so she stood up and hoped that just keeping busy would kick-start her brain. She finished her filing, gave reception a tidy up and then came back and put on her coat. Tate got up slowly.

'Not gonna say "I told you so"?'

'I'll walk down with you. I need to lock up.' A thousand tiny movements to stop herself putting her arms around him.

At the bottom of the stairs, he stopped. 'I read this all wrong, loused up again. Need your help here, Gracie. You got any advice?' He was looking towards the door of Far & Away as if it were an undertaker's.

She wanted to put her hand on his back and say it would be all right.

'I'd suggest asking to talk to her out here,' she said gently. 'That way you won't embarrass her in front of Bernice, but Bernice will be close if you need her. Esther is bound to be upset.' His eyes widened at that. 'But you have to be honest, Tate. Not brutally honest, but honest enough that you don't leave her any room to think there's hope. Be kind, but honest.'

He nodded and before she knew it she had placed her palm on his face. 'Be brave,' she said and didn't wait to see his expression. She walked very quickly away and didn't look back.

After two hours at the Wallace Collection, talking about Marie Antoinette and the world of French painting but thinking about her mum and dad, about Gilbert and Esther, and most resolutely trying not to think about how Tate's skin had felt under her hand, Grace grabbed some lunch and then went to the Shillingsworth. She glanced out into the courtyard at the strange bent-over unicorn–man figure before going to get her fill of the icon. She wished they'd put an attendant permanently in the room. Surely they could see it needed protecting?

She sat and looked at it for a while but found it hard to

meet the eyes of the mother or the baby. Hadn't Grace promised that it would never happen again? Yet here she was poised to throw all her self-control away again. She moved nearer to the icon, hoping to draw some strength from it. If she concentrated hard enough, would she have the willpower to turn her back on Tate?

As she walked towards the entrance to meet her group, she told herself she felt more resolute, but there was a tinny, hollow sound to it.

Her group today was small – a husband and wife from Lancashire and two ladies from Scotland. They set off round the eclectic mix of paintings, Grace trying to bring some cohesion to 'Big Ideas in Twentieth-Century Art' but finding it hard, like wading through thick mud. Images of her mother crying and the paint on the stair carpet kept tumbling into her brain, along with pictures of Esther patting her mouth and Tate sitting quietly, listening to Violet and calling her 'ma'am'. She jolted back to her group – at least *they* were still paying attention.

'So, in this painting,' she said 'would anyone like to show us how Nash achieved such a strong sense of claustrophobia?'

'By lying. By pretending, pretending, pretending. Walking around like butter wouldn't melt in your mouth . . . but look at you, look at you!'

That didn't seem any kind of answer to Grace until she recognised the voice. Esther. Esther standing, hands balled into fists, eyes wide. 'How . . . how could you, Grace? Right under my nose? He told me. You and him. Sleeping together.'

The couple from Lancashire looked at the women from Scotland and, as if in some unspoken agreement, they all moved away from Esther. Grace, on the other hand, felt as if she were frozen. *You and him. Sleeping together?*

'We were going to go to South America,' Esther cried out and Grace came back to life and tried to go to her, talk softly to her, but she got batted away.

'Esther, please,' she tried, 'come on, I know you're upset. Let's go and find Bernice, let's take you outside.'

'Go to hell, you whore!' Esther shouted and charged out of the room.

The group watched Esther go and then turned back to Grace. She felt they expected her to say something. She wasn't sure she could: her legs were trembling and she didn't know if it was just adrenalin, worry about where Esther might be headed or anger, complete skull-crushing anger, about what Tate had said in his letting-Esther-down-gently-but-firmly speech. The idiot. He was an idiot – how could she have been tempted to think anything else? When she saw him next she was going to . . .

She stopped thinking because she could hear him. Oh God, she had his voice in her head.

'Um,' the man from Lancashire said, 'do you think we could get on—'

'Shh,' Grace held up her finger. It was definitely Tate's voice getting closer.

'Now, look,' the Lancashire accent had become more strident, but it didn't matter; her tour group didn't matter, because there was Tate coming into the room, his group following behind him. Of course he was. Why wouldn't he be? This was on one of his routes. Maybe he'd even gone out of his way to come here because he knew she'd be here. To get under her skin a bit more.

He looked delighted to see her and his expression got down into her chest, but it didn't change a thing – she was still going to kill him.

'You complete and utter fuckwit!' she screamed the length of the room, and she knew it was too late. However hard she tried to fight him, it didn't matter anyway. He'd pushed her down the slide and now nothing could stop her descent. Everything was falling away from her, as she hurtled downwards without a brake.

Tate stopped smiling and his tour group stopped moving.

'Gracie, what's wrong?' he said, frowning. 'What did I do this time?'

'Where would you like me to start?' She was still screaming. 'Did you think it was funny? Were you trying to create some kind of "happening"? What the hell did you tell Esther?'

'Esther?' he said, looking around, worried. 'You've seen her? What did she say?'

'All kinds of things,' the man from Lancashire confirmed, tutting.

'You all right?' Tate said coming towards her, 'She didn't upset you? Hell, I better get on the phone to Bernice.' He was hunting in the pocket of his stupid coat. 'I thought Esther was cool about it. She seemed to take it OK.'

She got right up close to him so quickly he stopped hunting around in his pocket and seemed a bit taken aback.

'She did not take it OK,' Grace said, baring her teeth at him. 'She seemed to think that you and I were sleeping together.' Tate went a bit pink and that annoyed her even more, so she poked him hard with a finger and one of his group took a photograph of her.

'Put the camera away, Flora,' Tate said, 'this isn't part of the tour.'

Grace threw her head back and laughed like a hyena at that, unconcerned at the way she was the focus of everyone's attention. She didn't even care that the sound of feet moving quickly from outside the room suggested attendants were on their way.

'Priceless, priceless,' she crowed, 'they think it's art! That just about bloody sums up what you've taught them. What they've seen. Why not take them down the park so they can watch dogs sniffing round each other's—'

'OK, that's enough,' Tate said, catching hold of one of her arms. 'Show over, guys. Full refunds later. Just have a stroll round by yourselves while my colleague and I have a word.'

An attendant came up to them. 'You'll have to go outside,' and Tate said, 'Great idea,' and he was behind Grace, pushing her forward with his body, still holding on to her arm as they headed for the sliding doors to the courtyard.

She tried to struggle free, saying, 'I'm not going out there,' but one moment they were on the gallery side of the doors, the next on the courtyard side.

'Just calm down,' Tate said, letting go of her and sliding the door shut behind him. 'You're gonna get us banned from every gallery in London.'

'*I'm* going to get us banned? You've got a nerve. Everything was all right till you came here. Everything was fine.'

'You sure about that, Gracie?'

'Shut up!' She appeared to have moved on to screeching now. 'Shut up. You're always digging and prying and trying to work out an angle on me. This isn't about me. What did you tell Esther?'

She saw him straighten up and lower his chin. He stared her straight in the eye. 'I said I was sorry she believed I liked her more than a friend would like a friend. I apologised that I'd given her the wrong idea . . . that it wasn't her fault, that I had a bad habit of getting people all fired up.' He paused. 'I told her she was a nice woman but there couldn't be anything between us because I really, really liked someone else.'

'Not listening. Not listening,' she said putting her hands over her ears.

'Then I'll have to shout.' He was coming towards her and she could hear him clearly. 'I told her it was more than liking; I'd fallen hard, out of the blue, hit by a truck.'

Grace skittered backwards, took her hands from her ears. 'Shut up,' she screamed.

'Nope.' He was still coming forward. 'Didn't say your name, though. Esther must have worked it out.' His smile slowly returned. 'Everyone could work it out, Gracie. And honey, it was you who told me to leave no room for her to hope, so I told her we'd been lovers for a while.'

He must have heard her sharp intake of breath. He stopped walking and the look he was giving her reached right down inside her and shook her apart. 'Oh, come on,

Gracie. All I did was jump the gun, fast forward to what I wanted to happen. Jeez, you must know that and you're driving me mad 'cos I sense you want it too. You want it but you're too scared to say it.' He tilted his head. 'So, you gonna look me in the face and say I'm wrong?'

'You're wrong,' she wailed at him but she couldn't look him in the face to say it and he laughed.

'Told you,' he said and then she did look at him and he had a determined expression on his face. She started to move again, and so did he. 'Stay away from me. You're horrible!' she shouted. 'Cocky, obnoxious, a show-off, a charmer, lazy, untrustworthy—'

'Get it all out, Gracie,' he said, not looking the least bit bothered, ''Cos I don't think you're talking about me there? Sure that's not some other guy?'

She glanced down because her feet felt wet and for a second she feared she was on the beach, but it was too cold for that.

'No, not another guy. You. Wreaking havoc and walking away from it.'

He was in front of her, had his hands on her arms again, trying to pull her towards him. 'Nope, that's not me. Feels like you're making me pick up the bill for what some other guy's done to you.'

She jerked free of him, her anger gone now and in its

place a sickly panic. 'You said "bill".' She was flapping her hands about and couldn't seem to make them behave. 'Why did you say "bill"? "Picking up the bill"? Americans don't say "bill" – they say "check".'

'Come here, stop it . . . look, I have no idea what . . . hey, come back . . . whoa there! Gracie, stop. Don't . . .'

In her rush to get away from him, she had forgotten about the slowly turning unicorn and she stepped back into it and felt a great smack on the back of her head that reverberated down her neck and into her shoulders. She saw Tate reach for her and she was down on the ground.

She wasn't aware of pain, just that her back felt wet, and her first humiliating thought was that she had wee'd herself. But as she struggled to sit up and put her hand on her head, that was wet too. She held up her hand. Red water.

'Oh God, not again,' she said, 'not again. You see, you see . . . this is what happens. I get carried away, let passion take over and people get hurt. Look at that figure. Look, it's me, bent over in that bathroom . . .'

'Shush, shush.' Tate was down on his knees, unwinding the scarf from around his neck, pulling her into his shoulder. She felt him pressing on the back of her head. 'It's OK, OK, you get a lot of blood with head wounds. Always look worse than they are. Shush, it's going be fine.'

His face didn't look like he was one hundred per cent sure of what he was saying and then she felt him jump as something clunked against the glass of the door, making it tremble. 'What the . . . ?' Tate started and she turned and saw people putting their hands to their mouths, stumbling about, and attendants running. She recognised the man from Lancashire pulling open the sliding door, his eyes streaming. An alarm started to wail, bouncing off the walls of the courtyard.

'It's happening again, isn't it?' Grace said, struggling to get up. 'I need to get her out of there.' She wasn't moving. Tate was holding on to her jacket.

'Gracie, you can't go in there,' he said, 'it's full of tear gas and whoever's doing this isn't gonna think twice about swatting you. Out here's the safest place. I've got you. I've got you.'

Grace looked at him with a great clump of her jacket in his fist and that green, penetrating gaze skewering its way through her heart and knew he had, indeed, got her.

CHAPTER 28

It seemed to Grace that all she'd done since the second robbery was sit on a variety of chairs.

First there had been the chairs in A & E where she and Tate had sat side by side and he'd held her hand tightly. Her head hurt and so did her neck, but neither of them pained her as deeply as the realisation that another icon had gone and now she had no one left who really understood. There were scores of other icons in London, but none like those two. She'd bonded with them and now they were lost.

Tate asked her now and again if her vision was all right? Was she feeling sick? Could he get her anything? But mostly he kept quiet; uncharacteristically quiet, as if today had been too much even for him. They didn't talk about what he'd said to her in the courtyard or what she'd said back to him, and now, with the way her head and neck were hurting and the shock of the icon being ripped away from her, she wasn't completely sure any of those words had been spoken out loud.

Tate got up at one point and said he'd better ring Alistair. He came back, screwed up his face and said, 'Not a happy man,' and was silent again. The only time he seemed himself was when the nurse asked her how the accident had happened and she said she'd been hit by a unicorn.

'That's gonna really make them think you've got concussion,' he said. 'Better say it was half-unicorn, half-man.'

She didn't have to have stitches or stay in overnight, but they did say someone needed to keep an eye on her for the next twenty-four hours. She got her mobile out sharpish after that and rang her father to come and collect her. Tate waited with her till he arrived, called her dad 'sir' and then went. She watched him go. He wasn't walking like he normally walked. It was as if his boots had become too heavy for him.

After that, she sat on another chair in her flat while her father subtly tried to ask her questions about the robbery without appearing to. 'So, those attendants in the gallery, Grace, tough day for them. You know any of them?' and 'Any blinds you noticed?'

When she started to feel sick, she knew it wasn't the bang on the head – it was his constant badgering and the lingering paint and white spirit fumes.

Only threatening to get her mother to come over made him back off, and she was left to lie on the sofa and field a variety of telephone calls from people who'd just heard the news. In the end she turned her mobile off, put the duvet over her head and thought about the icon. When she had exhausted herself, she slept. Whether her father did check on her during the night or it was just luck she was alive in the morning, she would never know.

The next day she sat on a chair in the police station while she made a witness statement. The police would have come to the house, but Grace felt that if they saw any of her father's extensive diagrams and notes about the earlier robbery at the Paddwick Gallery, they would both be arrested on the spot. And if they'd looked under her bed . . .

The young police officer who talked to Grace was extremely interested in the fact that she and Tate had been present at the previous robbery and had been observed arguing before that one too. He was careful what he said, but she could sense his agitation – as if he felt he was on to something important. She asked him if he'd already interviewed Tate, but he said he couldn't discuss that.

'I did get injured,' she pointed out.

'We have no witnesses to how that happened, other than Mr Jefferson,' he replied.

She decided it was best, from then on, to be more circumspect about what she said. When she emerged from the room, her father was outside chatting to some of the officers he knew and she hoped to God he wasn't sharing his theories about signalling via gallery blinds.

After that it was back to the sofa. At some point her mother *did* arrive and, for a large part of the visit, Grace pretended to be asleep.

Now it was Monday morning, and although Alistair had said she didn't have to come into work, she wanted to. It hadn't taken long for her to wish she'd stayed at home. She was sitting on a chair in Alistair's office and Gilbert had been summoned to sit on another one, and the fact that Alistair had changed his tactics and was not huffing and puffing while planted in the middle of her office floor told her that this was going to be extremely unpleasant. The way he had his arms folded, his head bowed and was rocking back and forth in his chair was also a bit of a giveaway.

Gilbert mouthed, 'He's lost it,' at her and Alistair jerked upright, said, 'I heard that, Gilbert,' and then they were off. Gilbert got it in the neck first and had to admit under some heavy questioning that he'd been too hungover to fulfil his tour obligations. Alistair rounded that conversation off by telling Gilbert he wasn't indispensable and if he got himself a reputation for being unreliable, he'd soon find the work drying up. Grace could feel the outrage coming off Gilbert, but he clamped his lips shut and didn't express it. It was her turn next and Gilbert tried to be a gentleman and leave, but Alistair was on a roll.

He wanted to know just what her problem was? Why she imagined it was acceptable to fight with another guide, abandon her clients mid-tour (all of whom had complained and demanded a refund, by the way) and bring the company into disrepute with the galleries and all the other organisations who recommended them to visitors? He'd spent a lot of time trying to mend bridges, call in favours and field calls from the odd smart alec hotel concierge asking if it was true that each Picture London tour came with a free fight, a tear-gassing and a robbery? What did Grace think of that?

Before she could start telling him what she thought, he said, more softly, 'And don't think I'm just picking on you. I rang Tate over the weekend to tear a strip off him. I know you got hurt, Grace, and it was good of you to come back today, but really I did expect so much more from you.'

Grace gulped at that, wondering if the tears she'd been waiting for were going to come now, but the gulp was all she got, so she said the right things, promised it would never happen again; reasoned, placated, calmed. It was all an act: she knew that someone had taken the tray on which she had laid out all the neat, interlocking pieces of her life and kicked it high up into the air. Kicked it with great big biker boots and she couldn't promise anything.

When Alistair released them, Gilbert took her into her office and gave her a hug. It felt slightly strange, as if he were uncomfortable but determined.

'How's the head?' he asked when he let her go.

'Fine, more or less. To be honest, I was glad to come back today. Mum came round in a flurry yesterday upset I hadn't rung her right away. So, while Dad stayed in the kitchen being huffy, I had her sitting by the sofa doing Reiki massage on me and sobbing.'

'It's nice she was so upset about you.'

'It wasn't me she was upset about, it was . . . someone else . . . oh, never mind, Gilbert. Enough of Parenting for the Self-Indulgent and enough about my head. How's yours?'

He rolled his eyes. 'Head is better, Grace – it's had a while to recover. But conscience still bothering me. I wasn't particularly pleasant to you before Tate and I went out.'

'I dropped you in it with Bernice.'

He raised an eyebrow and pursed his lips as if weighing something up. 'You did, and she explained the whole of China to me, but you did it only after I had provoked you with my truculence. Your actions were understandable; mine were not. I turned on you, Grace. Showing off in front of Tate.' He went and stood by the window. 'I'm sorry. I'm an old fool.'

'You like him, don't you, Gilbert?' she said gently. 'Tate?'

He nodded. 'But not in *that* way, Grace. Not perhaps in the way you think. It's just he reminds me of Tony – all that life. He doesn't worry about saying the right thing, nor about standing on anyone's toes. When we were out with his friends it was refreshing – they don't shut up; they're like a load of birds. They argued, they got overwrought, they hugged, they made up. Do you know, we spray-painted a wall at some point during the evening? Can't remember exactly when. We had a limbo-dancing competition, which I am very afraid I might have won. We mooned a CCTV camera. It makes going home and having a lamb chop every Tuesday seem . . . well . . .' He laughed and Grace sensed it was at himself. 'Then you catch sight of yourself in the mirror behind the bar and realise you're old enough to be any one of their fathers. Grandfather even.'

'Gilbert, you're not that old.'

'I think with Tate I was looking for youth, not a *particular* youth – does that make sense?' He turned to her as if willing her to understand. 'I feel life's rolling along out there and I'm locked away from it. Marooned. Moth-balled.' A wave of the hand. 'But perhaps that's better than killing myself trying to keep up.'

She went to him and placed her hand on his arm. Nothing too familiar, too huggy-huggy.

'Gilbert, life doesn't need to pass you by. You can get back out there.'

'No. I'm a carer now; can't imagine being cared for.'

'That's maudlin, Gilbert, not like you.'

He looked pained. 'It was, wasn't it? But I wouldn't even know how to make the first move these days.' He held his hand up so quickly she hadn't got time to get the name 'Samuel' out. 'Don't, Grace,' he said firmly. 'I appreciate what you might be about to suggest, but just don't.'

He took his watch out of his pocket and sounding falsely breezy said, 'Well, better go. I have to be at Westminster Abbey soon. You take it easy today, Grace. Alistair's doing your three o'clock? Good. And I don't think Tate is due in. But if he is, no fighting, hmm?' He was choosing his words carefully. 'You know, Grace . . . you and Tate—'

'Don't Gilbert,' she said. 'Just don't.'

Grace sat at her desk after Gilbert left, but the day had an end-of-term feel to it, as if everything she tried to start would not get finished, so she went downstairs to see what had happened to Esther. Bernice said she was taking a break from work for a while. She might still make it to South America but there was a cousin, a woman, who would probably go with her.

'Where did she head off to after she left the gallery?' Grace asked.

'Heathrow. She rang Sol and me to go and collect her. She was just sitting there watching the planes.'

That would have been a sad image for Grace to hold in her head if Bernice had not snorted and said, 'At least she didn't try and buy one of the bloody things and sit in it outside Blond Boy's house.'

'Bernice, that's not very . . .' Grace stopped as she saw her father go past. She caught up with him by the window on the stairs.

'That American lad not in?' He glanced up towards Picture London's door. 'Because I've got a theory, Grace.'

'No, Dad,' she said wearily, sitting on the windowsill.

Her Dad's eyes were bright, his movements rapid. He perched on the sill next to her like a very excited bird. 'Think about this, Grace: every time there's a robbery, you and he . . . well, you're a distraction, right? It's happened twice – too much of a coincidence. Police think that, must do. So, what if he planned the fights?'

'No—'

'First time,' he held up his thumb as if hitch-hiking, 'he starts it simple as simple. Then gets you out pronto. Second one . . .' A finger joined the thumb. 'Makes sure he turns up at the gallery same time as you, gets you out again and bangs you on the head into the bargain. He distracts people enough for the tear gas to go in and then bish, bosh.'

'That's rubbish, Dad. He didn't know we'd have a fight the second time. How was he to know Esther was going to turn up?'

'Could have sent her to the gallery for all you know. Just to provoke you. Then there's this.' With a flourish her father drew out a notebook and opened it. 'Know where he lives? Thought not. Ribbonfield Mansions – lovely square behind the British Museum. Flat on the first floor. The whole first floor. Must be worth three million at least. How's he afford that with just a few tours a week?'

'Perhaps it's not his flat.'

Her Dad gave her a tap on her knee with the notebook. 'Good girl, logical reasoning. It's *not* his flat. Know who it belongs to? One Sergei Ledvinova. Know who he is? Neither do I. Not really. All I know is Nadim's done a bit of digging and Sergei's a businessman – plastics. But . . . no, listen, Grace, listen. He's a keen collector of art. Particularly with a religious theme.'

'What?' She had been about to get up off the window-sill and be very dismissive, but that last fact, on top of the one about the flat, felt more than just puzzling – it was worrying.

Her father tilted his head, looking even more like a bird.

'Plus, Tatie boy is acting like he's got something to hide. We've been following him and he comes out of here—'

'What? Hang on. Following him?'

'Since the first robbery. I didn't want to mention it before, didn't want to worry you. Besides, you might have inadvertently alerted him that he was being watched.'

'And he's been doing what?' she asked, wishing as she spoke that she hadn't, but still having a morbid curiosity to find out.

'Well, nine times out of ten he nips down side streets, doubles back and we lose him. Then when one of us waits near his flat for him to come back, he doesn't pitch up till about two in the morning.'

'He's a young guy, Dad. He'll be out clubbing, or . . . with a woman.' She hated saying that last bit and hated, even more, that she hated it.

'Yeah, that's what we thought.' Her Dad's eyebrows were having a field day. 'But he leaves all that crowd behind in the pub . . . except the night they all headed off with Gilbert. Did you know Gilbert went out with them?'

'It's hardly an offence, Dad, staying out till the early morning, nipping down side streets.'

'And he goes out every morning again at six. Regular as clockwork. Where's he going then? And he does that same nipping about and doubling back. Why's that?'

Grace didn't know and it hurt her head to think about it.

Her father eventually left her with a warning that she should keep an eye on Tate, report back anything that seemed fishy.

His voice was still in her head when she sat down on the sofa in reception, too confused and headachy to get any further. She got a bottle of water from her bag and popped a paracetamol out of its silver bubble and swallowed it down. Her father was barking up the wrong tree – he must be. She popped out a second tablet and sent it to join the first. There was a big difference between being overconfident and stealing icons to order.

She thought of the way Tate had watched her in Gilbert's bedroom and in the office before the bombshell of Esther's plane ticket. She remembered the intensity of what he had said in the courtyard of the Shillingsworth. The determination with which he'd moved towards her. Being cradled into his shoulder. She remembered him lying on the sofa she was sitting on now and felt something awful and exciting twist around in her belly, and it made her forget to breathe and then have to pull in a great lungful of air to stop from feeling woozy.

She went to check the answerphone to distract herself. Nothing of any interest. There was never anything of any interest.

Why was Tate living in a wealthy Russian's flat? What had he been doing before he came to work here? If Alistair had obtained any references, got any kind of background information on him, she could have double-checked it. But could he be a thief? A real, heavy-duty, tear-gas-people thief?

The phone rang and she sent the box of paracetamol skittering to the floor.

It was Emma. Something was wrong – she could hear it in her voice as she asked Grace how she was, said what a terrible run of bad luck she'd had to be caught in two robberies, asked if she should be back at work. And then Emma was crying, great guttering sobs just like Felicity's. Grace waited silently, knowing what was coming.

'There's more money going out, Grace, and, you know, I thought that what you said, about the Christmas present, well, it might be true but . . . but I've started finding things. Oh God, it sounds such a cliché . . . lipstick, Grace – not on his collar, on one of his cuffs – and a receipt, in the pocket of his trousers – I know, I know, I shouldn't have been nosey – for a shop called Julietta's. Have you heard of it?'

'No.' Grace glanced towards the filing cabinet where Gilbert had stowed the carrier bag. She couldn't help it. She glanced towards the office door, checking Alistair wasn't there. She couldn't help that either. Stupid, stupid Alistair. A receipt in his trousers – another vital piece of paper he'd mislaid.

'It's a lingerie shop, Grace. He spent ninety-five pounds in there. And . . . I know that might be for me for Christmas, but what with that and the lipstick and the longer hours . . . I don't know any more. I want to ask him but I'm afraid of what he might say. Oh Grace, if he was having an affair, you'd tell me, wouldn't you?'

'Yes . . . yes, of course I would. If . . . if I knew anything for definite.'

Emma was on that hanging phrase like a dog. 'For definite – what does that mean? That you think he is but you're not sure?'

Grace tried to say something, anything, but it wouldn't come and to her horror she found herself putting the phone down, cutting Emma off. She had just ended the call. Her friend had rung her, a cry for help, and she'd put the phone down.

She pushed her chair back slowly and went out of her office and towards Alistair's. His door was open and his welcoming expression died away as he caught sight of her face.

'I've just had Emma on the phone,' she said, and she didn't know how she was going to say the next bit, but once she'd started it felt like a release. 'She's worried you're having an affair – the long hours, the money going. Look, I don't want to get involved in this, but I am. I've tried to cover for you and explain it away, even to myself, but I can't any more. I'm already stuck in the middle of Mum and Dad's mess; I can't bear this too. I'm sorry if you're affronted because nothing is going on, but please, please talk to Emma.'

Alistair's phone began to ring and both of them stared at it. Did Alistair know it must be Emma? It went through to the answering machine.

'I have to go and do your tour,' he said, still staring at the phone.

'No, you need to ring Emma back. I'll do my tour. I'm fine. I've just taken some paracetamol, they'll see me through.'

As she closed the door of Picture London behind her, she heard the phone ringing again.

CHAPTER 29

'Well, look who's here.' Lilly came out from behind the ticket desk and chuckled, a not particularly friendly sound. 'Not got your fight partner with you? Heard he'd given you a knock to the head?'

'That's not true,' Grace said, 'I walked into a sculpture.'

Beneath her make-up, Lilly's face suggested she knew better and Grace decided to let it go. She had a lot of things she was trying not to think, worry or get angry about, and so she just added Lilly's annoying behaviour to that list. It was a pretty full list and she supposed she should fret about that too, except that would make it even longer.

She positioned herself on the flagstones near the clock with the loitering man in the powdered wig on it. If she examined him more closely, she was sure she'd discover that he had green eyes. She kept her own eyes on the double doors. She couldn't remember who was going to be on this tour. Had there been eight or nine names on the piece of paper she'd run off for Alistair earlier?

'So, things are getting back to normal here,' Lilly said, 'if you count us all being interviewed again as normal. And the police have been poking around all over the place. They've even been down in the drains.' She did a dramatic look towards the top of the staircase. 'Poor Norman's gone off with stress. Not surprised – had to put up with all that extra attention 'cos of his wife.' There was a sly look towards Grace. 'Bad luck you being in both robberies. Police'll be interested in that.'

Grace approximated a brave smile in response and Lilly steamed on. 'Heard your company's only got one life left. Better be a good girl today. I'll be keeping an eye on you.'

Grace was glad to be saved the hypocrisy of another smile by the arrival of people who wanted to buy some tickets and Lilly went back behind the desk to serve them. Grace resumed waiting. She felt surprisingly calm down here, her recollection of the actual robbery hazy, but she knew that when she got to the part of the tour where she usually diverted to see the icon, the memory of its loss would sink its teeth into her again.

She was watching Lilly apply her lipstick when the double doors opened and in they came: eight people, all different shapes and colours and sizes, who she assumed were her group, so she hiked on yet another smile and gave them her spiel about the fantastic things they were going to see.

Upstairs she was meant to start with Renoir – she always started with him – but she dragged them along to Manet instead; they would never know. And there she was, standing in front of the woman who was standing behind the bar at the Folies Bergère, and both of them were looking as if their minds were elsewhere.

She felt herself drift further away as she explained when the painting had first been exhibited and how old Manet was when he painted it, and then she was thinking of poor Emma and of her mum, of the icons ripped from the walls, of Gilbert going home for his lamb chops on a Tuesday. She was thinking of Bill too and how Tate was another one who looked like a beach boy but was actually a bonfire. No, not a bonfire, don't think of that.

The way people were looking at her made her understand that she'd stopped talking, but she couldn't remember one single thing about the picture behind her. She saw the glances run around the group as they realised that what they had interpreted as a pause was turning into something more embarrassing.

'It has bottles in it, this painting,' she tried. 'Champagne and beer. English beer. What does this tell us? Yes, what indeed? Well, lots of things. Many, many things. It tells us that . . .' She came to another halt and turned round to the barmaid as if she could help her out. 'It tells us—'

'It tells us that the bar was frequented by people of all classes, *and* by British tourists, 'cos we all know how the British like their beer.' Tate did a slalom to get round the group and arrive by her side. 'Sorry I'm late, folks,' he said, 'but Gracie here has been kind enough to start you off, now I'm gonna take the reins for a while. Just give me a second.'

He steered her over to one of the benches, and she felt him press gently on her shoulders to make her sit. He had on what he'd been wearing that first time she'd seen him, his greatcoat slung over his shoulders. She saw genuine concern in his eyes. 'What you doin', Gracie, honey?' he whispered. 'Tryin' to kill yourself?'

He sprinted back to the group and she watched him talk them through the painting, his hands emphasising and illustrating what he was saying. He did her trick of picking someone to come up close to the painting and tell everyone what they saw, and when they said, 'Some feet on a trapeze,' he professed complete astonishment, said no one had ever noticed that before. Had them all laughing, had them in the palm of his hand.

She knew that she was in the palm of his hand too.

She followed him round, as he'd done with her on that

first day, and she saw Lilly come into the room and check on them. She seemed disappointed that there was no fighting yet.

Tate carried on talking, laughing, entertaining, but every now and again he would stop and defer to her: 'Gracie, as the expert, you wanna add anything?' Once or twice she did and he beamed at her, giving the group the impression that nobody could explain things as well as she could.

He was lying: she knew he was much better at this than she was. He wasn't hiding behind a wall of reserve keeping everything locked down; he would joke, nudge, and ask people about themselves, get them to trust him.

So, he'd make a good con artist . . . but a thief? Maybe being a con artist was enough. Distracting people, getting them to open up, relax. She wished her head wasn't throbbing again – it made it difficult to think this through properly.

At the end, as he said his goodbyes in the courtyard, the group seemed loath to leave. His hand was full of the tips they had given him.

'Thank you for helping me,' she said when the last person had gone. 'You were good in there. Really know your stuff.'

'Chicago's a great teacher.'

'You brought it alive.'

'I'm a good actor. Like you, Gracie.' The penetrating look

was getting an outing again and then he did a big sigh, the kind where your shoulders hunch up and then come down and you blow the air out through your lips. 'You know what?' he said. 'I can't go back to this snippy-snippy stuff any more.' There was a lift of an eyebrow. 'I gotta keep my big mouth shut and not keep trying to get you to spill your guts and you gotta stop looking like I came in on the bottom of your shoe. Deal?'

There she was saying, 'Deal,' and holding out her hand. He put the money he was holding into it and closed her fingers, one by one, over the notes. It should have seemed too clever – a nicely contrived image – but it didn't; it felt like something delicate and tender.

'You've earned the money, you should keep it,' she said, but he seemed more interested in keeping hold of her hand. The only way she could get him to let go was by starting to walk. Hard to think when someone was looking at you like that.

As they neared the archway, her mobile rang.

'Sounds like you just got a signal?' Tate said. 'Wanna answer it?'

She juggled getting the money into her purse and getting the mobile out of her bag. It was her father. She moved away from Tate a couple of steps, mouthed 'sorry'.

There was no 'hello' or 'how are you?' when she answered

the call; just her father plunging straight into, 'I need you to do something, Grace. That American lad, you're with him now, aren't you?'

She moved further away from Tate.

'How do you know that?' She tried to keep her voice down and did what she hoped was a subtle scan to check if there were any familiar figures loitering about.

'Stop looking, Grace, and just listen. I need you to keep him busy, just for an hour or so.'

'Dad, what is this? What are you playing at?'

She saw Tate had taken out a pack of cigarettes and flipped open the top. He looked across to her, glanced back down at the cigarettes, seemed to hesitate and then flipped the top of the packet closed again. He couldn't get the packet back into his pocket cleanly, as if he were fumbling and it made her want to go and help him.

Her father's tone was wheedling. 'Just an hour, Grace. Go to the pub, talk about art. You can do that. Just till seven.'

'That's an hour and a half.' An hour and a half in a pub with Tate? She felt her throat tighten at the thought of that.

'It's for a good cause, Grace. What if he *is* involved in this robbery lark? That would mean you were doing a public service, stopping any more paintings getting stolen.

You know how you love those paintings. It's not fair that someone's going to hide them away in a private collection. Stop you looking at them. Come on, Grace. Just keep him busy while I go and check on something.'

She glanced back at Tate, who had the cigarette packet back out and seemed to be repeating the open, look, hesitate, close process.

'Will you stop badgering me if I do, Dad? I can't think properly . . .'

'I won't ask you to do anything else.'

'All right, all right. Just till seven. And don't do anything daft. Or dangerous.'

'Course not.'

'Trouble?' Tate said, coming towards her as she put the mobile back in her bag. The lights were shining off his hair. He was like an angel who'd fallen into a theatrical outfitter's. She saw how people were looking at him, even here in London. It made him seem more dangerous. Not angelic at all.

'Just my dad.'

He nodded and wrinkled his nose. 'Yup, dads can be tricky.'

'Not as tricky as mums.'

He laughed at that and there it was firmly established now – that connection. A bond.

'So.' He shrugged. 'How are you doin'? Can't believe Al sent you out to do this today. Not sure you should even be back at work. Neck still sore? Head still hurting?'

'Comes and goes.'

'Yeah?' His gaze travelled from her hair, down her face to her neck and then back to her eyes. 'It's there at the moment, your head. Looks fine to me. More than fine.'

She walked under the arch and out into the street where the lights were burning up the dark and the traffic was rushing past and Grace wasn't certain she could go through with sitting in a pub next to Tate and making polite conversation about art. She knew how to argue with him – that was safe – but talking properly?

He stopped. 'You look like you could use a drink, Gracie, but you don't drink, do you? So . . .'

Inside her, the old Grace yawned and stretched. 'I know a pub that serves really good water.'

He gave her one of his straight-down-the-line smiles. 'Water it is then.' His laugh came out like a breath.

They walked away from the worst of the traffic and the worst of the crowds and in the pub he kept looking back at her as he waited to be served, as if he expected her to get up and go. Yet when he brought the drinks to their table, his 'You mind, ma'am?' with a nod at the space next to her had a confident, almost demanding, tone to it that made her think of a gunslinger again – which, she thought, must make her a saloon girl. She felt her sense of caution roll further out into the long grass.

'Careful,' he said, as she lifted her glass, 'I got you fizzy. Sure you can handle it?' There was a challenging look in his eyes and that awful and exciting something was twisting inside her again. He didn't seem interested in his drink, didn't seem inclined to stop looking at her face. She glanced at the clock behind the bar. Barely quarter to six.

She felt stupidly self-conscious and tried to bolster up her resolve by remembering the reasons why her father was suspicious of Tate. He stomped all over her careful thinking with a low, 'Sorry I'm staring. Couldn't stop thinking about you this weekend, Gracie. Worried about you. Kept remembering that moment you hit your head. My fault. Pushing and pushing at you when it's none of my business. Saying all that stuff to Esther. I don't back off, that's my problem. One of them.'

She studied him as he talked. A strong, open face. Yes, definitely more of a cowboy than a beach boy, except those green eyes were too cat-like, too willing to take things beyond far. But far enough to steal the very things she loved?

'I should have seen Esther was getting too . . . you know.

Should have read that sign: *Handle With Care*. Messed up Gilbert a bit too, maybe . . .'

He gave her a look to check what she might think about that but she wasn't thinking about Gilbert; she was looking at Tate's eyebrows, how they were light brown, and how one of his lips still had a mark where Violet had nipped him.

He caught her looking and she dropped her gaze to his hand resting on the table.

'You have paint under your nails,' she said and was surprised that she didn't feel panicky or sad or angry as she usually did when something reminded her of Bill.

She saw him pull his hand back before hesitating and letting it remain there.

'Yup,' he said, 'just getting some bits and pieces ready for the installation, you know.'

'Did you find a location? The other evening, with Gilbert?'

'No, got waylaid. Plenty of time.'

He was so close to her she could feel him all the way down her side. He was looking at her lips. And then something over her shoulder took his attention and he did one of those double-takes she'd last seen when he was trying to understand what the hell Alistair was on about.

She turned to see Nadim at the bar, a pint of orange

juice held to his chest in one large hand, one foot on the brass rail at the bottom of the bar. He was working hard at looking nonchalant – it made him seem as if there was something caught between his neck and his collar.

'The damndest thing,' Tate said frowning. 'That guy . . .'

She turned back round quickly.

'I swear . . .' Tate started again. 'Looks familiar. Can't think where . . . but I swear . . .'

She got up. 'I think I need to go to the toilet. I won't be long.'

As she passed Nadim, she flared her eyes at him and whispered, 'Outside.'

He emerged on the pavement, and she harried him round to the side of the pub.

'What on earth are you doing? One, you're in a pub – what would your wife say if she knew? And two, has Dad asked you to keep an eye on me?'

Nadim was a jowly man and his mouth made a downward curve.

'Well, he might have. But now, Grace, he's gone quiet. Not answering his mobile. He's left me deep undercover with no operating instructions.'

How had she ever thought her father's interest in crime was better than an interest in morris dancing?

'I think you should go home, Nadim. Tate nearly

recognised you back then; he was trying to place you. Go home.'

Nadim was reluctant.

'Go home,' she said again. 'Or I might just tell your wife next time I see her that I saw you drinking vodka and orange. A pint of it.'

She left him professing it was just orange and rejoined Tate. He was fiddling with a beer mat before he saw her, and when he did, he stood up and smiled, his teeth very white in the gloom of the pub.

She really wanted to drink a double Scotch. Just standing there, straight down in one. She could do with a cigarette too. Any kind.

Then she stopped craving anything but Tate, because his smile had become something dirtier, and she saw his gaze do a trip down her body and back to her eyes again.

For the first time she let him look for as long as he wanted. She didn't cut short his access or pass off the way she was looking back at him as if it was something that had happened by accident. His cocky 'let me in' look seemed to melt away the longer they stood there, until it was obvious even to her that what he'd said before she'd got thwacked on the head was true – he wanted her. She saw him shift his stance and the look changed again as if, suddenly, he were unsure of himself.

Without them discussing that they were going, she was lifting up her bag and he was picking up his coat and they were outside. Grace didn't even care if they found Nadim was still standing there.

Tate was looking at her lips again.

'Really want to kiss you, Gracie,' he said, struggling into his coat. 'If you don't want me to, better say something now, because in a minute I'm not gonna be able to hear anything but the blood rushing in my ears.' He was moving as he spoke; she felt his hands find her waist and he was pulling her towards him. Whether she would have said stop if he'd given her the opportunity, she would never know, because suddenly his mouth was on hers and the feel of his lips made all the things she'd tried to keep a lid on force their way into her mind for a few disorientating, gut-churning seconds, before they spiralled away again, God knew where, and she kissed him back. It was a tentative kiss on both their parts and he pulled away after the briefest of time. When she opened her eyes, he was still right up close, his breath seeming laboured.

'Jeez, Gracie,' he said, both hands coming up to hold her face. 'If I kiss you the way I want to, it's gonna kill your neck.'

He could not have possibly known how much she was

turned on by that – it made her feel desired and precious to him, and when he brushed her hair back off one cheek and lightly kissed her there, the old Grace was awake, prowling around, looking on and saying, *He's gorgeous. What are you waiting for?*

'It would probably be easier if I was lying down,' she said, looking at him from under her lashes, and she saw she had surprised him. If anything, his breath seemed more laboured.

'Cab?' he said and she almost shouted, 'Yes.' He was pulling her to the edge of the pavement, then he was out in the road, waving his hand about.

'Where to?' he called over his shoulder as the taxi came to a halt.

'Wherever's closest.'

'Ribbonfield Mansions, Grantham Street,' he said to the driver and pulled at the door to get her in, leaping in behind her.

Grace had a moment of clarity in the taxi when she remembered that she was still meant to be in the pub keeping him busy and that he might be a thief and, even if he wasn't, he was absolutely the wrong man for her to be with, and then Tate put his hand on her thigh and she wanted him to kiss her properly. It was difficult to get the angle quite right; she couldn't turn her head much, but

Tate proved to be both imaginative and determined. Even with the seatbelts on.

He was kissing her in a way that made her realise just his mouth wasn't going to be enough. When he pulled the collar of her coat aside far enough to allow him to drop kisses at the base of her throat, she felt his blond hair tickle her neck and expected it to stir up memories of Bill, but it didn't – it stirred up heat and a sweetly excruciating tightness in her belly.

'Oh, that is so . . .' she exhaled and knew that if he kept on kissing her like that, if the traffic continued to move so slowly, she might do something from her old days. She imagined taking off her belt and taking off his and telling him to lie back on the seat and . . .

She caught the taxi driver's eye as Tate was pushing up her sleeve and kissing down the inside of her arm to her wrist, before slowly taking her middle finger into his mouth, and the look he gave her definitely said, *Don't even think about it on my seats.*

He dropped them outside a terrace of white houses with columned porches and Grace thought, *Dad's right, this is a bloody good address. How can he afford to live here? There's no such thing as a free place to sleep. What's he doing to earn it?*

'You live here?' she asked, and Tate said, in between

kissing her neck, 'Long story, Gracie, and there's a few other things I need to tell you as well. We could talk about them now, or I could take you upstairs and see what you've got on under this serious old coat.' He was opening it as he spoke, trying to get her shirt free of her trousers.

We should talk about it now, sensibly and calmly, her brain said, while her mouth murmured, 'Upstairs,' and he hustled her up the steps and through the front door. The hallway was silent and smelt of expensive candles and polish, and they raced up the stairs, him pulling her by her hand as he bounded ahead. His keys were out of his trouser pocket; he was fumbling with them and he took long enough trying to get the right one in the lock that Grace had time to think, *This is going too fast. All I know is that he turns me on and I need him and he's going to tear my heart out – and he might be a crook.*

Then the key was in the lock and she couldn't remember any of the questions she'd been asking herself.

'Normally have trouble getting it in, do you?' she whispered in his ear as he waltzed her in through the door and kicked it shut behind him.

'Nope, never. Usually slips in nicely,' he whispered back in a way that intensified the heat she was feeling, the tightness in her stomach and her desperate, desperate urge to feel all of his skin against all of hers.

He went to punch in some numbers on the burglar alarm and stopped.

'That's weird . . .' but he didn't finish talking because she had taken off her coat and when he heard it hit the floor, he turned to look. She started to unbutton her shirt.

'Jeez,' he said and she was being pulled along the hallway. 'Kitchen, sitting room, library,' he reeled off and Grace saw marble worktops, huge sofas and even larger chandeliers flash by.

Here was a bed that you probably needed a sat nav to find your way across, a wall of wardrobes, wallpaper good enough to frame.

'Let's get that head of yours somewhere soft.' He helped her very gently on to the bed. He was taking off his boots, kicking them across the floor, then taking off his socks as she started to undo more of her shirt buttons.

'No, no, no,' he said, nodding at what she was doing, 'I get to do that. Hate that freakin' shirt – gonna tear it off and ball it up and chuck it out the window.'

He was pulling his own shirt up and over his head and Grace saw his belly and chest appear bit by bit. He tanned easily, she could tell, and imagined his body moving through water, coming up out of it, drips beading and pooling in his belly button so she could lick them out.

He came back to the bed, got on it and straddled her hips. He was grinning down at her.

'Comfy?'

'Yes, but if you chuck my shirt away, these have to go too.' She tugged at his pinstripe trousers.

'These? Why these, Miss Surtees, have been in ma family for generations. We routed the British in these trousers and now I'm gonna do the same to you.'

They didn't move straight away after that, both getting used to this new way of being with each other. Not talking, just looking.

Then he was undoing the last of the buttons on her shirt and kissing each bit of her that was exposed, but he didn't throw her shirt out of the window when he peeled it off because suddenly, brazenly, she had removed her bra. It seemed to take his mind right off the shirt, which fell from his hands and then slid from the bed to the floor.

'Work of art, Gracie,' he said, not moving. And then, after gabbling that he was never letting her wear clothes again, he was undoing her trousers and pulling them down over her hips. She felt his mouth move over her thighs, his tongue making runs that finished with a kiss. Slowly he moved from one to the other, gave each its due attention, particularly along the place where her knickers met flesh. And then he was easing them down as well. She closed her eyes and if her neck hadn't been so delicate, she would have arched her back as she felt his hands on her bare hips.

He made a noise of appreciation and when she looked he seemed dreamy, mesmerised.

'Blonder than me,' he said and lowered his head and kissed her. That was the moment the real Grace came roaring back.

She reached down and put her hand in his hair, tugging just enough to get his attention, and soon she was helping him get his trousers off, helping him get his pants down, and he wouldn't leave her mouth alone as she wrapped herself around him, holding him as he said, 'Gracie, Gracie, you're all naked in my bed, everything stripped away.' And she was there, there in that actual moment, not removed from herself like the poor barmaid at the Folies Bergère. She was kissing him back – she couldn't leave his mouth alone either, or his neck or his chest or his shoulders . . . God, his shoulders.

Quicker and quicker now, she was letting herself lose control and opening up for him. She helped him roll on a condom and took him in, sensations bombarding her as she caressed him with her tongue and her hands and felt him move over and inside her doing the same. She heard him say, 'That's . . . wow . . . Gracie. Jeez.' Then he wasn't talking any more and she was being noisy and they'd both forgotten they were meant to be careful with her neck and her head, and she forgot she was meant to be careful with everything. Instead they just absolutely, frantically, went for it.

Lying on top of her afterwards, with both of their hearts hammering, Tate said, 'That was one hell of a tour, Miss Surtees. Now I'm gonna need a neck brace too.' Rolling off her, he lay by Grace's side and she turned to face him. He was looking at her as if he'd known all along that they should be lying here like this. But it was not a smug look, just a supremely happy one. She felt his hand on her breast; saw the silver of the ring on his thumb against the pink of her nipple.

'You young men,' she said, playing an imaginary chord on his arm with her fingers, 'think you know it all.'

He nodded and she loved the way it made his hair move.

'Certainly didn't know there was so much fire under that ice, that's for sure.' He moved his hand from her breast and pushed her hair out of her eyes. 'Wouldn't want to see it disappear again. Your eyes are even more beautiful when they haven't got all those extra layers of darkness in them.' His tone was sad, and he reached for her and pulled her closer, kissed her on the mouth. 'Not gonna keep asking you what happened, but if you ever wanna tell me . . .' He frowned and turned his head because there was a definite clunk from one of the wardrobes; she'd heard it too. Now there was a kind of scrabbling and Tate was off the bed, his head tilted slightly while he walked along the wall of wardrobes as if trying to work out where the noise was coming from. He stopped, backtracked, caught hold of a door handle and pulled sharply.

There was her father, bent over as if he had just toppled sideways. One hand was over his eyes. 'I told you to keep him busy,' he said, 'not bring him here. And where the hell's Nadim? He's meant to be shadowing you.' But Grace wasn't listening; she was too preoccupied looking at the icon held in her father's other hand.

CHAPTER 30

Grace had known falling for Tate would make her life go to hell in a handcart. She just hadn't realised it would happen so quickly or so drastically.

It had been half past five in the afternoon when she agreed to go for a drink with him. Now it was one the following morning; from the taxi window she could see only the odd staggering or homeless soul.

So, in seven and a half hours she'd given up fighting her attraction for Tate; had heart-wrenchingly lovely sex with him while her father hid in his wardrobe; seen him arrested; been questioned by the police in the presence of a solicitor; had her fingerprints taken; and, finally, been released on police bail pending further enquiries. She guessed Tate was still in the police station somewhere. At least she was only fighting guilt by association; he had the bigger problem of explaining how there was a stolen icon in his wardrobe. Or, rather, two stolen icons – the other one was in there too; her father had just dropped it when he'd fallen over sideways, hence the clunk.

So, nine years of living a quiet, well-ordered life and she'd ended up sitting in an interview room having her entrails picked over by the police.

They would probably turn up with a search warrant for her flat later, find the paintings under her bed and put her down as a major art thief.

Served her right – she knew all this chaos would happen.

To go with all those new experiences, Grace also had a severely trampled heart. She'd spent so long stopping herself falling for Tate that, when it had happened, she'd plummeted like lead – straight down; no hesitation or deviation. Which was why, even faced with the solid proof of what he'd done, it was hard to pull up from the nosedive. She should concentrate on the choking, tear-gas-filled chaos he'd helped create at the galleries. On all the subterfuge and lies. Where was the outrage that he'd stolen the things she loved?

Instead she kept thinking of what had taken place on that bed and what had happened after her father had stumbled out of the wardrobe.

Almost at once, the police had started hammering on the door to the flat, summoned by her father from within the wardrobe – God, they must have been making so much noise not to have heard him. At the sound of knocking, Grace had scrambled, clumsily, under the duvet and her father had gone to open the door. Tate had stood there, naked, looking first at the wardrobe and then at her.

'*Keep him busy*?' he'd said, repeating her father's words as if they were only now making sense to him. '*I told you to keep him busy*,' he'd repeated. He seemed empty and kicked. 'Is that what this was, Gracie? Keeping me busy?'

She'd said 'no' quickly, but he fired back, 'So, you had no idea your dad thought I stole the icons? Didn't know he was following me?'

She had floundered at that as 'no' was a lie and 'yes' was worse, and saw him press his lips together and slump down on the bed with his back to her. She knew he'd now remember how she had talked to her father on her mobile just before she had agreed out of the blue to go to the pub with him.

She'd wanted to put her arms around him, press her lips to his shoulder, but now there were police in the room and her father was whispering to her to say nothing, that she didn't want to implicate herself any further. Although how it was possible to implicate yourself more when you were already sitting up naked in a suspect's bed, having obviously just had sex with him, she didn't know.

When they took him away, Tate didn't even look at her.

He had his head down and, once again, it seemed as if his boots were too heavy for him.

The stark desertion of the streets mirrored how she felt, but she didn't know if it was because she'd fallen for Tate and he was a thief or because of that look of anguish he'd given her when he thought she'd just been using him.

Still, in the end he *was* like Bill – except Bill had only stolen her heart . . . Tate looked as if he'd gone for that and the icons. All she'd got in return was a cut head and a sore neck.

She tried hard to find any silver lining in the huge dark, thundering cloud that seemed to be centred over the taxi and heard her mother say to her father, 'So brave of you, anything could have happened.' Ah, there it was, that patch of silver: her parents were speaking to each other again.

More than speaking. Her father was sitting in the flip-down seat, her mother opposite him, and Grace saw how they were both leaning towards each other. Felicity had turned up at the police station with the solicitor and now she kept touching her husband's arm, doing that overly expressive face of hers as she listened to the whole history of how Tate had been captured. She had her hand on his thigh by the time he explained how he'd got access to the flat. Turned out he'd discovered the woman who cleaned it had once tried to pull a fast one on the insurance company he'd worked for. She'd been so eager to keep that bit of her past quiet from her new husband that she'd agreed to hand over the key and the code for the alarm.

'Never expected to find the actual paintings though, Fliss,' her father was saying. 'Was just looking for clues, you know. Nipped in the wardrobe when I heard Tate unlock the front door, hoped he wouldn't notice the alarm had been switched off.' Fliss was gazing at him as if he were James Bond, and Grace could almost see her thinking, *Jay? Jay, who?*

Grace might as well have been invisible, but that was a relief. She wasn't sure that she and her father were ever going to be able to look each other fully in the face again after what he'd heard her doing on that bed. And as long as her mother was occupied fawning over her father, she would not start rubbing Grace's back again and saying, 'I knew you were in trouble with Tate, didn't I? Such a bad, bad boy,' as if what Grace had done was bridge-burningly wild and romantic. If Grace heard Felicity say that once more, she was afraid she would do something that would get her plonked right back in the police station.

The taxi stopped at the lights and Grace saw her mother squeeze her father's thigh provocatively, and the prospect of going back to her flat with them seemed an ordeal too far today. She bore it for the rest of the journey and even while they were bustling around in her kitchen, making tea and toast, but when they started talking in whispers and her mother had reached giddy giggling stage, she got her biscuit tin out of the cupboard and left the room. She could go and hide under a hot shower but the prospect of washing the smell of Tate from her body made her drift to the sitting room and out again, along to her bedroom, and then brought her to a halt in the hallway. She stared at her messy walls and carpet, before going to ring for another taxi. She left her parents a note explaining where she'd gone, but had a feeling they wouldn't miss her for some time – there was an unnerving silence from the kitchen.

The building was dark and she should have felt scared going through it, but the gloomy silence chimed more with her mood than the billing and cooing of her parents. Clutching the biscuit tin, she went up the stairs, remembering how she and Tate had stood there in the gathering dark. From the window, the unlit Christmas decorations were tawdry, just clusters of light bulbs on wire. She climbed up to the door and unlocked it, primed to turn off the burglar alarm, but saw light coming from under Alistair's door. She checked the alarm and found it off. Just like in Tate's flat.

'Alistair, is that you?' she called and got a single, 'Yes,' in reply. He was lying on his back in a sleeping bag, his jacket folded up to make a pillow. He looked like a depressed slug and Grace remembered that, in what seemed like another life, he had been on the point of answering a call from Emma.

Emma. Grace had been a lousy friend to her.

She wondered when Alistair was going to ask her what she was doing in the office so early in the morning, but he either didn't care or had no idea what time it was.

'Alistair,' she said gently, 'I have some really difficult news to tell you. Tate . . . well, it seems that somehow he's mixed up in the two robberies.'

She expected him to struggle out of his sleeping bag, shocked, incredulous. She waited for a flurry of additional questions. There was no reaction. He was blinking and breathing but that was about it.

She upped her volume. 'Tate has been helping someone steal the icons. Those arguments we had, they were probably staged. Anyway, he's in it up to his neck because they've found the missing icons at his flat. It's a big flat, an expensive one. Belongs to a Russian.'

'Well, that's just bloody brilliant,' Alistair said to the ceiling. '*That* just about puts the tin hat on it. Anything more? Gilbert been nicking lead from the roof of the

National Gallery? You running a prostitution ring in your lunch hour?' He turned to look at her. 'And the police, I can expect a visit from them, can I?'

'I think so.'

'Fantastic. Can't wait for that. Tate a thief. Marvellous. Marvellous. Well that's the company down the toilet too.'

Too?

'It might not be that bad, Alistair.'

He shook his head vehemently as if he didn't want to be comforted. 'The company was on shaky ground before this, everyone pointing the finger. Now they'll ban us from everywhere . . . won't even be allowed to walk past the art hung on the railings by the park. They'll all want to know if I checked Tate out, where he came from, references, qualifications. All the things you said I should look into. Why didn't I listen to you, Grace? I didn't bother with any of it, went on my instincts.' He started to laugh as if he'd forgotten she was there and now the sleeping bag looked more like a straitjacket to her.

When he appeared to have exhausted himself, she asked him if he'd talked to Emma.

He nodded, just one sharp motion down and up.

'And how did it go?'

His turned a face towards her that plainly said, *I am*

sleeping in my own office in a sleeping bag, how do you think it went?

'I'm really, really sorry. Should I ring her and—'

'No. She wants to be left in peace to think.' He was back talking to the ceiling. 'It's been a shock. She needs time to get used to the idea.'

Grace thought that was a strange thing to say. The *idea*? Having an affair seemed more like an action than an idea. And 'get used to' made it sound as if this thing with the other woman was going to continue. Well, Emma wasn't French; there was no way she was going to put up with Alistair having a long-term mistress.

Grace checked Alistair's body language to see if she dared ask him any more. Difficult when everything from his neck down was encased in puffed nylon.

'So . . . you told her about the affair?' she tried.

He pulled the sleeping bag up higher.

'No,' he said, 'I told her about the cross-dressing.'

How much later it was when Alistair said, 'You can close your mouth now, Grace,' she didn't know. Probably only seconds, but in those seconds Grace had re-examined all of Alistair's secretive behaviour and seen it quite, quite differently. It was like one of those optical illusions that you viewed one way and saw a young, attractive woman, but viewed another and saw an old lady with a hat. Only in this case there was no young woman. Never had been. There might possibly be hats, though.

'How long has . . . ?' she began, before having a go at, 'Emma, she . . . ?' then finally settling on the more solid shore of, 'I understand now what you were keeping in this cupboard and, before that, your briefcase.'

He nodded. 'And when there was no one in the office, I'd come back here and be Stacey.'

'That's what she's called . . . your—'

'Yes. She's been coming to me for years. Since I was a boy.' She heard the defensiveness go out of his voice. 'I just love the feel of the clothes, Grace. The wigs. They calm me. I like looking pretty. I like being feminine. I like shopping for underwear and make-up.' His laugh was at himself. 'Tied myself in knots trying to hide my shopping trips.'

'Right. But . . .'

'I'm not gay, Grace,' he said gently, 'that's what you want to ask, isn't it? Or some permutation of that question. Do I feel trapped in the wrong body? Would I like to be a woman? No, I'm not gay, not bisexual. It makes me happy, makes me feel more like myself a lot of the time. That doesn't mean I don't love Emma. I do. I desire her, all those things.' There was a movement as if, inside his sleeping bag, he was shrugging. 'As they say, it's complicated.'

Grace was fearful of asking something insensitive, but she didn't need to worry: Alistair seemed eager to talk, unprompted.

'I loved my first wife, too,' he said, 'but Gemma couldn't cope with it. My fault – I should have told her before we got married, but you're so scared, Grace. You find someone you love and you don't want to lose them, but you can't fight this other need you have . . . She wasn't mean about it, Gemma; in fact, she felt guilty that she couldn't live with it. She'd always thought she was really open-minded, a live-and-let-live kind of person. Sure it was the guilt that made her give me the lease to this place.'

'So, the guy upstairs?'

'Her dad? Yeah, he knows.'

Alistair's face was suddenly crumbling. There were tears and he pulled the sleeping bag higher up around him while struggling to sit. It felt natural for Grace to put her biscuit tin on his desk, get down on her knees and help him – a big, lost man in a slippery sleeping bag.

'I don't know what Emma will do. I should have told her earlier. I'm such a coward. But you see, after Gemma I didn't think I should be with anyone, not in a full-time relationship. Then I met Emma and just hoped it would all go away, that I could fight it. Sometimes I do: I have regular purges of all my stuff, try to tell myself it's over. Keep everything locked down.'

Grace looked across at her biscuit tin.

'It always comes back, the urge . . . no, the *need* to buy, to dress up.'

Alistair sniffed loudly. 'You end up skulking around and being furtive when really you're desperate to tell the people who love you and take a chance that they'll come to understand.' His smile was brave and totally unconvincing. 'You hope they'll even see it as just another thing that makes you who you are.'

While he got himself back under control, Grace pictured Emma's reaction and wondered whether she would come to think of this as just another facet of the man she loved.

'I've disgusted you, haven't I?' she heard him say and she rushed to assure him he hadn't.

'It's just it's such a complete surprise, and what with being in the police station all evening and a lot of the night—'

'Why were you there?' he said, snapping back into boss mode.

'I told you, I was at the flat with Tate. It looks bad, you know, me being at the robberies, then at the flat. I've been released on bail, and I think if Dad hadn't been there, they might have kept me longer.'

Alistair was struggling to get out of the sleeping bag. 'But this is dreadful, Grace. I'm so sorry. I wasn't listening properly. Tell me again. You must be dead on your feet.'

Alistair continued to wriggle about and as he emerged, bit by bit, she saw he was dressed in a blue velvet skirt and a green blouse.

It didn't seem as strange as she thought it might. Perhaps that was because he had forewarned her, or perhaps after the day she'd had, nothing would ever seem strange to her again.

'That's a nice blouse,' she said, 'it suits your eyes.'

He gave her an uncertain smile before kicking the sleeping bag away. Now it no longer looked like a straitjacket but like a discarded chrysalis and Alistair was a colourful, slightly dishevelled butterfly.

CHAPTER 31

It didn't take long for the news of Tate's arrest to spread. The first indication was a call from Gilbert, who had arrived to do his nine o'clock tour at the National Gallery and was told he wasn't going to be let in; he'd have to ring his office.

Gilbert's response to the news Grace gave him was a series of exclamations and strangled noises – and she was only giving him the edited lowlights.

'I'm coming right round,' he said. Grace looked at Alistair, who for now had changed back into his uniform of chinos, striped shirt and lace-up suede shoes, and knew there were a few other revelations Gilbert was going to have to get used to at some point. Alistair was as monumentally miserable as you would expect a man to be whose marriage and business were imploding.

Grace worked through the list of people who were booked on tours that day, informing them that they wouldn't be happening. Money would be returned. After that, when the phone rang, they took it in turns to pick it up and put it right back down again.

'Most of the calls will just be people shouting at me,' Alistair had explained when he'd done it the first time. 'Real trouble will come and find us.' Grace knew that was true. Hadn't it already? Anything urgent would come up those stairs or appear on her mobile. Not that she was paying any attention to that either, unlike Alistair who was holding his like a charm. She guessed he was waiting for a sign, any sign, from Emma.

That made her feel wobbly, fretful . . . something.

So did looking at Tate's chair, but still tears would not come. It was as if being hit on the head by the unicorn had sent her tear ducts into shock; all that happened was her nose ran.

To occupy her mind, she turned on her computer and saw the emails from her sisters. The titles were enough: *Mum, a new stage in self-expression*, *Dad and how to nurture him* and *Lines to lie on broken hearts*. She had no idea what development in Felicity's involvement with Jay they were referring too, but whatever it was, it was out of date already.

She was about to delete them, shaking her head at her sister's collective stupidity, when she thought of her mother getting fooled and fleeced by Jay and of her own experience with Tate and didn't feel superior any more. She let them stay.

Gilbert arrived with the flurry of questions she had expected to receive earlier from Alistair, and as they waited for the police to tank up the stairs and the phone continued to ring and not be answered, Grace filled him and Alistair in on what had happened in the flat, leaving out the sex, but putting in her father.

Gilbert wasn't fooled by the leaving out bit.

'So, you and Tate?' His eyebrows had a knowing lilt. 'You started off by fighting and finished by . . . how would you describe it, Grace?'

'Getting on better. We were getting on better.'

'Until your father pops out of the wardrobe like some demented cuckoo in a clock. That must have taken some explaining to Tate?'

When she didn't reply, Gilbert said, 'I feel there are some gaps in your story, Grace, but goodness, Tate a thief? Hard to believe it of him. He seemed so open . . . and Corinne and Joe and that clingy one, are they involved?'

Grace only felt capable of hunching up her shoulders in answer and Gilbert kept on repeating how he couldn't believe it of Tate, until she was relieved when Alistair got up and said, 'Where are those bloody police? This is torture.' He completed a couple of tours of the room, avoiding the rocks that were now all over the place, before standing on his tiptoes and peering out of the window, his head pressed to the glass to get a view first up the street and then down.

Gilbert's mobile rang, which made all three of them start. 'Sorry, it'll be Vi,' he said, but on answering it, he didn't talk about the normal things he talked about with Vi. He ended with a hurried, 'Of course.'

'Violet's not ill is she?' Grace said when Gilbert's phone was back in his jacket.

'No . . . and it wasn't Violet. It was Tate. They've released him. Not been charged. He's going home to grab a shower and then he wants to see us. Acar's.'

'Released? No charge? Well, come on then, let's get down there,' Alistair said.

Grace leapt to her feet at the promise of seeing Tate again.

'Uh, Grace.' Gilbert's tone was delicate. 'Not you. He expressly asked *not* to see you.'

Grace spent the time that Gilbert and Alistair were at Acar's clutching her biscuit tin and forming a close relationship with the sofa. For the most part she was face down on it, but she did roll over on her back to ring her father.

Felicity answered. 'You've just caught me. I'm going home. On. My. Own.' The huffiness level was high, which alerted Grace to the fact that James Bond had fallen off his pedestal. Might even have shot himself in the foot. Or somewhere higher.

'I'm in pain here, Mum,' she said and got straight back, 'Don't talk to me about pain. My aura's throbbing, I can feel it.'

'Now, Grace,' her father said when he was put on, 'I want you to know that everyone makes mistakes in life. Sometimes the evidence seems to point one way but, well, I won't bore you with the facts—'

'Yes, you will. You bored me with your fantasies; the least you can do is bore me with the truth. Wait a minute.' She got a tissue out of her sleeve and wiped her nose. Still running. Still no tears. 'Right. Talk until I tell you to stop.'

Grace heard a slamming noise from her father's end of the phone and presumed it was her mother storming out.

'Turns out,' her father said, 'the police found where the Paddwick Gallery icon was late last week, just after that other one got nicked. It was *still* in the gallery. Ingenious really. There's a cabinet where the defibrillators are stored, but whoever put it in put a false back on it. Nice gap between the back you can see and the one that's snug to the wall. And guess what? Same story at the Shillings-worth.'

There was a long pause during which Grace wanted to

reach down the phone and shake her father to make him hurry up.

'Police knew whoever put them there was waiting for an opportunity to get them out and away, so they did round-the-clock surveillance in both galleries and just before closing time at the Shillingsworth yesterday, about seven, some bloke has a heart attack. Had it conveniently close to the defibrillator. First aider goes to assist, bystanders cleared away, ambulance turns up, carts bloke off to hospital.'

Her father could not hide the enthusiasm in his voice and Grace wondered how her mother and father, two people who appeared to be grown-ups, had such a poor grip on the reality of other people's emotions. He was chuckling now, actually chuckling while she was lying here suffering.

'Police stop the ambulance just round the corner and find the icon in it . . . not a real ambulance or real paramedics; not even a real heart attack. Take everyone in for questioning and they cough up a load more names. So, couple of hours later, they round up the guy who fitted the cabinets, a couple of the Shillingsworth's security guards, and three guards and an attendant from the Paddwick Gallery. Oh, and a Hong Kong businessman living in Windsor who was running the whole thing. Funny really, you and Tate were at the police station when it was all going on.'

'Yes, really, really hilarious, Dad. So tell me, Hercule Poirot, Tate has just been released. I'm assuming it's without charge?'

'Ah, yes. Not involved at all . . . now, don't make that noise. I was wrong about him, I'll admit it.' A pause. 'Oh, and those icons in his wardrobe—'

'Don't say it, Dad, I don't want to hear it.' She stopped and sniffed. 'I can't hear it.'

'But—'

'Dad!'

'All right, all right. But, I was wrong about Norman too: he had nothing to do with it . . . Attendant called Lilly. You know her?'

Grace put the phone under the sofa while her father was still talking.

Later, when she was lying on her side, she debated whether she should retrieve her phone and call Mark. Trouble was, she didn't know what she needed to tell him, except that sleeping with him wasn't going to work for her ever again.

She knew now why Tate had that paint under his nails, but if she didn't hear anyone say it out loud, she wouldn't think of him standing there, lovingly . . .

She closed her eyes tightly and clung on to the tin, trying to empty her mind of everything, and suddenly Gilbert and Alistair were standing over her. She sat up and tried to make sense of the time on her watch.

'Sorry . . . I was really tired. You've been gone a long time.'

She could not stop herself listening for biker boots on the stairs, even though she knew from their expressions that Tate would not be coming.

'Gilbert, can you handle this?' Alistair seemed uncomfortable. 'There's something I want to do in my office.' He swung his arm half-heartedly, more golf than baseball now, and trudged into his room.

Gilbert rolled his eyes. 'Like a wet weekend. What on earth is wrong with him today?'

'How's Tate?' She hadn't been able to hold it in any longer.

Gilbert sat down by her side. 'He's very tired, very shaken up by the whole thing. He'd been allowed his one phone call and had used it to talk to his mother. She was extremely distressed.'

Grace felt as if this was personally her fault. She imagined Tate's mother out in America still holding the phone long after the call was over.

'Poor man has no idea why he's been released, except

an officer mentioned that there had been new developments. We bought him a couple of beers and Alistair asked him about the big flat . . . and the Russian, and he held up his hands in that way he has . . .' Gilbert said fondly, 'and announced he had a few things to explain – not things he'd lied about, but omissions he'd made. Grace, what's wrong?'

Grace realised she must have been squinting at him, her head was throbbing again.

'Head and neck hurting. Falling asleep on this sofa hasn't helped.'

'Paracetamol?'

'Finished them. Look, never mind. Go on.'

Gilbert pinched his nose between thumb and forefinger as if it would remind him where he had got to. 'Turns out he's not really "into" modern art – installations, happenings, all that. He paints with oils, mainly portraits but other figurative work as well. This Sergei, the one who owns the flat, saw Tate's final show in Chicago, bought some of it, and when he heard he wanted to have a bit of time in Europe, struck a deal – he'd let Tate use his flat rent-free in London and, if Tate could show he was prepared to work to pay all his other expenses, well, then Sergei would know he was serious about travelling and learning. He's going to fund him to have six months in France

– there's a very good portrait painter Tate wants to study with in Paris and someone else in Marseilles, can't remember what his speciality is.'

'Oh God.'

'Indeed. All that enthusiasm for modern art was something of an act. I mean, he says he likes it, but it's not his first love. He just overheard Alistair in a pub saying he was looking for someone to do modern art tours and knew he could wing it. On top of the tours he's been doing cleaning, late shifts, early shifts.'

Grace understood now why Tate had spent so much time asleep on the sofa. She wished he was here now.

Gilbert sighed. 'As we said on the way back, we made an awful lot of judgements about Tate based on how he dressed.'

It was fitting that Alistair chose that moment to come out of his office. He was wearing the blouse and skirt ensemble again but this time he had shoes on with it, strappy and quite high. Totally inappropriate for work.

Gilbert stared, slid his gaze from Alistair to Grace, and there was the slightest widening of his eyes.

'This is Stacey,' Grace said, indicating Alistair with her hand. Gilbert was still looking and not talking. There was a certain slackness to his jaw, as if it had dropped open but by keeping his mouth shut he was hoping to disguise it.

'Any question you like, Gilbert,' Alistair said in his deep voice.

Gilbert slowly shook his head. 'I wouldn't know where to start.'

Alistair lowered himself into one of the leather chairs and Gilbert kept checking on him as though he needed to establish that what he was seeing was real.

'I seem to have completely forgotten my thread,' he said, giving Alistair's legs another hasty check. 'Had I got to the bit about Tate being followed? No? Right . . . well, in one way, he was pleased to find out that the people who had been hanging about were friends of your father. You see, with Sergei being Russian and rich, he worried they might be some Russian mafia types. Said he spent a lot of time trying to shake them off.' Gilbert laughed. 'He'd got to the point where he was thinking of going to the police, which is pretty ironic . . .'

Gilbert was building up to something unpleasant, Grace could sense it, and in an effort to stave it off she told them both about the phone call from her father.

'That explains a lot,' Gilbert said. 'Lilly, eh? Hard to credit it, although I could never warm to her. And no Russian connection at all?' He glanced across at Alistair and Grace could see the effort he was making to act as if he were completely unfazed. 'This is good news for the business, though, isn't it Al — um, Stacey?'

'Yes, I suppose so,' Alistair said without much enthusiasm. 'Bit of a nerve the galleries barring us when it was their own staff on the take. Could probably screw them for some compensation for loss of earnings.'

The old Alistair would probably have been on his feet and rushing for a phone, but this one continued to sit with his 'wet weekend' face on. Gilbert turned back towards Grace and mouthed, 'God save us,' before a more serious expression settled over his features.

'My dear, Grace,' he said, giving Alistair another guarded look, 'I hate to be the bearer of bad news, but having been on the receiving end of a lot of it in my time, I know that getting it straight is better than a big tour round the houses while everybody tries to avoid eye contact. So, Tate seems to think you set him up, that you distracted him long enough for your father to get into his flat. He was a gentleman and didn't supply details, but he looks crushed.'

Grace pictured those green eyes with the light gone out of them and retrieved a tissue from her sleeve. She held it to her nose and waited, and then lowered it again.

'Is there more?'

'Yes. About the icons found in his flat.'

'Please, please don't mention them,' she said, because

she knew what they were, had known it ever since she'd heard the original icons had been found by the police.

Gilbert's hand was on her knee.

'He painted them for you, Grace,' he said, gently, 'you must know that. He couldn't bear to see how sad you were when the real ones got stolen. He thought it was a way to show how he felt about you. He still wants you to have them, you know, when the police let them go.'

Grace didn't bother with the tissue this time and it wouldn't have lasted long anyway because she was heaving up great sobs and tears that coursed down her face and plopped on to the leather of the sofa. She was allowing herself to imagine Tate copying the icons to make her happy, the paint she'd seen under his nails evidence of his love for her.

She remembered the times she'd never even given him a chance because he reminded her so much of Bill, and yet he wasn't anything like Bill. All that work Tate had been doing, while Bill had sneered at getting out of bed before lunch.

She cried on, with Gilbert now and again patting her knee and saying, 'That's it. Cry it out' and Stacey saying, 'Yes, you have a good cry, Grace. Bottling things up never does you any good, believe me.'

She did take the lid off the biscuit tin then. Why not?

How much further could she slide? She, Gilbert and Stacey shared the whisky and Grace and Stacey the joints, even though any potency the dope had once possessed seemed to have dried to nothing. It must have done, because Grace didn't even find it funny when Gilbert put on the cheese-cloth shirt or Stacey stowed the cigarettes away down the front of her blouse 'for later'.

All she could think about was how life had been skewed and twisted: the copied icons were a token of something genuine from Tate, whereas what she'd given him on that bed must now, to him, seem just tawdry and fake.

CHAPTER 32

There had been no response to the messages she had left on his voicemail or the trip round to his address to ring on the bell and look up at the blank windows of his flat. Following a nasty, raw showdown with her father, she had persuaded him to write to Tate to explain that she'd had absolutely no idea that his plans had included invading Tate's wardrobe. It felt like getting one of your parents to write a letter excusing you from PE. Still no response. She was left explaining, to a void, what elements of her behaviour had been an act and what most certainly had not.

Increasingly desperate for some king of contact with Tate, she hunted out Joe, Corinne and Bebbie in the White Hart, but they hadn't seen Tate for days. Bebbie gave her a look that said, *Now you know how it feels.*

Standing in the pub, she'd wanted to gravitate to the bar to drown her despair, but after the whisky and the joints she'd been heartily sick and couldn't face even the smell of alcohol. Perhaps nine years of sobriety had made her allergic to any kind of drug? Was she stuck being a goody two-shoes forever? Back in the office, she put the biscuit tin on the floor and stamped down on the lid with the heel of one of those goody two-shoes until the whole thing was a buckled mess.

Putting it in the bin, she knew it was a symbolic act, but of what she wasn't certain.

She wasn't certain what she was meant to be doing at work either, really. Even though they were no longer black-listed, Picture London was still not functioning properly – Gilbert was the only one doing any tours. Grace still had a tendency to burst into tears whenever she passed any kind of painting, particularly portraits, and Stacey had long periods of time when she just stared at the carpet. Emma had been in touch to report that she was going to Italy with her parents for a week or two to think things through. Stacey would have been more optimistic if Emma had mentioned coming back afterwards.

Emma was another person who wasn't returning Grace's calls. Grace was trying to ignore a few herself – mainly from her sisters. They were now fully up to speed with Felicity's escapade, but this had taken second billing to Grace's 'return to the world of the heart' as Serafina had dubbed it. There was delight that Grace was still capable of such a monumentally wild and rash act and, even better, was laid low by love. They revelled in it and seemed particularly happy to tell her that if she had followed her emotions (female) instead of her brain (male) right from the start, she would once again be in the arms of an artist – inspiring, loving and nurturing him.

Grace found that really helpful.

Felicity had finally got the message that this latest drama might not be about her and her throbbing aura and seized the chance to play a major supporting role with gusto, appearing at odd times to dispense unasked-for advice and offers of 'emotional counselling'. This had driven Grace, the night before, to sleep in the office, reasoning that one sofa was very much like another. Besides, she felt closer to Tate there than anywhere else. Seeing his chair made her feel that at any minute he might walk in and sit on it. That happy image only stayed in her head a few moments before it was replaced by the one of him nodding at the vast bed in his flat and saying, *That's what this was, Gracie, keeping me busy?*

Her phone told her a text had been delivered and she snatched it up, merely to find another of Zin's poems. Lines that were meant to be uplifting had been arriving every day. This latest effort was particularly enamel-rotting: *The soul that has never loved has never lived, and heat once given forever lives on lips.*

Grace texted back: *Never mind heat forever living on lips, what about fathers forever living in flats? Got a poem to help me with that???*

Grace had company at night in the office – Stacey, still on the floor. Grace believed that it was some form of self-inflicted penance. She had a perfectly good bed at home, albeit without Emma in it.

Grace studied her now, sitting in the easy chair and working through more paperwork about refunds, and wondered how she walked in those shoes. The dress was good, suited her, and she'd had a shave and put on some enthusiastic make-up. Strangely, it wasn't the lipstick and eye shadow Grace found most disturbing; it was the wig. It was blond.

Stacey still looked like Alistair, though, even when Grace squinted at him, and she wondered whether it was important to him to feel he could pass as a woman. She decided now was not a good time to ask that question, but did offer to help Stacey with her make-up next time.

The more she saw Alistair dressed as Stacey, the less of a jolt it caused. Perhaps one day she would even be able to think about what she had on under that dress. She looked again . . . no, that day hadn't yet arrived.

She watched Stacey chewing the end of her pen. It certainly took enormous courage to sit there looking exactly how she wanted to look. She had the biggest balls Grace had ever seen in a dress.

When Stacey had finished the calculations, she passed Grace the paperwork and tottered back to her office. When Grace looked up next time, Alistair was standing there.

'I'm going for lunch,' he said, fiddling to do up the buttons on his shirt collar.

'Not ready to go out as Stacey yet?'

He shook his head and said, 'One day,' which made her feel incredibly sad and stirred up all kinds of thoughts about people not being who they really were and trying to cram their real selves back into a box . . . or a locked cabinet . . . or even a biscuit tin.

Grace scanned the work she'd been given, correcting a lot of it, but all the figures began to blur and she put her head down on it, not caring if she smudged everything and ended up with ink all over her face. What was the point in carrying on with this controlled version of herself when Tate had reminded her there was so much more to life?

'Neck so bad you can't even keep your head upright any more?' a voice asked right by her desk and she detached herself from the soggy paper and slowly sat up, even though she felt as if everything that used to be muscle might now be made of jelly. She wiped her eyes with the palm of her hand and took a good look at him.

He had on his greatcoat, with the collar up, and he might just have ridden in from the range, his hair all mussed up and especially blond against the blue of the material. She remembered how his hair had brushed against her chin when he kissed her neck and it caused a laugh to try and fight its way up inside her, a kind of glad-to-be-alive, glad-to-know-him laugh. She met his gaze and the laugh turned tail and went back down her throat.

'Got your messages,' he said and crossed the room to sit in his chair. He wrapped the coat more tightly around himself, his hands in his pockets, and stretched out his legs. 'I got your dad's message too. Gonna get any from Fliss? Your sisters?'

Before he would have delivered those lines with a laugh or a grin. Now they were coming out straight. It didn't feel like a good sign.

'I know I've really hurt you,' she said softly. 'I'm really, really sorry.'

He nodded, a kind of thinking nod, but didn't say anything, leaving her a big gap in which to jump and repeat all the things she'd tried to get into her messages.

'I really, really had no idea how far Dad's theories about you had got, Tate, please believe me. And, in no way is this an excuse, but being hit on the head, well, it didn't improve my ability to think logically. I should have just told him to leave you alone, but some of what he was saying seemed to make a weird kind of sense. Not the wardrobe thing. That would never have seemed anything other than mad.'

Tate had his chin down as he twisted the seat of the chair to the left and then to the right. She didn't know if it indicated irritation.

'And, please believe me, I had no idea that he was going to be at your flat . . . if I had, do you honestly think I would have let you take me there? It would have been the last place I'd go.' She lowered her head to try to see into his eyes. 'When you kissed me in the street, it was scary and wonderful and I didn't want it to stop. Everything from there on was real. Me.'

He lifted his chin, but his expression was still watchful and she knew she was beginning to sound as if she was pleading. She needed to see a spark of light in those green eyes.

'I don't know what else I can do to make you believe me,' she said bleakly. 'I just want to hold you and kiss you and say I am so, so sorry for all that time I wasted being defensive and snotty.'

She felt she was losing him.

'Please Tate, talk to me. How can I convince you it was the real me in that taxi, in that bed?'

'Easy.' His stare was direct and challenging. 'You can tell

me about Bill because I sure as hell wanna slug him, but I don't know what for.'

The word 'Bill' felt like another thump to her head. 'Bill?' she squawked and then tried in a flurry to think this through. He knew about Bill. But what did he know?

'Yeah, Bill,' Tate said more forcefully. 'Bill Jackson, the painter. Is there another Bill you lived with?'

Ah, so he knew that.

'How . . . how did you find out about Bill?'

'Had a visit from your mum and dad 'bout an hour ago and boy, have to say all bets are off about which one of them is more nuts than the other. Your dad told you his theory about Jack the Ripper? Man!'

She heard only snatches of what he was saying. Why, why had her parents suddenly decided to be interested in anyone but themselves?

Tate must have guessed she wasn't listening because he said, 'You in there?'

'They told you?'

'Yup. Your dad said he knew he'd loused things up, wanted to put it right. Fliss said you came back from Spain with a broken heart, hadn't been the same since. Kept playing it safe – work, life. Men.'

The one time she'd have liked them to display their usual self-absorption and they'd gone and—

'Grace.'

The hard edges of that 'Grace' made her panic. How should she play this? He was going to ask her to tell him everything.

'Thing is, it was those damn signs again,' he was saying, 'you were sending them out, I wasn't reading them. You looking queasy in front of Bill Jackson's painting; all that jabbering about checks and bills before you clonked your head.' He stopped. 'So, you gonna tell me now or am I gonna have to tip you upside down and shake you to get it all out?'

The expression on his face showed he probably would.

'I . . . this is hard . . .'

'Come on, I've gotta hear it from you.'

'All right, all right,' she said, struggling to think how to get everything in a believable order. 'Look, I met Bill when I was eighteen, just before my A-levels. I was on a school trip to a gallery. He was mooching about in there looking like a tramp, a beautiful tramp with a great shock of blond hair, these tatty blue overalls, fingers covered in silver rings.'

She saw Tate glance at the ring on his thumb and frown. It made her feel hesitant about going on, but on she went.

'One look and it was all the clichés – like being struck by lightning, the whole world falling away, you name it.'

She glanced at him to see if he was still frowning. 'I mean, with a mum like mine and older sisters who were already passion junkies, it was bound to happen. I was ripe for the *coup de foudre*. Ripe for starring in my own heartbreaking love story. He was the call of my wild. So . . . I left the gallery with him, left school, left home. Rang Mum to tell her and you'd have thought I'd just got into the best university.'

'Great parenting.'

She loved him more for saying that and tried to put it all in a smile. He did a kind of grimacy thing back but his frown had, at least, gone.

'Yes, some of Felicity's finest mothering skills came into play. Practically whooped with delight when I told her we were off to Spain. I was eighteen, Bill was forty.' She shook her head. 'Anyway, we went to Spain, Bill had rented a big, slightly dilapidated villa in San Sebastián. He loved the resort: great food, great location and respectable enough for him to have something to rebel against.' She knew Tate understood that.

She shrugged. 'It was wonderful for about a year and a half. We'd get up late in the afternoon and I'd swim and lie in the sun while he painted. We'd smoke a bit, drink a lot, he'd paint some more, we'd go out till early morning. We got in with a good crowd – lively. They were all

nationalities – other artists, writers, musicians, a few Aus-
tralians doing the Europe tour. Bill's son lived in a flat in
the town too for a couple of months. Just passing through.
He was a sculptor, though not a very good one. Anyway,
what more can I say? It seemed like a fairy tale – I was
Bill's lover, his muse, he couldn't get enough of me.'

'You can hurry this bit along,' Tate said gruffly.

'Even in winter it was beautiful: the beach deserted and
the skies stormy and us wrapped in layers of clothes and
blankets in the villa. And then suddenly it wasn't so good.
Flipped from feeling like bliss to being like barbed wire.'

She remembered the month they went from Bill reaching
out while he was painting to make sure she was still there
to finding a woman asleep on the sofa in his studio wearing
only his coat.

Tate sat forward in his chair. 'Stop thinking about it and
get it out, Grace. Come on, the quicker you say it the easier
it will be.'

She thought how young he was. How lovely to be so
certain, so glib.

'Bill started bringing other women to the villa; some I
knew, and others I didn't. If I got upset, he said I was being
small-minded, bourgeois. He said I was still the one . . .
just not the one and only.'

'Dickhead,' Tate said with feeling.

'No, he was just being Bill – passionate to the point of making you feel like you were burning and then leaving you charred and broken to go off and find someone else to incinerate. I loved him *so* much; this wasn't how my love affair was meant to go.'

She was surprised to hear herself laugh. 'He had me wound round his little finger. Makes me sick now how grateful I used to be when he came back to me still smelling of someone else. My heart was his and he knew it.'

'I'm not warming to Bill. How long did he dick around?'

'Long enough to make me sick with myself, him, everything.' She stopped talking as she tried to think how to finish her story about her and Bill because she couldn't go on to the place their relationship had really died. If she did, he'd be up and out of his chair and gone. He wouldn't look at her in the same way as he'd looked at her on that bed.

'What happened in the end?' he said.

'I had enough,' she said slowly. 'We called it a day. I came home. I went to college, resumed my A-levels, got a place at Edinburgh to do History of Art, got the job with Picture London.' She wished she'd paced that last bit better – it sounded as if she were reading from a list. Tate obviously thought so too.

'Just like that,' he said.

'Yes.'

'So, when did he burn the paintings?'

'What?'

He shook his head; she could tell he was losing patience. 'Did a bit of googling when your mum and dad had gone. Bill Jackson was in Spain for two years, and the woman in the gallery said he burned his paintings when he was in Spain. The explanation by that painting said he did it during a particularly turbulent period in his life. So I'm guessing you were either there or he did it because of you.'

'We had an argument, he got really drunk, that's how it happened.'

He leaned back again and studied her, and under the pressure of having those green eyes on her, all those mannerisms that showed she was lying leaked out.

'Don't treat me like an idiot, Grace,' he said. 'This story you're giving me, it's not the full one, is it? Lots of bits missing. Know how I know? 'Cos it's nine years down the line and you're still carrying this love affair around. See, Fliss might think that having your heart broken is enough to explain all this . . .' he waved his hand at her, at the desk, at the office. 'But I don't buy that. This is more than a broken heart. This is something that's left you so guarded it's making you wall yourself up. Isn't that the phrase? You're hemming yourself in, brick by brick. You're even going around acting like an unpaid slave in a business you could run twenty times better than Al. Why is that, unless your self-confidence has taken such a kicking you can't see how fucking brilliant you are? Or you've got so badly broken, you think the slightest bit of pressure's gonna bust you apart again?'

At that moment Grace felt the two conflicting emotions of gratitude that he understood her so completely and horror that her deepest fears had been uncovered.

'I like my job,' she said pathetically.

He snorted. 'Yeah? Well, that's great. Another big lie, but hey, I'm pleased for you.' His tone grew harsher. 'See, if I keep getting these lies, if you won't tell me what happened, my mind's starting to think all kinds of things. Not just about what might have happened, but how you feel about me.'

'Tate—'

'You've already proved you didn't trust me with your dad's wardrobe act, but hey, I can't blame you for jumping to conclusions. You know hardly anything about me and, well, if I didn't exactly lie, I didn't tell people everything – about Sergei, the flat, what I painted. But not trusting me with something from your past is different. What do you think I'm gonna do, sell it? Or are you holding yourself back 'cos you think I might be like Bill?'

When she didn't reply, he pushed his chair back and got to his feet. 'Oh, that's it. I get it. I'm like him and so I'm not to be trusted. Well, that's kind of insulting, Grace. I'm not him, I'm me. The one and only.' He flung open his arms, but without a smile to round off the gesture it was too bitter.

'No, no. It's not about you, it's about me,' she blurted out. It came across all whiney and she wasn't surprised when he shook his head and plonked himself back down in his chair and laughed.

'That's it? That's all I get? Something people say to explain why they wanna split up when they don't wanna get to grips with the real reason? What the hell does that even mean, Grace?'

She stood and came round the desk. Should she push it, take a step nearer to him? 'I know you're not him, Tate, I know that, but you've got that same walking-on-the-cracks way of looking at life and that's what scared me about you . . . and then in the pub, in the taxi, in the flat I just decided I'd chance it, I'd fall off the edge—'

'That's how you see being with me, as falling off the edge?' He was looking at her as if she'd slapped him.

'No . . . yes . . . please, Tate, that didn't come out right. I've fallen in love with you – really, really fallen. I can't get enough of you. I want to be with you. These last few days without you have been as if someone's turned off a light. But, please trust me on this. I don't want to go back over things I put away a long time ago. Please don't keep pushing me. I don't want to keep harking back to the past. Isn't it enough that I love you in the here and now? That I'm so, so sorry that I didn't trust you? Isn't it enough that you've fallen for me too – enough to copy the icons? It's the loveliest thing '

'No, it's not enough.' He shoved his hands in his pockets as if he was scared he'd touch her otherwise. 'It's pretty good, Grace, I'll give you that, but I want more. I've got a right to ask you about what went on with Bill stinkin' Jackson because whatever he's done to you has come back to bite me. It's made you distrust me from the first time we met . . . all this holding yourself back, all this order, routine, reining yourself in. That girl I saw spinning around in my chair pretending to be a gunfighter, she was real. I could see it in you from day one; she's the one I fell for. Why's she hiding, Grace?'

'I can't . . . I can't tell you. Please, it's painful—'

His eyes were stormy, his hands out of his pockets again, underlining what he was saying. 'What, more painful than being arrested, having to call my mom and tell her, thousands of miles away, that I was in trouble? Hearing how sick with worry she was?'

Her head, her chest, her stomach felt as if they were being compacted. She didn't speak.

'Tell me, Grace,' he said harshly. 'What really happened?'

'I can't. I really can't.'

'Why? 'Cos it makes you feel vulnerable, like you made me feel vulnerable? Know what it feels like to make love to a woman and then have the police pile in while you're still naked, still got the scent of her all over your skin?'

She couldn't even begin to answer that. She was gulping.

'This is bugging the hell out of me, Grace. If you won't even meet me halfway . . .'

She could see he was really trying not to lose his temper. She wondered, if she leaned over and kissed him, could she heal this, make it all go away?

'Did he hit you?' he asked suddenly, the anger coming out in the force of his words. 'Assault you . . . worse?'

'No, nothing like that.'

He made a harsh noise as if that had been his best shot and he had nothing left. She could see he was trying to take his hurt and work it into something less sharp, but then his face settled into an expression that made her feel like he'd walked out of the room already and she closed her eyes. She gave a start and opened her eyes when she felt him lay the palm of his hand gently on her face.

'I feel like we're in the Last Chance Saloon here, Grace,' he said, with a look as if willing her to understand. 'I can't be with you if you won't tell me what this is all about. It's a huge, great hole in what I know about you, can't you see that? I mean, I'd tell you everything about me if you just asked – first kiss, things I'd do differently, what I'd look back on my life and say I'm proud of, ashamed of. All the big stuff, I want to share it with you, because meeting you, falling for you, wow, it's been frustrating and maddening and crap-ass wonderful. I liked how you watched over everyone else – even when you were being snitty, I liked that – Gilb, Al, Vi. Liked it even more when I saw Fliss, saw how you were the mom in that relationship . . . it rang so many bells with me, Grace. You're kind and loving and caring and I thought I could trust you. A rock-solid pair of hands. A true heart. 'Cos you know, I've had it with flakiness, that casual letting everyone else go and hang because you've got to express your innermost self. Sticks right here.' She thought he was going to point to his throat, but he was pointing to his heart.

'You made me feel as if someone had turned up the power on all my senses, and I spent a while wondering if it was because I was kicking against you, trying to get a reaction, but it wasn't, Grace. It was just 'cos I loved you. Seemed like you were someone who might bat for me for a change.' He smiled and then it was gone. 'But here you are hiding a big part of yourself away as if you feel I'm too young or stupid to cope with it – whatever *it* is. And now . . . now you're talking about you and me as if I'm gonna demolish you. What way is that to start anything?'

'Tate, please . . .'

'You don't get it, do you?' he said, 'I need to know how he broke your heart so I can mend it properly.'

'Oh, Tate.' She reached up and put her hand on his. It was such a wonderful, wonderful thing to say to her and she was so tempted to take a chance. But then the guilt and shame came back. How could she see that handsome, open face change under her words? That would be harder to get over than him walking away.

She was trying to commit to memory how his skin felt when it was no longer going to be on hers.

'I don't know how else to reach you,' he said and he slid his hand out from under hers and it was gone. He was glancing over her shoulder like he was already thinking how he was going to make it to the door. He looked as if he'd just been taught a horrible lesson by life.

She tried to get him to sit down again. 'Please, Tate, people don't have to know everything about each other. I love you, I want to be with you and maybe, maybe I'll tell you it all when—'

'I don't want "maybe", Grace, it's not enough. I want "yes", "definitely", and I want it now. I want all of you. I've had years of promises that get broken; years of feeling second in line behind whatever passion was grabbing Mom at that moment. Whatever guy was grabbing her. Lots of superficial love, you know, lots of "my darling, clever boy", but none of that helping you see where the big bear traps are hidden, pulling you out when you fall in them.'

He glanced towards the door again and she sensed there was a lot more he wanted to tell her but didn't have the strength. He was still looking at the door when he said, 'Listen, I'm heading off to France quicker than I'd planned, as soon as Sergei and his lawyer have sorted out if I'm free to go. I was gonna ask you to come with me. I *still* want to ask you, but not like this, Grace. Not if you won't trust me enough to confide in me.' He suddenly bent forward and gave her a peck on the cheek. 'I love you, Grace, but I'm not coming round begging again. I've done all the running in this, kept on trying even though you kept on knocking me away. This is it. Your turn now. If I'm an edge, if that's how you see me, well, you gotta jump.'

He started to move away and then stopped, but she could tell from his face it was not a reprieve. His shoulders had dropped and she saw his chest rise and fall as it had done when she watched him sleeping.

'If you can't do what I want you to do for us, please, for fuck's sake, do something for yourself – get yourself a job that doesn't involve taking out the trash and putting the magazines straight and getting some guy's ass out of the fire who earns about five times what you earn. If you're gonna stay here, get Al to face up to what you do and either pay you for it or get another person in to do all that crap.' He reached up and mussed his hair about. 'Or . . . I could help you get some money together, maybe become Al's partner . . . I don't know . . . or you could go somewhere else – another company, more money. But do yourself a favour: if you're gonna stay, stop treading water, huh? Because, Grace, someday you'll just give up and drown under all this handmaiden stuff.'

She remained standing where he had left her and was still there when Alistair came back from lunch. He didn't say anything, just got her to sit down. She put her head on the desk again and it could have been a replay of the scene before Tate had visited her, except at least then she'd had some hope that she could be with him, and now she didn't.

CHAPTER 33

'So, New Hampshire next or you wanna go for a biggie?'

Violet pondered and said, 'Montana, I would like to go for Montana.' She giggled. It felt a bit naughty Tate being here during the day without Gilbert. Without Grace.

Tate got up and walked across the squares of paper as if they were stepping stones and had a look through the pile of scrapbooks. Montana filled three and he brought them back to the sofa, stone-stepping very neatly on his return journey.

They went through mountains and ranches and lumber, through Glacier National Park and the Battle of the Little Bighorn, Tate reading all the snipped-out bits of paper and now and again telling Violet things she didn't know. He had a nice voice to listen to, and now the mice seemed to have gone quiet, it was good to have some noise in the house.

She hadn't even been afraid when he'd turned up and done Grace's knock but wasn't Grace. They'd laughed about that when she'd let him in, although she felt his laugh didn't sound right. She expected that was because Grace and he had, as Gilbert said, 'fallen out'.

Violet knew it was something to do with the robbery and the fact that Grace thought Tate had stolen the Russian Ivons, which was plainly ridiculous. Anyone could tell that he was a good boy, although she would have liked to have seen his hair a bit shorter. Tate said it was also because Grace wouldn't let go of her secrets and Violet nodded despite not having the foggiest idea what he meant.

When they got to the last page of Montana, he closed the scrapbook with that same kind of action her mother used to use when she had finished telling them a bedtime story.

'It's been great going through these with you, Violet,' he said. 'Taken my mind off . . . lots of other things. But we won't be able to do all of the US. This is going to be my last visit.'

'Until when?'

'Until a long time.' His smile was a good one but she felt it had shrunk since that first time he had come here, although maybe that was because his lip wasn't swollen any more.

'I'm going to France,' he was saying, 'day after tomorrow. To learn a bit more about painting.'

Violet remembered Mr Lewis on the corner. 'My neighbour

is a decorator. You could get him to talk to you. Think of the money you'd save not going to France.'

He explained to her that it wasn't that kind of painting and she realised she'd been silly and laughed, although she was still rather sad that he wouldn't be calling again and a bit put out too. She had moved all the scrapbooks down to the sitting room after all.

When he didn't speak he reminded her of how droopy Grace had been when she'd visited. And then, out of the blue, he asked her whether she'd ever been in love.

That was easy. 'Of course. With my mother and with Gilbert.'

He was still droopy. 'Hurts, doesn't it?' he said and she agreed with him to be polite. She didn't remember it hurting at all; it was very straightforward.

'And . . . has Gilbert ever been in love?' he asked next, and she had a think about that; she said he'd probably loved their mother and she knew he loved her.

'No one else?'

Violet said 'no' and saw Tate open his mouth and then close it again.

'Did you want to ask something else?' she said.

'No. Old me would have. New me is reading the signs. Got Grace to thank for that.' He really shouldn't twist his mouth like that – the wind might change.

'Anyway, gotta go,' he said finally. 'It's good you love Gilbert and he loves you, 'cos you know, Vi, love comes in all shapes and sizes.'

He stood up and so she did too.

'I want to give you a big old hug, Vi,' he said, 'but know you'd hate it, so shake on it?'

She wasn't sure about the hand he was holding out but he said, 'That's paint under my nails, not dirt,' and so she did shake it – just a quick touch and away again. She surreptitiously wiped her palm down the back of her skirt afterwards.

As they walked to the door, he asked if she'd like him to send her some postcards from France? Suggested she could collect them and start a French scrapbook after she'd finished with China.

She said she expected China to take quite a while, but that yes, if he washed his hands before he wrote them and perhaps put each one in an envelope to send, that would be a lovely idea.

When he was putting his boots back on, he said he was sorry to be saying goodbye to her and to Gilbert. He didn't say he was sorry to be saying goodbye to Grace.

She watched him wander off down the path. Those boots could do with a polish.

Gilbert came home not long after that. The way he shut the front door didn't sound promising.

Another droopy person.

'You look very tired,' she said to him, 'can I make you some tea?'

'It's Grace,' he replied being really rather rude by not answering her question. 'I popped in earlier; she's still very upset. Not nice to see. I don't know what to do for her . . . she won't talk about it. She's pretending that everything's under control, everything's fine.' He was playing with the arm cap on the chair, which he knew irritated her. 'So stupid,' he said, really tweaking it. 'She's lovely, he's lovely, but it looks as if it's doomed. Makes you think . . . *carpe diem* and all that.'

She didn't know what he was doing talking about fish – it was casserole tonight. He was always trying to change the nights they had things. She left him putting the arm cap straight while she made a pot of tea. When she came back he was still looking sad, so she told him about Tate's visit.

'He said he was very pleased that you love me and I love you, Gilbert.' She would have liked to laugh then, because Gilbert gave her one of the looks he used when he thought she hadn't been able to undo the top on her pill bottle. 'And he said love comes in all different shapes and sizes.

I think he might have been drinking before he popped round.'

Gilbert nodded and frowned while he drank his tea and then he was burbling on about love too. 'It does, it does,' he said, 'comes in all different shapes and sizes. And it stretches.'

She had to ask him to repeat that last bit because she felt they'd veered into talking about elastic bands.

'It means,' Gilbert had said, playing with that blessed arm cap again, 'that you can love one person and then if another one comes along who you want to love, that's all right, because there's enough love to go around. It stretches, doesn't have to be rationed out.'

She wasn't quite sure what he was talking about now, and didn't know why he had to peer at her like that as if she had something on her face. She went and checked in the mirror and when she came back he was still peering at her.

'Do you want to tell me something, Gilbert?' she had asked, but he said he didn't; he just wanted her to try and remember what he'd said about love stretching and not having to be rationed.

She said she would and got a piece of paper off the bookshelf and wrote it down. That seemed to really cheer him up and they had a good old evening after that. Cluedo. Twice.

CHAPTER 34

Grace watched the gay man in traditional tweeds and the heterosexual man in a dress playing chess and doubted whether her next place of work would be as interesting. A few more days and Picture London would be moth-balled.

Alistair was flying out to see Emma in Italy; there had been hours of phone conversations and the signs were, if not good, then promising. But they needed time to talk, away from the pressures of the business.

Gilbert was fulfilling the last of their tours because Alistair said it was important to maintain the goodwill attached to the Picture London name, for when it reopened. He hadn't pressed Grace to help Gilbert out and she'd been grateful for that. From next week she was finished with art – she was moving forward to history (if that was chrono-logically possible) thanks to Gilbert. He'd alerted her to a management job at Capital H for History, a company that had a baffling love of puns but a full programme of tours and thus a constant need for someone with Grace's organisational skills. It was full-time and meant a proper wage and an office of her own.

Grace picked up her mobile and checked it again as she'd been obsessively checking it since Tate had left her. Nothing from him, and anything else she was ignoring. Except she had read the short text Emma had sent which suggested that, in their relationship at least, she had been forgiven for holding on to a secret. All the same, she knew it would be some time before Emma's life resumed any of its old habits, including pizza with friends. As Emma had so succinctly signed off: ☹ *other wman = hsbnd.*

She saw that Stacey was trying to get her attention without Gilbert noticing. Her look clearly said *help* because there was a pile of her black knights, bishops and rooks by Gilbert's elbow.

'Queen to e 4,' she mouthed and Gilbert said, 'Stop it, Grace, and . . .' He tapped Stacey's hand as she went to move the queen: 'Stop it, Stacey.'

It was a friendly tap because Gilbert got on better with Stacey than he ever had with Alistair. Gilbert said there was much less of that *Monarch of the Glen* posturing from Stacey, plus she had better taste in shoes.

Grace carried on putting files into storage boxes and shredding anything that didn't need to be kept. When, or if, Picture London ever got going again, it would be somewhere else. Alistair was giving up the lease, cutting more ties with the past.

Gilbert finished trouncing Stacey and came to help Grace with some files. 'Nice that we'll still be seeing each other,' he said, 'even though I suspect I'll have to keep touching my forelock when we meet. Do you get an armband showing your title?'

'I will make one myself.'

'You probably would. But they're not a bad bunch there, although maybe not as colourful as here.' He arched an eyebrow and they both looked across at Stacey, who was tidying away the chess pieces.

'I'm looking forward to the change,' she said. She welcomed the certainty of history with its secure dates and unchangeable facts and she need never look at another painting again. Slightly ironic that she was happy to look at other people's history and not her own.

When she had gone for the interview she had not expected to get the job. When she got it, she thought she would panic at the prospect of all that extra responsibility and turn it down, but in a moment of rare clarity she realised that she was being asked to do much less than at Picture London for a fair bit more money. There even appeared to be a personal assistant called Heather, who cheerfully said she did all the 'odds and sods' nobody else wanted to do.

Gilbert was looking at her. 'He hasn't gone yet, you know,' he whispered. 'There is still time.' He glanced at his watch. 'Just.'

'We're trashing that file,' she replied, trying to take a green lever arch one out of his hand.

Gilbert wasn't giving up the file. 'Grace, stop being so stubborn and go and talk to him.' They had a tussle over a piece of office stationery because it was more socially acceptable to fight over that than for Gilbert to put her in an arm lock to make her see sense and for her to slap him so that he would leave her alone.

'Oh, keep it then,' she said, letting go. 'And don't nag, I've stabilised.'

'If stabilised means you appear to be eating and drinking fresh air and Stacey has a slightly better grip on grooming and make-up than you do—'

'I'm cleaning out the office, Gilbert. I'm dressing down. Don't make me out to be—'

'Functioning on the surface, but underneath falling apart?' Gilbert said archly, pursing his lips. 'Well, I think stability is highly overrated, particularly in this case – standing firm is just plain wrong, Grace. Tate believed your innocence about all that wardrobe stuff so I can't see what else is stopping you two getting together.'

'Things, Gilbert. Things.' She waved away what might have been another attempt to interrupt. 'I have a new career to look forward to, and please, I don't harangue you about . . . people at the National Gallery who I think might—'

Gilbert had his hand up now. With the other one he gave her the file. He looked a bit heated. 'All right, all right. But the two things are not the same. I've been burned once *and* there's Violet.'

She didn't want to talk about burning. She just had to get through today, then Tate would be gone and things would return to how they were. Whenever she thought about being brave and telling Tate everything, she felt sick, clenched in on herself. Then guilt and shame surfaced and she realised it was hopeless. She would never forgive herself so how could he be expected to forgive her? She couldn't stand to have him look at her with disgust. It was a simple choice in the end – she could lose him when he went to France, or right now by coming clean. On balance, letting him go was better.

'Here,' Gilbert said, giving her a handkerchief.

She tried to concentrate on the positives. She already had her flat back – breaking down at regular intervals had shifted her father where logical argument had failed. Whether he was talking to her mother, or she to him, she didn't know. She was having a rest from family for a while, particularly the dramatic, crime-obsessed ones and those inclined towards poetry.

At lunchtime she went out into London, a drizzly, sky-bearing-down-on-the-tops-of-buildings place today, and walked to Green Park. Most of the trees were bare and the leaves on the ground were like litter – too many feet had kicked through them, too much damp and grime seeped into them. She did a rough circle of the park and thought of Tate. Always thinking about him and sometimes thinking about Mark and wondering if she had been wrong – perhaps she could go back to what they had? Mark didn't want all of her like Tate did. She could live with him all her life and he wouldn't ask her those difficult questions.

She dropped in to see Bernice on the way back. Sol was just putting on his coat; it was one of his days for helping now Esther was taking it easy.

'Cheese and chutney?' he said to Bernice who was on the phone and she gave him a thumbs-up. 'Anything for you, Grace?' he called over his shoulder on the way out.

She waited for Bernice to finish talking and because she couldn't bear to look at the brochure for the USA lying on the desk, covered it up with one for the Caribbean.

With Bernice off the phone they talked about Alistair, Bernice fishing for the reason why he was taking a break and Grace evading the nets and hooks without giving anything away. No change there then.

'I've seen you looking better,' Bernice said when Alistair had been exhausted as a topic of conversation. 'Sure you did the right thing?'

Under an earlier interrogation, almost as probing as the ones Grace had endured from her father, she had admitted to Bernice that she and Tate had had a fling, but that she had decided not to take it any further. This was true in a way.

'I'm not sure of anything,' she said truthfully, 'except that the kind of life Tate will be leading doesn't work for me. I need more stability, a settled routine. With someone like Tate I'd start off drifting and end up falling. You're really lucky, Bernice; I look at you and Sol and think what a good team you make . . . both pulling in the same direction, wanting the same things. You're working so hard together to build something solid – the business, your house, your marriage. Lovely to have found someone dependable who's completely on your wavelength.'

Bernice had been holding a magazine in her hands, idly flicking through it as Grace talked and suddenly, in one swift movement, she hurled it towards the wall, where it fell in a swirl of spine and pages.

'You think?' she said in a dull, dead voice.

Grace stared at the magazine, not really sure what was happening here.

'You think?' Bernice said again, almost aggressively. 'How about I tell you then that I have no idea what I'm going to do when the garden is finished. That'll be everything exhausted. House done, garden done, nothing else to hide behind.' Bernice's eyes were black, shiny. She flung her hands up. 'I suppose I'll have to move again then, won't I? My whole life I'll be doing up houses and moving on. Till. I. Die.'

'I thought . . .' Grace didn't know what she thought and was frantically trying to read Bernice. 'Doing up the house,' she tried again, 'I always thought it was a labour of love. And that, you know, next thing, maybe would be . . .'

Grace was building up to saying *a family* when Bernice snapped, 'That bloody house is the only thing we've got in common.' She put one of her elbows on the desk and the hand of that arm was balled in a fist. She was tapping her mouth with it, which reminded Grace of Esther. It was as though she was trying to stop anything else escaping. It didn't work.

'He's lovely, Sol, don't get me wrong, Grace, but God, I should have lived with him longer before I got married. You get swept along, don't you? People asking you when you're going to set a date, all that. And then it's like the whole of my family is marrying into the whole of his

– know what I mean? One big happy family. Before you can blink it's all signed and sealed. Organising the wedding, doing the house up gave us plenty to talk about, which was good, otherwise there would have been a great big yawning silence. Curtain poles, hand-blocked wallpaper, hard landscaping – I tell you, Grace, I've been clinging on to them for dear life.'

Grace felt punch-drunk, as if there was too much information that she had to revisit and re-evaluate in the light of what Bernice was saying. Just as she'd had to revisit Alistair's behaviour.

'But . . . but . . .' she said, aware she was sounding like a faulty motor scooter.

Bernice sat back, shook her head. 'Know what makes it harder, Grace? He has no inkling of how I feel. Worships me, loves what we've got. So what do I do to put this right, when he's done nothing wrong?'

'Bernice, I had no idea. I'm really sorry.' Grace would have tried to pat Bernice's hand or even put an arm around her but she looked volatile, like she might swat her away as Esther had done.

Bernice got up and retrieved the magazine, before chucking it again, this time on to Esther's desk. 'He'll be back soon,' she said, 'I better get on.' Just for a second she caught Grace's eye and Grace saw despair.

Bernice sat back down and hung her head but when Grace tentatively touched her on the shoulder, she said, 'No, don't. Don't be kind. Just keep an eye on the door.'

Grace went to the window, each one of Bernice's sobs feeling like the pull back and then forward of a saw.

'Please, Bernice, is there anything I can do to help?' she asked when the sobbing had stopped, thinking as she asked what a very stupid question that was.

Bernice opened her drawer and wiped her eyes on some of the fabric samples she still had in there. She took in a few deep breaths and widened and then scrunched up her eyes.

'How do I look?' she said.

'As if you've been crying.'

Bernice nodded and picked up her handbag and took out a mirror, some make-up wipes and a mascara wand and laid them on her desk.

'I'll tell him I jabbed myself in my eye while I was freshening up my mascara. Then I had to take it all off.' She picked up a wipe and dragged it back and forth over her eye until it was a smudgy mess. She turned her face to Grace. 'Look believable?'

'Kind of.'

'"Kind of" is always enough for Sol.'

Grace came away from the window and sat down again.

'Bernice, are you sure there's nothing I can get you? Do?'

'You can make damn sure that you want all that routine and stability, 'cos otherwise one day, Grace, you might wake up in bed with someone and you'll know in your bones you've picked the wrong man and the wrong life and all the pair of you can talk about is stuff that bores your bloody backside off because he doesn't have the language to talk to you about the things you really yearn to talk about, the things you really yearn to do – like lying in the desert at night and looking up at the stars, or feeling the ground spin under your feet as you whirl round and round just for the joy of being alive.' Grace knew that if Bernice had not run out of breath at that point she would have kept right on listing things. 'You'll discover, Grace, that he'll be here . . .' Bernice put out one hand, 'and you'll be here.' The other hand she put out was a good distance away from the first one. 'Blond Boy might be young, and God knows he's made some mistakes, but he opened the cage a bit, didn't he?'

They heard the street door open and Grace knew Bernice wanted her to go.

'Here you are,' Sol said, coming back in. 'Oh, love, what have you done?'

Bernice was again rubbing her eye with the make-up wipe.

'Jabbed myself in the eye.' She clicked her tongue. 'Hurt like hell, made it water. I'm taking it all off now.'

'Poor you. Never mind, grubs up.' He put a plastic-wrapped sandwich on Bernice's desk, 'Cheese and pickle and . . .' He reached into his carrier bag with a flourish and pulled out a pot. 'Special treat: caramel trifle. 2 for 1 deal.'

'Lovely.' Bernice's smile was wide and generous and only Grace knew it was a great big stinking lie. She got up and said she'd see them later and left the office, and the building, her legs feeling shaky underneath her.

She walked slowly at first, not sure her legs were up to anything quicker, but the more she thought of people living shut-down lives, having to pretend and play a part, she speeded up. Alistair, how long had he had to do it? Gilbert? Vi too? And now Bernice. Esther losing all control suddenly seemed preferable.

She pictured Bernice again, sitting there with her smudged and distraught racoon eyes. Living with someone you didn't love, letting someone go who you did, was there a difference? Think Grace, think.

Would that be what a life with Mark held? Or could it be worse? She thought of Violet and Gilbert's sterile and ordered house. Routines. Right ways and wrong ways of doing things.

She was walking fast enough to make people scoot out

of her way and found herself cutting along the bottom of Shaftesbury Avenue and down towards the National Gallery.

Samuel was in the Peter Paul Rubens room. She called him over.

'Hey, Grace. You OK? Haven't seen you for a while. Gilbert said you'd had a knock on the head.' He was looking at her head, his brown eyes all concern.

'It's Gilbert I want to talk about,' she said and realised she was out of breath. 'Sorry, been rushing. You like him, don't you?'

Samuel scanned the room before shepherding her to a part of it that was less crowded.

'Is Gilbert all right?' he asked.

'He's fine and I'm sorry if I've misinterpreted things and if I'm speaking out of turn, but I've . . . well, I've just messed up something and I don't think I can put it right. I'm too scared to put it right, too petrified of what the truth will do. So I'm going to have to embarrass you and Gilbert instead.'

Samuel suddenly laughed, his teeth a flash of white against his skin, and Grace remembered the way Tate's hair had blared out against the blue of his coat.

'You wanna sit down?' Samuel asked and Grace said she didn't and she told him about Gilbert. She told him how he and Tony had wanted to live together but Gilbert's mother had been ill and then died, which would have left Violet on her own, and how Tony had given Gilbert that horrible choice – Violet or him. She told him how Gilbert had felt he could only honourably choose Violet and now he was living this half-life, Violet unaware he was gay and jealous of anyone who she feared might take him away from her.

Samuel listened and said at the end, 'I have a mother. Eighty-five . . . still trying to find me a wife.' He chuckled and it made him seem like a grown-up, taking life's knocks and still able to see the joke. She wondered how he'd managed to stay that way.

'Gilbert's quite shy under all that armour,' she said and she could tell Samuel understood, but just in case, she added, 'I shouldn't have told you any of this, but doing the right thing doesn't always lead to happiness, does it? And, Samuel? If you do ever get as far as meeting Violet, take her some of those gloves, the ones you use for handling precious paintings.' She had another thought 'And some of those blue plastic overshoes. She'd love those.'

Outside the gallery she saw that the drizzle had stopped and she peered up at Nelson, and with something that felt like a cramp in her chest she remembered Emma Hamilton and the baby she and Nelson had had and kept a secret.

She began to walk back the way she had come, thinking of what Bernice had said and of a life filled with home-decorating superstores, worrying about whether to swap energy providers, or where to find the cheapest parking. She could not imagine Tate doing any of those things, but she could imagine him arriving in Paris later that evening and going to a bar, doing that weird handshake, kissing the women, making friends, bounding along down the avenues and boulevards eager to try and sample and meet and share. All that energy fizzing away over the Channel. Without her.

She reached for her mobile. 'Please, please answer,' she said, the street around her feeling oppressively small with all her anxiety bouncing off the walls of the buildings. She could barely keep her feet still, wasn't sure she'd even be able to hear when he answered, let alone speak.

'Hi, not here right now. Leave a message,' Tate's voice said.

A message? What to say, what to say?

'Tate, it's Grace. I'm sorry. I'm scared, so scared, but I want to tell you . . . everything. Please . . . look, I'm going to come to the airport . . . I know, I know, it's a cliché, but I don't care. I'm going to come and if you've already gone . . . perhaps I'll just get on a plane and come out to Paris . . . except I don't have my passport. Oh sod that, that's a detail. That's Grace talking. I mean the sensible one. Look, I need to talk to you and please, please try to understand that I was young and . . . No, I need to see your eyes when I tell you this. I have to go, get a taxi.' She stopped talking and finished the call.

She was wasting time. But where was she heading? She didn't know if it was Heathrow or Gatwick. She rang Tate again. Got his voicemail service again. 'I don't know where to come,' she cried, 'I'm, I'm going to guess it's Heathrow. I'm going to Heathrow.'

She finished the call and walked to the edge of the kerb to try to flag down a taxi, but she was in the wrong place, the traffic was against her, buses blocking the flow. She moved further down. No go. She crossed the road. She knew she was pacing the pavement, back and forth, back and forth.

'Just stop,' she screamed at a taxi as it went past, a fare already sitting in the back. More cars, buses, a motorcycle. 'A taxi!' she screamed at the road. 'All I want is one sodding taxi!'

She saw a couple give her a wide berth on the pavement and then her phone was ringing. She snatched at it, fumbled with it, dropped it and picked it up, jabbing at the answer button.

Tate's voice in her ear. She heard London fall away from

her. What was he saying? Was he saying something nice? No, he was saying it wasn't going to work. Just like that, flat. She sat down on the pavement, not because she intended to, but because her legs did.

He'd given up waiting for her; she'd left it too late. She felt bombarded by the noise of the traffic and the people, by the smell of petrol and the lights. How was she going to live here now? Go back to that other Grace?

Crashing misery, fear, self-loathing, regret – all the horsemen of her particular apocalypse trampled over her.

'It's not going to work?' she said into the phone. 'Really? I . . .'

'Nope. 'Cos I'm catching the Eurostar – doesn't go from Heathrow. I mean, it's fast, but it's never gonna achieve take-off.' There was a pause. 'Where are you, Gracie?'

She felt the horsemen wheel away as she registered that 'Gracie'.

'I'm sitting on the pavement.'

There was a laugh. 'That the best way to get to Heathrow? Which pavement exactly? Wanna narrow it down? Lot in London.'

She looked at the street sign because she couldn't remember where she was. 'Start of Pall Mall.'

'Advance to Pall Mall, eh?' She heard him talking to

someone. 'OK, driver says can be there in about fifteen minutes.'

'Driver?'

'In a taxi, Gracie, on my way to St Pancras. Just caught me. Sit tight, I'm comin' to get you.'

CHAPTER 35

By the time the taxi pulled up at the kerb Grace had passed through hope many times and each time it seemed fainter, the outlines less believable. When Tate stepped out on to the pavement, she thought that it was too cruel seeing him again like this, before joy took over in the form of breathy little voices saying, *Look how his lips are, remember?* and, *Of course, his eyes are* that *shade of green. The only shade of green they could possibly be.*

He smiled and it almost knocked her to the kerb before she told herself everything was up in the air as of this moment; that wonderful smile might still slip away from her. She took a step backwards and to the side as he approached and he copied her so that they still ended up face to face.

'I need to get in the cab in twenty minutes, a half hour at a stretch,' he said. 'So, we can use that time like bees doing a hive dance, or you can start talking.'

'I need to sit down.'

'Again?' He laughed. 'OK.'

She headed towards the doorstep of the nearest building. She could hear the taxi still idling, traffic passing, the city carrying on as normal. She focused on the two scuffed biker boots. Scanning up the purple and black checked trousers, past the silver ring to the sleeves of the greatcoat, she arrived at a chunky black jumper. Another few angles of tilt and she was past the hair to the eyes.

'Time's wasting,' he said and sat down on the pavement in front of her, crossing his legs. He was all tease and cheek. She could tell he thought this was going to be resolved lickety-split.

'Come on, Gracie. Spill. God I've missed you. Missed those eyes, brown, deep, sooooo sexy. Here, would it help if I held your hand?' He reached for it and she pulled away and tucked both her hands under her legs. She didn't want to put her hand in his and then feel him withdraw it sharply later.

His face didn't look so cheeky now; a little tense around his mouth and eyes, but his tone was still upbeat.

'Gracie, come on. I know it'll be painful, but once you've told me, it's gone.'

'Painful and then *you'll* be gone.'

'Doubt it. Go on.'

This is what she'd been running from, not just when he

tried to make her tell him in the office, but way back since that day in Spain in the upstairs bathroom.

'All right,' she said, feeling the cold from the stone she was sitting on start to creep upwards. 'When Bill started sleeping with other women, I fell apart. Big time. I was drinking heavily, smoking dope a lot of the time. Just lying by the pool, becoming more and more needy. I got worse. Soon I wasn't just drinking heavily; I was turning into a drunk. Long hours with my good friend Rioja – nice general anaesthetic but means you spend a lot of time with your head down the toilet.'

'Poor Gracie. No wonder you came home in such a state.' He reached over and pulled one of her hands free. 'Jeez, you're cold.' He blew on her fingers and it felt wonderful and torturous, because any minute now she was certain he was going to drop that hand.

She laughed bitterly. 'Bill used to point me out to his latest love as I lay sparked out by the pool. I was flaky, Tate. Really flaky. Remember how you said I was a "safe pair of hands"? Well, I wasn't.'

He nodded, so sweetly earnest. 'Yeah, I remember, but you need to cut yourself some slack. You were young, your heart was breaking, you were in a foreign country living with a dickhead.' He gave up trying to blow on her hand and sandwiched it between both of his. She really wished he hadn't; it was making it worse, feeling his skin like that, the heat coming off him.

'The thing is, Tate, when I give in to passion and let my heart rule my head . . . I lose my way. And when I slide and slip, I really go. Bad things happen.'

'Like calling me a fuckwit in front of all those people.'

'No, I'm talking about really bad things. In Spain, because I let myself go, it was horrible and it was all my fault and . . . '

'Hey, hey, take it easy.' He was up on his knees, hands on her shoulders. 'Gracie, whatever you did just tell me. You think I'm going to judge you? Or be shocked?'

'Yes, I think you will. No, don't say anything, just listen.' She waited for him to sit back down.

'In my crazed state, I had a moment of insight – Bill was loads of things, but the main one was competitive. He always had to be the centre of attention, head of the herd. He got so jealous if any other artist got more publicity or a better deal than he did.'

She tried to gauge what Tate might be thinking from his expression but couldn't. 'Anyway,' she went on briskly, 'I figured that if I slept with another man, he'd get jealous and want me back. I chose his best friend, Patrick, because, I'm ashamed to say, I knew he'd always had a bit of a thing for me. It got a good reaction. Patrick and he fell out and

Bill was all over me again.' She put her hand to her mouth and took it away again. 'God, this is so hard to tell you, Tate. Using Patrick like that was disgusting.'

'Second honeymoon last long?' Tate asked, looking off down the street.

'Couple of weeks. And when it had cooled again, Bill said I should keep experimenting with new men. We could still get together from time to time, I could stay living in the villa, but really I should follow my instincts from now on.'

'My instinct at this moment is to tell Bill he's a turd.'

She reached out and patted his knee. 'Thank you. I should have done that and then left. Instead I hung around – guess I couldn't face going home and getting all that chest-beating from Mum about turning my back on such a funny, rebellious, maverick genius as Bill. And I still loved him.' She clicked her tongue. 'Young idiot.'

'Not disagreeing with that.'

'I tried to tell Bill I didn't want an open anything, but he brushed my objections aside. So I thought I'd show him how wrong he was and how much seeing me with other men would hurt. My behaviour got wilder. I started to work my way through the men we knew – although to be honest, they were starting to avoid me and Bill; they knew a train wreck when they saw one. Then it was strangers I met in bars, on the beach. I'd invite them back to the villa, hoping to get a reaction from Bill. Nothing. He was besotted with a seventeen-year-old Portuguese girl at that time. Said she made him paint better than he ever had.'

Tate said something under his breath that sounded vicious and she hoped it was aimed at Bill.

'I was still losing large stretches of time to drink and I started experimenting with heavier drugs. Mainly pills, coke.'

'Heroin?' He had on his ancient face again.

'No . . . well . . . I smoked it once or twice, but I was too scared of it. Zin, she got into it when she left school. Boyfriend. I saw what it did, how hard she had to struggle to get clear of it . . . on methadone for a long time.'

'She's clean now?'

'Oh yeah. Completely gone the other way. Her body is a temple. But it took it out of the family. Felicity was a brick, though; the one time I've seen her put herself at the back of the queue. Now I'd say her and Zin are the closest of us all.'

She stopped talking as a woman with a small dog on a lead came past. The dog seemed all skin and no hair and when it sniffed at Tate he shooed it away, giving the woman a look that told her to move it along.

'So, you were sleeping your way through northern Spain . . .' Tate said, when the dog had been jerked away.

'Yes. And now it seemed that everything I did created a kind of chaotic backwash. There was a guy selling necklaces on the beach. We had sex on the sand when the front was deserted, except it wasn't and someone called the police. I got away without being recognised but the guy got picked up. They sent him back to North Africa. I went with a pickpocket in town, Ramón, who, surprise, surprise, stole all my cash. So I slept with his brother too and when Ramón found out, he stabbed him in the leg. Turned out he was capable of more jealousy than Bill.' She was starting to feel a bit sick because she could see Tate was having a hard time keeping a neutral look on his face.

She ploughed on. 'Was on a bike with one guy, coming back from a trip up in the hills. We had a crash. He broke both his legs; I just bounced I was so drunk. I picked up a businessman, God knows how – I was looking a wreck by then – and while he was sleeping I nicked his bag. Thought there might be some cash in it I could use for drugs. When I found out there was only some files, I threw it in a skip. Turned out he worked for a military contractor, shouldn't have taken the files out of the office. He lost his job . . . big fuss in the Spanish papers.'

Tate nodded slowly when she stopped, his lips pressed together. 'How many?' he said eventually.

'How many would be too many?'

He didn't answer, seemed to be watching the small dog and its owner who hadn't made much progress along the street. Grace watched them too until they went into a building.

'The ones I can remember . . . twenty or so. Over about three months.'

'Oh well,' he said before surprising her with a hearty, 'Way to go, Gracie.'

'What?'

'Well, it's going some, but it's not major league stuff. And the things that happened to the guys weren't just down to you. They had free will, Gracie – their decisions as much as yours. Seems to me women are always getting the "Jezebel" label stuck on them when we all know it takes two to tango.'

'Are you listening to me? I was out of control. I wasn't getting any pleasure from it, doubt I was giving any either. And know what my *pièce de résistance* was? I slept with Bill's own son. That's how bad I was. Kept the worst till last. His own son.' She wondered why she was so desperate for him to judge her.

'That'll hurt,' was all he said.

'It did, Tate. More damage. I am so, so ashamed of myself. Scott he was called – a horrible, spoilt brat, just a couple of years older than me. I had some weird idea Bill would come to heel this time, and Scott was on some kind of kick to hurt Bill . . . that father–son thing–'

'Yup, know all about that. Go on, Gracie.'

'We did it in the pool where we knew Bill would see us from his studio. He went ballistic, nearly drowned the pair of us. Upshot was Scott left San Sebastián next day with a broken jaw and Bill had a couple of cracked ribs, a broken foot and a sprained wrist.'

'Hope it was his painting arm.'

'Is that all you can say?'

'How about, "Jeez, what a nice family"?'

'And I split it up,' she almost screamed. 'I don't think they've ever spoken since. What kind of woman does that? It was like I was collecting scalps . . . hoovering up men. I mean, God, where would I have drawn the line?'

'Calm down, Gracie. Just get on with it. So, Bill chucked you out?'

She took a deep breath and forced it back out quickly, trying to steady herself. 'No. Forgave me. Said he admired my spirit, what I was prepared to do to get his attention again. We went back to how we were for a good couple of months.' She paused and thought about how attentive Bill had seemed and knew she wouldn't be able to keep the bitterness out of her voice. 'Except we didn't really go back

– I was just desperate to interpret it like that. He wanted me by his side all the time. He even let me hold his paints as he worked in the studio. It took a while for me to realise that he was using me as a kind of nurse with benefits. He couldn't hold his paints himself his wrist was so bad. He couldn't even get dressed or walk to a bar without my help. Great, eh? Lover to nurse via whore.'

'Don't want to hear you calling yourself that, Gracie,' Tate said sharply.

When she didn't reply he reached out and gave her a nudge. 'You wanna hear a few things about my past to make you feel better? He rubbed his hands together. 'OK, I had a thing with two women at once when I first when to college.'

'Two-timing is hardly comparable,' she said miserably.

'No, you don't get it. It was one of those *ménage à trois* things. Like your sister.'

She had a vision of two women coiled around Tate and knew she had no right to feel the jealousy she was experiencing.

Tate was grinning, rolling his eyes in an exaggerated fashion. 'Kid in a sweet shop to start with and then like piggy in the middle. Sex was great, emotional meltdown not so good.'

'Jealousy and back-biting?'

'Back-biting and front-biting. Stereo angst. Made you feel better yet?'

She shook her head and steadfastly watched a bus pass, seeing the poster on the side blur.

'Oh Gracie, Gracie,' he said softly. 'Come on, look, here's another thing. Racked up a load of debt on my course and this guy said he knew an older woman needed a handyman. I go round to her apartment – big, swanky place and turns out it wasn't the apartment needed a hand.'

Grace stopped watching the traffic. 'You mean—'

'Yup. And you know what? She paid well. And I tried to give value for money.'

'How old was she?'

'How old's too old?' he shot back with a grin. 'Oh, come on, Gracie. Get over it. You slept around a lot, screwed a father and son and, yeah, some bad things happened, but you didn't set out to make them happen. You weren't killing and maiming and all those really bad things people do to each other. You were lost and lashing out. It's not worth dragging about like a chain.'

She wished she could hold on to this moment of forgiveness – keep soaring for as long as possible before the big dive.

'That's not all,' she said bleakly. 'There is more. Worse.'

He nodded his head as if indulging her. 'Then get it out.

Offload it so we can talk about some happier things, like why you love the icons so much.' He leaned in closer. "Cos I have to tell you, I think this is one time I've been paying attention to the signs.'

Oh God. She hadn't expected to arrive by this particular route, but here they were. She felt as if he'd just pressed the button in a lift and they were hurtling down from the top floor.

'And what do they mean, Tate?' she said very slowly.

'I think they mean you want to settle down, have a family. It's that security thing again, isn't it, that need to feel settled? That's why you're so passionate about them, popping in between tours to get your fill. And hey, I don't know if I'm ready for all that yet, but it's not a turnoff, Gracie, not—'

'No, Tate. You've got it wrong. It's not about wanting a baby, it's about losing one. Mine and Bill's. I got pregnant during that time I was being his nurse and then I had a miscarriage and it was my fault. Utterly. Absolutely.' She stopped, then wound herself up enough to speak again. 'When I visit the icons I'm trying to say sorry, ask for forgiveness. It's all I can do . . . that and keep myself on a tight rein, make sure I never slide again.'

She wasn't sure he'd understood what she was saying because she had fluffed the end bit, her voice cracking, and she made herself keep looking at him to see how bad it was. He was standing up quickly. She saw him walk to the taxi, and she thought that was it – the last view she'd have of him. But he wasn't getting into it; he was talking to the driver. She heard the engine die. Saw the driver pick up a newspaper and start to read it.

He was back with her.

'You'll miss your train,' she said.

'Forget the train. Move over.' She shifted and he sat next to her. 'Tell me about losing the baby, Gracie. Tell me how it was your fault.'

She wished she had a tissue, but she used her coat sleeve instead.

'It was my fault because I was so badly out of control that it took me a long time to realise that I wasn't feeling lousy because I had a hangover, or I hadn't eaten for a day, but because I was pregnant. I'd been on the pill since I left England . . . but I guess I was throwing up so much by that point, the protection it was offering was barely nil. By the time it got through to my addled brain that I hadn't had a period, I was about seven weeks pregnant.' She turned to him. 'I should never have allowed myself to get pregnant in that state.'

'Allowed?' He was looking confused. 'I don't think you mean that, do you? It was sheer chance . . . you were playing

Russian roulette with all that sex and hardly any protection. It could have happened with any of those other guys, couldn't it?'

'No. With those other guys I always used a condom as well. I didn't with Bill.' She saw his disbelieving look. 'What? Weren't you listening when I told you what low-lifes some of them were?'

He burst out laughing. 'So, even when you were drunk out of your skull, high as a kite, you were careful?'

She nodded. 'Felicity always drummed into us that it was romantic to be barefoot and pregnant, not barefoot and HIV positive. Or syphilitic. One of the few lessons she taught me. Barefoot and pregnant by your one true love was the ultimate goal in her book.' She looked at the pavement. 'Barefoot! Can't remember the last time I took off my shoes outside.'

'But what about Bill, Gracie? How come you didn't get yourself an all-over condom before you went back to bed with him? He wasn't a "true" love, he was a philandering shit. He must have been racking up the partner miles.'

'Yes. That fact kind of went under my radar. Blinded by passion, you see, and Felicity's brainwashing. And I was so grateful to be back in his bed that I conveniently forgot the women who had been filling in for me.' She checked on his expression and couldn't read it. 'Anyway, luckily, miraculously, I only caught one thing from Bill – a baby, and he really wasn't pleased about it.'

'No shit.'

'Babies were a drain on his creativity. He hadn't hung around to help bring up Scott; he wasn't getting saddled in his forties with another child.'

'So he wanted you to have an abortion?'

'Yes. To go back home and have it. Get rid of me and the baby in one go, I think. But that was never going to happen, because within a couple of hours of me looking at the test result and thinking my life was ruined, I suddenly wanted that baby more than I wanted Bill. More than I wanted anything. Can't describe it . . .' She allowed herself to think back to that time, to feeling as if she'd done something miraculous and now the world wasn't going to be about her for a while; it was going to be about what she could give this baby. She wiped her eyes on her sleeve and didn't care that when she sniffed it sounded thick and unpleasant.

'Told Bill I was having the baby and I wasn't going back home like some disgraced serving wench. I dug my heels in. He went into sulk overdrive and I, well, I started trying to clean up my act. No drinking, no smoking, steered clear of the drugs . . . proper meals at proper times.' She smiled grimly. 'Didn't happen overnight. Struggled with it. But I was getting there. And I got the villa cleaned top to bottom.

Ordered all sorts of baby books too. I was going to bask in the sun, getting fatter and fatter and learning how to be a good mum. A mum who was nothing like Felicity. I wasn't just going to love this baby; I was going to teach it everything.' She wiped her nose on her sleeve again. 'Used to talk to it in the night, tell it that I was going to protect it and watch it grow into a good person. Keep it away from all the mistakes I'd made.'

'Steer it round the bear traps and pull it out when it fell in them,' Tate said sadly and she watched him until she felt ready to finish.

'Wasn't to be, though. Six weeks later it was all over. I still can't look at yellow tiles . . .'

She swallowed hard when she felt his arm come round her, seeing herself hunched over in the upstairs bathroom unable to comprehend how the bit of sky she could see through the window could still be blue or grasp the reality of what was happening to her. All she knew was that something so tiny, barely there, was knocking a hole in her by going.

'Yellow tiles?' Tate asked gently.

'We had them in the upstairs bathroom.' That was all she could say.

Tate kept quiet for a while, just holding her before saying, tentatively, 'You might have to go back through some of that, Gracie sweetheart, because I'm still missing how it was your fault.'

It all came out in a rush. 'The drink, the cigarettes, the drugs, staying up all night, not eating properly, the mess and dirt in that villa. I never gave the baby a chance . . . it was no different than waiting for it to be born and holding a pillow over its—'

Tate's arm came off her shoulders and he was turning her towards him.

'Take a breath, Gracie, and listen to me. First off, women lose babies for all kinds of reasons, particularly early on. All kinds of reasons. So, if you'd lived like a saint you might still have had a miscarriage. My sister, she had one and she's so shiny and healthy you could eat off her.'

'You're just saying that to make me feel better.'

'Don't, Gracie,' he said so severely that it made her jerk back. 'Don't be a smartass. This is my sister we're talking about. I've never got to know her as well as I should, but I saw her right after it happened and it was real pain she was going through. Right to the bone.' He put his hand on the back of his neck and rubbed it. 'Did everything by the book before she got pregnant and afterwards. Same end result.'

'But I didn't do everything by the book,' she shouted, wishing he'd understand. The woman with the dog was coming back and she stepped into the gutter to avoid Grace. She remembered how, when her life had been under control, she had done that with the Special Brew man.

'Gracie,' Tate said forcefully. 'You didn't do it by the book, but you didn't do any of that other stuff on purpose either. Having a miscarriage brings enough guilt with it as it is and you're putting all this extra stuff on top? Surely Fliss, your sisters, they've said the same as I'm saying?'

She shook her head. 'I've never told anyone. You're the first.' Even now she wasn't sure she could say *I lost my baby* in front of anyone but Tate.

Tate looked as if he'd just seen something horrible.

'You are kidding me? *Nobody* has helped you with this?' He had her hand again. 'Gracie, my sister took months to get over it, and I'm not sure "get over" is the right expression. She's got a little girl now, a healthy one, but I know she still has that one day a year when she goes off on her own. Remembers. And she's had family and friends to talk it through with. You should have had help.'

She was going to say she didn't deserve help because that was the next line she always said to beat herself with, but she glanced at Tate and saw his eyes were filling with tears.

'What are you doing?' She couldn't keep the wonder out of her voice.

'We Americans call it crying.'

'But why?'

'Because it's so damn sad,' he said smearing the tears that were now running freely all across his cheeks. 'No help? Not even in the hospital?'

'Not really. I didn't speak the kind of Spanish you needed in that situation.' And she hadn't missed the looks from some of the nurses, nurses who she'd seen in the bars around San Sebastián.

Tate sounded even sadder. 'This is crap. All this time you've tried to cope on your own and ended up blaming the one person you should have taken care of and been kind to before anyone else.'

She continued to watch, feeling as if she was trying to find a way through her own emotions while interpreting his. She wasn't picking up any signs of disgust or even disappointment – if you're disgusted you don't cry, do you? She almost couldn't bear to have hope. She thought of the bathroom again, the rush to the hospital, the noise and activity and then the long drop into silence. It had felt like a pit with a spike in it, just for her, and every time she thought of what she'd done, that spike was still lodged in her guts.

'I think the baby, the one in the icons, is watching me. Judging me,' she said. 'Asking me how I could be so callous. So careless with a life. I should have—'

'Nope. Should have, would have, could have . . . all crap. It just happened.'

'Tate, please.'

'Please what? Agree that it was your fault because you've got to the point where guilt and shame feels like somewhere familiar and warm to live? No way, Gracie, I'm hauling you out of there.'

'How can you really think it wasn't my fault?' she said incredulously.

'Shouldn't the question be: how can I really think it was?'

She didn't answer. She had scrunched up her face to try to keep everything from spilling out into wet, guttering sadness. She heard Tate sigh.

'OK, different approach. I'm gonna be blindingly honest. Would that help? It would? Well, here goes. This is my head talking, not my heart. No, I don't think a diet of Rioja and weed and all that other stuff is a particularly good start for a baby, but babies survive worse – doesn't do them much good, but they make it to getting born. And there are a million reasons why what happened to your baby happened. You gonna go through all of them and feel responsible for each one? Or you gonna do the sensible thing and howl at the moon because sometime's life is just a bitch and takes the very things from you that are gonna hurt the most?'

She considered that for a while, every now and again checking his face to see if his expression was changing to something more critical. If anything, the warmth in his eyes seemed to be intensifying.

Was it possible to think back on those days in Spain without them being slicked in black, sticky guilt?

They watched a man in a suit walk by, surreptitiously checking on their faces as if he was worried that their emotion would leak out and touch him. Tate squeezed her hand.

'Howling's gotta be better than this, hasn't it? And, come on. I'm sensing there's something else. Am I right?'

She nodded. 'I . . . I was the one who burned Bill's paintings. I built the bonfire. I hurled them on.'

He did a good job of trying to look as if that didn't shock him but he had cut the blood supply off to her fingers he was gripping her hand so tightly.

'I told you when I go I really go.'

'Yup, you did. Jeez.' He gave her a sideways glance. 'So . . .'

'When I came back to the villa after leaving hospital, Bill couldn't cope with how I was. He was fine with emotion on a canvas, daubing great swirls of despair in paint, but not the real, standing-in-the-bathroom-sobbing kind. I think he felt guilty too, but in him it came out in bluster.

And I spooked him. Suddenly I seemed to be more of a grown-up than him. I was sober and sad – he couldn't handle that.'

Tate made a noise but didn't say any actual words.

'One evening Bill lost it completely. He was ranting about how he knew I blamed him for what had happened and really I should just get over it – after all, it was for the best.' She pulled her knees up to her chest and hugged them. 'You can imagine how good that was to hear. He just kept spouting about how he was a free spirit; nothing weighed him down, not even his paintings. Boasted that he'd even destroy them if he suspected they were trapping him.'

'And you called his bluff.'

'I went to the bottom of the garden, to an area of scrub, and piled up a load of brushwood. It was so dry it went up really fast and I ran to the studio and grabbed the nearest painting. *Two Sidewinder Days in Madrid* it was.' She heard herself laugh. 'The look on Bill's face was worth it. And you know what, Tate? It felt so good to see it go up. Felt right. He ought to lose something he'd created and cared about like I had.' She remembered how the thick oil paint had made the flames spark into different colours.

'Bill had followed me out and just stood there watching. I asked him if it hurt seeing his painting burn and he said it didn't. I could tell he was lying. Always a liar about how much of a rebel he was. I roasted another painting and he still stood there, his hands twitching as he tried to fight the urge to salvage something.'

'Weren't you tempted to pick him up and hurl him on?'

She managed a smile at that. 'I did throw a lot of his clothes on, but he wasn't in any of them. After that second painting I would probably have stopped, if Bill hadn't suddenly rushed into the villa and come out with a box. He upended it into the fire and I saw it was all my baby books.' She stopped talking for a while and let Tate pull her in closer.

'After that I got three of his smaller works and immolated them, but I could feel my rage subsiding and I just felt weary. I needed to sleep but he told me I should finish the job. When I said "no", he went and got one of his best pieces and chucked it on. Said he was going to show me what real courage looked like.'

Tate slapped his leg. 'Love it. He even had to be top pyromaniac.'

'Yes, he did. He just kept bringing them out and burning them. When I felt that I was so tired I was likely to fall in after them, I left him to it and went to bed.'

Tate gave a low whistle. 'All of his Spanish period up in flames.'

'Not quite. When I woke up next morning, the villa smelling of smoke, ash blowing about in the garden, I knew everything was over. I went home not long after. By the end of the year Bill had taken himself off to Mexico, but before he went he'd been busy. A couple of months after I got home, a big crate was delivered to the house in Newham. It had six new paintings in it – a record of our love affair from those blissful times on the beach to the gut-stabbingly awful trauma of the last months. The letter with them said Bill had painted them in the empty villa, wanted me to have them to make up for how he'd been. Said he regretted the way it had ended, how he'd been about me, about the baby.'

'That was big of him. And so that painting last week?'

'Sold it while I was in Edinburgh. I had no idea that it was on loan until I saw it with you. Another two I sold to a banker in Houston. The other three are still under my bed. Selling some meant I could get a nice flat, pay off a lot of the mortgage. It also gave me the freedom to take a job that I liked rather than one I needed for the money. You see, for a long time I wasn't any good with pressure or stress.'

She was seeing that bonfire again. 'Oh God, I can't believe I burned those paintings. Is that what love becomes?'

'No. And stop feeling guilty. Bill got what he deserved

and, really, he could have stopped you at any point if he'd wanted. A guy who can break his own son's jaw isn't gonna be backward in getting his own way. He goaded you. It was all down to him.'

'Have you taken a course in forgiveness?' she said, putting her hand to his face.

'Yeah, but it didn't cover Bill. I'm thinking of going back to that gallery, pulling his painting off the wall and putting my foot through it.' He laughed and there was so much warmth in it Grace felt it defrost her a little.

'Right,' he said, taking hold of her hand and waggling it about. 'Gonna tell me you're responsible for the fall of the banks? Climate change? Volcanoes erupting in the Pacific? No? Well, great. Means we can go to Paris then.'

'Just like that?' She heard the panic in her voice.

'Exactly like that.'

She looked at the taxi and saw the driver had reached the sport's page of his newspaper. 'The train will have gone.'

He snorted. 'Don't think so. Got over an hour yet.'

'But you said I had twenty minutes, half an hour at a stretch.'

'Only 'cos I knew if I told you the real amount of time we had, you'd fight me for that long. Figured I'd go for the shorter fight.'

'I'm not sure I can do it, Tate. Even if I come round to thinking I'm not responsible for losing the baby and destroying the paintings, I still feel happier when I have structure, guidelines, rules, routines . . . without them, I don't know where I'll end up. I mean, look at the last few weeks: I started opening up to you, letting my grip loosen and everything went wrong. The robberies, Gilbert, Esther—'

'Alistair dressing up in women's clothes.'

That stopped her in her tracks. 'How do you know about that?'

'Picked the lock on his cabinet when he was out. Boy, they were big strappy shoes.' He planted a kiss on her hand and let it drop.

'You picked the lock? That's so . . .'

'Bad,' he said with an evil smile.

She was finding it hard to remember why she couldn't go with him.

'You didn't make any of those things happen, Gracie. I made Esther have the hots for me. I got Gilbert drunk. Everything else would have happened anyway. You've just fitted everything into that negative theory in your head, like your dad fitted me into his theories.'

She looked at the taxi driver. He was on the back page.

'I can't go. I'm starting a new job. A proper one. They'll be expecting me. I'll be letting them down.'

'They'll live. Got time to get someone else in.'

Tate was standing up and he pulled her up too.

'Gracie, you're a bat-shit crazy woman, but 'cos you're the bat-shit crazy woman I love, I'm gonna humour this Surtees Theory of Chaos. First stop in Paris is a stationer's. Wall planner, notebooks, little sticky, coloured tags. We're having rotas, rotas for everything, even sex. And boy, I'm going to keep you so busy you won't have time for spinning out of control. You're a natural organiser, Gracie, a manager par excellence. And you speak French, don't you? So either you can get yourself a grown-up job, or you can manage me – I'm not dicking around with painting like it's a hobby or a sideline. Besides, I'll need you to do all the translating and interpreting. I can only say, "Vouz avez des seins magnifiques," which I'm sure as hell gonna be using a lot on you, but it's not gonna get me far with any potential clients. Might even get my face slapped. Proper wages, Gracie, though. You're not being my handmaiden. And . . .' There was the subtlest of pressure changes in the way he was holding her. 'Maybe, when you feel up to it, we could find some head guy to sort out all that guilt you're carrying around. You know us Americans, we like to spill it all out and pay top dollar for the privilege.' Another, stronger hug. 'No, you're not gonna have a minute free to slide anywhere and I'm gonna carry a handrail with me at all times so you can't fall off the edge.'

'Now you're just being silly.'

''Nother thing, Gracie – I'm not Bill. He was a lazy sonofabitch and I'm not. Look at me: managed to paint, hold down two jobs, get arrested and fall in love with you.'

Her heart did a double beat at the way he said 'love' and he took her hand again and wrapped his around it. She let him, feeling the warmth start to spread down her fingers and into her wrist.

'Know what else? His paintings are crap. Too showy. Bonfire was the best place for them.'

She loved the way he'd got himself into a temper on her behalf.

'Come on, Gracie, get in the cab.'

'I've got no clothes.'

'Excellent.'

'No passport.'

He pulled it out of somewhere in his coat. 'Your dad brought it round that day he and Fliss visited. Hung on to it . . . still had hope.' He opened it and raised his eyebrows. 'So, I worked out you changed your name by deed poll. What's the real one? Truth now.'

God, she loved him; she must do if she was prepared to tell him this: 'Tahiti Supernova Larkspur.'

He looked as if he'd chewed something really cold. He

closed the passport. 'You know, Grace is a really, really good name.'

'Gracie's better.'

He grinned. 'Now, get in the cab.'

The prospect of such happiness still seemed unlikely. Could she really just go and not worry about the consequences? Maybe leave some of that guilt on the pavement?

'Perhaps it would be better if you went first and I came out when you're settled?'

'Don't think so. You're gorgeous, I'm desperate for you, we're going to Paris. Get in the cab.'

'Tate . . .'

'Come on, you're going to be the grain of sand in my oyster: so irritating, I can't help but make pearls.'

'I have no idea what you're talking about.'

'Me neither. But what about this, Gracie? Understand this?'

His hand was on the skin at the base of her neck and the longer he kept it there, the more she felt the heat rolling and twisting in her.

'Ohhh,' she said, her breath coming in hard. 'I feel like I flung myself on that bonfire. And you?'

'Hand on fire, arms, groin, chest. Colours flashing in front of my eyes.'

'Is that "color" without a "u"? Because if it is, that's another reason for me not to come. We don't even speak the same language.'

'True, but actions speak louder than words.' Suddenly he was kissing her, deep, urgent kisses, his tongue pushing into her mouth and his hands in her hair, and she was inside his coat, her arms locked around him. They stopped when it seemed like one of them might suffocate. 'French kissing, Gracie. Loads more to come. Now, get in the cab. I want to take you to Paris and paint you.'

'In sand and blood, like Bill?'

'Nope,' he said into her neck. 'I mean paint *you*. There's a shade of blue I want to start with at your wrist, like ice in your veins. Then a darker blue further up your arm, growing darker and darker until it's red flame. Then, Gracie Surtees, I'm gonna take the finest brush and paint your nipples – haven't decided what colour yet, but whatever colour I choose it's gonna end up on the sheets, on my mouth, everywhere.'

'That's disgusting,' she said, feeling every nerve-ending blow with the thought of it.

'Sure as hell hope so. Get in the cab.'

She was still hesitating and he narrowed his eyes.

'Time to step up to the plate, Gracie. Stop pushing me away. Get in the cab.'

'Yeah, get in the bloody taxi, love,' the driver shouted, throwing his folded paper on to the passenger seat.

Tate was moving away from her.

'I can't wear cheesecloth,' she shouted after him.

He frowned. 'OK . . . whatever that means. OK, no cheese-cloth.' He gave her one of his tender looks, opened the door and climbed in.

'And you won't let me fall?'

A definite, 'No,' came back to her.

Grace looked at the open door as the taxi started up again and thought of the risk and uncertainty, all the things that could go wrong. She thought of Capital H for History waiting for her on Monday morning and her flat, the paintings still under the bed, and Mark and all the reasons she couldn't just up sticks and leave. And then suddenly, decisively, she kicked her shoes into the gutter, left one, right one, and sprinted towards the open door.

ACKNOWLEDGEMENTS

Thank you to Steven Davidson for advice on police procedures; to London Art Tours for information generously given which I messed about with shamelessly to fit my plot (sorry), and to the Courtauld Gallery for being inspiring and uplifting – I have borrowed its setting and some paintings, but that's where the resemblance to my fictional Paddwick Gallery ends. An honourable mention too for Shanna Wells – her local knowledge of Rhode Island was invaluable, and apologies to Texan friends Leah, John and Evan. You are nothing like the Baldridges.

Huge gratitude, as always, to my agent Broo Doherty (sound judgement, calm voice, wicked humour) and to Charlotte, my former editor at Quercus, who saw the book part of the way through the edit process and to Jo, my new editor, who completed the process. To Nicola and Kathryn – I really appreciate your hard work and patience in the face of my vagueness.

And now, the kind of thanks that can't really be put into words, but I'll have a go.

All my love to Matt, Kate and Becky for their support, understanding and the enthusiastic way in which they embrace wherever this writing takes me. And to my sisters Ruth and Anne – I couldn't have chosen two better ones this last year or any other year. TFFS.